ALSO BY DAVID BALDACCI

MEMORY MAN SERIES

Memory Man
The Last Mile
The Fix
The Fallen
Redemption
Walk the Wire
Long Shadows

ALOYSIUS ARCHER SERIES

One Good Deed
A Gambling Man
Dream Town

ATLEE PINE SERIES

Long Road to Mercy
A Minute to Midnight
Daylight
Mercy

THE CAMEL CLUB SERIES

The Camel Club
The Collectors
Stone Cold
Divine Justice
Hell's Corner

JOHN PULLER SERIES

Zero Day
The Forgotten
The Escape
No Man's Land

KING & MAXWELL SERIES

Split Second
Hour Game
Simple Genius
First Family
The Sixth Man
King and Maxwell

THE SHAW SERIES

The Whole Truth
Deliver Us from Evil

WILL ROBIE SERIES

The Innocent
The Hit
The Target
The Guilty
End Game

STANDALONES

Absolute Power
Total Control
The Winner
The Simple Truth
Saving Faith
Wish You Well
Last Man Standing
The Christmas Train
True Blue
One Summer
The 6:20 Man

SHORT STORIES

Waiting for Santa
No Time Left
Bullseye
The Mighty Johns (A Digital Novella)

DAVID BALDACCI

LONG SHADOWS

GRAND CENTRAL
PUBLISHING

LARGE PRINT

New York   Boston

Grand Central Publishing
Hachette Book Group
1290 Avenue of the Americas, New York, NY 10104
grandcentralpublishing.com
twitter.com/grandcentralpub

First Edition: October 2022

Grand Central Publishing is a division of Hachette Book Group, Inc. The Grand Central Publishing name and logo is a trademark of Hachette Book Group, Inc.

The publisher is not responsible for websites (or their content) that are not owned by the publisher.

The Hachette Speakers Bureau provides a wide range of authors for speaking events. To find out more, go to www.hachettespeakersbureau.com or call (866) 376-6591.

Library of Congress Cataloging-in-Publication Data has been applied for.

ISBNs: 978-1-5387-1982-4 (hardcover), 978-1-5387-1981-7 (large type), 978-1-5387-3980-8 (international), 978-1-5387-1979-4 (ebook), 978-1-5387-3977-8 (signed edition), 978-1-5387-3976-1 (BN.com signed edition), 978-1-5387-3975-4 (B & N Black Friday signed edition)

Printed in the United States of America

LSC-C

Printing 1, 2022

*To Ginny and Bill Colwell,
two very special people,
for all you have done for so many*

LONG SHADOWS

CHAPTER

I

"WHO THE HELL IS THIS?" barked Amos Decker.

He had been awoken from a sleep far deeper than he usually achieved. The insomnia had been getting worse, and it was adding nothing positive to his already unpredictable temperament. He hadn't looked at the phone number on the screen before answering it. In his line of work, calls came at all times of the day or night and not always from those on his contact list.

"Amos, it's Mary Lancaster." Her voice was low, tenuous. "Do you remember me?"

Amos Decker sat up stiffly in his bed and rubbed his unshaven face. He saw on his phone screen that it was nearly three in the morning.

"Since I pretty much can't forget anything, it's not likely I'd forget *you*, is it, Mary?" He patted himself on both cheeks, working to remove the fuzziness from his mind. Then his thoughts settled on the timing of the call, which was in itself a warning.

In a tense voice he added, "Mary, is something wrong? Why are you even up now?"

Mary Lancaster was Decker's former partner in the Burlington Police Department in Ohio. A while back she'd been diagnosed with early onset dementia. The disease had spiraled continually downward, as her brain deteriorated and dragged the rest of her along with it.

"I'm fine. Couldn't sleep."

To Decker, she didn't sound fine at all. But he hadn't spoken to her in a while, and this might just be how she was now.

"I have trouble with that too."

"I just wanted to hear your voice. It just seemed so important to me right now. I've been working up the courage to call you."

"You don't ever have to worry about calling me, even in the middle of the night."

"It's so difficult to understand time, Amos, night and then day. But then, everything is very difficult for me to understand right now. And ... it's so very frightening because ... every day there seems to ... be less and less of me ... th-there."

He sighed as the tragic sincerity of her words hit him especially hard. "I know, Mary. I understand why you feel that way."

"Yes. I believed that *you* would."

Her tone had firmed up a bit. Decker hoped it was a positive sign.

He leaned against the creaky headboard, as though

using the wood to fortify his own spine in dealing with this unexpected development. Decker surveyed the dark confines of his small bedroom. He had lived here for years, but it looked like he was just moving in, or else was simply passing through.

He was a consultant with the FBI. Long before that he had suffered a near-fatal brain injury while playing professional football. His altered brain held two new attributes which, up to that point, he hadn't even known about and had no reason to: hyperthymesia, or perfect recall; and synesthesia, which caused him to pair certain things with unlikely colors. In his case it was dead bodies linked with a shade of electric blue. After his football career ended he had become a policeman and then a detective in his hometown; thus, seeing dead bodies was not all that unusual.

He and Lancaster had successfully partnered on many cases. Having a perfect memory was a godsend for a detective, but a thousand-pound ball-and-chain for a human being. Time did not heal any of his past miseries. If anything, they were more intensified.

He lived in an apartment in Washington, DC, in a building owned by a friend of his, Melvin Mars. Decker had first met Mars while the man was on death row in Texas. He had proved Mars's innocence, and Mars had received a substantial financial windfall for his wrongful incarceration. He'd used some of it to buy the apartment building. Mars had recently married and moved to California.

Decker's longtime FBI partner, Alex Jamison, had been transferred to New York and found what looked to be love with a Wall Street investment banker. His old boss at the FBI, Ross Bogart, had retired and was learning to play golf—badly, he had heard—in Arizona.

That meant Decker was now alone, which he knew he would be one day. The phone call from his old partner was thus welcome, even at this hour.

"How are you, Mary? I mean, really, how are you?"

"So-so," she said. "Every day is a...challenge."

"But you sound good."

"You mean I can put sentences together. The...me-medications help me with that, sometimes. This is one of those times. I'm...not usually like this. I'm usually...*not* good."

He decided to reroute the conversation. "How are Earl and Sandy? Sleeping, I suppose." That was Mary's husband and their daughter.

"They went to visit Earl's mother in Cleveland. She's not doing well. Probably won't be long for this world. She's old, and gaga like me, actually."

"You don't sound gaga to me, Mary."

"Yes, well..."

"Wait, if they're in Cleveland, who's staying with

you?" The last time he had visited her, there had been an aide helping out.

"I'm okay right now, Amos. It's all right for me to be here."

"I don't know, Mary. I don't have a good feeling about this."

"You don't have to worry about me."

She sounded almost like the old Mary. Almost.

But there was something else going on here that he didn't like.

CHAPTER

2

DECKER PUT HIS LARGE BARE feet on the cold wood of the floor. "I've been meaning to come to visit you. It's been too long. But you sound better...than last time."

"Yes, it has been too long. Far too long. But not you. *Me.*"

Decker straightened up and eyed the window, where the city lights winked lazily at him in the darkness. "I, uh, I don't understand," he replied. "I guess I'm still half-asleep," he added by way of explanation, but she wasn't making much sense.

"This...is a terrible thing I have...in my head. It's...awful."

"I know, Mary. And I wish you didn't have to deal with it." He stopped and struggled to come up with more sympathetic words; it was a task that would have been easy for his old self, and nearly impossible for his current one. "I...I wish there was a cure."

"For you, too," she said. "There is no cure for you, either." In these words he could sense her seeking some level of solidarity with him in diseases of the mind that would end up doing them both in.

"We're a lot alike in that regard," he agreed.

"But also *not* alike," she retorted in a tone she hadn't used before. It was an escalation of sorts, at least he took it that way.

Decker didn't know how to respond to that, so he didn't. He sat there listening to her breathing over the phone. In the ensuing silence he could also feel something building, like thrust did on an airplane about to take off. He was about to break the silence when she did.

"Does it keep changing?" she asked in a small, measured tone.

He knew exactly what she was referring to. "It seems to," he answered. "But everyone's mind changes, Mary, healthy or not. Nothing is static. Normal or not, whatever *normal* is."

"But you're the only one I know who truly...who could maybe understand what I'm going through."

He heard a sound over the line and thought she might be slapping herself in the head, as though trying to dislodge in there what was slowly killing her. He tried to think of something to say, to draw her back to the conversation.

"But I thought you were getting counseling. It helped me. It can help you."

"I did get counseling. But then I stopped getting it."

"But why?" he said as his anxiety rose higher.

"They told me all I needed to know. After that, it was a waste of time. And I don't have any time to waste, Amos, not one *fucking* second." She let the blunt epithet hang there in the ether like smoke from a discharged gun.

"Mary, please let me know what's wrong. I can tell something's happened."

Sharp as a pistol shot she barked, "I forgot Sandy today. Right before they left to go to Cleveland. I forgot her."

"People forget names all the time, Mary," said Decker, sounding a bit relieved. He sensed this was where the conversation was intended to go when all was said and done. He didn't think this when next she spoke.

"I didn't forget her *name*. I…I forgot who she *was*." There came another lengthy pause where all Decker could hear was the woman's breaths and then a sob that was so dry and drawn out it sounded like she was strangling.

"Mary, are you—"

She continued as though he hadn't spoken. She said, "I just remembered her before I called you. And only because I looked at a photo with her name on it. I forgot I had a daughter, Amos. For a time there was no Sandy Lancaster in existence for me. Can you understand how…terrible that is?"

He could almost sense the tears tumbling down her sallow cheeks.

"I was this close to . . . to not. Ever again. Forgetting my own child. My flesh and blood."

"You shouldn't be alone, Mary. I know what you said but I can't believe that Earl—"

She cut in. "Earl doesn't know that I am alone. He wouldn't want that. He's *normally* very careful about that."

Decker stood, rigid in hushed anxiety. Her response was stealthy and, far worse, coolly victorious. He could feel clammy sweat forming all over him.

"Then who's with you? The aide?"

"She was, but I made her leave."

In a bewildered tone he said, "How exactly did you manage that? She shouldn't have—"

"I have a *gun*, Amos. My old service automatic. I haven't held it in years. But it fits my hand so fine. I remembered the gun safe combination, can you believe that? After I forgot pretty much everything else, I remembered *that*. I suppose it was . . . an *omen* of sorts," she added offhandedly.

Every muscle that Decker had tightened. "Wait a minute, Mary. Hold on now."

"I pointed the gun at her. And she left, very quickly. Right before I called you. I woke her up, you see. With the gun. It makes you wake up fast, you know that."

Decker was now more *awake* than perhaps he'd ever been in his life. He glanced wildly around trying to think of something, anything. "Look, Mary, put the gun away right now, just put it down. And then go and sit as far away from it as you can, and just close your eyes and take deep breaths. I'll have someone there in two minutes. No, *one* minute. Just one minute and help will be there. I won't disconnect from you. Stay on the line. I'm going to put you on hold for just a sec—"

She wasn't listening to any of this. "I forgot my daughter. I forgot S-Sandy."

"Yes, but then you remembered her. That's the point. That's... You have to keep..."

Decker clutched his chest. His breathing was ragged, his heartbeat gonging in his ears, flailing pistons of disruptive sound. He felt a stitch in his side, as though he'd run a long distance when he hadn't taken a single step. He felt nauseous and unsteady and... helpless.

He thought fast. Surely the aide would have called the police. Surely, they were already on their way there.

"What about tomorrow?" she said, interrupting these thoughts. "Will I remember her tomorrow? Or Earl? Or you? Or... me? So what does it matter? Can you tell me that?"

"Mary, listen to me—"

"She was crying so hard, my little girl was. 'Mommy doesn't know who I am.' She said it over and over and over. She was so sad, so unhappy. *I* did that to her. To my own little girl. How can you hurt someone you love so much?" Her tone was now rigid, unforgiving, and it froze the surging blood in Decker's body.

"Listen to me, Mary, listen closely, okay? You're going to get through this, okay? I'll help you get through it. But first you have to put the gun down. Right now." Decker put a hand against the wall to steady himself. He imagined the gun in her hand. She might be staring at it, considering things. The floor under his bare feet felt fluid, rocky, a ship's deck in pitchy seas. He searched his mind for the right words that would draw her back from the edge she was on, that would make her put down the little automatic that he knew she had killed at least one man with during her professional career. If he could just come up with the right words that would let this episode end well when it could so very easily go the other way.

He was about to speak again, to convince her to wait for help. He had his lines ready. He was about to deliver them. They would make her put the gun down, he was sure of it.

Then he heard what he had prayed he would not hear.

A single shot, which he believed—because he knew

Lancaster—had been delivered with deliberate care and competent accuracy. She would have chosen the temple, the chin, or the open mouth as her entry point. Any one of those would get the job done.

And then came the oppressive thud of Mary Lancaster's body hitting the floor. He was certain she was dead. Lancaster had always been a good planner, results oriented. Such people excelled at killing themselves.

"Mary? Mary!" he shouted into the phone. When no response came, his energy wilted. *Why are you screaming? She's gone. You know she is.*

He leaned back against the wall and let gravity transport his big body down to the floor, similar to the one on which Lancaster's corpse was now lying.

He was alive. She was not. Right now it was a difference without significant distinction for him. He sat there as his little room was lit by the electric blue of a death that had touched him from nearly a thousand miles distant.

Years ago Amos Decker had once come within a centimeter's width of a trigger pull of shooting himself in the mouth and ending his life.

But right now, part of him was as dead as Mary Lancaster.

CHAPTER

3

ASHES TO ASHES, DUST TO dust. And other assorted bullshit, thought Decker.

That was the way it always ended. That and a deep, unforgiving hole closed up with dirt. A suited Decker, usually comfortable only in jeans or wrinkled khakis and a loose sweatshirt, stared down at the eternal berth-to-be in the ground. It would soon be filled with Mary Lancaster's boxed remains.

It was a chilly, drizzly day in Ohio. For this area it was very normal weather in spring, the vestiges of winter clinging like a dewy spider's web to a frosted windowpane. The crowd here was large; Earl and Mary Lancaster were well-known and well-liked, and Sandy had made many friends at her school. Decker eyed numerous former colleagues from the local police force, who all stared dourly at the ground.

Alex Jamison had been on assignment and unable to come, but had sent a card and her condolences. Ross Bogart had done the same, along with flowers.

They hadn't known Lancaster that well, but Decker still wished they could have been here with him. He usually eschewed company, but not today.

The casket had been closed. The gunshot had been fired upward through the mouth, leaving Mary Lancaster beyond the magic of the mortician's cosmetics, and thus unviewable.

Decker looked over at Earl Lancaster, ashen faced and lost and old looking, as he clutched the hand of his teenage daughter, Sandy, who was learning disabled. The girl's eyes darted here and there, processing the world in her unique way. She might not understand death the way others did, Decker knew, and that might be a good thing, at least right now. But, at some point soon, she would realize her mother was gone. And she would wonder when her mother would be back. And Decker did not relish being in Earl's position to have to explain what had really taken place when that gun had fired. There would be no good way to do so, he thought. But it still had to be done, because Sandy deserved an explanation.

Sandy suddenly caught sight of Decker, broke free from her startled father's grip, and ran over to him. She stared up at the giant man, her face sparkling in a sea of gloom.

"You're Amos Decker," she declared brightly.

This was a game that they played; well, *she* did.

And Decker always answered as he was about to now, though it was not easy to form the words this time.

"I know I am. And you're Sandy Lancaster."

She grinned and cracked, "I know I am."

As soon as she finished speaking, Decker's features crumpled.

I forgot who she was. For a time there was no Sandy Lancaster in existence for me.

Mary Lancaster, at least in her mind, could not have committed a graver sin than not remembering that her daughter existed. He was certain that was what had placed the finger on the trigger and given her the strength to pull it.

He felt a nudge on his hand and opened his eyes to see Sandy's small, slender fingers curling around his long, thick ones.

"Amos Decker?" she said again, watching him carefully, perhaps too carefully. For some reason he knew what she was going to ask, and it panicked him beyond all reason. "Where's my mommy? There are so many people. Do you see her somewhere? I need to talk to her."

Decker had never lied to Sandy, not once. He couldn't lie to her now, so he said nothing.

"Sandy!" Earl came running over and took his daughter's hand. "Sorry, Amos."

Decker waved this apology off, turning to the side to

wipe his eyes. Then he leaned close to the other man and spoke into his ear so Sandy wouldn't hear.

"I'm so sorry, Earl."

Earl gripped Decker's arm. "Thank you. Um, we're having a little gathering at the house right after the service. I hope you can come. Mary...would have wanted that."

Decker nodded, though he had no intention of going. Earl seemed to read this in his features and said, "Well, it was good to see you."

Decker glanced at Sandy to see her gaze riveted on him. He saw betrayal in her features, but that might have been due to his own sense of guilt placing it there.

Earl said softly, "The police told me...that she called you. Thank you...for trying."

"I wish I had been more—"

"I know."

He watched them walk off to the car provided by the funeral home. The rest of those in attendance began straggling away, some flicking nods and glances and sad smiles his way. No one approached him, though. They all knew the man too well.

And then Decker was alone because he preferred it that way.

As the cemetery workers started to lower the coffin into the hole precisely dug for it, Decker turned and walked mechanically along through the graves until he reached a certain spot beside a certain tree. He did not need a perfect memory to find this place. He simply needed a bereaved heart. This was a difficult pilgrimage for him. There was probably no other kind.

Cassandra Decker. Molly Decker. Mother and daughter. His wife, their child. The love of his life, his flesh and blood, taken from him by a murderer's hand. The flowers he had laid here on his last visit had long since disintegrated, much like the bodies lying below. He brushed these fragments away and knelt down next to the twin graves.

Once, when he had been here visiting his dead family, a dying man named Meryl Hawkins had wandered out of the woods and demanded justice from Decker, in connection with the first case Decker had worked as a homicide detective. Decker had accepted the challenge, and in doing so had proved his younger self wrong and his older self correct. And Hawkins had been given justice, however belatedly, and posthumously.

Decker had also tracked down his own family's killer.

He had served justice in both cases, but it was, without doubt, a hollow outcome, marred by the fact that the justice was delivered too late for the victims. No amount of justice could return the dead to the living; the satisfaction gained from learning the truth was dwarfed by the loss.

He said the words he needed to say to his wife and child, and then rose from the cold ground and glanced to the left. There was an empty plot there.

Mine. He had come close to filling it on several occasions, once by his own hand, while staring at his murdered child as she sat, in death, in her own house.

Will my perfect memory fail one day and I'll forget I had a daughter?

He had still been on the line when the police had arrived at Lancaster's house. He had talked first to the officer, and then the detective, a man he knew from the old days. There had been sadness exchanged on the loss of a life well known to them, a grudging acceptance of the choice made, and of the motive behind it.

He walked back to his rental car. His flight to DC was scheduled for the next morning. He had no idea what would await him when he got there.

And Amos Decker wasn't sure he cared anymore.

CHAPTER

4

THE LETTER WAITING FOR DECKER was from the Cognitive Institute in Chicago, or CI as Decker and everyone else there referred to it.

He had gone there the month before for some routine tests, which they had done on him annually ever since he had been there as a patient after his football injury.

He put his suitcase down inside the door of his apartment, and tore open the letter with his thick finger.

It was several pages long, which surprised him. Usually, they were much shorter. But usually there was nothing really to tell him. This time was different.

He sat down and read it through twice, though his perfect memory had already imprinted all of the contents in his mind forever.

He slowly tore the pages into strips and threw them into the trash can.

Well...okay.

His phone buzzed. He looked at the text and groaned.

He was to come to the Washington Field Office immediately, or so commanded his superior at the Bureau. He glanced once at the trash can where the destroyed letter rested and then grabbed his car keys and walked out the door.

* * *

"Amos Decker, meet your new partner, Special Agent Frederica White," said John Talbott in a voice that sounded like a game show host introducing a new prize.

The massive Decker looked all the way down at the five-foot-three-inch Black woman, and she looked back up the mountain at him. It was unclear which one was more surprised by this announcement.

"New partner?" said Decker, glancing at Talbott, who had taken over for Ross Bogart. "I didn't ask for a new partner. Alex—"

"Special Agent Jamison is not coming back, or at least not anytime soon. And so we have transferred in Agent White from Baltimore to work with you."

White had never taken her eyes off Decker. Her expression was unreadable. She was in her midthirties, lean and wiry, packing about 105 pounds on her petite frame. Her caramel-colored hair was cut to

FBI regulation length and held in place with a pair of tortoiseshell barrettes.

Decker noted the small hole in her left nostril for a stud, although FBI regulations forbade the wearing of any such item while on duty. At the end of her right jacket cuff he could just make out a greenish mark protruding from under the cloth.

A tat.

She had on two-inch zipper boots that lifted her within a foot of his height. No stilettos for FBI agents, despite what the TV cop shows had their female actors wear. Black jacket and slacks, white shirt, buttoned to the top. No cleavage—ditto on the TV shows. Thin lips, green flinty eyes, slender dark eyebrows atop them, a sharp-edged nose, high cheekbones, jutting chin—the woman was all sharp edges.

"You *can* shake hands, you two," said Talbott encouragingly.

The two did not shake hands. They just stood there like they were afraid one was trying to get the jump on the other.

Talbott, a man waiting for the full pension and the exit door that came with it, smiled deeply, and said in a fake cheery voice, "I'll just leave you two to get to know each other better."

The door closed behind him.

"I didn't ask for this either, just so you know," said White.

"Then why are you here?"

She gave him the full hiked-eyebrows treatment. The hole in the side of her nostril quivered with something, maybe suppressed energy or rage.

"I was unaware I had a choice since the Bureau signs my paycheck. But I didn't know I would be partnering with you until thirty seconds ago."

"Then we have that in common," said Decker. "But I don't want to work with a new partner."

"So *you* have a choice?" she said.

"Apparently not."

"I know Alex Jamison. She's a good agent. She told me things about you."

"Why? You said you didn't know you were partnering with me until just now."

"Word gets around, Decker. Don't think there's another one like you in the Bureau."

"What did she tell you?"

"Between me and her. By the way, I go by Freddie, just in case you were wondering."

"Is this enough getting to know each other? Because I've had my fill," he said.

"Good enough for me, but if we walk out of here now Talbott will just make us have lunch together or something, and I doubt you want that."

Decker edged over to the window and looked out on a cloudy day, his thoughts just as muddled. He detested change, and here he was being hit by it on all sides. He could either leave the Bureau or endure a new partner named Frederica/Freddie. Which scenario would be worse? He didn't know.

"I heard about your old partner back in Ohio. That was a real tragedy. My sympathies," added White. She sounded sincere.

Decker didn't turn around. "She was a good cop. She didn't deserve to go out that way."

"Does anybody?"

"I can think of a few."

"Anything you want to know about me?"

He turned to her, mildly intrigued, and said, "What do you think is important?"

"I'm divorced. Got two kids. My mother lives with us, helps to take care of them. I grew up in Philly. I had three brothers, and I have one sister."

"Had?"

"One brother died by gunshot during a shootout with another gang, and one's in prison until he's an old man. My oldest brother is an attorney and works for the Public Defender's Office in Boston. My sister has her own tech business and lives in Palo Alto in a house worth more than I will ever make in my life."

"You always this open with strangers?"

"You're my *partner*. You have to have my back and I yours. Okay, to finish my personal highlight reel, I went to Howard University for my undergrad. Got my master's from Georgetown. Joined the Bureau thirteen years ago. I've fired my gun twice in the line of duty. I'm small but I hit above my weight and I bite really hard. Got a double black belt in karate not because I love martial arts, but because I hate getting my ass kicked, both physically and symbolically. I do not tolerate idiots or laziness or bullshit, and I encounter way more of all three than I need to right here at the Bureau. I like to know where I stand at all times. As a person of color and a woman on top of that, I find it a necessity to my future well-being, and that of my family. And nothing is more important to me than that."

"How old are your kids?"

"Nine and twelve. Daughter and son, respectively. Calvin, named after my father. And Jacqueline, but she goes by Jacky."

"Do you share custody with your ex?"

"I was still carrying Jacky when my ex decided marriage and fatherhood were not for him. I have full and permanent custody. Calvin doesn't even remember his father and that's a damn good thing."

"You still live in Baltimore?"

"I was *working* in Baltimore until this morning."

"Plan to move here?"

"If I can afford anything down here, which I doubt unless I want to live in the nosebleed seats. And I'll wait and see. Sometimes new assignments don't stick."

"Yeah, sometimes they don't." Decker said a silent prayer on that one.

"What about you?"

"What about me what?" he said.

"Anything to share?"

"If you spoke to Alex, you know all you need to know about me."

"But nobody tells it as good as the person himself."

"I don't tell anything remotely good about myself or anybody else."

White took this shot and fired off one of her own. "You know, you're smaller than I would have thought."

He looked down at her. "I'm a wall, only not one you *lean* on."

"It's just that Alex made you out to be nine feet tall and eight hundred pounds. Compared to that description, you're sort of shrimpy. I can't help feeling disappointed. But nevertheless, are we good to go, *partner?*"

Decker said with all due candidness, "At this point, I don't really give a shit."

"You always this way with the people you work with?"

"Initially, yeah."

"Well, let's work quickly through initially then."

Decker looked her over. "I'm sure you're a fine agent. I have nothing against you. But change like this is not my thing. And I've had more of it in my life than most people."

She glanced up at his head. "Football player? Cleveland Browns? I hate the Browns. I'm an Eagles girl through and through. Hate the Baltimore Ravens, too, and that's all I see now."

"I don't really follow football anymore."

She glanced at his head once more. "Yeah, I guess I can understand that."

The door opened and there stood Talbott. His features grim, he did not seem remotely like the cheerful man from a few minutes ago.

"You two have your first case. You're heading to Florida. Right now."

"What happened?" said Decker.

"A federal judge and her bodyguard. They're both dead."

CHAPTER

5

THANK GOD FOR MOTHERS," SAID White as she settled in her plane seat next to Decker. "Especially on short notice."

"She takes care of the kids while you're traveling?"

"Yep. Otherwise, I couldn't do it. Childcare is outrageously expensive, even when you can find it. Lucky she was a young mother. Still got a lot of energy."

"Five kids will age you fast."

"She worked, too, as the assistant principal at the school where we all went. My dad was a cop in Philly. Never made that much money."

"Is he retired?"

"He died in the line of duty."

"Sorry to hear that."

"My mother got a big settlement from the city."

"Why was that?" he said curiously.

"Because the dude that shot my father was also a cop, who didn't like the color of my dad's skin. And then the department tried to cover it up and make it look like an accident. This was twenty years ago, I was still in high school."

"Civilizations don't always progress, they some-times regress."

"Didn't expect that from you."

"Why not?" he asked.

"I don't know, to tell the truth."

After the jet lifted into the air, White said, "You read the email they sent about what happened in Florida?"

Decker nodded.

"What do you think?"

"I don't think anything. Somebody else's version of the facts in an email doesn't mean anything to me. I need to see it for myself."

"Well, what I got from it was this was an inside job, or at least the killer knew things he shouldn't have."

"You're making assumptions that aren't justified yet."

"Like what?" she asked.

"That it was only one killer. And that it was male."

"I was just speaking generally."

"I like specifics much better. So explain why you think that," he said.

"The person or *persons* knew the judge's routine. No forced entry. Her personal security was killed without him fighting back. That tells me that he didn't perceive what was happening as a threat. The judge was killed and there was no sign of a struggle. She didn't try to call for help."

"So she might have known whoever it was who killed her. The guard too."

"But why let someone in if they just killed your protection?" White asked.

"She either didn't know that had happened, or something even more devious was going on. She's divorced. Ex lives in the area."

"Right. So the ex-hubby's a possible suspect."

"Spouses, and particularly exes, always are."

"Don't I know it," replied White.

The plane started shedding altitude an hour and a half later, and they landed at the Southwest Florida International Airport near Fort Myers. A rental car was waiting for them.

White drove while Decker wedged himself into the passenger seat of the midsize four-door.

White glanced over at him as they pulled into traffic. "Sorry, it's all they had. Shortage of rental cars these days."

"I've never ridden in one that was remotely comfortable, so my expectations are nonexistent."

"Agent from the local RA is on the scene," she said, referring to an FBI Resident Agency.

"I know."

"The bodies are still there, too. They're apparently holding them for us."

He glanced at her. "Are you trying to screw with me?"

"No, I'm trying to be informative."

"Don't."

"Alex *said* you could get testy."

"You haven't even seen mildly annoyed, much less the other side of the Rubicon."

"Thanks for the information," she replied. "I like to know where I stand."

He recited from memory, " 'As a person of color and a woman on top of that, I find it a necessity to my future well-being, and that of my family.' "

"Alex also said your memory could be frustrating at times, but she worked around it."

Decker looked out the window at the bright sky and said, "I never liked Florida. When I played ball at Ohio State, we would come down to play Florida and Florida State and Miami. Hated every second of it, and not only because their players were so much faster and athletic than we were."

"Why? Too much heat or too many old people? Or both?"

"No, it's because I'm just a lunch pail guy from the Midwest."

"Meaning?"

"I hate sand."

CHAPTER

6

THEY DROVE UP TO A gated community in the town of Ocean View, which was situated about half an hour north of Naples. The roar of the breakers from the nearby Gulf shared the ride with them.

"This place looks like a postcard," noted White as she stopped the rental at the guard hut.

"Not where we're going it doesn't," replied Decker.

The guard came out of the little shack. He was in his forties and walked with a swagger more befitting a Navy SEAL than a luxury community rental cop gatekeeper.

"Can I help you?" he said as White rolled down her window.

She flashed her FBI ID pack.

"White and Decker. We're here regarding the murder of Judge Julia Cummins."

"Right, right," said the man as he eyed Decker.

While White was still in her black suit with the white shirt, Decker had on khakis and a faded dark blue sweatshirt.

"You must have come from up north," said the guard. "It's almost never sweatshirt weather here."

"Have you provided the list of guests and residents who entered here over the last twenty-four hours?" said Decker.

"Provided to who?"

"The cops," said White.

"They haven't asked for it."

"Okay, we're asking for it now," said Decker.

"I'll have to check with my supervisor."

"Then go ahead and make the call while we're waiting, because we need that info now."

"Don't you need a warrant for that sort of stuff?"

"Did you kill the judge and her guard?" said White.

The man took a step back. "What! Hey, no way."

"Then we don't need a warrant. People coming through this gate have no expectation of privacy. And this is a murder investigation. So we need to know who came through here and when during the last twenty-four hours at least."

"So make the call to your supervisor," said Decker. "And bring the information to the judge's house. We'll be waiting for it."

"Uh, okay."

"And open the gate," said White.

"Oh, right." The man quickly did so, and they drove through.

"If that's the quality of the security here, I'm surprised only two people are dead," noted White.

"Well, there might be more that we don't know about yet," said Decker.

Cummins's home was large and of Mediterranean design with white stucco siding and a red tile roof. It was situated on a shady, quiet cul-de-sac. The plantings were mature and well tended. This tranquility was marred by police and unmarked cars parked all over, and yellow crime-scene tape vibrating across the front yard in the brisk breeze.

Decker noted a blue sedan parked in the driveway. "Might be the dead security guard's ride."

"How do you figure that?"

"Every other ride here is either a police cruiser, or has Florida government or federal plates."

"Could be Judge Cummins's car."

"A woman who owns what looks to be a two- or three-million-dollar home is not driving a dented-up ten-year-old Mazda. And she would have pulled it into one of those three garage bays, not left it in the driveway. And check out the bumper sticker."

White read it off: "The Feds are watching you."

"Not something you'd typically see on a *federal* judge's car."

They parked at the curb, cleared the security at the

front door, put on booties and vinyl gloves helpfully provided by a member of the forensics team, and stepped inside.

Decker was immediately hit by a searing vision of overpowering electric blue. This was his synesthesia working overtime. His whole life, in fact, was represented by an overactive memory plus sensory pathways that had crossed streams like a clover exit off a highway.

He put a hand against the wall to steady himself because when the electric blue hit him, it made his balance momentarily say bye-bye.

Deep breaths, in and out.

When White looked at him she didn't say a word, which made Decker instantly suspicious. He would have to deal with that later. His new partner was getting on his nerves by just being silent.

The short, stocky man marched into the foyer of the house like he was a CEO entering a boardroom for a meeting. He was in his late forties and dressed in pressed slacks and a navy blue jacket. His tie and shirt were immaculate. His hair looked like it had been pressed with an iron. His features were sharp, his expression sharper still.

And he was just the sort of stuffed-shirt official prick that Decker detested.

He flashed his cred pack. "FBI Special Agent Doug Andrews out of the Fort Myers RA."

Of course you are, thought Decker.

"And you are?" Andrews said.

White produced her cred pack. Decker just stared at the doorway.

"And this is Amos Decker," said White. "We just flew in from DC."

Andrews's expression soured. "I wasn't told they were sending in agents from out of town. I was just told to hold the bodies here. I wasn't given a reason."

"Well, *we're* the reason," said White.

Andrews looked at Decker's casual dress and said, "I didn't see your ID, what was the name again, *Decker?*"

Decker looked around the grand foyer. Delicately furnished with expensive items arranged just so. Custom paint and wallpaper. Antique grandfather clock ticking away in one corner. Rugs were thick and colorful and no doubt expensive. He could smell death in every corner of the place. This was not his imagination. Dead bodies were decomposing in the near vicinity and the foul smell was unmistakable.

He saw a bloody palm print on a wall leading to the stairs. On the stair runner were other blood marks. They had number cones next to them, the mark of the forensics team's doing its processing. He saw chalky fingerprint powder everywhere. He could hear the clicks of cameras and the murmurs of conversation. Everything was going as it should. Now he had to deal with this asshole, which he didn't want to do.

Without looking at the man Decker said, "We were sent down to assist in the investigation."

"We have the matter well in hand. And I—"

Decker walked past him and into the next room.

"Hey!" barked Andrews as Decker disappeared around the corner.

He looked back at White. "What the hell is with that guy?"

"Like me, he's just here doing his job. And if you have a problem with us being here, you're going to have to take it up with HQ. But right now, we're going to work, just like you."

She followed Decker into the next room.

Andrews hurried after her.

CHAPTER

7

DECKER HAD EXPERIENCED CRIME SCENES galore
during his time in law enforcement. And he remembered every detail of each one. This one looked both
routine and also unique in certain respects.

This was the judge's study or home office. Book-
shelves, a desk, a small leather couch, a wooden
file cabinet, a sleek desktop computer, and a table-
top copier. One window looked out onto the rear
grounds. Paintings on the wall, nice knickknacks,
a colorful Oriental rug over wooden floorboards.
Nothing looked disturbed, no evidence of a frantic search for something, or a robbery or struggle
having taken place. Everything neat, tidy, in its
place.

Then, on the floor, a body. But not the judge. A
man. Obviously, the security guard. Private, not a
U.S. marshal as was usually the case with a federal
judge. He was in his thirties, lean, six feet, close-cut
brown hair that rode like a soft cap on his skull.
He was not wearing a security guard's uniform, but

rather a dark tailored suit and a white shirt with a red blotch in the center and two holes as the cause of the blood, and his death. Someone was taking no chances.

The edge of his holstered gun poked out from his jacket. Decker knelt down and checked the suit label: Armani. He looked at the watch on his wrist: Cartier. The shoes: Ferragamo.

Interesting.

The dead man was spread-eagled on the floor, sightless eyes looking up at the small chandelier hanging from the ceiling. He had a couple days' worth of beard stubble. Even in death, his features were handsome, if now very pale. His expression was one of surprise, if a dead person could hold such an emotion. And some could, Decker knew.

He eyed the forensics team doing their thing. He approached one, a woman in her forties dressed in blue scrubs and masked as she entered some information on an iPad. White followed.

"You the ME? Got a preliminary cause and time of death?"

She glanced at him in surprise and then looked around until she saw Andrews standing in the doorway. He grudgingly nodded at her as he walked up to stand next to Decker.

"I *am* the ME, Helen Jacobs. We're looking at a pair of GSWs to the chest, looks like they pierced the heart. Death instantaneous. TOD is between midnight and two a.m. last night."

White said, "Any signs of forced entry?"

"None," replied Andrews. "And who called you guys down here, Agent White?"

"SAC John Talbott out of the WFO. Give me your number and I'll text you his contact info. I thought you had been informed."

Andrews did so and White sent him the info.

"Anything taken?" asked White.

"Still checking. Nothing readily apparent."

"Name of the deceased?" asked White.

"Alan Draymont," replied Jacobs.

"We understand he was private security," said Decker. "Who with?"

"Gamma Protection Services," answered Andrews. "We contacted them and will set up an interview."

"Wearing a suit and not a uniform?"

"Gamma has a number of levels of protection. They do mall, warehouse, and office security, assignments like that. For protection at this level, they have higher-skilled operatives."

"Higher skilled? Like the dead guy?" said Decker, eyeing him closely.

"Like the dead guy," Andrews shot back. "Nobody's perfect."

White said, "Why a bodyguard? Was she getting threats?"

"Checking on that with Gamma," said Andrews a bit petulantly.

"And if so, why not a U.S. marshal?" said White. "That's the way it usually works with federal judges, right?"

"Again, checking on that," said Andrews, now huffily. "But the judge could hire private security if she wanted to. She could afford it."

Decker looked at him. "You knew her?"

"Acquaintances. I live in Ocean View. It's sort of a small-town vibe here."

"Did Draymont fire his weapon?" asked White.

"It's still in its holster," replied Andrews.

"And the killer or killers could have put it back there *after* he fired it," noted Decker.

Andrews stiffened and said, "We'll check."

"Any trace of the killer?" White asked.

Jacobs answered, "Most of the prints we've found so far belong to the judge, and a few to Draymont. There are some others, though, that we haven't identified yet. No footprints that we could find. There's a low-pile carpet runner on the stairs that didn't show any trace. And hardwood floors here in the study, upstairs hall, and the deceased's bedroom. Tough to get anything from that. It hadn't rained or anything, either, so no shoe impressions that we could find."

"And the judge's body?" asked Decker. "How did she manage to do the stairs after she was wounded?"

Jacobs looked at him curiously, then said, "You saw the blood trail on the stair runner when you came in, and on the hardwood floor leading out of here."

"Hard to miss with your little cones set out. But it was really the bloody palm print on the wall next to the stairs. I assume that must be the judge's, since two shots to the chest means Draymont wouldn't have made it out of this room under his own power."

Jacobs said, "I think she was stabbed once down here and the killing took place upstairs in her bedroom."

"Let's go," said Decker, not liking the two words *I think*.

They avoided the evidentiary trail on the carpeted steps and reached the second-floor landing, where Andrews led them into the bedroom.

"Killer didn't step in the blood from downstairs?" asked White.

"No, he was careful about that," said Jacobs.

Judge Julia Cummins was lying on her bed wearing a short white terrycloth robe. The robe was open, revealing the woman's black underpants and a white camisole. Someone had put a blindfold over her eyes, but then cut out holes in the cloth where the eyes were. There was blood all over her clothing, and on the bedspread and also on her hands, the bottoms of her feet, and her knees.

"She's been stabbed repeatedly," said Jacobs. "Ten times by my unofficial count, not counting defensive wounds. COD was blood loss due to the stabbings."

"So she was downstairs where she was attacked, ran up here, and the intruder came up and finished her off," said White.

"Appears to be that way," said Jacobs cautiously.

"Stabbing someone that many times is personal," noted Decker.

Andrews interjected, "But we have a ways to go. It's a complicated crime scene."

Decker eyed the twisted covers and took in the fact that the mattress was out of alignment with the box springs.

White must have been reading his mind. "Looks like a struggle took place there."

"You mentioned defensive wounds?" asked Decker, noting the cuts on the woman's forearms.

Jacobs said, "Yes. It's natural for a person getting attacked with a knife or blunt instrument to use their arms to block the blows. Multiple slashes. However, the wound to her lower sternum was probably the fatal one. From the location and depth, it likely cut right through her aorta. I'll know for certain when I do the post."

"Any trace under her fingernails?" asked White.

"None that I could find on a preliminary exam. I'll look closer when I do the post."

"Blood on her hands, knees, the bottoms of her feet?" noted Decker.

Andrews said, "Explained by the fact that she was attacked downstairs, stepped in her own blood, maybe fell, and got blood on her knees. Ran up here. Mark on the wall by the stairs where she no doubt put her hand to steady herself, and spatter on the stair runner."

"Any signs of sexual assault?" asked Decker, who did not look convinced by this theory as the blood spatter images from the stairs and the study marched across his mind's eye.

Jacobs replied, "I did a prelim. No signs of that. I'll know more once I get her on the slab. But I don't think she's been sexually assaulted."

Decker looked at the blindfold. "Nice of the killers to leave us this little symbol."

Andrews stepped forward. "Why blindfold her but then cut the holes so her eyes are showing?"

"The blindfold was most likely put on post-mortem," noted Jacobs.

"Of course it was," said Decker abruptly.

"You said symbolic?" said White, looking at the blindfold.

Decker said, "The lady was a judge. Justice is supposed to be blind. Only with her, I guess it wasn't, or at least in the opinion of her killer, since they made sure she was seeing clearly, or as clearly as the dead can."

Andrews sucked in a sharp breath. "Shit, that could be true."

"Where did the blindfold come from?" asked Decker.

"From the judge's closet," answered Jacobs. "It was taken from a set of handkerchiefs she had."

"Any trace of the killer left in the closet or here? Footprints, residue of blood spatter from stabbing the judge?" asked White.

"We've found nothing so far. We're still dusting for prints, and we'll take the prints of family and friends for elimination purposes, of course."

Decker said, "So this might have been heat of the moment. The killing certainly seemed to be. And the killer used the judge's handkerchief instead of bringing one already fashioned as a mask. What'd the killer use to cut the holes?"

"We've found nothing that had blood on it that would have been used."

"The killer might have used the knife to do it and then took it with him or her," said White, who then noted the card in an evidence bag next to the dead woman. "The card was found here?" she asked.

Jacobs nodded. "It was actually placed on her body."

White looked at the card in the clear plastic bag. "'Res ipsa loquitor.'"

She glanced over at Decker, who was watching her.

"Any paper or pen here match the card and the ink?" asked Decker.

"The pen is generic, but we've found no match here on the card so far," said Andrews. "The killer might have brought it."

"Any prints on the card?" asked White.

"No."

"If the killer brought the card, that *does* smack of premeditation," noted White.

"Yes, it does," said Decker. "But that coupled with the mask and the frenetic stabbing makes this a very contrarian crime scene."

Decker looked around the space and noted a photo on the nightstand.

In the picture was the deceased, and on either side of her a man and a teenage boy.

Andrews picked up the photo with his gloved hand and said, "That's Judge Cummins, of course. And that's her ex-husband, Barry Davidson, and their son, Tyler. Looks like this was taken at the club, judging by the background."

"The club?" asked White.

"Harbor Club. It's right down the coast, about five minutes. They were members. Well, the judge was."

"And her ex and her son? Where are they?"

"We contacted Barry Davidson. He lives nearby."

"Alibi?"

"He was with his son. It was the week he had him."

"So his son is his alibi?" said Decker.

"Yes. I understand the boy is devastated."

"How old is he?"

"Seventeen."

"Do you know the ex and the son?" asked Decker.

"I've met Barry Davidson."

"And you know this club, obviously, since you recognized it in the photo."

"Yes. I belong to the Harbor Club, too."

Decker eyed the man's costly suit and shoes. "Is that your Lexus outside?"

"Yes, it is. What about it?"

"Nothing. Is the Mazda Draymont's ride?"

"Yes," answered Jacobs, looking anxiously between the two men.

Decker said, "So, what's your theory on what happened here last night, Agent Andrews?"

Andrews glanced at White and then took a moment to compose his thoughts. "I think it seems reasonably clear. Since there was no forced entry, either one of the doors was unlocked or the person or persons was let in. The fact that the judge was in her underwear leads me to believe that Draymont was shot first. The judge, on hearing something from her bedroom, put on a robe, came downstairs, and was attacked. She ran back to her room, probably to lock herself in, but wasn't able to. They killed her here. Then they left the card and put the blindfold on her."

"If Draymont let the person in he must have known them. Either on his own, or because they knew the judge," said White.

"But if the murders occurred between midnight and two, that would be pretty late for a visitor," observed Decker.

"Could Draymont have been in on it, let the person in, and then had a change of heart, or the killer intended on leaving no witnesses behind?" said White.

Andrews said, "That's certainly possible."

"Who called the police about the bodies?" asked Decker.

"They got a call from the neighbor next door, Doris Kline. She went out on her rear deck this morning to drink her coffee and read her iPad, and saw the back door of Cummins's house open. She went over to make sure everything was okay. It was after nine at that point. And the judge was normally on her way to court before then. Kline walked in the rear door, went into the kitchen and then through to the study, where she saw Draymont's body. She ran back to her house and called the cops. They found the judge's body, too, and called us in because of her federal status. I've already contacted the U.S. Marshals Service to loop them in. I've been busy here, but I plan to interview Kline next."

Decker nodded absently and surveyed the room once more, imprinting every detail onto his memory cloud, as he liked to refer to it now. When he'd first learned he had perfect recall he'd named it his "hard drive," but times changed and he had to change with them.

His hyperthymesia was an amazing tool for a detective, but it was also overwhelming at times. He had been told that there were fewer than a hundred people in the world who had been diagnosed with the condition, and Decker would have preferred not to have been one of them.

Most people with hyperthymesia concentrated their recall on personal events, memories from the past, mostly autobiographical in nature. Because of that, Decker had learned that they often tended to live in the past as well because the stream of recollections was unrelenting. While Decker certainly had some of that, too, his memory recall was different. Pretty much everything he heard or saw or read in the present was permanently encoded in his mind and could be pulled out at will.

He turned to Jacobs. "TOD on the judge?"

"Approximately the same range as Draymont. Midnight to two a.m. I might be able to get a little tighter on the parameters, but that time box is looking pretty solid."

He handed her his business card. "Let me know

about Draymont's gun and the possible sexual assault."

"All right."

He looked at Andrews. "We told the guard at the entrance gate to get us the list of people who came through over the last twenty-four hours. He was going to bring it here."

"I had planned to do that," said Andrews.

"Good, we're operating on the same wavelength. While we're waiting for him, let's go talk to Mrs. Kline."

He walked out of the room.

Andrews whirled on White. "How long have you and Decker been partners?"

White checked her watch. "Oh, about six hours."

CHAPTER

8

DORIS KLINE USHERED THEM INTO her home after they knocked, and led them to the rear lanai. She was in her late fifties with permed hair and too much makeup, at least to Decker's mind.

But what the hell do I know?

Kline had on a pair of white slacks and an orange shirt with the sleeves half rolled up, revealing taut, tanned forearms, mottled over with coppery sunspots. She was skinny for her five-foot-eight height, and the woman was a smoker, which might have been a factor in her thinness. A pack of Camels and a purple Zippo lighter sat on the table on the screened-in lanai, which overlooked the backyard. Beyond that were some slender palm trees and compact shrubbery. A pool was situated in front of them. From the smell it was apparently filled with saltwater. Through the screens enclosing the space, Decker noted a well-trod path down to the beach, with the dull gray stretch of the Gulf just beyond that. Seagulls swooped and dove across the clear sky looking for things no human could see.

The house was smaller than Julia Cummins's place and hadn't been kept up as well. The stucco was damaged in several areas, and the outdoor heat pumps heavily rusted from the heavy salt air had drawn Decker's notice. The lawn and landscaping hadn't seen much attention, either. He didn't know if that was simply the result of indifference or a lighter wallet than the judge had had.

"Were you the only one in your house last night?" asked Decker.

Kline blew smoke from her nose and nodded as she reached for a glass of what looked like orange juice, but Decker smelled the alcohol in it.

"I was. I'm divorced, my kids grown and off. I don't go out much because my ex left me with lots of bills and not enough alimony. He had the better lawyer, unfortunately."

"Can you take us through this morning?" asked White, her eyes widening, apparently at the woman so casually revealing this personal info.

"I came out here around nine, saw the rear door was open, and that seemed strange. At that hour of the morning Julia had usually long since left for court, and she really never used that door. She just went right from the house to the garage."

"Did you know her well?" asked Decker.

"We were neighbors and good friends for years."

"I'm sure you're upset about what happened," interjected White.

Kline tapped ash into a crystal bowl, her lips firmly set. "I'm not a crier. But I'm very distraught that Julia is dead. I cared for her. A lot. We were good friends. We would vent to each other. But I've seen a ton of shit in my life. The best defense is just to keep it at arm's length, at least that's my take."

"So, you investigated and found the body of the man in the study?" said Decker.

"Scared the crap out of me. I ran right out and called the police. They were here in maybe three minutes. There's a station not that far from here."

"You knew the dead man?" said White.

"I'd *seen* him at Julia's. I never spoke with him."

"Did the judge discuss with you why she needed security?"

"Not really, no. I guess all judges get threats and stuff. Hell, these days, who doesn't? Look at social media. I could post something about saving orphans and I'd be attacked as a sex-trafficking pedophile. People are such animals online."

"But did she actually say it was because she had received threats that she had the bodyguard?" asked Decker.

"No, I don't believe she did. I guess I just assumed."

"Last night, did you hear or see anything?" asked

White. "Say between midnight and two, or even before or after that? Flash of headlights turning into the drive next door? Gunshot? Screams or raised voices? Sounds of a fight?"

She shook her head and sharply cleared her throat. "I use a CPAP machine at night, and I take an Ambien. I wasn't going to hear anything."

"Do you have an alarm system?" asked Decker.

"Oh sure. But I don't usually turn it on."

"Why not?" asked White curiously.

"Well, we have a gate and twenty-four-hour security."

Decker said, "So did the judge. Plus her own private bodyguard. Clearly wasn't enough."

Kline looked less sure of herself and tapped ash into the bowl. "I guess I see your point."

"How about the neighbor on the other side of the judge?" asked Decker.

"The Perlmans? They're in New York. They left last week and will be back tomorrow."

"They knew Cummins?" asked Andrews.

"Sure, we were all friends. Maya, that's Mrs. Perlman, was a retired lawyer, so she and Julia had that connection. Trevor is her husband; it's her second marriage. Oh and I think they were the ones who told Julia about the protection service she ended up using."

"Why was that?" asked White.

"I'm not entirely sure, but I think the Perlmans had used them in the past. I don't know why. You'd have to ask them."

Decker and White exchanged a glance.

"Do you know the judge's ex and their son, Tyler?" asked Decker.

"Yes. Barry and Tyler Davidson. Cummins was Julia's maiden name. She kept it after they were married. Saved her some paperwork after the divorce since she didn't have to change it back. They all lived next door until the breakup. Barry still lives nearby. When I was married, we would all go out together. After our divorces Julia and I would still go out, or else have a girls night in. We'd either cook, or do takeout with white wine and Hallmark movies. Although lately she seemed a bit different."

"How so?" asked White.

"Over the last year or so she wanted to go out more. Dinner, dancing. Hitting the club scene. She was dressing, well, how shall I say, a little younger than she had been. Don't get me wrong, she looked fabulous. She was a decade younger than me. She seemed to be having fun. Why not?"

Her lips started to twitch and tears suddenly clustered at the corners of her eyes.

"And they had shared custody of Tyler?" said White quietly.

She dabbed at her eyes with her hand. "Yes, one

week on and off. But Tyler will be going to college in about a year and a half, so it would have ended then. With Julia gone I guess it ends right now..." Kline set her drink down and stubbed out her Camel. She put a hand to her face and let out a sob. "I'm...I'm sorry, I th-think it just h-hit me that she's really g-gone."

White produced some Kleenex from a pack in her pocket and passed them across.

Kline wiped her eyes. "Thank you." She collected herself and continued in a husky voice, "Julia was very nice. Very caring. After my divorce she was so supportive."

"She talk to you about any problems lately? You ever see any strange cars around or people you didn't recognize loitering?" asked Decker.

Kline shook her head and finished her drink in one gulp. "No, nothing like that. Again, this is a gated community so they keep the riffraff out, or at least they're supposed to."

"You never really talked about the bodyguard? Seems strange between close friends."

She lit another Camel and blew fresh smoke out. "Look, I tried to ask her about that a couple of times, but she shut it down. I respected that, so I didn't push it. I just figured it was crap someone in her position had to put up with."

"To confirm, she actually told you about the guard, but didn't say why he was there?" asked Decker.

"That's right."

"When was the last time you saw Barry or Tyler?" asked Andrews.

"Tyler was here last week when he was staying with his mom. Barry, I saw about three weeks ago. He had come by for some reason. Maybe to pick up Tyler."

"How does Tyler usually get here from his dad's place?" asked White. "Did his parents drive him back and forth?"

"He has his own car, a BMW convertible, and a gate pass, so he usually drives himself. But sometimes his father brings him, or Julia would drive him back to Barry's condo. A couple times I've seen an Uber drop him off. And he has a bike, too. It's not far, a couple of miles."

"So that's the last time you saw Barry? About three weeks ago?" asked Decker.

"No, now that I think about it, I saw him at the clubhouse. Oh, about a week or so ago."

"The Harbor Club?" asked Decker.

"No, we have a clubhouse here and a golf course. Very challenging. Do you play?"

"No. Why was he there?"

"Well, he was playing golf, nine holes, and then he had lunch. I said hello to him."

"So he's still a member?" asked White.

"Oh, yes. He retained all of that even after the

divorce. In fact, it might have been part of the divorce for all I know."

"What does he do for a living?"

"He runs his own company. Investments, that sort of thing. Does quite well. And Julia's house is beautiful. Pool and big lanai. I have that, too, on a smaller scale, but I don't have the money to really keep it up anymore," she added bitterly. "I'm going to have to downsize at some point."

"Was he the major breadwinner in the marriage?" asked White.

"I wouldn't say that. Before she was a judge, Julia was a high-powered lawyer, made a ton of money. And she also came from serious New York money. Trust funds and all that. Her father was a Wall Street bigwig. She got millions from him in inheritance. She was an only child. She wasn't even fifty yet and now she's dead." Kline shook her head, her expression one of misery.

"Do you know who the beneficiary is of her estate?" asked Andrews.

Kline refocused. "I would guess Tyler, but I don't know for certain. He's their only child. I can't believe she'd leave a dime to Barry. You'd have to check with her lawyer to be certain."

"Do you know who that is?" asked White.

"Duncan Trotter. I know because he handles my stuff, too. Julia recommended him, in fact. His office is on Pelican Way, off the main street in town. He can tell you everything about that." She sat back. "Anything else?"

White exchanged glances with Andrews, who shook his head. Then she looked at Decker, who was staring at the sky through the screened roof.

"Decker, you got anything else for Ms. Kline?"

"Why the divorce?" asked Decker.

"Mine?"

"No, Julia and Barry."

Kline shrugged. "Why does anyone get divorced?"

"That's what I'm asking."

"There were issues, just like any marriage. Barry could tell you more, but it would just be from his perspective."

"And what was *your* perspective? You said you were good friends. When married, you all socialized as couples. You shared very personal information. You must have an opinion," said Decker.

"Why do you care about that?"

"Not to be too blunt, but most wives who are murdered are killed by their husbands. Same holds true for ex-wives and ex-husbands."

Kline pursed her lips. Her look was clear: She did not want to go there. "Julia was as straight as they come. Barry, well, he cut corners."

"How?"

"He just wasn't much of a rule follower."

"Can you give us an example?" asked White.

"They were audited about five years ago. Turns out Barry got caught with his hand in the cookie jar, and they had to pay hefty fines and Barry almost went to jail. Julia had only just gotten on the bench. If that had come out before? She probably wouldn't have been confirmed. She filed for divorce shortly afterward."

"And she was upset?" asked White.

"More like livid. I think that hastened the end of what was already a troubled marriage."

"Why already troubled?" asked White.

"Barry never grew up. He wanted to be a college frat boy forever. Goofy and boozing and just having fun."

"Did he cheat on her?" asked White.

"Not that I know. I actually believe he loved her and only her."

Andrews said, "Okay, anything else, Decker?"

Decker had looked up at the sky again. When he didn't answer, White put her notebook away and rose. "Well, thank you for your time. We'll probably have follow-up questions."

"I just want you to catch whoever did this."

"We want that, too."

Andrews rose and looked down at Decker. "You ready, Decker? We're heading out."

Decker lowered his gaze to Kline. "Who told you the judge was dead?"

"What?" said Kline, looking surprised.

"You saw Draymont's body in the study, but you didn't see the judge's body upstairs?"

"That's right."

"Did the police come over here and tell you?"

"No. I just assumed. I mean, if Julia had been alive, she would have come over here. I would have seen her out in the yard. She would have called the police herself last night."

"So you just assumed she was home last night?"

"Yes, that was why the guard was there, I presumed." Decker nodded and rose. "Okay."

"I'm not sure I appreciate the allegations in your questions," Kline said irritably.

"That's okay. People never do."

CHAPTER

9

THE SECURITY GUARD AT THE gate was waiting for them when they returned to Cummins's house. He held up some printed-out pages.

"Here you go, everybody from the last twenty-four hours."

Andrews reached for the pages but Decker's arm was longer and he got to it first.

"Thanks. Can you give us a summary? With some local color?"

The guard said, "Well, we obviously had lots of people who live here come and go. They don't have to sign in."

"But I saw there are electronic tags on some of the cars with the name of this development on them. So there should be a *record* of homeowners coming and going, right?"

"They're in that stack I just gave you."

"Thanks. The summary?"

"Oh, well, there were well over a hundred visitors' cars during that period of time."

"Is that a lot, a little, right on target?" asked Decker.

"It's a little high, but that was because of the golf tournament."

"That was played yesterday?"

"Yes."

"And what documentation do visitors need to get through the gate?"

"They have to be on the guest list, called in by a homeowner, or have a temp pass. The contractors go that route usually, though some of them who come really frequently have permanent gate passes."

"What form do these permanent passes take?"

"Form? I don't understand."

"Do they have the electronic strips on their windshields that trigger the gate like the homeowners do, are they paper on the dashboard, or what?"

"Well, they can be either/or, actually."

"So the paper ones will have no record of who was actually coming and going?"

"No. I mean, we don't keep a list, we just check to make sure the paper pass is still valid. And we keep a count of vehicles coming through. And contractors are supposed to be gone by six p.m.," he added.

"What if a car or truckload of people comes in? Do you do a head count to see how many come in on paper or electronic passes?" Decker asked.

"What?" said the guard, looking confused.

"He means," said White, "if five people come

through the gate in one vehicle, do you make sure the same five people go out in that same vehicle?"

"Um..."

"So the answer is no," said Decker, eyeing the papers in his hand like they were dung.

"Right."

"And guests who come in after hours?"

"They have to use the call box to phone an off-site security service that will check to see if they're on the list."

"And people who bike and walk up here?"

"Well, they're usually homeowners or their guests."

"So you only check vehicles?"

"Well, yeah."

"Is there camera surveillance here?"

"Um, yeah, but the cameras keep breaking down. Salt air, I guess. But this is a really safe place."

Decker sighed. "Not anymore it's not. Did you see anyone who looked suspicious or who previously asked about the judge or otherwise seemed nervous or out of place?"

"No, but you should check with the off-site service, too."

"We will," Andrews assured him. "Thanks."

The man got back into his white Honda with SECURITY stenciled on the side and drove off.

"The security situation here is not as good as the residents probably think it is," noted White.

"It's also typical for this type of gated community," said Andrews. "The super-rich have whole other layers of sophisticated protection."

"Too bad for the *merely* rich," said Decker. "Let's go talk to the ex and the kid."

"They're waiting for us at their condo."

"Kline said it was about two miles from here," Decker said.

"That's right," replied Andrews.

White said, "And the ex has a security strip on his car, presumably."

"If so, and he came here last night, it should be in those records," noted Andrews. "Which I think I should keep charge of."

Decker glanced at White before handing the batch of papers over to Andrews. "Knock yourself out."

"You can ride over with me," said Andrews. "I can bring you back here after the interview. Where are you staying?" He led them over to his Lexus.

"DoubleTree," replied White. "We haven't checked in yet."

"It's not that far. Has a nice restaurant."

"How well do you know Barry Davidson?" asked Decker.

"Look, if you're trying to get me knocked off this case because of some made-up conflict—" snapped Andrews.

"The only thing I'm *trying* to do," cut in Decker,

"is *solve* this case. If you have any helpful information?"

Andrews glanced at White, who said, "We're not in a competition, Agent Andrews. If the positions were reversed, I'd be irked, too. But we're following orders, just like you. So let's just try to get along and nail the sucker who did this."

Andrews shot Decker a look.

"What she said," said Decker.

"I don't know him that well. We've played golf together exactly once, and that was a tournament where we were paired up. I've had some casual conversations with him over the years, but that's it."

"Guy have a good rep in his line of work?"

"Nothing that I've ever heard to the contrary. I actually have some friends who are clients. They seem very pleased."

"And you didn't know about the tax thing five years ago?"

Andrews looked uncomfortable. "There was some local scuttlebutt about that. But I wasn't involved."

"And the kid?"

"He's a junior in high school, already got some solid college interest for football. I've watched him play. He's really good."

"Ever in any trouble?"

"Straight as an arrow as far as I know. I'm friends with several of the local cops. They never mentioned anything involving him. I think Tyler knows he has a shot at the big time and doesn't want to screw it up. He's an Honor Roll student."

"You seem to know a lot about him," said White.

"He's sort of a local sports hero. He's nationally ranked at his position. And he won the state heavyweight wrestling title as a sophomore. Now he concentrates on football."

"Sounds like a real stud," said Decker.

White said, "Decker played at Ohio State, and then for the Cleveland Browns. But I'm not going to hold that against him."

Andrews looked up at the huge Decker. "Is that right? The Cleveland Browns? And then you became a cop? Odd career trajectory."

Decker glanced at White. "And getting odder by the minute."

CHAPTER

10

THE DRIVE TOOK THEM PAST picturesque scenery, wide beaches, birds roaming the skies, high-rise condos, and oceanfront estates lurking behind sturdy gates and high walls. And all the way Decker ignored this and just stared out the rear window, seeing only images in his head.

His wife dead, his daughter dead, years and years now in the grave. Just recently, Mary Lancaster departed by her own desperate hand. And the very much alive Alex Jamison and Melvin Mars and Ross Bogart all moving on with their lives.

And here I am with a new partner and... this. Two more murders, the puzzle that always comes along with it, the interviews, the questions, the lies in response, more questions and confrontations and just plain bullshit that both the innocent and guilty continually spew out. And then it gets solved and off I go to the next one.

From Florida to North Dakota and all points in between.

He turned to see White staring at him from the front passenger seat. The woman had seen a slice of life that Decker never would. It had no doubt made her tough, ferocious in defense, but crafty and cagey and knowing she had to play by a set of rules that were biased against her to a degree that should alarm everyone but somehow never really did.

"I'm not sure I have enough in the bank to offer up cash for your thoughts," she said, tacking on a smile.

Decker looked away. In his mind's eye he saw Mary Lancaster lift a trembling hand with a gun in it to her mouth, insert the barrel, close her eyes, and end her life in one of the most tragic ways possible.

Then, instead of Lancaster's face, Decker saw his own countenance. He was staring at a toilet on which sat his daughter. Father and daughter were barely a foot away from each other. One staring helpless, crushed beyond all conceivable human limits, the other staring back at him and seeing nothing because the dead could not. He had taken out his service pistol and laid it in his mouth. The muzzle of the Glock had felt metallically bitter, the barrel oil leaching onto his tongue. He had looked at Molly and then closed his eyes. His finger had slipped to the trigger and it would have only taken a couple foot-pounds of force to propel him into death with his daughter and wife. Such a simple move, one he had done thousands of times on the gun range, and several times while doing his job in the field.

And yet, unlike Mary Lancaster, he had pulled the gun free and waited for the cops to show up.

Had I been too cowardly? Had I lacked the courage that Mary had in abundance? And she left her daughter and husband behind. An option I didn't have, and one I don't think I could have taken.

"Decker?"

He broke from his thoughts to see White staring worriedly at him. This annoyed him.

"How much longer?" he brusquely asked Andrews.

"Coming up to the security gate now."

"Does anybody around here live in a place without a guard gate?" asked Decker. "Is it *that* fucking dangerous here?"

Andrews eyed him in the rearview, as though checking to see if Decker was perhaps joking. He said, "I don't have a guard gate in my neighborhood. I guess I don't make enough money."

"Has anyone spoken to the Davidsons yet?" asked White.

"Local cops. Just to inform them of Cummins's death. They deferred the rest to us."

"We'll need to establish alibis," said White. "And what about a search warrant for the ex's condo?"

"The woman's body was just found this morning," said Andrews. "Let's take it one step at a time. And we have no grounds for a search warrant."

"Yet," amended Decker.

They cleared security and took the elevator up to the fourth floor of the condo building with a broad view of the Gulf on the rear side. The elevator doors opened and they were in a small vestibule with one large wooden door. Andrews knocked on it, and a few moments later they heard footsteps approaching.

The teenager was large, about six-three and two-forty. He was dressed in dark blue workout compression shorts, was barefoot, and had on a white tank top. Decker eyed his physique and noted the bulging quads and thick calves, the broad shoulders, the lanky, muscled arms. The kid already had a collegiate body, he assessed. Now if he had some decent wheels and quick-twitch muscle mass, he might have a nice college run. The NFL was a whole other matter. The funnel there got as narrow as a needle's eye.

"Tyler?" said Andrews, who showed the young man his badge and ID. He introduced Decker and White. "We understand your father is here?"

"He's drunk," mumbled Tyler, who looked to Decker like he was on something though his pupils looked normal. "Shit-faced." He shook his head, his expression pained and his eyes bloodshot from crying. "Is Mom really...?"

"Yes, Tyler, I'm afraid she is," said Andrews.

His big hands curled to knotty fists. "I'm gonna fucking kill whoever did this."

Andrews put a hand on his shoulder. "No, you're not, Tyler. It's our job to deal with this and we will. We will find whoever did this and they will never see another free day. I promise you that. Now we really need to talk to your dad."

"And you," interjected Decker.

Andrews frowned at this but nodded. "And you too. But please take us to your father."

Tyler turned and led them down a hallway. They passed an expensive-looking electric bike that was parked against one wall, its power pack plugged in.

"Nice ride," said Decker.

"My dad got it for me. Florida is pretty flat but when you're doing thirty-forty miles at a fast clip under your own power, the motor comes in handy sometimes."

Decker looked around as they passed minimalist furnishings and décor, lots of gleaming metal and glass, and walls painted white to take advantage of the strong Florida light. The rear windows gave sweeping views of the Gulf, where ships seemingly no larger than toys made their way slowly across the water, or else bobbed up and down at anchor.

Tyler pushed a door open and motioned them in.

Sitting in a leather recliner was, apparently, Barry Davidson. He had on jeans, a white polo shirt, and no shoes or socks. A glass with some dark liquid rested on his flat stomach with one of the man's hands wrapped loosely around it. His eyes were closed and Decker wasn't even sure the guy was awake. Or alive.

"Mr. Davidson?" said Andrews. "We need to talk."

Davidson made no reaction to this.

"Dad!" shouted Tyler, putting a massive hand on his father's shoulder and violently shaking him.

The glass went sideways, and whatever was in it spilled across the man's shirt and jeans. The eyes popped open and the recliner came forward, and Barry Davidson would have fallen to the floor if Decker had not been quick enough to catch him.

"What? Who?" said Davidson, shaking his head and blinking rapidly.

"It's the cops, Dad. The FBI. They need to talk to you!"

Tyler shook his head, a disgusted look on his face. He picked up the now-empty glass and placed it on a table.

Decker looked around the room and noted that it was set up as a home office with wooden file cabinets, shelving, a desktop printer-copier, a postage meter, and other office supplies and equipment arrayed around the space. A large computer screen with a digital webcam attached sat on a large glass-topped desk. He imagined the guy probably did a lot of Zoom meetings from here. French doors opened to a covered balcony.

Davidson rubbed his eyes, slapped himself a couple of times on the cheeks, and looked up at Andrews.

"I kn-know you, right?"

"Doug Andrews. We played golf together once, at the Harbor Club."

A still-dazed Davidson pointed a shaky hand at him. "Right, right, never forget a guy's game. You can hit it a mile but you putt like shit. Grips all wrong and you have too much backswing."

Andrews smiled embarrassedly at White. "Never considered quitting my day job."

Decker stepped forward. "We're here to talk to you about your former wife's death."

Davidson nodded, his head dipping and bobbing like he might be sick. White took a step back to avoid being in the pathway.

"Right, r-right," said Davidson. "She's...dead."

"Someone fucking *murdered* her, Dad," snapped Tyler. "Get your shit together, will you?"

Andrews put up a hand. "Come on, Tyler, your dad's been through a lot."

"*I've* been through a lot. Mom went through the

most of all. You don't see *me* getting stoned." He shot his father another disgusted look.

Andrews said, "A forensics team will be by later to take your prints."

"Why?" said Tyler.

"For elimination purposes. Your prints will be all over the house, Tyler, since you live there every other week. But we need to ID prints like yours and your father's so we can focus on any strange ones that might be there."

"I...I haven't been inside h-her house in a couple weeks," said Davidson, his eyes rolling around in their sockets. "When I went to pick up Tyler."

"We'll still need to take your prints," said Andrews.

"J-Julia's d-dead," Davidson said, starting to sob.

Decker put a hand on his shoulder. "Mr. Davidson, why don't you go grab a shower, and get some fresh clothes on. We'll make you some coffee and get some water into you for hydration to knock the buzz off and then we can talk, okay? It's really important. The first forty-eight hours are the most critical of all for any murder investigation."

He helped Davidson to stand and then looked at Tyler, who was staring out the window, his arms folded over his heaving chest. Decker glanced at Andrews. "Let's get him to the bathroom."

Tyler called out, "Bring me his clothes. I'll put them in the wash to get the stink of the booze out."

Decker and Andrews helped Davidson to the bathroom, got the shower going, and pulled out some towels and toiletries. They got the man stripped down and into the shower. Then Decker left him there with Andrews and gave the soiled clothes to Tyler. He followed Tyler to a laundry room, where he threw the clothes into the washing machine.

"Didn't know I was going to have to clean up after my dad," Tyler said sullenly. "I did my stuff earlier. I had my run early this morning with the guys and got soaked through. I'm a big sweater."

"Yeah, me too. But we have a lot more skin than most people."

"I guess."

He turned the machine on, leaned against the wall, and then abruptly started to sob.

Decker let him do so for a bit before saying, "Can I get you anything, Tyler?"

"N-no." Tyler wiped his face, composed himself, and suddenly eyed Decker's large frame. "You look like you might've played some ball."

"Ohio State. And the NFL, for the briefest of times. I was a walk-on with the Browns."

"*The* Ohio State University already offered me a scholarship. And I've got three other offers."

"Great school. Great program. Where else?"

"Alabama, Georgia, and Stanford."

"The best of the best. You want to play in the NFL?"

He shook his head. "I'm not at that level and never will be."

"Most young men your age wouldn't be able to make that sort of frank self-assessment. They usually think they're good enough."

"I've been making frank assessments all my life. I want to go into business. Silicon Valley. That's where a lot of cool stuff is happening."

"Well, they're all great schools, but Stanford is right where you want to end up. And they play a pro-style offense. So as a tight end, you'll get a lot of throws your way."

Tyler looked intrigued. "How'd you know I played tight end?"

"You've got the build, the height, and your hands have calluses and abrasions all over them, especially the palms and the fingertips."

"I could be a QB."

"QBs throw the ball, they don't catch it. You get that level of toughened skin from frequent high-velocity impacts with the pigskin."

"Wide receiver, then."

"You're too beefy to play wideout. Those guys are slim with lightning in their shoes. And a high school coach would never waste a guy your size on that position. You could play any slot on the line with your beef. And they'd use you as an extra lineman on running plays."

"Yeah, I pretty much do exactly that. What position did you play in college?"

"OLB," said Decker, referring to outside linebacker.

"*You're* big for that."

"I've put on weight since then, but I had decent wheels. They tried me on the D-line, but even back then those boys were all three-twenty plus. And I wasn't athletic enough to hold my own at two-sixty against O-lines where the tackles made me look like a middle schooler. OSU plays in the big leagues and the NFL is another planet. With the Browns I did most of my field time on special teams. I was never going to be a starter."

"Guys we play against in high school are running four-threes like it's nothing."

White said, "Well, not to put a stop to the shop talk, guys, but...?"

They turned to see her standing a few feet from them.

Decker glanced at her and said to Tyler, "You want to talk here or somewhere else?"

"How about the beach?"

White hiked her eyebrows at Decker. "You mean out on all that *sand*?" she said.

"Fine," said Decker. "Why don't you wait here, Agent White? And let them know where we went."

White was about to protest, but then she glanced at Tyler and slowly nodded. "Sure, I can let you *footballers* have some alone time."

The two big men walked off, leaving White to sit down in a chair and wait, her lips pursed and her gaze hanging on Decker's broad back.

CHAPTER

II

I'M...UM, I'M SORRY ABOUT your mother," said Decker as they reached the sand and headed south. Decker had taken off his shoes and socks and rolled up his pants. Tyler had slipped off his flip-flops and was carrying them. Decker was awkward at social encounters like this. As a young man, before his brain injury, he could be empathetic and consoling and even glib. Now, on the other side of his near-death experience, he was none of those things.

"I think I'm gonna wake up and she'll be there waving at me."

"I can understand that. So, when was the last time you actually saw your mother?"

"I stayed with her last week, this week I'm with my dad."

"Tough going back and forth?"

"It was at first, but then I got into a routine. Well, I did with Mom. Dad never has had much of a routine."

"So you saw her last a week ago?"

"No, I had lunch with her three days ago, at the golf clubhouse where she lives."

"Wasn't she at the courthouse then?"

"She had the afternoon off, she said."

"She seem okay, no problems?"

"Yeah, she was fine."

"Did you ever meet her private bodyguard?"

"No. When I was with her last week, she didn't have a bodyguard around."

That remark caught Decker by surprise but he decided not to comment on it. "But at some point did she tell you that she had one?"

"Yeah, she mentioned it at lunch. I asked her what was up."

"And what did she say?"

"She said it was over some stupid stuff from being a judge, but she didn't want to take chances."

"She wasn't more specific?"

"No. But she'd gotten threats in the past and nothing had come of it."

"Were you worried that you might be in danger while you were over there?"

"I'm a big guy, I can take care of myself. But I always worried about my mom. Lots of psychos out there, you know."

"When you were over there, did you ever see anything weird?"

"Nope. By the time I got home after school, I

was pretty beat. Usually ate dinner, listened to some music, did my schoolwork, and then hit the sack."

"You on a year-round workout schedule?"

He nodded. "We were runner-up for state, so everyone's gunning for us. The team that beat us lost half their starters to graduation, while we're still stacked. I was first team All-State as a junior. And even though I've got my scholarship offers, my take is I've got to be even better than I was last year. Weight room, cardio, playbooks, passing and blocking drills. Never stops."

"Same way in college. And in the pros, it's your life."

"Maybe I'll make enough money to buy my own team one day."

"There you go. So you never saw or heard anything else troubling your mother?"

"Except for my dad."

"What do you mean?" Decker said sharply.

Tyler suddenly looked fearful. "No, hey, I just mean, well, he's like a little kid who never grew up. Nothing wrong with that. He just loves life, you know?"

"I get that, but was that the reason for the divorce?"

"Yeah, and there was some dumb tax issue that she was really upset about. This was about five years ago, after she became a judge. She filed for divorce pretty soon after that. I didn't really get it. I mean, blow up a marriage over taxes? They both had plenty of money. Anyway, Mom didn't like Dad's lifestyle after the divorce, and she didn't want Dad having his girlfriends stay over while I was with him. She didn't think it was right."

"What did you think about that?"

"Well, I have to admit, it was nice seeing the young ladies running around the condo in T-shirts and pretty much nothing else, or tanning themselves on one of the balconies or by the pool, but it did get old after a while. I mean, it was my dad! And they were only in it for his money anyway. Even though he does keep himself in decent shape, he's almost fifty. Twentysomething ladies don't go for that without the cash to back it up."

"So, you were with your father last night? Here?"

"Yeah. I got home around seven. We had dinner, watched some TV, and I finished some schoolwork. Then I went to bed."

"What time?"

"About ten thirty or so. I was beat."

"And your dad?"

"I heard him talking in his office. My bedroom's right next door. He has clients all over the world, so he operates in different time zones. Kept waking me up when he went on the Zooms. It's like he thinks he has to talk loud because they're in Asia and shit."

"Happen to check the time when you woke up?"

"It was off and on. And I didn't go back to sleep

right away. Once was around one or so. I remember because I was thinking I had to get up at six to go for my run and I was pissed."

"Okay."

"And another time was after two. I remember looking at my Apple watch. And then again close to three."

"Okay."

"And while I was trying to fall asleep I heard him in his office *before* then walking around and practicing his pitch, you know, what he says to his clients. He does that all the time."

"So let me get this straight: You heard your father either on a Zoom call or walking around and practicing his pitch when, exactly?"

"Well, pretty much from like before midnight until almost three."

"You mean you *never* fell asleep?"

"Okay, yeah, I did. Around three when I heard him get up and leave his office. So he might have left the condo after that but I don't think so. I heard him pass my room and then his bedroom door opened and closed. It has a weird squeaking sound. Then I heard his shower start up."

"He showers at three?"

"Like I said, he keeps weird hours because of his business. And he sweats like I do, especially when he's dealing with clients. He says they're very demanding. And the showers help to calm him, let him get relaxed for bed. And he usually has a drink before he goes to bed."

Decker took all this in. "Okay, thanks for that."

"He cared for my mom. A lot. This blew him away. He's been crying all morning and drinking like a fucking fish." He paused and looked out to the water. "I think part of him is also terrified that he's the sole parent now. He can't drop all the responsibility on Mom anymore. She really did it all with me. SAT prep, schoolwork, doctor's appointments, making sure I was all set for the prom, helping pick out colleges, dealing with recruiters, riding my ass on grades. She never missed one of my football games. And when I was younger I played every sport and she was right there. She even coached one of my Little League teams."

"Sounds like a superwoman, considering she was a lawyer and then a judge."

"Yeah, we were all real proud of her when she got to be a federal judge. The freaking president of the United States had to nominate her. I mean, is that cool or what?"

"Pretty cool."

Tyler shook his head. "Now what's going to happen?"

"You're going to finish high school, go to a great college, and make your mom proud."

"But with her not here, I'm not sure I can keep my shit together anymore."

"Any time you start thinking that, think about all the things your mother did to get you ready for life. It was worth it to her, so it has to be worth it to you. It shows respect."

Tyler looked at him funny. "Sounds like you lost somebody close, too."

Decker eyed the young man and saw in him a bit of his younger self. Supremely confident in his athletic abilities, unsure of everything else.

"We've all lost somebody close, Tyler. It's how we deal with it that counts, because if you mess that up nothing else really matters."

12

I HAD A ZOOM CONFERENCE with a client in Hong Kong from two a.m. to around three. Before that I was speaking with another client in Beijing from midnight to one. I prepped for the Beijing meeting from around eleven fifteen on, and for the Hong Kong meeting after the Beijing call. They're both twelve hours ahead of us. Then I grabbed a shower, had a scotch, and went to bed."

Barry Davidson had showered and changed his clothes. After a couple cups of coffee and two bottles of water, he seemed more composed and focused. They were back in his office. Tyler had left to get some air.

"We'll need to check any video recordings you made and talk with those folks," said Andrews.

"Do you really consider me a suspect in Julia's murder?" snapped Davidson.

Decker said, "Spouses and ex-spouses are always suspects until their alibis are established."

"I never went near Julia's place last night."

White glanced at Decker. "Okay, let's move on from there, Mr. Davidson. In speaking with your wife, did she voice any concerns, was she having problems with someone? Maybe a case she was over-seeing?"

"Julia and I don't…didn't really talk much about her work. I'm not a lawyer, and that world is pretty foreign to me. And she never really got what I did for a living, though it provided very well for us."

"I understand your ex-wife also came from money, and lawyers and federal judges make good income," said White.

"I'm not saying I was the major breadwinner or anything, although I made far more than her salary. As a judge, she was dramatically underpaid, in my opinion."

"Have to take that up with Congress," noted Decker. "When was the last time you saw or talked to her?"

"A few days ago. She wanted to remind me about Tyler taking his allergy meds. He needs to get on it early with spring starting. I'm on Zyrtec year-round myself."

"And you *saw* her last when? You mentioned you were at her house a couple weeks ago to pick up Tyler."

"Julia wasn't at the house then. Let me think a

minute. Yeah, it was at school. About a week ago. There was an awards program at school. Tyler was getting the student-athlete of the year."

"Nice," said White. "I'm sure you were both proud."

"He works hard and deserves it. I was never much of an athlete in high school, and I didn't do any sports in college. He gets some of his size from me, but Julia was a great swimmer and tennis player. His athleticism definitely came from her." He looked up at them, his face a tapestry of misery. "How...how did she die? No one told me."

White exchanged a glance with Decker, who said, "She was stabbed, Mr. Davidson."

"Oh my God." He put his head in his hands.

Andrews pulled out his phone. "Something was left beside her body."

Davidson looked up. "What?"

Andrews held up his phone. "This note."

Davidson looked at them. "'Res ipsa loquitor'? Sounds like Latin. What's it mean?"

"We hoped you could provide some information about it, and also about any enemies she might have had."

"I don't know Latin. And she had no enemies that I knew of."

Andrews said, "I did a preliminary check of her past trials. She's overseen a number of drug cases, syndicates, gangs. Some pretty dangerous characters."

"I...I guess. I just never focused on that," said Davidson.

"And she had a personal bodyguard. Any idea why?" asked Decker.

"Tyler mentioned something about that after he had lunch with her, so I texted Julia to see what was up. She never got back to me."

Decker nodded, looking thoughtful. "Do *you* have any enemies?"

Davidson looked up in surprise. "*She* had the bodyguard, not me."

"Maybe she was more cautious. So, any enemies?"

Davidson looked away. "N-no. No enemies. Look, I...I need to end this interview. I'm going...to be sick." He rushed from the room.

They walked outside and stood around Andrews's car.

"Anything from your talk with Tyler?" asked White.

"Confirmed his father's alibi in all respects, so unless the kid is lying to cover for his old man, which I don't think he is, Barry might be off the suspect list if the TOD holds. Tyler said he never saw any security guard around his mother's place while he was there. But he did say his mother told him about it, and that it was about some stupid stuff having to do with her job. That's probably Tyler's word choice, not the judge's."

"How would he not see a guard there?"

"Well, if the guard was outside the whole time, and he arrived and then left while Tyler was sleeping, it could be the case. We need to get that info from the company."

"So the ex may be free and clear?" said White.

Decker said, "Not necessarily. We could be looking at a murder for hire. Then his alibi is meaningless."

When Decker got into the car and closed the door his phone buzzed. He recognized the number.

It was Earl Lancaster.

CHAPTER

13

EARL, IS ANYTHING WRONG?" SAID Decker anxiously.

"It's Sandy, Amos."

Decker felt his gut clinch. "Sandy! What's the matter? Is she okay?"

"I tried to talk to her about her mom. But I could make no headway."

Decker relaxed. "Earl, the police department has some really good grief counselors. They can talk to Sandy—"

A clearly desperate Earl Lancaster interrupted. "We've tried that, Amos, it was no good. The thing is—"

"What?"

"Sandy wants to talk to *you*."

"To me!"

Decker looked up as Andrews started the car. White was looking at Decker curiously.

He lowered his voice. "Why does she want to talk to me?"

"Because she says you never lie to her."

"The thing is, Earl, I'm down in Florida on a case. I can't get away right now."

"That's okay. She just wants to *talk* to you. Can you do it now? She's very insistent."

Decker looked up at White, who was still staring at him. "She wants to talk to me now? What am I supposed to say?"

"That—" Earl's voice dropped. "That her mom had to go away but will always be looking down on her, watching her, something like that." Decker heard a noise. "All right, Sandy, all right, here he is."

Decker heard some shuffling as the phone was passed over.

Then Sandy's voice came on. "Are you Amos Decker?"

Decker thought about clicking off. But then he imagined Sandy's small, hopeful face and he just couldn't. "Yeah, Sandy, this is Amos Decker."

"I want my mommy, Amos Decker, but nobody will tell me where she is. Will you tell me where she went? Please?"

As per her nature, Sandy was speaking loudly, and by the expression on White's face she could hear it all. She noted Decker staring at her helplessly, and quickly looked away.

Decker said, "She...your...mommy had to go away, Sandy."

"No! That's what they said, but Mommy would

never, ever go away without saying goodbye to me. She loves me. You're lying to me and you never lie." She began to cry.

Decker thought about the words Earl had suggested he use but he knew that Sandy would see right through that and things would only get worse. She might have mental disabilities, but in some ways she was far sharper than he was. And this was one of those ways because it dealt right with the heart.

"Sandy, will you listen to me?"

"Not if you say Mommy went away, I won't," she said in a choked voice.

"Do you..." Decker could barely believe he was about to say this, but he could think of nothing else. He didn't want to fail Sandy, as he had her mother. "Do you remember my daughter, Molly? You two played together."

Sandy's tone instantly brightened. "Sure, I remember Molly. She was very nice to me."

"And then you remember that Molly went away one day, right?"

"R-right."

"I didn't want her to go away, but she had to because, well, it wasn't her choice. She didn't want to leave me, but something made her."

"Mommy said something happened to her. That someone hurt her."

"That's right. Someone hurt my daughter and she had to go away, Sandy."

Andrews caught White's eye. He looked distraught and shaken. She shook her head and put a finger to her lips.

"And so did Molly's mommy," said Sandy. "I remember."

"Yes, Molly's mommy, too, they both went away at the same time. Someone made them go, they didn't want to."

"Did they say goodbye?"

"Sandy, close your eyes."

"What, why?"

"Just close your eyes, please, it's important."

"Okay."

"Are they closed?" asked Decker.

"Yes."

"Now, think of your mom. What is she doing?"

"She's smiling at me. She always smiles at me."

"That's right. Every time she talked to me about you, she was smiling. Because your mom loved you more than anything, just like I loved my daughter."

On this, White made a fist and pushed it against her mouth. Her eyes were closed, but some tears trickled out.

"Do you see Molly when you close your eyes?" Sandy asked.

"Yes, I do, all the time. I see her mommy, too. And I

think that's why they, and your mom, never said good-bye. Because when you say goodbye like that, it means they won't see us again. But they will. You see her right now. And I'm closing my eyes and there are Molly and her mom. I see them right now and they're smiling at me. So, no goodbyes. They're always there, Sandy. We just have to close our eyes and say hello and then they come to us. They're right there, with us. All the time."

"Hi, Mommy," said Sandy. "It's me, Sandy."

"And even if she doesn't seem to say anything back, Sandy, in your mind you know everything she would say. Molly always called me *Pops*. So right now I hear Molly calling me that."

"Mommy calls me Sandy-dandy."

"I know. And she's probably calling you that right now."

"I can hear her. I really, really can. It's me, Mommy, Sandy-dandy."

"Yeah, I can hear her, too."

"I'm going to go show her some new dresses that Daddy got me."

"I'm sure she'll love to see them."

"You really are Amos Decker, aren't you?"

"Yeah, I really am Amos Decker."

For better or worse.

A few moments later Earl came on. "My God, Amos, I don't know what you said, but she's totally changed. She ran upstairs laughing her head off and saying 'Sandy-dandy' over and over." He paused. "Amos, you still there?"

"I'm here."

"Thank you so much."

"Yeah, look, I gotta go."

Decker clicked off and stared down at the phone.

Andrews gave White a questioning look.

She said, "Take us back to our rental. I think it's time we checked in at the hotel and had some food. And, maybe, a *drink*."

As the car pulled away White glanced surreptitiously at Decker.

The man just kept looking at his phone.

CHAPTER

14

I WON'T ASK YOU IF you want to talk about it, because I know what the answer will be."

Decker and White were sitting in the dining area of the DoubleTree. Their meal was done. Decker had a beer, while White fingered a glass of merlot.

Decker ignored this and finished his beer. He was standing up to leave when she said, "I had three kids, Decker. Now I only have two."

He sat back down. "What happened?"

"Rival gangs going at it out on our street. They spewed rounds all over the place. One came through the wall of our house. My son, Donte, had sat up in bed when he heard all the noise. Bullet caught him right here." She placed a trembling finger to her left temple.

"I'm sorry. When did it happen?"

"Five years ago." She paused and looked down. "He was my middle child. I had my kids right in a row. My biological clock was ticking. I knew

I wanted three. I thought I could handle it, FBI career and all. Until my ex walked out the door when I was still carrying Jacky. Luckily my mom came to the rescue. I…I wasn't home when it happened. I was away on an…" A sob broke through, but she quickly quelled it. She wiped her mouth with her napkin and looked up, but didn't meet Decker's gaze. "Away on an assignment," she finished.

Decker tapped his fingers nervously on the table. He didn't want to break the silence because he was unsure about what to say. But finally he decided to say something, because he sensed that it had taken a lot of courage for White to make such a gut-wrenching admission. And she deserved something in kind from him.

"Sandy is my old partner's daughter. She has some mental disabilities, so she couldn't really understand about her mom. That's why her dad called me. Sandy and I…we sort of have a trust thing going on."

"What you told her was really good, Decker. It was pretty much spot-on for the situation."

"I don't normally talk about what happened to my family. It's just not something I…do."

"I don't, either. But I just thought we needed an icebreaker."

"Fair enough."

"They say time heals, but I'm not sure about that. Not at all."

"Time doesn't necessarily heal, but it allows perspective, and the fading of the loss. But not for me." He placed a finger against his head. "I can't forget. Not even a little bit. Nothing fades, nothing gets better. It's a new movie release every day, but it's the same movie."

"But you can remember the good times too, right? Better than the rest of us can with ours. I'm starting to fade on some of that stuff with Donte. I don't want it to, but I've got two kids and a career that suck up all I've got."

Decker rubbed at his mouth. "It doesn't make up for it. It's not apples to apples."

"I can see that. And I can also see that you are done with the personal stuff, so let's get to the professional. Impressions today?"

Decker automatically reengaged. "Barry Davidson is not being truthful about something, I just don't know what. Tyler is confused and hurt. I want to talk to Gamma Protection Services and see why they were guarding the judge. And I want to know what the note represents. 'Res ipsa loquitor.'"

"I've heard it before, but I Googled it to be sure. Legal jargon. Means something like 'The thing proves itself.'"

"Right, I checked that too. Must be important, at least to the killer, which makes it important to us."

"You think it stems from her caseload, something in the past? The blindfold, too? Maybe some defendant thought she screwed them. Justice *wasn't* blind, that sort of thing?"

Decker said, "Tyler thought her getting protection had something to with her position as a judge. But she might have not been straight with him about that. It might have something to do with her ex-husband. Barry Davidson has money, a thriving international business. He likes to party, have the young ladies over, or so Tyler told me. He might have screwed with somebody or embezzled some funds from a shady client, and this was the result. They get back at him by killing her."

"Or, like you suggested before, he could have hired someone to do it. Either way, we need to check his financial records."

"Andrews is already on that. But let's discuss the possibility that someone else killed her because they had a beef against Barry."

"But why kill the judge and not him?" asked White.

"You kill him, maybe you don't get your money back."

"If so, and he knows who it is? And maybe that's what he's not telling us?"

Decker said, "He'll either eventually tell us, go

after them on his own, keep his mouth shut because he's afraid—which would get my vote—or disappear because he's scared shitless."

"I like how you summarize things. So neat and orderly."

He eyed her cagily. "Jamison told you about the electric blue, right?"

White did not answer. She just kept watching him steadily.

"When I walked into the judge's house and had my little 'moment'? I saw the look on your face. Death equals electric blue. You knew that. I could read it in your face."

"She did tell me, yes," White conceded.

"And this was not just idle chatter from a long time ago. You called her *after* you got assigned to partner with me."

"And to her credit she didn't want to tell me anything. She's totally loyal to you, if you have any doubt about that. But I used my girl-agent-to-girl-agent card."

"Anything else I need to know from the girl-agent exchange system?"

"I'll let you know if it becomes relevant." She paused. "Does that tick you off?"

"No, it's actually the only thing you've said so far that made me smile."

She gaped. "You smiled? When? Because I didn't see it."

"I do it internally."

She smiled resignedly. "Of course you do."

They went to their rooms.

* * *

White immediately phoned home and talked to her mother and then her kids.

She had a lot to catch up on even though she hadn't been gone that long. It was good to hear their voices, especially now, with so much change going on in her life.

While she was doing that, Decker sat on his bed and stared out the window, where the sun had long since faded, but he could hear the roar of the Gulf through the glass.

He closed his eyes and once more envisioned the gun in Mary Lancaster's hand. He watched as she lifted it to her mouth, inserted it between her lips, letting the muzzle rest on the tongue, because it was very awkward to hold a gun that way. Then her finger would slip to the trigger. She probably closed her eyes, let her mind wander to wherever it needed to.

And then...

He opened his eyes, rose, and walked over to the window. The ocean view was inspiring: vast, sprawling, infinite, smooth, yet somehow chaotic, clunky, unpredictable to him. After he'd lost his wife and child, Decker had only wanted to be left alone. Part of him still felt that way. Yet part of him was terrified of having no one left, either. Sometimes it was just him...and his mind.

My ever-changing mind. Just like the rest of my life. Always fluid, never stable. And according to the good folks at the Cognitive Institute, the ride is going to get a lot bumpier.

Later, his phone buzzed. He didn't recognize the number and it wasn't in his contacts because no name came up.

"Decker," he said.

"Agent Decker, this is Helen Jacobs. I'm the medical examiner?"

"I remember you, Ms. Jacobs. So, Draymont's gun?"

"Had not been fired. But there's something else."

"What?"

"He *was* killed by two gunshot wounds to the heart, I confirmed that."

"But?" prompted Decker.

"But I also found what looks to be a wad of cash crammed down his throat."

CHAPTER

15

DECKER ROUSED WHITE FROM HER room and they drove over to the medical examiner's office, a one-story, low-slung concrete building that was so ugly it seemed unjust to bring someone's remains here to be legally cut up.

Helen Jacobs met them at the front door. She had on a long white lab coat, and her hair was done up in a bun and covered with a blue surgical cap.

White said, "Did you contact Agent Andrews as well?"

"Yes. But he didn't answer, so I left a message."

"Let's go," said Decker impatiently.

Jacobs led them down a long corridor with scuffed white walls, cheap laminate flooring, and feeble fluorescent light. She unlocked one door with her security card and ushered them in.

This room was outfitted with stainless steel tables, sinks, and lots of drains, Stryker saws, scalpels and other medical instruments, a tool that looked like a crowbar, organ scales, iPads resting on rolling tables, and mikes dangling from the ceiling so the medical examiners could record in real time their thoughts and findings.

Against one wall were the rollout beds behind closed cabinet doors: the wall of death, as Decker always saw it.

The electric blue had hit him as soon as Jacobs had unlocked the door. He noticed White noticing him, but the look he gave the woman caused her to glance sharply away.

On one dissecting table was Alan Draymont. He'd already been cut up, though the incision that had sliced a Y-shape across the front of his torso had not yet been sewn back up. Exposed were the man's innards. Decker saw that his organs had already been removed and then repacked inside the body cavity in viscera bags.

His scalp had been cut away and draped over his face; the skull had been cut open, and the brain removed.

Jacobs used a gloved hand to pull the skin back, reconstituting the man's face.

She used forceps to open the mouth wide and then directed a light inside the opening.

"You can see it now. I didn't want to remove it until you got here."

The two agents, White on tiptoes, bent over for a look.

"You sure it was done postmortem?" he said.

"Pretty sure, yes."

He glanced at her. "Pretty sure?"

"The gunshots to the chest clearly killed him. The loss of blood shows that his heart was beating normally when that happened. There were no signs on the body of restraint, defensive wounds, or a struggle, though."

Decker's mind leapt ahead of her words. "Meaning a man getting a wad of cash shoved down his throat is going to at least struggle against it."

"It would be like he was choking to death," added White. "He'd fight, or they'd have to restrain him first."

Jacobs said, "And he'd have gag reflex and there would be evidence of that in his larynx and on his tongue and other indicia. None of that is present, only the abrasions one would find by ramming an object like this down someone's throat *after* they were dead."

Decker eyed White and said, "Some sort of message? Punishment or revenge?"

"That would make Draymont the target and *not* the judge," said White.

"Who's to say he wasn't?"

"And they had to kill the judge because...?"

"She came downstairs, saw what was happening, and was attacked. She fled upstairs, where they finished her off." He stopped. "But then why the note and blindfold left with the *judge*?"

"Maybe that was just meant to throw us off," suggested White.

Decker said to Jacobs, "Get the wad out of his mouth."

She used another set of forceps to accomplish this and the money slowly emerged from the dead man's mouth, the last thing that would ever pass through that portal.

She laid it on a clean cloth on a side table.

Decker put on a pair of latex gloves he pulled from a box and gingerly started to unfold the money.

"That doesn't look like George Washington or Abraham Lincoln or Andrew Jackson," noted White as she peered around him.

The currency had the images of a white-bearded man looking out and a dark-bearded man staring to the left.

"Národná Banka Slovenska," Decker read off. "Pätdesiat. It's worth fifty of something."

White pulled out her phone and typed in a search. She waited and then the result came in.

"It's Slovakian. The Korun was the currency until the end of 2008. Now they use the euro. The two guys are Saint Cyril and Saint Methodius."

"So the personal bodyguard of a murdered federal judge had old and no longer legal tender Slovakian banknotes stuffed in his mouth after he'd been shot to death?" said Decker.

He unrolled all of the bills, counted up the amount, pulled out his phone, and translated the money into dollars using an online currency calculator.

"At the old exchange rate it's worth less than fifty dollars."

"But it's now worthless," noted White.

"It looks like someone was making some sort of a point," opined Jacobs.

"We need to find out all about Alan Draymont," said Decker.

"His employer, Gamma Protection Services, would be a good place to start," replied White.

CHAPTER

16

THE NEXT MORNING THEY TOOK Interstate 75 east and drove the roughly two hours to Miami, where Gamma Protection Services had its headquarters. It was in a sleek high-rise near the water. Agent Andrews had been filled in on the cash found in Draymont's mouth and had driven over with them.

As they headed up in a glass-enclosed elevator, Decker said, "Protection services must pay really well."

"Ever thought about jumping over to that side?" asked Andrews.

Decker glanced at him. "No."

"The dollars are a lot better."

"I have nothing I want to buy that badly."

At the solid front doors of the protection agency they showed their creds to a camera after being prompted by a voice over an intercom, and were buzzed into the large foyer.

The place was glass and metal with sleek, low-slung couches in bold colors. Nattily dressed men and women hurried by looking important and busy.

They were asked to wait in a conference room that held broad views of the Atlantic.

Five minutes later a woman in her late thirties walked in, trailed by four others, two men and two women who looked like carbon copies of each other: trim, young, and serious, with tailored suits. The men's ties were perfectly knotted, and the pocket squares matched the ties. The women's hair was sculpted, their dresses hit right at the knee, and their heels were a regulation two inches in height.

Decker observed all this and sighed. *Please let me get through this official gauntlet without saying shit I'll regret.*

The woman looked at him, White, and Andrews.

"Agent Andrews? It was the conference on cyber-security, wasn't it? We were on the same panel?"

"That's right," Andrews said, smiling. "These are my colleagues, Amos Decker and Agent Frederica White. This is Kasimira Roe, the CEO of Gamma."

She shook their hands and motioned for them to sit. Decker noted that her entourage didn't sit. They just stood against the wall, hands held in front and stared at the FBI intruders.

Decker ran his gaze down the line of clocks on

the wall showing times from different cities around the world. He was startled when he spied the fourth one.

"As you can imagine we are extremely distressed about what happened to Alan Draymont and Judge Cummins," began Roe. "It was unthinkable."

"Well, it happened, so not so unthinkable for *someone*," noted Decker.

She glanced at him. "And you're also with the FBI?" She ran her gaze over his khakis and wrinkled white shirt that he wore untucked.

"He is," said Andrews quickly. "From Washington, as is Agent White."

Roe lifted an eyebrow at this. "I would have thought you were more than equal to the task, Doug."

Decker observed Roe closely. She was around five eight, dark hair, and pale skin, lean and fit. She wore all black with black stockings and the two-inch heels. Her nails were professionally done, and her makeup was subdued but effective. Her brown eyes were luminous and alert, and they kept edging in his direction, he noted, like curious antennae. A guarded, complex woman, he concluded.

White interjected, "It's a federal judge, so reinforcements are expected. The U.S. marshals would normally be the active agency here, but Draymont was private security."

"And we'd like to know why she needed it," said Decker.

"I'm not really sure how I can discuss that without breaking professional confidences," replied Roe, looking directly at Decker.

"I would have thought they were broken as soon as the judge died," countered Decker.

She smiled demurely. "It's not as simple as all that, Agent Decker."

He didn't correct her on the agent nomenclature because it didn't matter to him. "Well, can you explain that to us?"

"Our relationship with clients is one of trust. It does not perish with the person."

"Well, since you failed to protect her, it might help us find out who killed her. I don't see why that would be a problem for you. Or her. Or her family."

Andrews, probably noting the annoyed look on Roe's face, said quickly, "I think Decker means that it's in all of our best interests to see that justice is done and that Judge Cummins's killer pays for their crime."

White chimed in, "And understanding what concerned her so much that she had to hire your firm might really help us get there."

Roe glanced back at the row of people behind her. One man hurried forward and whispered in her ear. She said something back and he nodded.

He returned to the wall, and she looked back at Decker and the others.

"We are checking on some things with our corporate counsel. Of course we want to cooperate fully, but we want to do so in a way that does not jeopardize any client confidentiality."

"Did she ask for Mr. Draymont specifically?" asked Decker.

She stared at him and said brusquely, "Not to my knowledge."

"We'd like something more definitive," he said.

"Right now, it's to my knowledge," Roe said firmly.

White said, "Did you meet with her over this matter, or was it an associate?"

"Full disclosure, I knew Julia Cummins through some functions, and organizations we both belonged to. But I did not handle this case. I'm not sure of the details regarding her matter. I assume that she retained the firm, otherwise Draymont would not have been at her home guarding her."

"Would it be better if we spoke with the person who *did* handle it?" asked Decker.

"We'll have to see. As I said, corporate counsel must be involved."

Decker eyed Andrews to see what his response to this might be. When he said nothing, Decker said, "Let me just be clear. I wasn't asking a question. Who is this person? We need to meet with them."

"I'm sure that you can understand we're all a little stunned at Gamma," Roe said sharply.

"Not nearly as much as Cummins's teenaged son who lost his mother," countered Decker.

"Yes, of course, I didn't mean to imply otherwise," said Roe hastily.

"And as I'm sure you know, speed is of the essence in an investigation like this. So the sooner we find out why the judge hired your firm, the better."

"Have there been new developments?" said Roe, looking at Andrews.

He began, "Well, as a matter of fact—"

Decker broke in, trying to keep his rising temper in check. "Is there *anything* you can tell us that might be helpful?"

Roe slowly drew her gaze from Andrews. "Alan Draymont was a good operative, never a problem."

"Did he have a family?" asked White.

Roe looked puzzled. "Why?"

"Just trying to cover all bases. And they would have to be notified of his death."

"As far as I know he was single. I don't believe he had any children, but we will confirm that. I apologize, but Gamma has gotten so big I can't know all of our people personally in every detail."

"Of course, of course," said Andrews.

"How long has Gamma been in business?" asked

Decker, again trying to hold his temper at his colleague's obsequiousness.

"Forty-three years."

"So presumably before you were born then?"

"Yes. My father, Kanak Roe, founded Gamma back then, under another name. It was operating out of a strip mall four blocks off Miami Beach. Now we have well over a thousand operatives in a dozen countries. With seven offices in Florida alone."

"It's been incredibly successful," observed Andrews, drawing a glare from Decker.

"What was your father's background?" asked White.

"He immigrated here with my grandparents as a child. He became a citizen, earned his undergraduate degree, and then joined the Secret Service. Later he started what became Gamma."

"And he's now retired?" asked White.

"No, he...A boating mishap, three years ago." She looked toward the window. "Far out there, in the Atlantic."

"Sorry to hear that," said White.

"That's when I took over running Gamma. I've worked here full-time after spending five years with the Secret Service. I followed in my father's footsteps, you see. Then I worked my way up here and was second-in-command at the time he—"

"When can we speak to the person here who dealt with the judge?" interjected Decker. "And we understand there might have been threats that she'd received. If so, we'll need whatever records you have on that."

Roe looked at him from under hooded eyes, and her lips curled in displeasure. "You're quite tenacious. You would make a good operative."

"Right now I'm just trying to be a good investigator. Is the person in this building? We can talk to them now. And any record of threats? We'll need copies."

"As I said, I will—"

"Yes, I know, check the file and talk to *corporate counsel*." He glanced at the people standing behind her. "Can you send one of them off to do that *now*? They don't look too busy. And we drove a long way to go home empty-handed. I'm sure you can appreciate that."

Andrews coughed and frowned, while White looked as resolute as Decker.

Roe flicked a finger in the direction of her team. They looked at one another for a few moments. Then one of them walked out of the room, tapping on her phone screen.

Decker once more eyed the clocks on the wall.

Roe turned to see what he was looking at.

"We have offices in all those places," she explained.

"Yeah, I get that. But I've never seen a clock for *Bratislava* before."

"It's the capital of—"

"—Slovakia," interjected Decker.

Both White and Andrews exchanged startled glances at this.

Roe said, "That's where my given name comes from. I believe its true origins are Germanic, but my father was Slovakian from Czechoslovakia. He left long before it was split into the Czech and Slovak Republics."

"Not easy to emigrate from there when it was under Soviet rule," said Decker.

"The Soviets taking over was the reason my family left. They wanted a better life." She smiled. "In Slovakian, 'Kasimira' means 'command for peace,' or something to that effect."

"And you have an office there?" said Andrews.

"Yes, a small one. I try to get out to each of our foreign offices every couple of years if I can. But I haven't been to Bratislava for three years now."

"Ever since your father's *mishap*?" said Decker.

She eyed him with a bit of alarm in her look. "Yes, that's right."

Decker was about to ask another question when the woman who had earlier left the room returned with another woman.

She said, "This is Alice Lancer. She can give you more information about Alan Draymont and Judge Cummins."

Decker looked Lancer over. She was around forty, medium height, blond, and slender, with attractive features and a no-nonsense demeanor.

But then her face turned the color of putty and the woman grabbed at her chest as she began to breathe heavily.

And a moment later Lancer fell to the floor, unconscious.

17

SHE'S BEEN TAKEN TO A nearby hospital," Andrews reported to Decker and White as he got off his phone.

They were standing in front of the building housing Gamma Protection Services. After Lancer collapsed, an ambulance had been called, and she had been taken away without regaining consciousness. Roe and her entourage had disappeared back into the secure halls of Gamma, and Andrews and the others had been escorted out by an armed man in a security uniform.

Decker said, "When can we talk to her?"

Andrews shrugged. "I don't know. Soon, hopefully."

"And the files on any threats?" Decker added.

Andrews snapped, "Look, Decker, a lady just collapsed. I'm hoping she's okay. Why not focus on that for a minute, okay?"

Decker glanced at White, who was giving him a curious look. He said, "Who else at Gamma can we talk to?"

"I think it was just the Lancer woman," replied Andrews.

"Out of this whole big, fucking company, she's the only one who knows anything?" demanded an incredulous Decker.

"That very well may be the case," said Andrews. "Need-to-know philosophy."

White said, "Maybe I'm being overly paranoid here, but is it a weird coincidence that the only person who knows anything faints dead away before she can talk to us?"

Andrews said, "Oh come on, that's a little out there, isn't it? I mean, these are legitimate people we're dealing with here. Gamma has a sterling reputation."

"What about the Slovakian banknotes and Kanak Roe being from there?" said White. "Just another coincidence?"

Decker said, "And for the record, I don't believe in one coincidence, much less two."

Andrews looked less certain. "Well, that one *was* strange, I will admit."

"I think it's more than strange. I think it's a clue that's screaming at us," said White.

"Well, let's not rush into anything," said Andrews. "We don't want to waste time chasing down the wrong alley."

Decker said, "Alan Draymont had old Slovakian banknotes stuffed down his throat. Gamma was founded by a guy from what is now Slovakia. His daughter's name is basically Slovakian, and they have an office in the capital city of Slovakia. If that's all a coincidence I'll retire from the FBI and go flip burgers somewhere, naked."

White snorted at this remark.

Andrews said, "Okay, I'm there with you. So does that mean this whole thing was directed at Gamma, and Draymont was killed because he worked there? And the judge was collateral damage?"

Decker said, "We need to determine if Draymont was a symbolic kill, or whether he was personally targeted for a reason other than his affiliation with Gamma."

"How do we find that out?" asked Andrews.

"By doing our job. What hospital did they take Lancer to?" asked Decker.

"They didn't say."

"Then call them back right now and find out which one. Because when the lady comes to, we're going to be there."

Andrews did so and said, "Okay, I got the info. We can drive over now. It's not far."

Twenty minutes later they were walking into Harden Hospital near Coral Gables. It was four stories tall and outfitted far more luxuriously than any hospital Decker had ever been in.

"Harden?" said Decker.

Andrews said, "It's a private facility and not cheap."

White said, "You can say that again. This place has a restaurant and a *spa*." She pointed to the electronic marquee in the lobby.

They approached the reception area, where a young woman in a sleek blue pantsuit and white blouse greeted them from behind a console outfitted with black granite and zebrawood. Decker felt like he was in a five-star resort, instead of a place for sick and injured people.

"May I help you?" the woman asked.

Andrews flashed his badge. "We're here to see Alice Lancer. She was just admitted."

"Yes, of course. Let me check on that."

She sat down in front of her computer and hit some keys. She looked at the screen and said, "She arrived here and has been processed, but apparently they haven't put her room number in the system yet. If you'll have a seat, I'll let you know as soon as they do."

Decker stared at the woman for a long moment before walking over and sitting down in one of the waiting area chairs. White and Andrews joined him there.

"I'm sure it won't be too long," said Andrews.

"It's already been too long," Decker pointed out. "And getting longer by the second."

White studied him as he kept glancing at the

front desk looking agitated. "What's on your mind, Decker?"

"One word."

"Which is?" said White.

"'*Apparently*.'"

Decker rose and went over to the front desk. The woman glanced up at him. "Yes? I haven't heard anything yet."

"Why did you say they '*apparently*' hadn't assigned her a room number yet?"

"Excuse me?"

"You used the word 'apparently.' That suggests some confusion or uncertainty."

The woman looked embarrassed. "Oh, well, it's just that we have quite a few empty rooms, and once you're processed, a room is assigned."

"Would the process rule out her being given a room? Like triage? Maybe they just let her leave."

"No, the record on the system didn't indicate that."

White and Andrews joined Decker, who asked the woman, "What does the record indicate?"

"That she was processed and admitted, but no room was assigned."

"Has that ever happened before?" asked White.

"Um, no, I mean, not very often."

"And when it *did* happen, what was the reason?" asked Decker.

"That the person refused the admission for some

reason. In other words, that they left AMA, against medical advice."

Decker said, "Where is the admitting done? We need to go there right now."

"But you can't, it's only for—"

White, who was obviously as out of patience as Decker, held up her badge and barked, "This says that you take us there *now* or you will be arrested for obstruction of justice."

The woman looked near tears. "Oh my God." She jumped up and said, "It's this way."

They followed her through a secure door, which she opened by holding a security card to the reader port on the wall.

They hurried down a long corridor and through another secure door. Laid out in front of them were a series of cubicles where people were inputting information into computers as other people sat in chairs next to them. Some folks were on gurneys parked against the wall. EMTs were standing next to some of them, apparently waiting for confirmation of their patient's status.

"This is the Admissions Office," she said.

Decker glanced around and then hustled over to a woman who was just getting up from her desk.

"We're looking for an Alice Lancer. She was just admitted here."

"I don't know who that is."

Another woman, sitting in the next cubicle, said, "She's gone."

Decker looked over at her. "Gone? Did she refuse admission?"

"No. Two police detectives came and took her away."

CHAPTER

18

I'VE GOT AN APB OUT," said Andrews. "And I've spoken to the Coral Gables Police. They have no information about a woman being taken from Harden Hospital by their people."

They were in the car outside the hospital.

White said, "So the detectives were bogus? The hospital staff said their badges looked real and Lancer went with them."

"At this point it doesn't look like they were legit," said Andrews. "What the hell is going on?" He eyed Decker, who was in the rear seat staring moodily out the window. "Any thoughts, Decker?" he asked.

"Clearly the lady didn't want to meet with us."

"You mean she faked the faint and then escaped from the hospital with the help of a couple of buddies?" said White.

Decker continued to look out the window. "It wasn't just her and a couple of buddies. It's not easy to pull something like this together that fast. You'd need resources that can act on the fly. And contingency plans."

Andrews said, "You don't think Gamma is involved in this, do you?"

"We didn't get to talk to apparently the only woman at Gamma who can tell us anything. And now we're out here and they're safely back in their little cocoon."

"Roe said they would provide copies of their records," countered Andrews.

"No, she didn't. She said corporate counsel would determine whether they could provide us anything," corrected Decker.

Andrews started and said, "Right, I guess that is what she told us."

"So don't be surprised if that counsel tells us Gamma can't provide the documents without going to court. And we all know how long that bullshit takes. The strategy of running out the legal clock has become pretty popular. And by then it may be too late." He turned to look at Andrews. "And when you called for an appointment with Roe, they had a chance to prepare. Whether it was just Lancer or some or all of them, I don't know. But they acted fast."

Andrews looked at White. "What do you think?"

"I think the question is, if we can't get the info we need from Gamma on a timely basis, where *do* we get it?"

Decker said, "Presumably the judge would have some documentation of the threats. They weren't found in her house, correct? Or on her answering machine, if she even had one."

Andrews said, "They weren't. But we're still checking her cell phone and computers."

"Then we might have to get them from the court," said Decker.

"I'll need to speak to our legal counsel," noted Andrews.

"I didn't mean *that* court, I meant Judge Cummins's chambers. The evidence might be there. And there are people she worked with we need to talk to."

"I was planning to do that," said Andrews.

"And pull any CCTV footage from the hospital. We might get a look at the guys who sprang Lancer."

"Okay, I'll get on that."

"And while we're in the area, let's go see where Alice Lancer lives."

"We don't have her address," said Andrews.

"Yes we do," said Decker.

"How?"

"I saw it on her admittance form to the hospital."

"You remember it correctly?" asked Andrews.

"I wouldn't worry about that," interjected White.

"We don't have a search warrant," pointed out Andrews.

"She's gone missing. Can we get by on a welfare check?" said Decker.

"I doubt that. And the locals do that, not the FBI."

"She's a potential witness in the murder of a federal judge."

"Doesn't matter. And to be clear, I'm not screwing up any prosecutions on a rookie Fourth Amendment fuckup."

Decker looked at the man with a little more respect.

* * *

Lancer lived in the village of Miami Shores, a half-hour commute north of the Gamma Building. It was a village of well-kept-up single-family dwellings, a couple of small commercial areas, wide streets, and lots of trees residing along them.

"It's a bedroom community for Greater Miami," explained Andrews. "And also has a lot of retirees. But you could say that about most places in Florida. You ever think about retiring here, Decker?"

"No. How much farther to her place?"

"It's the next street."

They turned into the driveway of a small bungalow with stucco siding and green-and-white-striped awnings over the windows. A short, squat palm was planted out front. The grass was clipped short, and the flower beds didn't have much in them. They got out, and Decker looked through the window of the one-car garage.

"Empty. Her car must be at work still."

"We don't have a search warrant, like I pointed out before," noted Andrews.

"But we can look around, right?" said Decker. "Until you file for and get a search warrant?"

"Yes. On the *outside*. And in plain sight."

They made a perimeter search of the yard and found that Lancer didn't really make much use of it. There was a small wooden deck on the rear of the house, but there was no outdoor furniture to sit on. The backyard looked as uncared for as the front.

Decker used his height to peek into some windows but couldn't see much.

"Can I help you?"

He turned to see a woman staring at him from the yard next door. She was in her seventies, gray haired, with a plump frame and wearing white sweatpants, a long-sleeved dark blue shirt, and orthopedic shoes. Glasses dangled from a chain around her neck.

They all showed their credentials.

She put on her glasses and drew closer. "The FBI! Has something happened?"

"And your name?" asked Andrews.

"Dorothy Steadman."

"Have you lived here long?"

"Over fifteen years."

"What can you tell us about Ms. Lancer?" asked White.

"I don't really know her all that well. I'm long retired. So our paths don't cross very often."

"When was the last time you saw her?" asked Decker.

"I saw her drive off this morning. I believe she works in Miami."

"Did she seem normal?"

"Yes, I mean, nothing looked out of the ordinary."

"Have you spoken with her lately?" asked Decker.

The woman considered this. "Oh, a few days ago. She was taking a walk. This was in the evening. We chatted for a few seconds. The weather, that sort of thing."

"She have many visitors?"

"Not that I've seen. I mean, occasionally."

Andrews took out his phone, brought up a screen, and held it up. It was a picture of Alan Draymont. "This man?"

The woman said, "Yes, I *have* seen him. He's been over to see Alice many times, at least that I'm aware of. I assumed they were dating."

"Did they seem romantically engaged?" asked White.

"Not particularly so. I just assumed. Has…has something happened to Alice?"

"We're trying to find out. What else can you tell us about her?" asked Decker.

"She lives quietly. She keeps to herself. Never spoke

of having children. I thought she had something to do with law enforcement."

"Why'd you think that?" asked White.

"I saw her getting in her car once, and she had a gun on her belt."

Andrews handed her a card. "If you think of anything else, please give me a call. And if you see Ms. Lancer back here, please alert me right away."

"Alert you? Is she in some sort of trouble?"

"Like we said, we're trying to find things out," said Decker. "Thanks."

As they got back into the car White said, "So Draymont and Lancer were maybe a couple?"

Decker said, "Draymont gets murdered, and Lancer fakes a fainting spell to get out of answering our questions. This is not a dating issue. This is something more than that."

"What could they have been involved in?" said Andrews.

Decker replied, "They both worked at Gamma. That might be the common denominator."

"You mean *involving* Gamma?" asked Andrews.

"Not necessarily. But let's keep an open mind, okay?" Decker added.

"It would be hard to believe that an organization with the sterling reputation of Gamma would be—"

Decker interrupted. "Yeah, go tell that to Bernie

Madoff's investors. And where'd you get that photo of Draymont?"

"From Gamma's website."

"And you need to file that search warrant request for Lancer's place."

"I'm on it," said Andrews, hitting a speed dial number and putting the phone to his ear.

"And now, we go to court," said Decker.

CHAPTER

19

THE FORT MYERS FEDERAL COURTHOUSE was on First Street. To Decker it looked like a lot of other federal courthouses he had seen, only this one had palm trees out front.

They cleared security with their credentials and were allowed to keep their weapons. They were escorted to the office of Ken Caine, who was the deputy U.S. marshal in charge of courthouse security. Andrews told them that Caine was a friend of his.

"We play golf together."

"Does *everybody* play golf in Florida?" growled Decker.

"It's one of the main reasons people come here, Decker," retorted Andrews.

Caine was in his fifties, with grizzled gray hair, and his blue blazer and gray slacks rode well on his fit six-foot frame. He struck Decker as a no-nonsense, no-bullshit kind of guy. But he had been wrong about that before.

Caine shook their hands and said, "Damn, I can't

believe that Judge Cummins is dead. She was the nicest person you'd ever want to meet."

Andrews said, "I know, Ken, it was a shock."

"What can I do to help?" said Caine.

Andrews explained about possible threats Cummins had received. And also that Cummins had hired Gamma to protect her possibly because of those threats.

"What in the hell?" exclaimed Caine. "Why didn't she alert us as to any threats?"

"You're sure she didn't?" said Decker. "I mean, not you but someone else here?"

"Any threat to a federal judge in this court is *my* jurisdiction. There are procedures in place. Judge Cummins has been threatened before. This is south Florida, violent gangs and drug smugglers abound here. And she had quite a few of those on her docket. We always protected her. I just don't understand why she didn't tell us."

"Did she mention anything to you about any recent concerns she had?" asked Andrews.

"No, nothing."

"And you didn't know she'd hired Gamma?" asked White.

"No, I did not," Caine said heatedly.

"Are you familiar with Gamma?" asked Decker.

"I know of them. I've been to some security conferences where Kanak Roe spoke."

"Do you know his daughter?" asked Decker.

"Kasimira? I've had some interactions, but I don't know her all that well."

"Still, what's your opinion of her?" asked Decker.

"She makes a lot of money."

"About her professionally?"

"She was with the Secret Service, so she knows what she's doing. Her father was excellent at his work. She's, well, she's more *business* oriented than he was. She's nearly doubled the size of the firm just since she took over. That big office building in Miami? She bought that two years ago. Gamma has the top six floors and she rents out the rest. Makes a fortune just off that."

Decker watched the man closely as he said all of this. *Is Caine jealous of Roe? It sure sounds like it.*

"Sounds like she's a smart businesswoman," observed White.

Caine said, "There's more to life than money. She maybe needs to check her priorities."

"Why do I never hear someone say that about a business*man*?" said White.

"We need to search the judge's chambers," interjected Decker. "And talk to her secretary, clerks, anyone who might be able to help us."

"I'll take you," said Caine, after glaring at White.

20

SARA ANGSTROM AND DAN SYKES," said Caine, introducing the two people in their midtwenties. "The judge's clerks for this term."

They were in the anteroom of Cummins's chambers.

Angstrom was tall, thin, and blond with pale skin and a dour expression. She was dressed in a dark jacket and slacks with a white blouse. Sykes was several inches shorter with a flabby build and black-rimmed glasses. His dark hair was longish, and he had a pen in his short-sleeved shirt pocket.

Decker looked them over and came away with a first impression of grief, then disbelief, and, finally, fear. They both said they had no idea of any recent threats against the judge.

"How about further back?" asked White.

Sykes said, "She presided over a RICO case about eight months ago. Local mobster with ties to a cartel in Mexico. Two of the defendants threatened her in open court."

Caine said, "And we provided protection for her

until the case was over and for two months after that. Then we reevaluated the risk and concluded it was no longer relevant."

"They could have just gotten around to acting on their threat," said Andrews.

White added, "We'll need to see the case files and related documents."

Sykes said, "Of course, whatever you need."

Decker turned to Angstrom. "Any idea who might have been involved in this?"

Angstrom looked alarmed. "Me? No. I have no idea. I mean, there was nothing about Judge Cummins's cases that was all that different from the other judges here."

Caine said, "That's true."

"How many judges are there?" asked Decker.

Caine said, "Over a dozen active district court judges, the same number of senior judges and over two dozen magistrates."

"And they're *all* kept busy?" said White.

"The Middle District of Florida was created in 1962," said Caine. "The first new federal district since the nineteen-twenties. It was done to alleviate the backlog of cases in the Southern District. Now the Middle District's caseload is larger. It covers a broad swath of Florida, both coasts to the inland areas. Fort Myers, Tampa, Orlando, Ocala, and all the way north to Jacksonville. So, yes, they're kept very busy."

Decker looked at the two clerks. "How long have you worked for the judge?"

Angstrom said, "I've been here nearly a year."

"I came on four months ago," replied Sykes. "The clerk before me got married and moved out of the area."

"And there's nothing on her docket *now* that might have prompted threats?" asked Decker.

"Nothing unusual," answered Sykes, and Angstrom nodded.

"Has she had any visitors here that seemed out of the ordinary?" asked White.

Caine answered. "No, nothing like that. Visitors here are usually family and friends or professional colleagues."

"And nothing since the RICO case?" said Decker.

"No," said Angstrom.

"Where's the judge's secretary?" asked White.

"She called in sick today," said Sykes.

Decker looked at Caine. "We'll need her home address."

He said, "Her name's Patty Kelly. She's been here for over two decades. Sharp as a tack."

"Good, maybe she can give us some sharp answers," said Decker. He looked at the clerks. "In the meantime, if you can send the judge's current docket to Agent Andrews? Filings, motions, case summaries."

"Criminal or civil?" asked Sykes.

"Both. People kill over money as much as they do anything else."

"Straightaway," said Sykes.

Caine said, "Should I post extra security over the other judges? They've been informed, of course, and I can tell they're worried."

Decker said, "I'm not going to tell you how to do your job, Marshal, but some extra guards can't hurt."

"Right."

"Now, we'd like to see her chambers."

Caine led them inside, and Decker stood in the middle of the room and looked around. It was large, befitting the stature of a federal judge: lots of polished wood, bookcases, a large desk, comfortable chairs. Decker looked over the photos on her desk. Several of Tyler at various ages. One frame held a handmade card with a funny face on it and a "I love you Mommy," scribbled in a young child's penmanship. Obviously, Tyler again. There were no photos of Barry Davidson.

In another frame were Cummins, Doris Kline, and another woman.

"Any idea who the third person is?" said Decker, holding it up.

"That's Maya Perlman," answered Caine. "She practiced before this court. Never before Judge Cummins, of course, because they were friends. She retired about a year ago."

"You know her?"

"Oh yes. Like I said, she had cases here, lots of them. So she was at the courthouse a good deal. Really nice woman, and a very fine lawyer."

"What was her practice?"

"Criminal defense."

"Interesting." Decker eyed the desktop computer. "Cummins's laptop and phone were at the house, correct?"

"Yes," said Andrews. "They're being examined. And we'll check this one, too."

Decker and White looked through the desk drawers while Andrews started searching through a cabinet.

Later, after they were finished, Decker went back out to the clerks. " 'Res ipsa loquitor.' Mean anything to you?"

Angstrom said, "It's a Latin term. It means 'Things speak for themselves.' "

Sykes added, "The concept is used in civil cases. Negligence, that sort of thing. Shifts the burden of proof to the defendant."

"Give me an example," said Decker.

"An animal part found in a can of vegetables. A plane engine catching on fire. An AC window unit in a high-rise falls out and kills someone. The result itself speaks to there being negligence or some illegal or actionable act by the defendant. In other words, it wouldn't have happened at all if someone didn't screw up. It's not applicable in criminal cases. There the burden of proof remains with the government at all times, of course."

They walked out of the courthouse with Patty Kelly's home address.

"Do you know Kelly?" Decker asked Andrews.

"No, not really. But I've never heard a bad word said against her. She's been with the judge since Cummins joined the court."

After a ten-minute drive they reached a neighborhood of well-kept modest houses with meager lawns, tall and short palm trees, and lots of rock and gravel accents in various colors. Decker assumed that was popular down here because rock and gravel didn't need to be watered and the sun couldn't kill them.

A late model red Kia SUV was parked in the driveway.

They knocked on the door and waited. Finally, they heard footsteps.

Only the person who opened the door wasn't Patty Kelly.

CHAPTER

21

Yes?" said the man, who was in his sixties, with salt-and-pepper hair, and a loose, couch-potato frame.

Andrews flashed his badge and said, "We're here to see Patty Kelly. And you are?"

"*I* am her husband, Steve Kelly. Is this about the judge?"

"Yes. How'd you hear?"

"Someone from the court called here this morning."

"And your wife?"

"Patty's not here."

Decker said, "She called in sick today."

"She didn't sleep well last night. She had time off she needed to take, so she did."

"Do you know where she went?"

"Maybe to the store. She mentioned last night she had some shopping to do. She was gone when I got back in the house from working outside. Probably went to just take her mind off the judge. She's been gone a few hours now."

"Can you call her?" asked Decker. "And let her know we're waiting?"

"Sure." Kelly took out his phone and called. It went right to voice mail, so he left a message. "I'm sure she'll call right back. She always does."

Five minutes later his phone had not rung.

Decker said, "Try texting her."

He did and they waited another five minutes.

"What store?" said White.

"Well, she was going to quite a few. But she usually saves the grocery shopping for last. At the Harris Teeter, just up the road. You might have passed it."

"What kind of car does she drive?" asked Andrews.

"White Toyota Camry. She's got a vanity plate. 'SUNNY.' As in Florida sunny."

Decker looked at Andrews. "Why don't you wait here in case she comes back. We'll check out the Harris Teeter. Whoever sees her calls the other." He eyed Kelly. "Got a picture of your wife handy?"

Kelly took a framed photo off the shelf and held it out. White took a picture of it with her phone.

Decker glanced at the photo. Patty Kelly was an attractive woman in her early sixties with white-blondish hair cut to the shape of her head. She had a trim figure and stood about five-five. Intriguingly, she looked familiar to him for some reason. And it was surprising that he could not pull that memory up instantly from his personal cloud.

Well, the Cognitive Institute said I was in for more changes. Maybe this is one of them.

He and White got into the rental and drove off to the Harris Teeter.

They were on the lookout for the white Camry with the SUNNY plates on the way there, but didn't see it. Decker drove through the parking lot looking for the car, while White went inside the Harris Teeter to search for the woman.

Twenty minutes later they both had come up empty. They drove back to Kelly's house. Steve Kelly had tried calling his wife multiple times without luck.

"Did she get any calls before she left?" asked Decker.

Kelly checked the landline, but the latest message on there was a recorded voice from the previous night announcing a great financial opportunity in gold futures if the Kellys called back right away.

"How about her cell phone?" asked White.

"I don't know. Like I said, I was out in back doing yard work earlier. I wouldn't have heard her phone ring from out there." Kelly looked at them nervously. "I'm sure she's...I mean, nothing could have happened to her, could it?"

None of them answered his question.

Decker said, "If you hear from her, will you tell her to call us?" He handed the man one of his cards.

"Right away. I'm sure she'll be back soon. Probably be back any minute now." As soon as he finished he looked off into the distance, his mouth agape, and his eyes slitted in worry.

As they drove away, Andrews said, "What do you think?"

"I think potential witnesses keep disappearing on us. Let's go to a place where that can't happen," said Decker.

"Where's that?" asked White.

"Alan Draymont's home. He's not there, but there might be something to help us."

"But he lives back near Miami," said Andrews. "That's over four hours roundtrip from here."

"You got something else to do today?" retorted Decker.

"What do you think about Mrs. Kelly?" interjected White.

"She worked with the judge, probably knew things about her nobody else would. And now she might have vanished."

"Surely her husband would have seen someone kidnap her," countered White.

"A phone call or text to lure her out would have done the same thing," replied Andrews.

Decker eyed him and said, "That's right. And if she doesn't turn up voluntarily we have to figure out who that might have been. I'd get her phone records ASAP."

Andrews got on the phone to do just that and

he said he was also putting out an APB on her and her car.

As they drove along, Decker closed his eyes and let everything they had learned, and not learned, settle over him like a layer of fine dust. Yet, frustratingly, all he could see in his mind was Mary Lancaster with a gun in her mouth. He opened his eyes and stared at the back of White's head as she steered the car.

This is not the time for my brain to go on some weird-ass emotional odyssey.

He watched as Andrews spoke to his folks at the FBI to get the necessary paperwork going to get into Kelly's phone records and also put out the APB.

Decker wondered how much longer he could keep doing this shit. Part of him didn't care if he ever solved another case. And that had never happened to him before. Was it Mary's killing herself? Sandy's desperate pleas to him? The fact that he hadn't held his wife, or kissed Molly on the cheek, in years?

His daughter would be a teenager now, in high school. Getting ready for the prom. Getting ready for college, maybe. Getting ready for life. Instead she was lying in a coffin next to her mom's grave. Through no fault of her own.

That buck stopped with me. Always with me.

Andrews put his phone away, "Okay, the ball is rolling on that." He eyed Decker. "Did you hear me?"

Decker glanced at the sun, the image of his dead daughter strewn all across its flaming surface. Decker could imagine his brain and imperfect memory burning up, just like the sun.

And maybe that would be the best thing that could happen to him. Because right now, he just didn't see this ride lasting much longer.

CHAPTER

22

ALAN DRAYMONT HAD LIVED IN an apartment about twenty minutes from Lancer's house. It wasn't in a sleek high-rise. It was in a three-story structure nowhere near the water. It looked old and worn out. And set up like a motel where the doors opened directly to the outside.

"They'll probably knock this thing down in a couple of years," noted Andrews. "Rezone and go up fifteen stories and maybe have water views; you can make a fortune."

"Yeah, and in twenty years *this* might be beachfront," noted Decker.

"That's not funny," shot back Andrews.

"It wasn't meant to be."

Andrews looked at White. "We're sensitive to climate change issues down here."

White looked in the direction of the water. "I guess I would be, too, seeing how close it is to you all. But I live in Baltimore. We got issues, too. Guess we all do. Only I'm nowhere near the Harbor. Way out of my price range."

"Roe said they had seven offices in Florida?" said Decker.

"Yeah, they actually have one in Naples."

"So if Draymont lives two hours away, why have him guard Judge Cummins? Why not use someone from Naples?"

Andrews said, "That's a good question."

White interjected, "If he was guarding the judge at night, did he sleep on the premises?"

"If he slept at all," said Decker. "He'd probably be up all night patrolling and then go crash somewhere while the judge was at work. But Gamma would have to foot that bill, I would think."

"I'll check on that to be sure," said Andrews.

They approached Draymont's apartment, which was on the third floor.

"Any problems with a search warrant here?" said Decker.

"There is if he lives with someone," pointed out White. "Who might have killed him. Then there is a Fourth Amendment issue, because even murderers have an expectation of privacy under the law. Go figure."

Decker nodded. "Right. So let's knock on the door and find out if he did live with someone. Because *consent* to search by someone legally authorized to do so is the best exception to a warrant requirement."

When they got to the third floor and approached Draymont's apartment, Decker pulled his gun and said, "Okay, that's maybe an opportunity."

The door was partially open.

Andrews and White had drawn their weapons, too.

Decker eyed Andrews. "Your turf, how do you want to handle this?"

"Me first, you left, White right." Andrews moved past Decker, shouted out, "FBI, identify yourselves. Now!" There was no response. "FBI, coming in." He kicked the door open, and edged into the front room. Decker was on his left wing and White on the right, their guns doing sweeping arcs in front of them.

"Shit," said Decker. "Somebody beat us to it."

The place had been turned upside down.

They made a quick search to make sure no one was there, dead, injured, or hiding.

Decker said, "Check with the management and see if anyone saw anybody here either last night or today, and also when was the last time anyone saw Draymont. And you'll have to dial up a forensics team. Since we're not sure if he lives with someone, get a warrant."

"Right."

The place was only about a thousand square feet,

Decker estimated. Little furniture, and what was there was cheap and old. It might have come with the apartment for all he knew. There were no personal photos that he could see, nothing to really show who had lived there.

Andrews returned about a half hour later after his questioning of management and other personnel.

"No one saw or heard anything. The place only has the manager and a handyman on-site. The manager had liquor on his breath and the handyman was working on his pickup truck in the back and didn't really seem with it."

"No maid service or anything?" asked Decker.

"Nope. People clean their own units. I tried the apartments on either side of Draymont's. Nobody answered. I taped my card to both doors with a message to call me if they know anything about Draymont. The manager said he pays on time and caused no problems. No visitors that he knows of, but I doubt he keeps close watch. And there's no one else on the lease other than Draymont."

"When we did the quick search I didn't see anything business related here," said White. "No home office, laptop. No files or documents."

"And his phone was not found on his body at Cummins's house," said Andrews. "People weren't taking chances. If they took his phone, they turned it off, because we couldn't track it. Same for Lancer."

"Let's get Patty Kelly's cell phone number and see if we can track it," suggested White.

"On it," said Andrews. "And I'll have the apartment secured until the warrant drops. Even if no one else is on the lease, I don't want to take chances that someone else might reside here."

"Good idea," said White.

Decker looked over the railing at the parking lot below. The day had produced a truckload of questions and really not a single answer. In fact, it was getting more complex by the minute.

This is going to take my A game. But I'm not sure I'm up for it.

CHAPTER

—————

23

THEIR HOTEL HAD A SAD four-seater bar and Decker was sitting in one of them cradling a half-empty bottle of Bud. He eyed the TV screen, where a hockey game was on. To him, it was a little incongruous watching heavily clothed men skating on ice with palm trees gently swaying just outside the hotel, and a temperature of seventy degrees at eleven p.m.

He took out his phone, placed it on the bar, and looked at the caller log. Mary Lancaster had phoned him at 2:58 in the morning. She would have roughly seven minutes left to live.

The image of the woman putting the gun in her mouth once more came to his brutalized mind. And he had just stood there without saying one damn thing to stop her.

When he had woken up in the hospital after the blindside hit on the football field that had ended his athletic career as well as the person he had once been, Decker had no idea what had happened to him. As the doctors explained about his dying twice before being resuscitated, it was as though they were speaking to him about someone else.

Traumatic brain injury, they had said. The extent of the damage was unknown as yet, they had told him. They had simply done their best to keep him alive. It would not be until weeks later that he would learn what had truly happened to him that day.

Then came the extended stay at the Cognitive Institute in Chicago, where he had met folks who had also suffered injuries to their brains. And for all of them that trauma had led to startling new mental superpowers.

Superpowers. Yeah, I can forget nothing, most of the time. I see death as electric blue and other shit sometimes as orange or pink or green. Big, bad numbers used to come to eat me. I'm as socially awkward as a fourteen-year-old boy with a face full of zits at his first dance. I get tongue-tied on things I used to do easily, like being funny instead of annoying, having a filter, being sympathetic, though I have gotten a bit better with that. I have the same body but not the same person inside of that body. It cost me my family, though, and because of that I can never forgive . . . me.

He closed his eyes, and his broad shoulders slumped as he felt the full weight of all that he was pondering.

"You want some company?"

He looked up to see White standing there. She'd

changed into jeans, a dark red blouse, and black ballerina flats that made her look very short.

"Free country."

She slid onto the seat next to him and glanced at his phone. The screen had gone dark.

"Waiting for a call?"

He pocketed the phone. "No."

She waved to the bartender and ordered a G and T with Bombay Sapphire as the critical ingredient. "We covered a lot of ground today. Crisscrossed the state twice, in fact."

"But didn't find out much," he amended.

"Early days yet. Got to start somewhere. And there are always lots of questions and muddling shit at the beginning."

"*And* at the end, depending on how things turn out."

Her drink came and she took a sip. "I looked you up, Decker. You have never failed to solve any case the Bureau put you on."

"My very first case as a rookie detective back in Ohio, I put the wrong man in prison. A bunch of years later he told me so. He challenged me to prove I was wrong and he was right."

"And did you?"

"Yes. But it was too late to help him. Someone killed him the same day he made his challenge. I found his body."

"And how did that make you feel?"

He finished his beer and waved for another. He turned to her. "How do you think it made me feel? It made me feel like shit. I carved years off a man's life because I fucked up. I went into a case with preconceived notions and I never deviated from them."

"Did you learn from that?"

"Yeah, I did, but too late for him."

She raised her glass. "Congratulations, you're not perfect."

"Is that what you think this is about?"

"What this is about is us trying to do our job to the best of our ability. When *I* was a rookie, I messed up chain of custody once. Then I wasted time on following dopey leads. Got torched on the witness stand twice by slick defense lawyers because I didn't prepare hard enough. This is not TV, Decker. We make mistakes. We're human. We don't always get it right. We don't always solve the case in one hour including commercials."

"Maybe you don't" was all he said to that. But there was so little energy behind it that White did not seem to take offense.

She said, "So, we got Lancer and Kelly missing. Draymont and Cummins dead. Ex with an alibi."

"Provided by his son and maybe some business associates on video. We need to confirm he really was on those Zooms. If all that hangs together, he couldn't have personally done the murders. But he could have hired someone, as I said before."

"The Slovakian cash in the mouth?"

"Either real and literal or an intentional distraction." *Or maybe both*, he suddenly thought.

"Motive for the ex?"

"We need to talk to Cummins's lawyer, Duncan Trotter. Might depend on where her money goes."

"Her neighbor thought it was going to Tyler, not Barry Davidson."

"Still could be a motive, since Barry might manage that money and burn through some of it until Tyler comes of age."

"He looks to be doing pretty well all on his own."

"Looks can be deceiving. And even if Tyler gets it all, there could be personal reasons for the killing that we don't know about yet. They *were* divorced and it didn't sound like it was all that amicable."

"True."

"And I've got a hunch Gamma is going to stonewall us on our queries."

"I gotta feeling Gamma is gonna stonewall us on a lot of things."

Decker nodded but said nothing. He stared at his fresh beer like it was a clue.

"Hopefully, we'll find something on the judge's computers or phone that will help us."

"Yeah," Decker said unenthusiastically.

She stared at him. "Alex described you as relent-less. You get going on a case and nothing, not God himself, is going to stop you."

He did a sideways glance at her. "And?"

"And, don't take this wrong, but you don't seem to be that guy right now."

He took a long swig of beer. "Maybe right now I'm not."

"Is it Lancaster's suicide?"

He rose, dropped cash for his drinks, and walked off.

CHAPTER

24

SHE WATCHED HIM GO, THIS huge man lumbering along. He had been described to her by many people she respected as far and away the most dogged investigator the FBI had. Yes, annoying, frustrating to deal with, fragile at times, cutting unnervingly right to the edge of the legal envelope. But the man got the job done. He would walk through walls and over anyone standing in his way, no matter who it was, or how high up in the pecking order they were.

And while he had been somewhat like that today, he did not look like that man right now.

And he was her brand-spanking-new partner.

She sipped her G and T but didn't really taste it.

Shit, am I screwed or what?

She pulled out her phone and called home. Her mother, Serena, answered. She asked about the kids, who were asleep at this hour.

"They're fine, but from the sound of you, *you're* not fine, Frederica."

Her mother had resolutely declined to ever call her daughter Freddie.

"Just the case. Issues."

"All your cases have issues, especially in the beginning. What's different now?"

"My partner is different." She went on to explain about Decker, including his brain trauma and personal losses. "He seems disengaged. And if this investigation goes into the toilet, so do I. I didn't want a transfer. I don't even know why they picked me to partner with him."

"You don't? Really?"

White's brow crinkled. "What exactly are you saying, Mom?"

"Do you remember what happened to you when Donte was killed?"

"How the hell could I ever forget that?"

"Well, you apparently have. Just think on that. And pray on that. I feel sure you'll get there in the end."

"How can you stay so positive with all the shit that's happened to our family?"

"You think we're the only family that's had bad things happen?"

"We've had more than our share."

"I know some folks that have lost *all* of their children to violence."

"A racist white cop put a bullet in Daddy's head

because Daddy stood up to him. And he didn't spend one damn day in prison for it because the department thought it would be really bad for morale, and so they covered it up to look like an accident. Yeah, we got money, but that doesn't cut it. It didn't bring Daddy back."

"Everything you said is exactly right, Frederica. And you will carry that with you for the rest of your life, as I will. But if you let it be what *leads* your life and defines who you are, then your existence on this earth will not be nearly as positive or productive as it could be."

"I don't get you, I really don't."

"Just like maybe you don't *get* your new partner."

"If he blows this, my trajectory gets stalled out real fast. My kids are going to college. I need to keep moving up."

"I got the money for college for your kids."

"No, that's *your* money. That's Daddy's money. I don't want it."

"You'd be so stubborn over that you'd risk your kids' not getting ahead?"

"They're my kids and I'll get it done for them. Just like you and Daddy did for us. You didn't have rich relatives help you out. And I'm not going that route, either. You didn't raise me that way."

"Just pray on it, Frederica, just pray on it."

White clicked off and just shook her head. She

hadn't prayed or been to church since Donte had been killed.

And I'm not starting now. Because where was God when Daddy got killed? Where was he when Donte died? Not anywhere near where I fucking live.

An instant later she felt both her pulse and blood pressure rise dramatically.

Shit! She'd started having these panic attacks a while back. It was never to do with work. It was always to do with her kids. And her conversation with her mother had put it all front and center again. She took deep breaths and willed herself to calm.

She'd never talked about this with anyone at work. She didn't want anyone there to think she couldn't handle herself, the pressures, no matter where they came from. She had thought about getting help, talking to a counselor, but then decided to try to manage it on her own.

She left her unfinished drink on the counter and went to bed.

And Frederica White didn't sleep any better than Amos Decker did.

CHAPTER

25

H<small>E COULDN'T GET THE DAMN</small> image of Lancaster putting the gun in her mouth out of his head. It was like a heartbeat you heard in your eardrum. It just wouldn't go away and you couldn't ignore it. Decker tossed and turned in his bed and finally gave up.

He rose, dressed, and headed out. He reached the beach. It was two in the morning. He wasn't fearful for his personal safety. He was a huge guy and carried a big gun. And anyway, he didn't give a crap right now.

He walked to the edge of the sand and peered out at the ocean, pounding and whirling and doing its thing, like it always did.

The sky held a scattering of stars, a few smoky wisps of clouds. At the higher altitude he saw the contrails of a jet crossing the Gulf on its way somewhere.

His gaze returned to the earth, and he drew in a deep lungful of salt air.

And he started walking on the sand. It crunched and compacted under his bulk, giving him some purchase. It felt good, for some reason. Loose granules coming together to form something solid. Or was that just wishful thinking from a tired, overwrought mind?

Yeah, that could definitely be the case.

He walked near the water and then plopped down on his butt, pulled his knees up, and wrapped his arms around them.

He and Cassie had taken Molly to Disney World once when she was six. It was the only time he'd been to Florida on something non-football related. The only time other than now.

They'd had fun and emptied their bank account. But it had been worth it. He remembered the character breakfast when Mickey Mouse and Donald Duck and Goofy and their pals had come by. Molly had been terrified at first, hiding behind her father and only peeking out at the costumed characters as they walked past.

But little by little, she had gained confidence, and come out of hiding. She'd held hands with Donald and had her picture taken with Mickey. Cassie had tears in her eyes, and even Decker, who didn't get any of this at all, picked his daughter up so she could kiss the tall Goofy.

It was a wonderful, if overpriced, trip, and it also felt like a million years ago. And in most respects, it was.

He snagged a shell and looked at it. It was white and gray and cracked and felt fragile in his huge hand.

So, what are you going to do, Decker? You got some dead bodies and a load of stuff to look at, most of which is total bullshit. There will be junk popping up that doesn't make any sense but I will have to make sense out of it. If I can. And I don't know if I can. Or if I even want to. And those are two big ifs.

He rose and kept walking.

Out over the waves he conjured images of people who had been important in his life. Unlike his wife and daughter, they were all alive.

There was Melvin Mars, once on death row and now leading a wonderful life with a woman he loved. There was Ross Bogart, now retired, but with whom Decker had solved dozens of cases. And out beyond them both was a young woman who was once a journalist back in Burlington, Ohio, and now was a full-fledged FBI agent, kicking ass and doing good.

He took out his phone and hit speed dial, hoping she would answer.

Alex Jamison did, on the very first ring.

"I was wondering how long it was going to take for you to call me," she said.

"I'm sorry for calling in the middle of the night."

"I'm in a car pulling graveyard-shift surveillance, and I can think of no one else I'd rather talk to than you. So, how is it going with your new partner?"

"It's going, but not well."

"Did you expect otherwise? You *are* Amos Decker, after all."

He found himself smiling at this remark. "I keep being reminded of that every day. Pretty sure it's not a good thing."

"She's a fine agent, Decker. Really sharp. She's got more experience than me. And she's been through a lot worse than I have."

"I know. She told me."

"She might have told you some things, not all."

"You sound like you're closer than 'Freddie' let on."

"Many female FBI agents are close, if not for real, at least in spirit. There aren't that many of us, at least in proportion to the guys."

"Is this where you tell me I have to give her a chance?" he said dully.

"No. This is where I tell you that you have to give *yourself* a chance. Freddie will be good, Decker, with or without you. I'm not worried about her. But I am worried about *you*."

"Because of Mary?"

"Because of lots of things."

"I...I got a letter from the Cognitive Institute. After my annual checkup there."

"And what did it say?"

"It said a lot of things."

"Bad things?"

"Not so good."

"Is it manageable?"

"They don't know, so neither do I."

"I'm sorry, Amos," she said, her voice suddenly splintering with emotion.

Decker shrugged at the waves and her remark. "It's not unexpected. Have to pay the piper at some point."

"Doesn't matter. You're flesh and blood. You feel things. More than most."

"The thing is, this case down here...it's complicated."

"Are any of them not?"

"I mean, really complicated. And I'm not certain...that I'm up to it."

Jamison said nothing for so long that Decker thought he had lost the connection.

"I have to admit, that one surprised me. You always somehow manage to."

"Not my intent."

"Let's get something straight. I don't care how complicated the case is, you're up to it, if you want to be."

"And therein lies the rub," said Decker.

"You once told me that without your work, you had nothing."

"Which is pitiful in and of itself, I know."

"I didn't tell you that back then, and I'm not telling

you that now. You don't make widgets for a living. You find justice in this fucked-up world we all live in. You give the dead a voice. You hold guilty people accountable."

"I used to think that. Now I believe I was just chasing something I'll never catch."

"You never used to believe that. I lost count of the number of times you told me that the only thing that matters is that when someone does something bad, they cannot be allowed to get away with it. Nothing else mattered, you said, if we let that slide. Because that one thing dictates the sort of world we will all live in. I know you remember that, even without a perfect memory."

"Stop saying that, Alex, because nothing about it, not one goddamn thing, is *perfect*."

"Which makes you just like everybody else. Look, I don't know what was in the letter from the Institute and you don't have to tell me. But if it is the worst, then you need to decide what you want to do. You're the only one who can answer that question."

"I...I need you, Alex."

"The truth is, you never needed me or anyone else to do what you do. I was the sometimes helpful sidekick who basically stood there in awe of what you were able to do time and again. And while I can't come back right now, I *will* come back."

"But what about this guy in New York? I thought it was serious."

"The fact is, he wasn't all he was cracked up to be. And I decided I'm not a big-city girl."

She fell silent and Decker could only hear her calm, measured breaths, unlike his.

"I don't know if I can do this, Alex."

"You absolutely can do it *if* you want to. And if you don't want to, there's nothing wrong with that, either. And I'll be right there supporting you. But knowing you as I do, if you walk away now, whatever you're feeling, you'll wake up tomorrow ten times worse. I can't say I know everything about you. No one really does about someone else. But I know you better than anyone else alive. And I know that I'm right about that. And so do you."

Another long silence ensued.

"Thanks, Alex," said Decker.

"I want you to know something. Something important. Something that I believe with all my heart, Amos."

"What's that?"

"*I* need *you*. As does the rest of the world."

CHAPTER

26

DECKER ROSE PROMPTLY AT SIX A.M., feeling refreshed, despite not much sleep. He looked out his window at the gathering dawn and reflected on his conversation with Jamison.

It had been wonderful to hear her voice. It had been humbling to hear the woman's words. He knew he had to get his shit together. And if he walked away from this, from the only thing he'd been good at since football, then what would he do with his life? To make himself get out of bed each day? To avoid once more sinking into the abyss of the past?

Decker was not a superstitious man. But right as he had gone to sleep, he'd seen his daughter, and Molly was trying to talk to him. Saying things he really couldn't make out though he had desperately tried to, because his exhausted mind had fooled him into thinking she was really there.

The thing was, Molly had never come to him in a

vision, not like that. Perhaps she could tell he was at a crossroads.

And I probably am.

He knew what his wife would tell him. "You're no quitter, you've never been a quitter. When shit got tough, you just brought a bigger shovel and left scorched earth in your wake."

And now maybe he knew what Molly was trying to tell him. And Jamison.

So he showered, shaved, brushed his teeth extra hard, changed into clean clothes, tucked his shirt in, and combed his hair. Next he put on his only jacket, a corduroy one with elbow patches. And while the jacket was old and not stylish, it was still a jacket.

He was waiting in the hotel restaurant at seven thirty sharp when White and Andrews showed up within a minute of each other.

White looked him up and down, noting the groomed appearance and the jacket. "You look ready for war, Decker."

"Maybe I am." He glanced at Andrews. "Let's grab some chow and coffee and go over what needs going over."

"The APBs have turned up nothing," said Andrews as they ate. "Kelly's phone must be turned off because we couldn't trace it. But search warrants are being issued for Lancer's and Draymont's homes. Should have them this morning, in fact."

"Good," said Decker. "And the entry log for the guard gate?"

"I have people going over that and noting anything that we'll have to run down. From what I've been told so far, there's not much there. It did show Draymont came through the gate around eight p.m. that night. I did confirm Davidson was on the Zoom calls with two clients at the times he says. And you said Tyler gave him an alibi for the rest of the relevant time period. We'll have to get an official statement from him."

"Right, but as I suggested before, what if Davidson hired someone to kill her?"

"I can check his financials, see if he made any large payments or took out a bunch of cash. Hit men like cash."

"Okay," said Decker. "What about Gamma and any info on threats received by the judge?"

"I got an email from their counsel late last night. As you hinted at, they said we would have to go to court if we wanted any information."

Decker flitted back through his memory cloud and thought about each time they had asked someone about threats to the judge. The result was confusing at best. "Okay, what else?" he said.

"I received the judge's trial docket info late last night and went over it. There seems to be no cases worth looking at, including the RICO one."

White said, "I was hoping there would be something there to tie into the blindfold and the weird note left behind."

Andrews finished his coffee and eyed them. "Any particular place you want to start today?"

"Why don't you and White collect the warrants and go check out Lancer's and Draymont's places."

On these words, White gave him a death stare that Decker avoided altogether.

"And what will you do?" asked Andrews.

"I'm going back to the judge's house."

"Why?" asked White sharply.

"To look at it again. We can meet back up later." He held up his hand. "Keys to the rental?"

White tossed them to him and added icily, "There you go, Decker, knock yourself out."

After he walked off, Andrews and White sat there in silence. Finally Andrews said, "Anything going on I need to know about?"

White continued to stare at the departing Decker before turning to Andrews. "If you find out, be sure to tell me."

CHAPTER

27

IT HAD BEEN A SHITTY thing to do to White, Decker knew. And he'd still done it. He had his reasons. He didn't know if they were good ones, but they were his.

And he'd gotten an idea in his head and had decided to just run with it. Alone. For him, sometimes alone was best.

He drove to Cummins's gated community and used his credentials to clear security; the same guard was there.

"Any of that stuff I dropped off help you guys?" the man asked.

"Working on it," said Decker as he tapped the gas and sped off.

The forensics team was still at the house. He put on his gloves and booties and made a beeline for the bedroom. The bodies had been removed but he had had Helen Jacobs email him the pictures of the deceased from the crime scene.

His personal cloud had been percolating last night

and early this morning. And when he had laid one memory plate on top of another, a number of inconsistencies had popped up. That was why he was here.

He opened the door of a bedroom down the hall from the judge's. It was as neat as a pin, a place for everything and everything in its place. He could tell this was Tyler Davidson's room only because of the two footballs perched on a shelf and some high school textbooks set out on a desk.

This looks nothing like my old teenager bedroom. I was a slob back then and still am. But Tyler was clearly focused and organized, at least while he was with his mom.

He returned to the judge's bedroom, sat in a chair, and took in the space, slowly, one section at a time. He slipped out his phone and went through the photos of Judge Cummins, one image at a time, from her toenails to her fingernails, hair, face, and clothing. He went into the bathroom and made a careful search of the drawers, counters, and cabinets. He did the same with her closet.

Then he sat in the same chair and looked at the images of the slain Alan Draymont. The twin bullet holes in his chest. The suit. All the rest.

One memory frame after another slipped through his mental process, with every discrepancy noted and analyzed.

Okay, I can finally feel it coming together.

He went downstairs and looked in the dishwasher and saw what he thought he would. The same for the recycling bin. The forensics team had made a note of all this, but no one had put it all together yet. Until now. Things were becoming apparent to him that he should have seen before.

Because you've half-assed this case up to this point, that's why.

Draymont had known Alice Lancer. He had been to her home. That was not unusual—they did work together. She was the one who had been tagged as knowing about Draymont's assignment with Cummins, and the threats. But his place had been tossed. And Lancer was missing. And so was Patty Kelly. He knew of no connection among the three of them, though he was now certain there had to be one.

Based on his memory analysis and what he had found here, he phoned Helen Jacobs and asked her a question. Then he asked her a more detailed query for which she did not have the answer.

"I'll get right on that," she had said, almost apologetically.

He had already checked the list of contents of the bathroom trash can made by the forensic team, and what he thought should have been on that list wasn't.

He stared down at the toilet.

Yep, probably flushed.

And if he was right about all this, the case would take on a whole different dimension.

Decker walked out of the house and saw Doris Kline lifting some groceries out of an old-model yellow Mercedes convertible.

"Need some help?" he asked.

She turned and saw him. "Sure, save me a trip."

He grabbed two bags while she carried one. His bags clinked. He looked in them to see the bottles of vodka, scotch, and gin. The lady apparently liked them all. He saw several boxes of crackers and a wedge of cheese poking out of her bag.

"Having a party?" he asked as he followed her into the house.

She looked at him slyly. "Yeah, a party of one, unless you're interested."

"On duty, sorry. Besides, I don't think it would go well with the eggs I had for breakfast."

He set the bags down on the kitchen table and looked around the space. Dark, not overly clean, dated furnishings, and just a sad air all around.

He glanced at her to find Kline watching him.

"What did you expect?" she said. "I told you my ex had the better lawyer. I got the house and he got the cash. Now he's traveling the world making whoopie while I can barely pay a high schooler to cut the grass."

"Doesn't seem fair."

"I was stupid. Still trusted him after he cheated on me, more than once. My fault."

"I think the fault lies with him."

She unscrewed a bottle of vodka and poured it into a glass. She added some tonic and mixed it with her finger. "I knew I liked you. Have you found out who killed Julia?"

"Working on it. Did you ever see Cummins and Draymont together?"

"Draymont is the dead guy?"

"Yes."

"Sure, I mean, he was over some nights the last few weeks."

"*Some* nights? So, not *every* night."

"Well, his car wasn't there those nights, so I just assumed he wasn't, either."

Decker sat down at the table and eyed her. "I know she was your friend, but I need to ask you something."

She sat down across from him and sipped on her drink while she gave him a knowing look. "You want to know if they were having sex?"

"Yes, but what made you think that?"

"He was young and handsome and she was still young and lovely and single and alone. I would've jumped into bed with that guy in a heartbeat. The men around here are mostly bald and fat. And all they want to do is play golf. Makes you lose faith in the American male."

"Anything more specific?"

She looked at him with a coy expression. "Just things that maybe a woman picks up on that men never do."

Decker sat back. "Let me tell you what *I* picked up on. He wasn't wearing a tie. Everyone in a suit at Gamma Protection does apparently. At that hour, he was *in* the house, not outside. There were two wineglasses in the dishwasher and an empty bottle of merlot in the recycling bin. The judge had makeup, lipstick, and perfume on when she was killed. I don't think she was asleep at all. The fingernail and toe-nail polish she was wearing was the same color as the bottle on her bathroom counter. She'd put it on that night, presumably, which you wouldn't really do unless you were expecting someone. It was a particularly hot shade of cherry red. It was also on one of the wineglasses."

Kline smiled. "Go on, Agent Decker. You're just hitting your stride, I can tell."

"There were clothes on the floor of her closet, all items of lingerie, as though she was thinking about what to wear that night. Some tissues were in the wastebasket with lipstick marks on them. Same color the judge was wearing. That was probably either the judge wiping off excess, or Draymont getting rid of kiss marks on his face. The bed covers were really messed up and the mattress was several inches off-kilter from the box springs. We thought that represented a struggle with her killer. But now I think it was two people being energetically intimate."

"At least she had fun before she left this world," said Kline thoughtfully, her lips trembling. She composed herself with a long drink from her glass. "And I must say, you're very observant. For my part, I had just seen a couple of times the way they looked at each other. And when I asked Julia about him she went overboard explaining how it was all professional. Which led me to think, 'She doth protest too much.'"

"You didn't tell us that yesterday."

"You didn't ask."

"Our questions were pretty general."

She lifted her glass. "Well, now you know."

"The security gate log showed Draymont arriving around eight that night. Was that his usual time?"

"Around that. Actually, I don't think he was here last week at all. And he'd been at her home two days before he was killed. At least I saw his car."

"Do you know when your other neighbors the Perlmans are getting back today?"

"Their flight gets in around eleven. They'll probably be here around twelve thirty or so."

"Have you told them about Judge Cummins?"

She shook her head. "I . . . I didn't have the heart to.

Maya and Julia were very close. It's not something you want to do over the phone." She finished her drink. "So, what will you do with that information?"

"Keep digging like I always do. The truth is worth it."

And as he left her, Decker reflected that it actually felt good to say that.

CHAPTER

28

"You were right, Agent Decker," said Helen Jacobs.

They were huddled over the body of Julia Cummins at the morgue. Decker's electric blue tsunami had come and gone, but left him a bit pale and shaken. He hated that reaction as much as he hated anything. It made him feel weak and not up to the task. And he knew others seeing it might think the same.

Screw synesthesia.

"She'd had sex before she died?" he said.

"Yes. I checked for that, as I said when I saw you at the crime scene. But I was really looking for an *assault*, considering that she was murdered. I went over her entire body. I checked for the usual finger pad bruising on her arms, legs, and neck, suction bites, especially on her breasts, petechiae in the eyes and palate, bruising to the inner lips and behind the ears, all places typically impacted by a sexual assault. I used swabs and a Foley balloon catheter to check her vagina. The physical structure of that part of the anatomy makes detection of an attack difficult, so I also used a colposcope and an ultraviolet light to do my exam. All the results came back pretty much negative for a sexual assault."

"And since you found no firm evidence of sexual assault, you proceeded no further on that line?"

"That's right. No assault meant no sex at all, at least in my mind." Jacobs looked embarrassed. "I should not have made that assumption. But I suppose I was influenced by her violent death. You never see consensual sex end that way. At least I haven't."

"She was also found dressed—in her underwear—but still dressed. Perps who commit sexual assaults don't usually take the time to re-dress their victims unless it's some sort of ritual killing."

"I guess that influenced me, too. And none of the clothing was torn or damaged, except by the knife strikes. In a sexual assault the attacker always tears some of the clothing, particularly the under-wear, to show his aggression and dominance. But once you texted I dug a little deeper. There were the smallest of signs around her vagina, just a bit of swelling. There was no tissue damage, or bruising, the sort of thing you see with pretty much every sexual assault. And when I went back and looked again, there was also very slight evidence of a vaginal lubricant."

"So the encounter was planned?"

"Apparently."

"Did the man use a condom?"

"He must have. There was no evidence of sperm in the vagina. I certainly checked for that."

"I think the condom was flushed, not that it would have mattered. She lived alone. And I think they both must have showered afterward. And then the judge put on the clothing she was later found wearing. There were damp towels and washcloths in the laundry bin in the bathroom."

"I guess that would make sense."

"Can you still get a DNA match?"

"I hope so from other detritus left behind when people have sex, even with a shower. And there should be plenty of it on the sheets, which we have here, and I can also examine the towels and wash-cloths. Do you have someone to match it to?"

Decker pointed to Draymont's body, which was lying on the other table. "That guy right there."

Jacobs's eyebrows lifted. "Okay, while I admit I missed the consensual sex piece, I never thought she would be sleeping with her bodyguard. But I guess it happens."

"Do you have Draymont's personal effects?"

She led him to a locked cabinet and opened it. Inside were a number of labelled plastic evidence bags.

"Clothes, shoes, wallet, other personal items."

Decker examined each one carefully. He already knew about the suit and watch and shoes. He opened the billfold. Inside were three credit cards, one a personal platinum Amex.

"Thanks."

"Her son came by to identify her," Jacobs volunteered.

Decker shot her a glance. "Tyler came? Not his father?"

"He said his father couldn't bring himself to come."

"Damn. How did that go?"

"I covered her right up to her neck, so he couldn't see..."

"Yeah."

"He cried. But he handled it pretty well, actually. Better than I would have."

"Life's a bitch sometimes," murmured Decker. "What about prints? Any luck?"

"We didn't find any we couldn't match. We found lots of Tyler's prints, but none in his mother's bedroom. And none of Barry Davidson's." She picked up her iPad and scrolled down. "We found several from the neighbor, Doris Kline. Prints from a maid service Cummins used. Some others we determined were tied to service companies, HVAC, plumbing, and other ones like that. Andrews had them checked out and all had alibis."

"But not Doris Kline, right?" Jacobs looked up.

Decker continued, "She lives alone. She found the bodies. She was home that night."

"Y-yes, I guess that's right. But do you think she could have done it? When I printed her, she seemed genuinely upset about the judge's death."

"I think anyone can do anything until it's proved conclusively that they didn't."

Jacobs eyed him strangely and then shrugged. "While you're here, there *is* something else I found."

She led him over to a computer set up on a countertop. "I examined the blood found on the stairs and on the palm print on the wall of the stairs leading to the upstairs bedroom."

"You mean the blood that came from the judge when she was attacked downstairs, and then fled upstairs to her bedroom where she was killed?"

"Well, that's what I thought, at first. But the blood-stains on the stairs and under the palm print weren't hers. They were Draymont's."

Decker glanced over at the two bodies, separated by a few feet in death, and perhaps by miles as far as the investigation was going.

"So the judge was not attacked downstairs?"

"Well, at least she wasn't *bleeding* while downstairs."

"So Draymont was probably leaving the house when he was shot. The judge came downstairs, prob-ably when she heard the two gunshots. She found the body, got his blood on her that way, and then ran back upstairs, leaving his blood trace along the way?"

"That seems to be the case," said Jacobs.

"But if the shooter was still there, why not kill her downstairs?"

"They might have tried to, but missed."

"There were no bullet holes found other than the pair in Draymont," Decker pointed out.

"Of course, that's right. And she was stabbed, not shot."

Decker rocked back on his heels. *She was stabbed, not shot. Why the hell didn't you see that discrepancy before, superpower memory or not?*

"What caliber killed Draymont?" he asked.

"Nine millimeter. Both slugs were still in him. They're in good shape for a ballistics match if we can find the gun."

She showed him the rounds that were in another plastic evidence baggie. "They were fired from a distance of over four feet. No powder burns or other markings on the body."

"Which makes sense. It would give Draymont no opportunity to wrestle the weapon away. Now, what can you tell me about the knife used to kill the judge?"

She brought up a file on the computer that showed the knife wounds on the dead woman together with a measurement scale.

"I'm estimating about a six-inch blade with a serrated edge."

"Four defensive wounds on her forearms and two on her hands?"

"That's correct. Unfortunately, there was no trace under her fingernails. She probably was focused on blocking the knife strikes and never got ahold of her attacker."

"Right."

"And, as I reported before, ten stab wounds to her torso, including the fatal one."

Decker shook his head.

"What is it?"

"Maybe nothing. Thanks."

He left and walked out into the heat and sunshine.

Gun, knife, impersonal versus frenetic. What the hell was I thinking? Well, you weren't thinking, were you?

You don't shoot someone and then chase down and struggle with a witness, and then knife her. She would have been screaming her head off, though with Kline on a CPAP machine and taking a sleep aid, and the Perlmans out of town, there would have been no one around to hear. Still, you would just shoot her, like you had Draymont. Bang, bang, no screams, no struggle. You didn't have to get close enough to stab her multiple times.

So they had one personal murder and one probable

nonpersonal murder occurring around the same time and in the same house.

Despite all the reasons why it could have never gone down that way, Decker was now thinking one thing.

We have not one but two killers. And as implausible as it sounds, I don't think either one knew about the other.

CHAPTER

29

AT AROUND HALF PAST TWELVE a Mercedes sedan pulled into the home's wraparound driveway and came to a stop. A man in his early seventies with neatly trimmed white hair and wearing a blazer and dark slacks got out from the rear driver's side. He was around six feet tall and thin. A tall, slender woman in her late fifties with long silvery hair and dressed in a billowy navy blue skirt and long-sleeved white blouse climbed out of the rear passenger side.

The driver clambered out, popped the trunk, and pulled out two rolling suitcases.

The man tipped him and took the suitcases.

As soon as the Benz pulled off, Decker steered his rental into the driveway.

He got out and said, "Mr. and Mrs. Perlman?"

Mr. Perlman turned to him. "Yes? Who are you?"

Decker held out his credentials. "Amos Decker with the FBI."

Mrs. Perlman glanced sharply at her husband. "FBI? What is going on, Trevor?"

Trevor glanced toward the house. "My God, what's happened? Have we been robbed?"

Decker drew closer. "No. But a crime *was* committed next door."

Both Perlmans looked around. "Which neighbor?" he said.

"Julia Cummins. Can we go inside and talk about this?"

"We just got back from a long trip," protested Trevor, indicating the suitcases.

"It won't take much time. Just a few questions."

Trevor said resignedly, "All right."

The interior of the home was spacious, with a flowing floor plan, lots of neutral colors, and an abundance of rear windows opening out to views of the Gulf beyond.

Decker noted the costly furnishings and oil paintings on the wall and the sculptures resting on pedestals, and thought that, unlike Doris Kline, the Perlmans had the money to keep their home up.

On the wall were photos of the Perlmans on a sailboat and another of Trevor Perlman at the wheel of a cabin cruiser with a captain's hat worn at a jaunty angle. They looked happy and carefree. When he glanced over at them now, they looked anything but.

Trevor put the suitcases in a corner and turned to his wife. "Maybe some coffee, Maya?" He looked at Decker. "Would you like some?"

"Thank you, yes."

After the coffee was made and given out, they sat on the lanai, where, with the press of a button by Trevor, a wall of glass opened up.

"Nice place," commented Decker.

"We like it," said Trevor. "Now, you mentioned a crime?"

"Yes, I'm sorry to have to tell you this, but it was a double homicide at Judge Cummins's home. She and her bodyguard were killed."

Maya gave a little shriek and nearly spilled her coffee. Trevor stared blankly at Decker, as though he could not have possibly just said what he had.

"Julia...was...killed?" said Trevor.

"Yes. And her bodyguard, Alan Draymont."

"Oh my God," wailed Maya. She stood up, staggered, and fell back onto the sofa with her eyes shut.

"Maya!" cried out her husband. "Maya!" He gently smacked her cheeks and glanced at Decker.

"Water, there's a fridge right over there."

Decker grabbed a bottle of cold water. With her husband's aid, Maya had come around and sat up. She drank the water and her color returned.

"I...I need to...compose myself."

"Of course," said Decker.

Trevor helped her from the room and then came back to the lanai and sat down.

"My wife and Julia were very...close."

"So I understand. I'm sorry."

"Do you...what in the hell happened?"

"As I said, someone killed her and her bodyguard. We have no suspects yet. How long have you and your wife been out of town?"

"For the last week. We were visiting some of Maya's children in New York. From her previous marriage," he added.

"When was the last time you spoke to or saw Judge Cummins?"

Trevor put his coffee cup on a side table. "I think I saw her a couple of days before we left. Just in passing. Just to say hello. Maya may have seen or talked to her before we left." He looked up at Decker, his face taut. "How...was she...killed?"

"I can't get into that. I understand that you recommended Gamma Protection Services to Judge Cummins?"

His voice breaking, Trevor said, "Y-yes, w-we did."

"Why was that?"

He sipped his coffee and composed himself. "Maya was a lawyer. A defense attorney. No lawyer wins every case. One she lost involved a man accused of sexually assaulting his wife *and* children. He was sent to prison. But he got out about six months ago. He apparently didn't think Maya had done a good enough job. He made threats. He even came by the house a couple of times. We got a restraining order. But he broke it. So we hired Gamma."

"Was it Alan Draymont?"

"I...I don't know. What does he look like?"

Decker produced a picture on his phone. "This is him."

Trevor looked at it and shook his head. "I don't know. It might be him. But it was more than one person. After a while, they blur together."

"I can understand that. How long did you have protection?"

"For about a month, I think."

"What happened to your wife's old client?"

"He attacked someone living in his halfway house and nearly killed the guy. He's back in prison awaiting another trial. Hopefully, this time they put him away for good."

"Do you think your wife is up to talking with me now? It'll save me having to come back."

"Let me check."

He went off while Decker finished his coffee. He rose and walked around the lanai.

Decker hadn't owned a home since the one his family had been killed in. After that, he'd ended up basically living in a cardboard box in the back of a

Walmart parking lot for a longer time than he cared to remember. You never think that would happen to you, until it did. And then your thinking changed measurably to, *I'm never going to get out of this nightmare.*

He had gained a hundred pounds from eating crap and not exercising at all. He could barely stand with the extra weight. And the only thing that saved him from remaining on the streets and probably dying there was waking up one day, seeing the cardboard ceiling of his "home," and realizing how ashamed his wife and daughter would be of him.

His recovery had not happened overnight. It had taken nearly a year. During that time he had gone to live at a local Residence Inn, and used the dining area as the office of his fledgling detective business.

When the first few clients came to him, he knew they were repulsed by what they saw in him. A huge, hulking, not overly clean man with a thick beard and nothing approaching an outgoing and engaging manner. The only thing that saved him was the fact that Decker was damn good at his job. He could figure out just about anything.

I hope that holds for this case.

"Agent Decker?" said a woman's voice.

He turned to see the Perlmans at the entrance to

the lanai. Trevor was holding his wife's hand. She looked pale but collected.

"I'm sorry about...what happened earlier."

"No need to apologize. It was a shock, I know. I won't take too much more time. Just a few questions if you're up to it."

They sat down across from him.

"When was the last time you saw or spoke to Judge Cummins?"

"I talked to her on the phone right before we left for New York, so about nine days ago. I was just giving her our travel details, in case of emergency. We always did that with each other."

"And the last time you actually saw her?"

"A couple of days before that. We had a drink, down near the courthouse."

"Did she seem okay, nothing troubling her?"

"No, she was fine."

"You practiced at that court?"

"Yes, but never before Julia, of course."

"I understand from your husband that a former client threatened you?"

"Yes, Gerald Garvey. He's the sort that gives defense attorneys a bad name. I knew he was guilty, but he was entitled to legal representation. I got him a sweetheart deal, but he didn't see it that way."

"And you hired Gamma Protection?"

"Yes."

"How did you hear of them?"

"I think it was someone at the courthouse. Plus, they're a well-known firm."

"Did you know Alan Draymont? Your husband didn't know if he was one of the people who guarded you."

Decker held up the picture of Draymont.

"Yes, he looks familiar. But, as you alluded to, there were several different people who protected us. Men and women. I don't remember all their names. They had credentials and everything, and we were sent a secure email with their names and pictures to verify their identities."

"Can you look up those emails?"

Trevor interjected, "Surely, you can get those details from Gamma?"

"You'd think, wouldn't you? But they're having some *personnel* problems right now."

She said, "I can look later. Right now, I just need to go lie down. This has been a terrible shock."

She rose and her husband stood with her. "I think that's all for now," he said.

He escorted Decker to the door and closed it firmly behind him.

Decker took in the sunshine and felt the warmth and heard the ocean and then the *thwack* of a golf ball from somewhere. On a cart path that cut through the trees, two people in their sixties rode past on bikes and waved at another couple drifting by from the other direction on their spiffy, decked-out golf cart. They all looked happy, content.

Decker walked back to his car.

I'm never moving here.

CHAPTER

30

As he was about to drive off, his phone buzzed. He didn't recognize the number.

"Decker."

"Please hold for Ms. Roe."

A moment later a familiar voice said, "Mr. Decker, it's Kasimira Roe. I wonder if we can meet?"

"I'm game. We didn't really finish the first time, did we?"

"No, we didn't."

"At your office?"

"No, at my home. It's on Miami Beach. I'll switch you back to my assistant and she can provide the address."

"When?"

"As soon as you can get here."

"Anything particular you want to discuss?"

"Just get here as soon as you can. I'll transfer you back."

Decker got the address, plugged it into his phone, and set off once more for Miami.

* * *

The high-rise looked ultramodern and expensive and super chic, thought Decker, which meant he hated it. He half expected Justin Bieber, or some other young celebrity he really knew nothing about, to walk out dressed in torn jeans that cost more than Decker had in his checking account and jump into a Lamborghini.

He cleared security after both the guard and concierge ran unimpressed gazes over his rumpled and distinctly uncool clothes and deeply scuffed shoes.

And this is my nice stuff.

He rode the elevator up and walked to a double set of white doors at the end of a wide hall.

He knocked, and the door was immediately answered by a young woman in a maid's uniform.

Jesus, do they really still make them wear that get-up?

The woman asked Decker to take his shoes off, which he did reluctantly, since his socks were not in the best shape and then there was the smell. He had always had sweaty feet. And the humidity here didn't help matters.

She led him down a plushy carpeted corridor that was outlined with soaring white columns. A wall of windows looked over the ocean. The other walls were covered with what looked to be some serious artwork.

The maid knocked on a door at the end of the hall, and a woman's voice said to come in.

Decker stepped into the small, intimate room with cushy furnishings and a gas fireplace that he imagined didn't see much work in this climate.

Roe rose from her chair. She was dressed in a white pleated skirt and dark blue jacket with a white blouse peeking out from underneath. Her shoes were flats. Her hair was tied back in a bun. She shook his hand and asked him if he wanted anything.

"Information," he replied as he sat down across from her.

"I checked you out, Mr. Decker. I hope you don't mind."

"I would've been surprised if you hadn't, knowing the business you're in."

She smiled and it was a pretty smile, he thought, lots of teeth and more girlish than professional woman. "May I be frank?"

"I prefer it, since I always am."

"You were described by just about everyone I talked to as possessing a motor that just won't quit, a deep desire to get justice. And for also being a royal pain in the butt."

"My language about myself wouldn't have been nearly as polite."

The girlish smile faded, and the professional shield came down. "Alice Lancer has not been located."

"That's right. Do you know a woman named Patty Kelly?"

"I don't believe so, no. Why?"

"She's Judge Cummins's secretary. Looks like she's done a runner, too."

She looked genuinely startled. "Do you think it's connected to Alice's disappearance?"

"What do you think?"

"I would *think* you can't rule it out at this point."

"Did you find a record of any threats against the judge? Or any reason why Cummins needed protection?"

"My people are looking at our records. But any disclosure has to be cleared through our legal counsel."

"But I was hoping for some professional courtesy. I came all this way, after all. At *your* invitation."

"Um, I'm going to have a glass of wine if you'd care to join."

"Never got into wine. But if you have beer?"

She rose, opened a glass door set in the cabinet, took out a bottle of open red wine, grabbed a glass from the overhead cabinet, and poured out a goodly portion into her wineglass. "Dos Equis okay?"

"Fine."

She pulled a bottle of beer from the fridge, poured it into a glass, and handed it to him. She resumed her seat and took a sip of her wine. "My father was the one who got me into wine."

"They made wine in Czechoslovakia?"

"No, in California. My father immigrated there

initially. As a teenager he worked in a vineyard for two years to earn money for college. Then he came east, went to college, joined the Secret Service, and then left to build what eventually became Gamma Protection."

"Sounds like he was quite a force of nature."

"He was." She stared out the window. "And I miss him dearly."

"I'm sure. So, you wanted to meet?"

She looked back at him, an expression on her face Decker couldn't really read. "I understand that a wad of old Slovakian money was found in Alan Draymont's throat."

Decker sat up straighter and eyed her, barely concealing the anger he was feeling. "And how did you find that out?"

"I know that you're upset by that. But I have resources everywhere, it's just the nature of the business I'm in."

"Resources are one thing, getting confidential information about an ongoing federal criminal investigation is something else."

"Is it true?" she asked.

"What if it were? What would that tell you?"

"You already know of my father's connection to that country."

"But even if he had any enemies, your father is beyond their reach. And why take it out on Draymont in any case?"

"As to your first query, Gamma and my father were interchangeable. He may be gone, but the company is still there."

"So they want to destroy the company your father built, you mean?"

"It could be. It's certainly one possibility."

"And as to my second query?"

"I don't know why they would target Alan Draymont. My initial thought was the most obvious. That the real target was the judge and he died defending her." She glanced up at him. "Could that still be true?"

"Anything's possible."

"But you think it unlikely?"

"With the cash in the throat? I doubt they just happened to be carrying expired Slovakian currency when they showed up at the judge's house to murder her."

"But it could be a device to throw you off the scent. To distract?"

"They would have to know Draymont was guarding her, and they might have known who employed him. How well-known was your father's background, that he came from Czechoslovakia?"

"Well-known enough. We have the clock in our office." She attempted a smile.

For Decker, this was an exercise in futility, since he already believed that there were two unrelated killers at the house that night. But he also might be wrong about that.

"Then your theory is that someone wanted to get back at Gamma. So they killed Draymont, stuffed his mouth with Slovakian money, then killed the judge to take out the witness?"

"It's one possibility," she replied.

"Why target Draymont? Out of all the agents you have? And why kill him when he's on assignment, which means they might well have to kill the protectee, too?"

She sipped her wine and looked thoughtful. "I know it might seem implausible when you say it that way."

Decker took a swig of beer. "When I say it any which way."

She stared at him. "So, what is your theory then?"

"Is that what this is about?"

"What do you mean?"

"You call me to meet, throw out a bullshit theory which I shoot down, and then you put me on the spot to tell you *my* theory to make me look smart. But you really want to find out where we are in the investigation."

She smiled demurely and set her wine aside. "Would you like to come and work for Gamma? We can use people like you."

"Don't think it would work."

"Why?"

"I don't wear ties. Except at funerals."

She sat forward, her expression more urgent. "I *am* afraid that this will have a negative impact on Gamma."

"And despite my winning personality, I don't do PR."

"The media has already picked up on the fact that one of our operatives was killed."

"I don't really care about your business. I just want to catch whoever killed two people."

"I can understand that, but I have a lot of people to think about."

"Okay, you think about them and I'll focus on my job."

"You're not very cooperative."

"Am I supposed to be with someone who's gotten information on a case she shouldn't have, and tried to con me into spilling even more without telling me a goddamn thing in return?"

She looked down. "I guess I deserved that."

Decker set the beer aside and rose. "I gotta get back to work."

"Could you...walk with me on the beach?"

"Do I really look like a beach guy to you?"

"Just for a few minutes? Please?"

CHAPTER

31

ONCE MORE DURING THIS TRIP Decker found himself on the sand.

Roe had taken off her shoes. Decker had stuffed his socks in his coat pocket. He towered over her as he did most people. They walked in silence for a minute or so until she stopped and looked toward the water.

"It was out there, somewhere."

"You never said how your father died."

"I didn't, did I?"

"Look, it's no business of mine."

"I didn't bring you out here because it was no business of yours."

He looked out to the horizon. "Okay, I'm listening."

"I think he went out to fish. My father loved deep-sea fishing."

"Was he alone?"

"I don't know."

"How could you not know?"

"Well, no one went out with him, at least that I know of. But that doesn't mean he was alone."

"Anyone reported missing other than him?"

"Not that I know of."

"Well, if someone *was* with him, wouldn't they have come back and told you what happened?"

"No one came back. The boat disappeared. They never found any bodies. They never found the cause of what had happened."

"You mean no debris, no oil slick to show if the boat went down?"

"They did a brief search of the area where they thought he might have been, but they did no underwater search because there was no evidence that the boat sank. And it's a huge area. And unlike a plane which has to file a flight plan, you don't have to file a plan for your boat trip. The regular fishing charters go to the same areas, but that didn't apply to my father, of course."

"Who reported him missing, then?"

"A friend of his who often went fishing with him. No one realized my father had not come back until the next day. He went out on a Saturday and no one noticed his boat was missing from its slip until later in the day on Sunday. Then, as I said, they sent a search team out to where they thought he might have been. They found nothing. But he might not have stayed in that location. The water is very deep out there. During the time he was gone, the boat could have sunk. But as I said, they found no evidence of that."

"Then how do you know he died?"

"Because I've heard nothing from him for three years. If he was alive, he would have contacted me. He has to be dead. My father would not leave me in limbo."

"Are there pirates out there?" asked Decker.

"There are smugglers. And he might have run into something like that. I had an investigation done along those lines, and it got nowhere." She turned to Decker. "Which is why the Slovakian money found at the crime scene has me...concerned."

"Because it might somehow connect to your father's disappearance?"

"And it might help explain what happened to him, after three years." She stopped and turned to him. "Because I have to know, Mr. Decker."

"You have a company specializing in investigating just this sort of thing, Ms. Roe."

"Please, call me Kasimira. And yes, I know that, but much of our work is *protection*. While we do have investigators, I would like a fresh pair of eyes on this, an outsider. And my people have *had* a shot at solving it over the last three years. They've come up with nothing."

"I already have a job," countered Decker.

"With this latest revelation about the money, you may not have a choice. I think somehow the murders of Draymont and the judge might be connected to my father's disappearance."

Decker looked down at his white wrinkled toes. "That's an interesting theory."

"Which might be proved correct, or not. But you can't discount it, not yet."

He glanced up to see a set of pleading eyes on him. "No, you're right. I can't. Yet."

"So you will look into it?"

"I follow the evidence where it takes me. And if it takes me in the direction of what happened to your father, that's where I'll go, too."

"Thank you, Mr. Decker. Thank you."

They walked back to her apartment after rinsing off their feet, and Decker put on his socks and shoes.

She held out a file. "This is everything I have on my father's disappearance."

Decker took it and said, "Your father was a child when he left Czechoslovakia?"

"Yes, that's right."

"So he personally couldn't have had enemies when he left there. What about the rest of his family?"

"He rarely spoke about them other than to say they were simple farmers."

"Did *you* know your grandparents? Were they politically connected, or wealthy? Were they with the KGB and the Soviets were pissed they fled the country with maybe a bunch of nuclear weapons secrets?"

"They died before I was born, so I never met them. But I've seen pictures, though. They *were* simple farmers. They would have meant nothing to the Soviet leadership."

Decker glanced at the file. "So, other things being equal, it was probably your father's enemies in *this* country that made him disappear."

"But the Slovakian money?"

"That could mean any number of things, Kasimira. But what I could use from you is a background file on Draymont and Lancer. What they did before coming to Gamma, that sort of thing. Think you can provide that without making us go to court?"

"I think I can manage that."

"Send it to Agent Andrews so he won't feel left out."

"But there's something else you need to know. My father was terminally ill. He had only months to live. I think that's why he wanted to go out on his boat. Maybe one last time."

Decker stared pointedly at her.

"Do you think that's important?" she said.

"I think everything in a case is important, until it's proven conclusively not to be."

"So you'll let me know what you find out?"

"I'll let you know what I *can*, but I will not tell

you anything that will jeopardize my investigation. Like someone else already did about the Slovakian money." He held up the file. "And just so we're crystal clear: Despite this, I haven't ruled *you* out as a suspect."

He turned and left Kasimira Roe and her chic Miami Beach condo in the sky.

CHAPTER

32

So, nothing?" asked Decker.

White eyed him as they stood outside Alice Lancer's neat little bungalow a half hour north of Miami. He had phoned her and driven directly there from Roe's condo in the sky.

"In official parlance the term is 'fuckin' zip.' Same at Draymont's apartment, which is no surprise, since someone had already searched his place." She looked at the house next door. "But there was something. A neighbor looked out the window and saw a car pull into the driveway. She described two large men getting out of the car and going into the house."

"When?"

"Right after Lancer disappeared."

"So they snatched her and came right here?" said Decker.

"Looks like it."

"And she didn't see Lancer?"

"No," replied White. "She might have been drugged and in the trunk for all we know."

"And the neighbor didn't call the cops?"

"She had no idea that Lancer had disappeared. But she said she was going to call the cops. Then one of the guys unlocked the door and they went in like they owned the place, so she thought they must be friends of hers."

"She get the license plate number?"

White shook her head. "But she gave us a description of the car."

"Well, at least she was more helpful than the other neighbor we talked to. So, had her place been previously searched, too?"

White said, "Not like Draymont's. But something tells me a search was made. And there was no laptop or desktop computer here."

"Did the neighbor see them carrying anything out?"

"No, she went out for a walk and didn't see them leave."

"Okay, so they're still a couple steps ahead of us. We have to change that at some point."

"And what have you been up to, Decker?"

At that moment Andrews walked out of the house.

"I'll fill you in, but later."

She glanced over at Andrews. "Okay."

"Decker," called out Andrews. "Long time no see."

"Yeah. I understand not much here."

Andrews walked up to them. "We're a day late and a dollar short. But the team is still in there processing. They still might find something useful. How did things go with you?"

"They're still going."

"I thought I'd go back to the office and write up my report so far and check in with the forensics folks. You two want to grab some dinner back in Ocean View later?"

"Yeah, that sounds good, we'll give you a call when we get back," said Decker. "We have to go report in, too. I'll drive back with Agent White."

Andrews gave them a thumbs-up and walked off to his car.

Decker led White over to the rental and they climbed in and drove off.

They had barely gone thirty feet when White unloaded. "I don't appreciate getting dumped by my partner."

"I can—"

"Shut up, 'cause I'm not done. In fact, I'm just getting started. I'm a good agent and I've been busting my hump for a long time and I don't deserve this shit from you or anyone else."

"Look, I—"

She stuck a finger in his face. "I'm not done, so shut the fuck up, Donnie!"

"Didn't take you for a *Big Lebowski* fan," said Decker, referring to the line from that classic film.

"If you ever pull that shit on me again, I will lay

your ass out so fast, you'll think Muhammad Ali came back from the grave and used you for punching practice. And I already told you I have a double black belt in karate, so I *can* lay your butt out. I don't care how big you are."

"I'm trying—"

She smacked him on the arm. "*Not* done yet, Decker. And as soon as this case is over, however it turns out, I'm getting the hell away from you. And then you can go and play your stupid little mind games and screw over somebody else, because I'm not having it. I am not putting up with your bullshit and you are not blowing up my career. Now, do you understand what the fuck I'm saying to you?"

Several moments of silence passed.

"Decker, I *asked* you a question."

"I was just making sure you were done."

"I hope to hell that I am."

"You're right. I screwed with you and I shouldn't have. It was my fault and I'm sorry."

"Why in the hell did you do it in the first place?" barked White.

Decker didn't answer right away. "I don't handle change well. And you're not Alex. But even with Alex, it was no picnic with her for a long time."

"Yeah, she told me. But you eventually warmed up to her. You gave her a chance. Why am I different?"

"You're not different. Maybe *I* am."

"Meaning?"

"Meaning, I don't know. But what I do know is we have a case to work, and it's going to take both of us to get there."

"And why should I give you another chance?"

"I can't think of a single good reason," he conceded.

White said, "Good. If you had tried to bullshit me I might have shot you."

They drove for a bit in silence.

"Okay, what did you find out today?" she asked.

He told her about his theory on Draymont and Cummins being lovers.

"The ME confirmed that she'd had consensual sex that night. And the physical evidence substantiates that it was probably with Draymont. DNA on the sheets will confirm. If so, he was probably leaving the house when it happened, while the judge was probably upstairs in bed. She heard the shots and raced downstairs."

"Shit, what made you think to check that?" said a stunned White.

"No one could confirm that there ever were any real threats against the judge. She'd been threatened before, for real. What did she do when that happened? She notified the U.S. Marshals Service and they assigned her protection. What you don't do is go out and hire your own protection. There would have been no need. So, another plausible reason for Draymont to be there was sexual. Doris Kline thought the same thing."

White shook her head, looking confused. "But why go through that sort of subterfuge? She was single. Draymont was, too."

"That's what we have to find out. I also spoke with the Perlmans. They just got back from New York. They weren't much help. They suggested Gamma to Cummins because Maya Perlman's former legal client made threats against her. They weren't around during the murders, so they didn't see anything. But Maya Perlman was really upset. She and the judge were close."

Next, he told her about his meeting with Kasimira Roe. "That's why I was in Miami and then drove up to meet you at Lancer's place."

"So, she wants *you* to find out what happened to her father?"

"And if I have to in order to figure out what happened to Cummins, I will."

"Do you really think there's a connection?" she asked.

"But for the Slovakian money stuffed down Draymont's throat I wouldn't."

"Did she mention anything about Lancer or Draymont? Or any records of threats?"

"I asked her and she passed the buck to 'her

people,' and 'legal counsel.' But I hope to get some quid pro quo in return for looking into her father's disappearance, which hopefully means we won't have to go to court to get the info."

"But Decker, if they were billing Judge Cummins for Draymont to be there, and I'm assuming they were, she must have given them *some* reason why she needed protection. And how could they assure it would be Draymont doing the guarding?"

"The thing is, I don't think he was there on behalf of Gamma at all. Doris Kline said he wasn't there every night. And we haven't found anyone to say he was there all night. I think Draymont was just there to have sex with Cummins. This wasn't running through Gamma at all."

"But when we met with them, why couldn't they just tell us that?"

"I guess they were expecting Lancer to do the honors and we saw what happened there."

"But wouldn't Roe know if the judge was a client or not?"

"Maybe not—it's a big organization."

"But you said the Perlmans recommended Gamma to Cummins, so she must have been looking for some sort of protection."

"I know. That's the part that's puzzling. And she might have talked to someone at Gamma about protection. But I don't think Draymont was providing it. Or if he was, he was also providing the judge something extra. But the fact that he wasn't there every night? And apparently no one else came to take his place on a rotation? Doesn't sound like a standard protection detail to me. But we can confirm it with Gamma, and by an examination of the judge's financial records. If she did hire them she had to be paying them."

"So could Draymont have been wrong place wrong time, even with the money found in his throat?"

"No. I think Draymont and the judge were killed by *two* different people, at two slightly different times."

White nearly came out of her seat. "What!"

He explained to her about the ME's confirming that the blood on the wall and carpet was Draymont's, not Cummins's.

"She comes downstairs, maybe after hearing the shots, and then she goes back upstairs. Why not call the cops from downstairs?" Decker wondered.

"But it could still be the person who killed Draymont who then went after her and prevented her from sounding the alarm."

Decker shook his head. "They were two totally different crimes. If you have a gun and want to silence a witness, you don't pull out a knife and kill her slowly while she screams her head off and fights for her life. And for her to get Draymont's blood on her means she had to touch him. As I said before, she probably heard the shots, went into the study, saw him lying there, touched the wound, maybe tried to perform CPR. Whoever shot Draymont wouldn't have stayed around to watch that. And if they had meant to kill her, they would have gone to find her, not waited for her to come downstairs. For all they knew she would call the cops from her room."

"That all makes sense. But the cut-up blindfold on her? And the legal phrase on the paper?"

"Could be something very personal to her, which would make sense if there were two separate killers. And but for the money in Draymont's throat and the very different criminal elements, I might think he was killed in protecting the judge and then they went and finished her off. But that's *not* how this played out. At least I don't think it did."

"And why not wait and fill in Andrews on this, too?" asked White.

"Because Roe knew about the Slovakian money in Draymont's throat. She said it came from her 'sources.' I think her *source* was Andrews."

"He does seem more deferential with her than I would like, but you can't know for sure he told her."

"We will."

"How?"

"I'm going to ask him."

"And if Andrews did tell her?"

He shot her a look. "Then you can turn into Muhammad Ali and use your double black belt to kick *his* ass."

CHAPTER

33

THEY WERE NEARING THEIR HOTEL when Decker's phone rang. It was Barry Davidson. He sounded frantic.

"I can't find my son. Tyler didn't come home from school today. I've tried his phone and left messages. None of his friends know where he is."

"Okay, just calm down. We'll be right over."

They cleared the gate and rode the elevator up. Davidson was waiting for them at his front door.

They could both smell the liquor on his breath as he hurried them inside.

"When was the last time you saw or spoke to him?" asked White.

"This morning, around eight. He was leaving for school."

"I didn't think he'd be going back to school so soon," noted Decker.

"He...he said he wanted to, to get his mind off things."

"You said you talked to his friends?" said White.

"Yes, one of them told me that Tyler had left school early. And Tyler hasn't answered his phone or returned my texts. He's usually very good at doing so."

"He might not have his phone with him," said Decker.

"He *always* has his phone," countered Davidson.

"The cops won't do anything yet, unless we have information that he might be in danger, or distress," said White.

Davidson slumped into a chair and reached out for what looked to be a glass of whiskey.

"And getting drunk won't help matters," pointed out Decker. "In case Tyler needs you."

Davidson withdrew his hand and looked guiltily at them. "I'm... I'm afraid he might... I don't know. Hurt himself."

"Did he ever talk about doing something like that?" asked White, a note of urgency in her voice.

"No, but he never lost his mother before," retorted Davidson.

"Does he have any usual haunts, places he likes to go, to think, or be alone?"

"Nothing particular, no."

"Any girlfriends?" asked White.

"He did, but they broke up a month ago. I called her, but she hasn't heard from Tyler."

"What's his normal routine?" asked Decker.

"He gets up around six and goes for a run, usually on the beach with some other players. Then he works out at the gym in the building here. I had to pay for extra weights, by the way," he added proudly. "They didn't have enough for him. Then he goes to school. Then he works out some more there. Then he comes home. He's usually here by six or so."

"Okay, but it's only seven thirty now," said White.

"But I've been calling him since noon. I wanted to see how he was doing and if he wanted to help me…help me pick out some music for his mother's funeral service."

"When did his friend say he left school?" asked Decker.

"Around two. But he didn't say where he was going."

"And they just let him leave?" said White.

"He only had a study hall left."

"Did he mention to you this morning about leaving school early, or going somewhere?"

"No, nothing like that."

"Did he take his car today?" asked White.

"Yes."

"Give us the address of his school," said Decker.

Davidson wrote it down and handed it to him.

"While we're here, can you answer a few questions about your ex-wife?" said Decker.

"What?" said Davidson irritably.

"Was your wife seeing anyone, I mean, romantically?" asked Decker.

Davidson seemed to shrivel in the face of this question. "I don't know. I...I always hoped that we might reconcile, you know?"

Decker glanced at White. "No, we didn't know. Care to explain?"

"We had problems. Julia seemed to think they were insurmountable."

"And you didn't?" said White.

"I'm probably a hopeless optimist," Davidson said with a grim smile.

"But your optimism didn't work. Did that bother you?" asked Decker.

"What's that supposed to mean?" barked Davidson.

"You wanted to get back together with your ex. She didn't. Now she's dead."

"I didn't kill her. I was here. Tyler confirmed that. And I had Zoom meetings."

"Before COVID, I thought 'Zoom' was just a verb," said Decker. "I wish it still was just a verb."

"Why aren't you out there looking for my son? Find him, goddammit!"

"You're not planning any trips, are you?" asked Decker.

"Why?"

"Don't."

34

You pulled his chain pretty hard in there," said White as they climbed into the car and set off. "Why was that?"

"I usually pull things to see if they snap."

"And Davidson? You really think he's good for his wife's murder?"

"He's got a motive, jealousy, if he knew about his ex and Draymont, but not the opportunity. But that becomes meaningless if he hired someone to do it for him."

"If a hit man did go to her house, there should be some record of a car going through the gate."

"There are certainly ways around that with all the holes in that wall."

"I suppose. But you think two different people killed Draymont and Cummins. If Davidson was still in love with her, he would have had motive to hire someone to kill lover boy, too."

"Yes, he would."

"But you don't think he did?"

"I'm not sure I believe he even killed his wife, much less Draymont. But I still think it was two different people. The fact remains, if the person who shot Draymont killed Cummins, then that person would have still been there. So why chase her upstairs with a knife? The shooter fired two nine-mill rounds into Draymont. I don't know of any pistol that only chambers two nine-mill rounds. The shooter would've had plenty of ammo to take her out."

"You make a compelling case, Decker, I'll give you that. Shooter shoots and then leaves. Judge rushes down and while she's trying to save Draymont a second person comes in with a knife and kills her."

"Or they could have used a knife from her kitchen. The ME described a six-inch serrated blade. Lots of kitchen knives match that description. We'll have to try to determine if any knives are missing."

"So Draymont's murder was premeditated, but Cummins's was spur of the moment?"

"Maybe," said Decker.

"If so, we're talking one incredible coincidence."

"And I don't even like your run-of-the-mill coincidences, much less *incredible* ones."

"I never pegged you for a sense of humor."

"Don't confuse humor with lack of a filter," he cautioned.

"Where are we going now?"

"To find Tyler."

"You mean, you have an idea where he is?" she said.

"I might."

* * *

Arriving at the high school they saw that the mascot was the Monarch.

"Monarchs, huh? Always thought that was funny in a democratic country," observed White as they parked in the visitor's lot.

"I've seen lots of funny things lately in a democratic country, and I haven't laughed at a single one of them."

They got out. When Decker headed to the rear of the school grounds, White said, "Where are we going?"

"To Tyler's world."

"Tyler's world?" said White as they walked along.

Decker pointed to the football stadium, where someone had turned on the lights illuminating the field. "There."

As they drew nearer, they could both see Tyler, clad in shorts and no shirt, running all over the field catching footballs being thrown by another young man.

They went through the gate and walked down the bleacher steps to the track that ran around the fenced-in field.

"Nice facilities," said White. "My high school football field was pretty much just a parking lot."

"Good wheels," said Decker as he watched Tyler run his routes. "Nice cuts."

"If you say so."

"Hey, Tyler!" he called out.

Tyler looked over at them, caught one more ball, wiped the sweat off his face with a towel hanging from his waistband, motioned to his friend that they were done, and trotted over. His torso was lacquered in sweat, every defined muscle shining brightly.

"Yeah?" he said, breathing heavily. He bent down, snagged a bottle of G2 off a bench, and guzzled it.

"Your father was worried about you. He's tried calling. You didn't answer."

"I left my phone in my car over there," said Tyler, pointing to a navy blue BMW convertible parked outside the fence at the other end of the field. "And I lost track of time. What's the big deal?"

"No big deal to me, but it was to your old man."

Tyler finished his drink and wiped down his arms and legs.

"You run nice routes," observed Decker.

"Yeah, I work hard on it."

"But you cut faster to the left than you do to the right. That's because you're right leg dominant."

Tyler stared at Decker, clearly interested now.

"In college, particularly the schools you're looking

at, you have to be balanced. Otherwise, the linebacker or the safety or, better yet, the corner who covers you will read that weakness within a few plays and he'll get the jump on the ball every time you cut right. Then it's an interception all the way. It's just a millisecond difference, but on a timed throw to a spot certain from the QB, he'll get there before you will."

"A college trainer my mom hired told me the same thing. He gave me some drills to work that out."

"Good. Keep drilling. But if you do eight reps to the left, do twelve to the right. Hack squat with your left leg a few more reps than your right to build up the muscle mass. Do balance drills with your left leg to try to reach parity with the right. Quick-twitch exercises to that side are a good idea, too, along with maxing out hip flexibility. That'll improve your rotation and range of motion. Lots of guys have that same issue. You may never get to complete parity, but you can get close, and your QB will love you for it."

"You know your shit."

"It was *my* life for a long time." Decker leaned on the fence. "How's your dad? Still drinking hard?"

"Drinking and maybe doping, too." Tyler suddenly looked afraid. "Hey, I didn't mean that. I don't want my dad—"

Decker waved this off. "We're not DEA. We're FBI. But your dad shouldn't do drugs because you pop a pill thinking it's Oxy and it's actually fentanyl and your next place of residence is a coffin."

"Yeah, I guess so. I'll make sure he's not doing any of that."

"You care about your dad, don't you? Despite being pissed at him."

"He and my mom were all I had. Now I just have him. So I want him to get his head on right and get through this."

Decker glanced at the BMW. "Nice ride. Mom or Dad get that for you?"

"Dad. Mom didn't like the idea. But I'm responsible. I don't drink. I don't do drugs. I go to school, play football, watch my p's and q's, and keep my head down."

"Then you're way ahead of me when I was in high school."

"And you made it to the pros," noted Tyler.

"I worked my butt off, but I got lucky, too. And my career didn't last long."

"You regret any of it?"

"Just my last play on the field."

"What happened?"

"Long story, not worth retelling. Give your dad a call before he has a heart attack, okay?"

Tyler looked down, seeming embarrassed. "I left my phone in the car on purpose."

"I know you did. You wanted to get away from

all the shit. Come out here, run some routes, think about nothing but catching the ball and going all the way with it."

Tyler glanced up and smiled. "I feel like I'm talking to an older version of me."

"In some ways, Tyler, you are."

CHAPTER

35

"WHERE ARE WE GOING NOW?" asked White as Decker turned onto the highway and rode it east, toward downtown Ocean View.

"Duncan Trotter, Cummins's estate lawyer. I made an appointment to meet with him this evening and go over who benefits from her death."

"You have been a busy boy. So, what do you think Trotter will tell us?"

"In many homicides, following the money is a pretty good philosophy."

* * *

Trotter was in his sixties with curly gray hair, a high, lined forehead, and a thin physique. He wasn't dressed in a suit, but rather a dark blue polo shirt and gray slacks. Instead of wingtips on his feet, he had flip-flops. His law empire consisted of a few rooms in a one-story office building a couple blocks off the town's main street.

They sat across from him in his cluttered office. He had told them when he answered the door that his secretary had long since left for the day. When they asked their questions about the last will and testament of Julia Cummins he commenced tapping some keys on his computer and then studied the screen.

"It was awful, awful about Julia. What a nightmare." His voice was thin and reedy and only carried a foot or so before fading away. Decker actually had to hunch forward to hear him. He could see, with that voice, why the man was not a trial lawyer.

"Yes, it was tragic," said White. "And we need to find out who did it. That's why we're here."

"Yes, yes, of course. I know Barry took it hard." He lifted his rimless specs to his forehead and gave them a knowing look. "He's never gotten over Julia, you know. Still in love with her."

"So the divorce was her idea?" said White.

"Oh, without a doubt. I'm not telling stories out of school, you understand. Common knowledge among our set."

"So you socialized with them?" said Decker.

"Yes. It's how you get clients. X refers you to Y and Y refers you to Z."

"Do you know Tyler?"

"Fine young man. Amazing athlete. He adored his mother."

"And his father?"

Trotter slid his glasses back into place. "Let's just say that in that relationship Tyler is the father and Barry is the child. Again, no tales out of school. Indeed, I have to wonder why Julia ever married him in the first place."

"Love makes you do crazy things," said Decker.

"So was that the reason for the divorce? Barry never grew up?" asked White. "A lot of women don't want to raise kids *all* their lives."

"I think that was one very significant reason. And when Barry hit forty-five, he had an early midlife crisis. Bought expensive cars, dressed like he was still in college, wanted himself and Julia to hang out with a far younger crowd."

"We were told that the judge might have recently had her own midlife crisis," said Decker. "Dressing hipper, going out more, dancing, clubbing?"

"Um, yes, I had noticed that, too. The hemlines got a little shorter and the heels a little higher. It was no business of mine and I'm in no way judging her choices," he added quickly.

"Did Barry ever cheat on her?" asked Decker. "We understand he dates very young women now."

"No, I actually think he loved Julia more than anything," said Trotter. "But Julia finally got tired of his 'new ways,' and then they had a tax issue that nearly landed Barry in jail. That was apparently the last straw for Julia. She filed for divorce shortly thereafter."

"Did you handle that?" asked White.

"Me? No, no, no. I don't handle divorce cases. Don't have the stomach for it."

"Did you find what you're looking for?" asked Decker in a prompting manner as he eyed the man's computer.

"Yes, yes I did. Now, Julia was a very wealthy woman."

"How wealthy?"

"Not counting her home, Julia's estate is worth over twenty million dollars, all of it in liquid assets, stocks, bonds. Just the income from the portfolio alone is over a million a year."

"And who gets it?" asked Decker.

"There are some charitable bequests and a few small gifts to various people, but the vast bulk of the estate is to be held in trust for Tyler Davidson."

"In trust. So who's the trustee?"

"Barry Davidson. He's also the executor. After the divorce, Julia talked about changing that, but never got around to doing so."

"What are the terms of the trust?" asked White.

"Pretty standard. The principal will be disbursed in three tranches. When Tyler is twenty-five, twenty-eight, and thirty-one. Until that time he can apply to the trustee for funds for education, starting a business, purchasing a home, that sort of thing. Pretty standard. Oh, and the home goes to Tyler as well, unless Barry decides to sell it instead. If he does, the proceeds will go into the trust."

"So Tyler is rich then?"

"Well, he certainly will be when the funds are disbursed, even after applicable taxes."

"And what does the trustee get out of it?"

"Reasonable compensation. And control over the trust funds until they are disbursed."

"Funny that Cummins would have kept her ex as trustee," said Decker.

"Yes, but as I said, she was going to change that."

"She actually told you that?"

"Yes. But she just didn't get around to it."

"That doesn't seem like the woman I've been learning about. She sounded efficient, organized, someone who executes on something promptly."

Trotter leaned back in his chair. "You know, you're exactly right about that."

"But she actually talked to you about changing trustees and the executor?" said White.

"She did, several times. And I reminded her once."

"What was her response?"

"That the time just wasn't right."

"What did she mean by that?" asked Decker.

"I don't really know. Maybe she thought Tyler would be upset if she cut his dad out as trustee. But the last time we spoke about it was six weeks ago."

"Res ipsa loquitor," said Decker.

"Excuse me?"

"The phrase. It's connected to Cummins's death. Did she ever use that phrase with you?"

"No, never. I haven't used it since I was in law school. And you say it figures in her death some way? How very strange."

"And getting stranger by the second," said Decker.

36

I DID NOT LEAK THAT information to Roe or anyone else," said Andrews angrily.

They were seated at an outside table of an Italian restaurant, where, by prearrangement, Decker and White had met the FBI agent for a late dinner.

"Well, she knew," said Decker.

"Then she learned it from someone else. Are you sure *you* didn't mention it?"

"I don't *mention* shit to anybody," replied Decker.

A visibly angry Andrews sat back and sipped from his glass of white wine.

"Anything come from the gate log review?" asked White in a calming tone.

"Nothing yet. And if Barry hired a hit man I don't think he came through the gate. I requested a warrant for his financial records, as I said. We should have those very soon." He put his wine down. "Now, we *did* receive info from Gamma on Draymont's and Lancer's backgrounds. Before coming to Gamma, Draymont worked in DC for the Capitol Police."

"Interesting transition, coming down here and going private," said Decker. "Draymont was way too young to be double-dipping," he added, referring to the practice of a government employee's earning his full pension and then going to work at another job.

"Maybe Gamma made him an offer he couldn't refuse," suggested Andrews.

"If they did, it would be nice to know," said Decker.

"You mentioned you met with Kasimira?" asked Andrews.

"I did. She wants me to figure out what happened to her father. That's why she agreed to release those files on Lancer and Draymont, because I told her I'd look into it under certain conditions."

Andrews looked surprised. "But that's not the case you're on."

"I'll only work on it if it connects with our case. I told her that."

"But how could it? Kanak Roe presumably died three years ago."

"And someone stuffed the currency of Roe's native land into Draymont's throat. That's either one hell of a coincidence or there might be some common elements between the two events, even though they're years apart."

Andrews fiddled with his napkin. "I guess that's possible."

"And what's the background on Alice Lancer?" asked White.

Andrews cleared his throat. "Lancer has been with Gamma for six years. Draymont about the same, by the way. Before going to work for Gamma she was a lawyer for a few years, then a communications director, and later a lobbyist at a political outfit in DC."

"So the same city and basically the same arena as Draymont."

"Yes. So they could have known each other back then."

White drank from her water glass and said, "Lawyer, and then communications director, and then a lobbyist for a political group, and now she works at a private security firm? Odd career trajectory."

Decker said, "It all depends on her personal goals."

She looked at Andrews. "Family? Draymont and Lancer?"

"Draymont's family is in Seattle. Parents still alive, and he has one brother. They've been notified. They're coming in to claim the body."

"And Lancer?" said White.

"We found out that Alice Lancer is an orphan. Her adoptive parents died in a plane crash over a decade ago. She has no siblings. And we really have no way of finding out who her biological parents were."

Something clicked in Decker's head when Andrews said this. *Okay, that's interesting.*

"So, dead end there," noted White.

"Seems to be. And there's no sign of Lancer or Patty Kelly. It's like they've disappeared off the face of the earth."

"Funny how that always seems to happen when someone doesn't want to talk to the cops," interjected Decker.

"What will you do next?" asked Andrews.

"We learned from Duncan Trotter that Judge Cummins's death resulted in her ex being the trustee of a twenty-million-dollar-plus fortune."

Andrews nearly dumped his wine. "Shit. I knew she was loaded, but not *that* loaded."

Decker's phone vibrated and he read the message that had just come in. "This is from the ME. I had a hunch about something and it turned out I was right."

"What was the hunch?" asked Andrews.

"That Alan Draymont wasn't guarding the judge, he was sleeping with her."

"What!" Andrews blurted out.

Decker briefly explained what he had found at the crime scene and also the confirmation from the ME. He also told Andrews about his theory of there being two different killers.

Andrews nodded, looking thoughtful. "I have to admit, the different methods of the killings were bothering me. You either see one or the other.

But Decker, Trevor Perlman said he recommended Gamma to the judge. And she told others, including her son, that she was having protection."

"Doris Kline told me that Draymont wasn't there every night. And no one else was taking up the protection. Funny way to guard someone."

"But then why go to Gamma at all if there were no threats?" asked White.

"Not really sure. But it looks like that's what happened. You don't sleep with your security guard. And your security guard doesn't just not show up to guard you."

"So she wasn't really afraid of anyone?" said White.

Decker glanced at her. "Oh, I think she *was* afraid of someone. And that person killed her."

CHAPTER

37

AFTER DINNER, DECKER SAT IN his hotel room staring at a wall.

He was not thinking of the case right now. He was thinking about the letter he'd gotten from the Cognitive Institute in Chicago.

Dear Mr. Decker, Your latest brain scans have shown various anomalies that will require further testing and monitoring. Preliminarily, new lesions are presenting, and it seems that previously unaffected sections of your cerebrum are at risk of being transformed in ways that . . .

Here, Decker stopped thinking about what the letter had said.

Lesions. Previously unaffected. Anomalies. Transformed in ways that . . .

Not a single bit of that sounded good.

Added to that was the fact that four men whom Decker had played football with or against in college and then in the NFL had died prematurely over the last three years.

One from ALS, or Lou Gehrig's disease, one from a heart attack, and another from a stroke caused by his Type-2 diabetes.

And the fourth man had died by suicide, with his brain donated to Boston University's CTE Center for further analysis to see if he had the disease. Which he did.

Realistically, how much time do I have left? I didn't play long in the pros, for sure. But I've played a lot of football, and the shot I took that day probably did as much damage as five years in the NFL would have.

He looked around the confines of the small room. *And is this really how I want to spend it?*

But he also knew he could not make any life-altering decisions right this minute. So he lay back on the bed and thought about the case. It was puzzling, as all cases were. But this case was different in that the more he got into it, the more puzzling it became. Even the things he believed he had figured out, namely that Cummins and Draymont had had a sexual relationship, and that they were dealing with two unrelated murders committed in the same house and within minutes of each other, became more inscrutable the further he went into it.

The foreign currency in Draymont's mouth seemed

to connect with Kanak Roe, or at least the Roe family. Kasimira seemed to think it was directly tied to her father's disappearance and apparent death three years earlier, but Decker had no evidence of that being the case. If the Roes had enemies in what was now Slovakia, had the killer or killers of Alan Draymont gone back there? If so, he had little chance of bringing them to justice.

And then there was Julia Cummins's murder. It was personal, unlike Draymont's. The multiple stabbings evidenced a frenzy fueled by hatred.

Was Barry Davidson, the ex who was, by all accounts, including perhaps his own, still in love with Cummins, also behind the woman's murder? The problem was the man's alibis were pretty solid. And if Davidson had hired a hit man, would that person have unleashed such a frenzied attack on the woman? With up-close encounters you could leave behind your DNA and other forensic markers. It made no sense.

But if Davidson was out as a suspect, who then? Was Cummins seeing anyone else? He doubted that Alan Draymont had been Cummins's only romantic interest since her divorce years before. She was young, attractive, a federal judge, wealthy. She would be quite the catch for someone.

He would have to have another go at both Doris Kline and Maya Perlman, to see if they knew of any other romantic partner out there. Or one who had been spurned or dumped by the dead woman.

Decker looked at his watch. It was late, but Kline might still be up. Perhaps Maya Perlman, too, despite her travels, and the crushing news of her friend's death. At least it was worth a shot.

He decided not to bother White, who had mentioned that she was going to help her kids with their homework over a Zoom call tonight.

He left the hotel and drove to the gated community. He had to show his ID to the security service via a video link, and then was allowed in.

He drove to Cummins's house and parked in the driveway. All police presence was gone, but the crime scene had not been officially released yet. He supposed Davidson, as the executor and trustee of his wife's estate, would have to come over at some point and decide what to do with the property and its contents. He doubted Tyler would want to keep a house where his mother had been brutally murdered.

Both the Kline and Perlman homes had lights on. He decided to try Kline first.

He knocked on the door but she didn't answer. He peered in the sidelights but saw no movement. Her car was in the driveway.

Is she lying in there drunk?

He had no cause to force his way in, so he walked over to the Perlmans' home and knocked. A few moments passed before a woman's voice said, "Who is it?"

"Amos Decker, FBI. Do you have a minute?"

"It's very late."

"It won't take long, and we're doing our best to find out who killed your friend. Speed is of the essence."

He figured a little guilt trip might go a long way.

"Oh, all right."

She opened the door. Maya Perlman was dressed in gray slacks, a light blue shirt, and sandals.

She motioned him in and closed the door. They sat in the living room, where the walls were the same color as her slacks.

"Is your husband around?"

"He's asleep. The trip took a lot out of us, and he's quite a bit older than I am. Second marriage," she added in explanation, not that Decker had asked for one. "So, what is it that you need?"

"Do you know if Judge Cummins was seeing anyone?"

"Seeing anyone, you mean as in dating?"

"Yes."

She sat back and let out a long breath. "After the divorce, Julia hunkered down, as it were. She and Barry had it bad the last few years. Lots of fights and arguments. She tried to make it work, she really did, but Barry had some sort of midlife crisis and thought he was twenty again. Right after Julia went on the bench there was some big tax issue because Barry had done something that, if not criminal, went right up to the line. After that, Julia was done."

"Yeah, I heard all that from others. And after she *hunkered* down for a bit?"

"I know she used one of those online dating apps. She had a few dates from those. None of them worked out, at least that I know."

"I'm sure she would have attracted interest around here."

"You'd think. But lots of older men like to be the center of attention and they also like to be the ones with the money. And her being a judge probably didn't help matters. They also like to be the professional king as well. And the men who don't care about any of that? Well, they bring their own issues."

"Getting her to fall for them so they can raid her piggybank?"

"Exactly."

"So, anyone she might have just run into somewhere and seemed to like? Or someone she ran into and it became a problem?"

Perlman sat forward, looking nervous. "You mean a big enough problem that he might have killed her?"

"The crime did have elements of being one of passion, of rage. You don't usually get that when someone is just trying to rip someone else off. And it's hard to fake, because, well, to do to Cummins what someone did? You have to be pretty damn angry."

She shuddered and sank back against the chair cushions. "Julia did tell me about someone she had known from her past. I mean, her past before she came here."

"Who?"

"Someone from New York. That person moved down here, while Julia was still married. After she was divorced, they went out for a while. It didn't last, but . . ."

"But what?"

"Well, Julia was upset when she spoke about it. She said he seemed very controlling."

"Do you know his name?"

"That's just it. I don't. She never told me for some reason, which was odd. She just spoke generally about it. And then it was over, and I never asked any more about it."

"Do you know who might know?"

"Doris might. She and Julia were very close. Closer than Julia and I were, at least lately. I think it might have been because I'm married and they were both divorced."

"Okay. Next question: Did you know the judge's secretary, Patty Kelly?"

"Just in passing. I never appeared before Julia, for obvious reasons. Why?"

"Just needed to ask."

She shook her head. "I can't believe this has all happened. It's like a nightmare that you can't wake up from."

"So, Alan Draymont? Do you remember him guarding you?"

"I believe that he did, yes."

"I need something more definitive than that. Were you able to find those emails from Gamma with the security personnel on them?"

"Yes, I can forward them to you."

He gave her his email address. "Thanks. That should confirm whether Draymont guarded you."

"Anything else?"

"Not for right now. You two will be in town for a while?"

"We were planning to be. But with a murder right next door?"

"Well, if you do decide to go somewhere, can you let me know first?"

"Why? Wait a minute, we're not suspects, are we?"

"We checked with the airlines. They confirmed you had flown to New York and returned *after* the murders."

"We were visiting my grown children from my first marriage. They both live there. They can certainly confirm we were there the entire week."

"Okay. But I might have to ask you some more questions."

She held up her phone. "Well, that's what we have this for, isn't it? With it, you can reach me pretty much anywhere on earth."

She rose. "Good night, Agent Decker."

CHAPTER

38

Mrs. Kline?" Decker was knocking on the woman's door again. "Doris?"

He took a step back and peered up at the face of the house. Her car was still in the driveway. He tried the door, but it was locked.

He walked around back and opened the gate. The upper deck where Kline had been sitting when she noticed Cummins's door open was unoccupied. He opened the door to the lanai and froze.

In the pool water something was floating. Or someone.

Shit.

He stepped onto the lanai for a better look. It looked like Doris Kline; he couldn't tell for sure. She was facedown.

He rushed forward, knelt down, and grabbed her arm.

She came out of the water, screaming her head off, until she saw who it was.

A stunned Decker let go of her arm and fell back

on his butt on the pool surround. Kline went under but came back up a moment later, sputtering and spitting out water.

When Kline saw him sitting there, she exclaimed, "What the hell is wrong with you?"

"I thought you were dead."

"I was *meditating*. I meditate in the water."

"Facedown, at this time of night?"

"My house, my rules. And a shrink I once dated told me about it. It's like being in one of those floater tanks. Well, I can't afford that, so I just use my pool. I float on my back and then flip over and hold my breath. I'm hoping it will improve my lung function. And you're lucky because I usually do this in the buff."

"Stopping smoking will *really* improve your lungs."

"I've stopped more times than I can count."

She climbed up the pool steps, revealing she had on a one-piece bathing suit with a short skirt. She dried off with a big towel that had been set on one of the chairs, then wrapped herself in it and sat down at a table. In front of her was a glass with what might be gin or vodka.

She took a pack of cigarettes off the table and lit one using her Zippo lighter. She blew smoke out, held up the drink, and said, "You want one? You can't be on duty at this hour."

"You got any beer?"

"In that fridge over there."

He snagged a Corona from a small fridge set up in the outdoor kitchen, popped the top, and sat down across from her.

She said, "Now, would you care to explain what you're doing here and why you thought it was a good idea to try to give me a heart attack?"

"I'm sorry about that. I came by before and knocked but you didn't answer."

"I've been on the lanai for the last hour. I like to come here at this time of night. It's so dark and quiet and peaceful."

"I was over talking to Mrs. Perlman. She didn't have the answer to something and thought you might."

She blew smoke out. "Okay, shoot."

He told her about the man Perlman had mentioned who had come here from up north.

"She said they dated for a bit, and when it ended, Julia was...troubled? Do you know anything about that?"

Kline nodded. "She told me about him. His name is Dennis Langley. They went to law school together. He moved down here while she was still married. He followed her around like a lovesick little puppy dog. After the divorce, he finally made his move. They went out. They had some good times. They might have had sex. Julia never shared that. And then, it was over."

"What happened?"

"Julia didn't want to continue it. She thought he was too controlling."

"That's what Maya Perlman said, although she didn't know his name. Why do you think she didn't tell Maya?"

"I bet Maya knows Langley, too, both being law-yers. And maybe Julia didn't want it getting around that she was dating the guy. Julia told me to keep it to myself, which I did. Until now."

"Where is Langley located?"

"He practices law here in town."

"What sort of law?"

"Criminal. He's good from what I heard. You think he might have killed Julia?"

"Wouldn't be the first time a guy who got dumped did something like that, would it?"

"What the hell is wrong with men anyway?"

"We're too used to getting our own way. And way too much testosterone. And then there's the lack of brains."

She raised her glass. "I vote for the last one."

"What can you tell me about Langley?"

"He's Julia's age, tall, handsome, outgoing, charm-ing."

"Sounds like quite a catch."

"Yeah, but from what I heard, so was Ted Bundy."

"When was the last time you saw him around here?"

"I've never seen him around here. But I know who he is, and I have seen him around town. It's been about six months since they broke up."

"And she broke up with him? That's what Cummins said?"

"Yes. Seems silly to talk about breaking up with people when you're in your forties and fifties. The same as having a 'boyfriend' at my age. But then I don't, do I?"

"Do you want a boyfriend?"

"Depends on the time of day you ask me. Or how many drinks I've had."

Decker smiled.

She smiled back and said, "I know we don't know each other very well. But I'm a quick reader of people and I wasn't sure you had a smile in you."

"Sometimes I surprise myself."

"I don't see a wedding band. Are you divorced? Or never married?"

Decker's smile faded. "Neither. I lost my wife a while back."

"Oh, I'm very sorry. And I made your smile go away. Just the sort of stupid thing I do."

He shrugged half-heartedly. "It's not stupid. It was a perfectly legit question."

"I'm sure you miss her very much."

"I do."

"Do you have kids? Do you take care of each

other? That can help. I know that from personal experience."

"I had a daughter. But I lost her, too."

"Omigod. Was it an accident? With the two of them?"

"It wasn't an accident. Someone...killed them."

Decker had no idea why he was telling her this, but for some reason it just felt right. Or necessary. Or something.

"Oh my God, I am so sorry." She reached out and gripped his hand. "But let me just say this. You were all together for a time. And that is something you can always hold on to. I...I told you my kids were grown and off living their lives. That wasn't entirely accurate. Three of them are. But I lost my oldest to cancer when she was barely six years old. I cried for maybe the next ten years. And then I stopped crying."

"Why?"

"Because I started remembering her when she was alive and healthy over sick and dying. I occasionally lapse." She held up her drink. "Like with this. But for the most part it's worked out okay."

"And you don't feel guilty for—"

"—for still being alive? Of course I do. But you can either get past that, or you can kill yourself." She eyed him keenly. "I would not recommend the latter. I mean, I really wouldn't."

"You sound like you speak from experience on that, too."

"I speak from more experience than is good for me. And if you really want to feel guilt, try taking your own life. It's like you're spitting all over their graves."

"Why is that?" asked Decker, looking at her intently.

"Because you're trying to take something away from yourself that was taken away from them *without* their consent."

"I've never heard it described that way before."

"I never thought of it, either, until it hit me right in the heart."

CHAPTER

39

BACK AT HIS HOTEL ROOM Decker sat down on the bed and opened the file Kasimira Roe had provided him on her father.

There was a photo of Kanak Roe included. He looked to be about sixty at the time the picture was taken. His face appeared like it was cast in marble with steel accents. A formidable, perhaps indomitable man. He had come to this country with nothing and built an impressive business. To do that you had to be tough and resilient and maybe ruthless, too.

He learned about the man's stint with the Secret Service, his guarding of multiple presidents. And then, instead of pulling his full time with the Service and locking in his pension, Roe had left and come down to Miami to start the protection business that would eventually become Gamma.

From the file Decker learned that the business had grown rapidly, and Gamma had a long list of impressive clients. And Kasimira had taken it to ever higher levels.

He then turned to the day that Roe had vanished. The man had left his boat slip in Key West for what apparently was planned as a day cruise.

The boat had sleeping quarters belowdecks and a small kitchen. Kasimira had told him that her father normally would go out in the early morning and return well before dusk to his home in Key West. But that day he hadn't come back.

He did wonder why a terminally ill, and presumably weakened, man would head out by himself to go deep-sea fishing. Decker had never done any deep-sea fishing, but he had watched people do it on TV. It took a helluva lot of strength and stamina to fight some of the big fish and land them. And to do so by yourself was difficult enough even if you were young and healthy.

But maybe, as his daughter had suggested, he just wanted to take the boat out one last time.

He hadn't been clear on why Kasimira would allow her father to do that, but in a note in the file she had explained that she only found out about her father's plans the next day, when he didn't return to the slip. As she had mentioned during their meeting, apparently the only person who knew what he was planning was an old fishing buddy of Kanak's, who had not been there that day, and thus didn't know his friend had failed to return.

There was no information on exactly what terminal

illness Kanak had, but Decker wasn't sure it mattered. The man had been given a death sentence, regardless of the cause.

He briefly imagined Roe setting off in his boat and heading out into the open ocean knowing he only had a few months left.

Will I come to that point, sooner than I want to? And what will I think about when the days grow short?

Decker believed he would think about his wife and daughter. About possibly seeing them again, if there really was life after death.

But Kasimira seemed to have been very close to her father, thus Decker deemed it unlikely that the man would leave her in the lurch like that. So had someone else prevented him from coming back from that trip?

He closed the file, sat back on his bed, and picked up his phone. He punched in a number that had been in the file. It was Kanak Roe's friend, the one he had told about taking the trip. His name was Daniel Garcia. The men had become friends, not over business, but over their love of fishing. It was late enough that he didn't expect anyone to answer.

"Hello?"

"Mr. Garcia?"

"Yes?"

Decker explained who he was and why he was calling.

"Yes, Kasi told me you might be phoning. How can I help you?"

"You can tell me what you know about Kanak Roe heading out that day."

"If I knew he wasn't coming back I would never have let him go."

"I understand that. Do you know what his illness was?"

"Pancreatic cancer. Nasty shit. They almost never catch it until it's too late. You got about a year to live after a stage-four diagnosis. Kanak had about three months left. He was on all sorts of meds and painkillers."

"Was he in any shape to take the boat out by himself?"

"I mean, the crap he was on, he could function. Yeah, he was in pain, but if you saw him you wouldn't know he was dying. Look at the *Jeopardy!* guy, Alex Trebek. He was working pretty much right up to the end. One tough dude. Same with Kanak."

"But did you really think he was going deep-sea fishing? I mean, that's not easy to do even when you're healthy and strong."

"Look, if I really thought he was going fishing on that boat I would have gone with him. That's at least a two-person job. No, he just wanted to take the *Kasi* out maybe one more time."

Decker had learned from the file that Kanak Roe

had named his boat after the nickname he used for his daughter.

"I see."

"The *Kasi* was a great boat. A thirty-eight-foot Scout with a twelve-foot beam. Triple Yamaha engines. Had a beautiful cabin, where most deep-sea fishing boats are bowriders. Sleeping berth, stove cooktop, flat-screen TV, shower, sink, and toilet, even an AC unit. And with the tri-engines that baby could really go. I've been out on it a bunch 'a times with him."

"And when he didn't come back?"

"I had to head out of town that day. I didn't get back until later the next day. Went down to the marina. The *Kasi* is two slips over from my bucket. Saw the slip empty and then started raising the alarm."

"Surprised no one did it before then."

"People come and go at all hours from that marina. And they don't have folks there twenty-four seven monitoring who comes and goes. But I called Kasi. She jumped on a chopper and flew down straight-away. Along the way she tried but couldn't reach her father. I went over to his house in Key West, but the place was empty. His SUV was in the garage. He must have taken a cab or Uber to the marina."

"Did he usually do that?" asked Decker.

"Sometimes, when he didn't feel like driving."

"So, his daughter didn't talk to him every day, then?"

"She usually did. But she had just gotten back from

a business trip. In fact, she had just returned to her place in Miami when I phoned."

"She said there were smugglers out there," said Decker.

"There are, but they don't do their thing during the day. And why would they bother another boat? Just make trouble for themselves."

"He might have seen something he shouldn't have out there."

"Maybe," Garcia said in a doubtful tone. "But then what happened to the *Kasi*? Hard to hide a fifteen-thousand-pound boat. And they never found any sign that it sank, blew up, or was scuttled. And it's hard not to have something hit the surface. Oil slick, debris. You can't pick up every piece."

And a human body, Decker thought.

"When was the last time you spoke with Kanak?"

"Two days before he went out. He talked to me about the trip. That's when I knew he wasn't going fishing. He knew better than that. I mean, you really got to have somebody at the wheel while you're fishing for the big boys. You use all sorts of different equipment, an array of poles and lines all over the place. And different baits, including surface, weighted and kite, downwind, upwind, teasers, dredges. Lot of stuff going on."

"How far out would you go?"

"Well, the marlins, sailfish, and yellowfin are usually

at least fifteen miles out, that's been my experience anyway. That's why they call it *deep-sea* fishing. We would go out about twenty to twenty-five miles. Water gets really choppy and bad weather can spring up, but Kanak was an old hand. We've ridden out many a storm together. Hell, we almost got blown to Cuba once. That was an experience. But the day Kanak went out there wasn't a cloud in the sky."

"But with his physical condition, weren't you worried about him?"

"To tell the truth, I didn't believe he was going out any more than three or four miles. Just to see the ocean up close one more time."

"What do you think happened to him, then?"

"Damned if I know. It's like he rode that boat all the way to heaven."

CHAPTER

40

THE NEXT MORNING DECKER MET White for a quick breakfast and told her about his late-night meetings with Kline and Perlman, and his call with Danny Garcia.

"Surprised Kline didn't mention Langley when we spoke with her the first time."

"In her defense, we really didn't ask her."

"So we need to talk to this guy."

"We do. I got his address."

"You want to roll Andrew into this?"

"Do we have a choice?"

"You really don't like him, do you?"

"He's not really my kind of guy."

"Am *I* not your kind of guy?"

Decker let out an exasperated sigh. "Don't pull my chain. I didn't get much sleep."

"This Langley might be interesting."

"He might be. Or he might be a dud. I'll give you the address. Call Andrews and have him meet us there."

* * *

Dennis Langley's firm operated out of an elegant brick townhome. The space was outfitted with costly furnishings and refined taste. Decker and White were escorted to Langley by a tall, lovely young woman named Rose, who described herself as "Mr. Langley's personal assistant, paralegal, office manager, and accountant all rolled into one." She had also told them, in answer to a question from Decker, that Langley had two young associates working with him.

Langley was, as Kline had described him, tall, handsome, fit, and dressed in an elegant fashion. His dark hair had a few gray strands that lent not a sense of age but of elegant gravitas. He welcomed them cordially and motioned them to chairs in his large office space. Decker noted the adoring look that Rose gave her boss as she slowly left the room, taking care to swivel her hips just so and run a hand through her long hair probably just in case her boss was watching.

Andrews sat next to Decker and looked fidgety and upset. Decker kept his gaze on Langley, while White put her hands in her lap and took in the entire room, which was as luxuriously appointed as the rest of the space. There was a wall of photos and certificates and shelves full of what looked to be awards from local bar associations.

"I was wondering when you were going to get around to me," said Langley. His voice, deep and baritone, was as far from Duncan Trotter's trembling falsetto as it was possible to be.

"You could have voluntarily come forward," said Decker.

Langley smiled. "Not in my DNA. But here I am now to answer your questions."

"You don't seem too upset about Judge Cummins's death," said Andrews suspiciously.

"We broke up a while ago. I'm actually seeing someone else. But don't get me wrong, Julia was a wonderful person and I hope you catch whoever did it."

Spoken like a man who knows he's a possible suspect, Decker thought.

He said, "Just to get the preliminaries out of the way, where were you between the hours of midnight and two on the night she was killed?"

"Well, I was in bed at that time, like most people."

"Can anyone vouch for that?" asked White.

"My girlfriend, Gloria. I was in bed with her at her place."

"Her last name?" asked White, her notebook open.

"Gloria Chase."

"And she lives where?"

"Here in Ocean View. About ten minutes from my office."

"We'll need to speak to Ms. Chase to confirm your alibi."

"You just have to ask."

"How often would you go over to Cummins's house when you two were seeing each other?" asked White.

"I never went to her house."

White blanched. "You were dating the woman but you never went to her house?"

"She never asked me to. I wanted to, of course, but she preferred coming to my place."

"Was your relationship sexual?" asked White.

"That's pretty personal."

"So is murder."

He sighed and sat back. "At my place quite a few times. And once, in a hotel."

"A hotel?" said Decker.

"We went to Miami. It was over a weekend." He paused and added, "Her divorce was apparently quite liberating for her."

"How so?" asked White.

"In law school she was quite the shy, demure type. Didn't even drink. I tried to date her then, but it went nowhere. Down here, all these years later, it was a different story. After her divorce she had become...well, you know, kind of...wild. Did what she wanted to do, how she wanted to do it."

"Yeah," said White. "With men I think they call it being secure in their own skin."

"Right," said Langley with a glib smile.

"We understand that the judge broke things off with you," said White.

"I saw it as mutual. We had some good times and then those good times ended."

"You were described as controlling," said White.

"I like to think of myself as forceful and decisive, but Julia was no shrinking violet. If she didn't want to do something, I wasn't going to convince her otherwise. The fact that we only had sex at a place of her choosing? I think that speaks volumes. I sure as hell wasn't controlling her."

"Do you own a gun?" asked Andrews.

"I do. I have a concealed-carry permit for it."

"Can you provide it to us?"

"For what? Ballistics?"

Andrews didn't answer.

"Sure, I can get it for you. It hasn't been fired in months. I just occasionally take it to the shooting range."

"Do you need a gun?" asked White.

"Well, the Second Amendment says I can have one regardless of whether I *need* one or not. And Florida law is very liberal on gun rights. And I'm a criminal defense attorney. My clientele can be violent. And when they don't like the job I did for them? And they have relatives and friends who might want to send me a message? So I bought a gun."

"Did you ever appear before Judge Cummins?" asked White.

"Come on. Julia would never have allowed that. We were friends from law school even before we started dating. She would have recused herself."

"So, you have a gun and you broke up with the judge who described you as controlling to someone," said Andrews. "And she had inquired about getting security because she had received threats."

"I also have an alibi. And I never threatened Julia. I would never have hurt her. And, like I said, I've moved on." He studied Andrews. "Come on, Doug. Just because I routinely beat the Bureau in court is no reason to come here and act all pissed off."

Decker glanced sharply at Andrews. "I didn't know you two knew each other."

Langley chuckled. "I'm president of the local criminal defense lawyers' association. I've gone up against the Feds more times than I can remember. My record speaks for itself."

"I will concede that you have gotten more guilty people off than not," said Andrews through gritted teeth.

"We can debate the guilty part forever. And they don't pay me to lose, Doug, do they?"

"Can we have the contact information for your new girlfriend?" said Decker.

"Rose can provide it. And you can send someone by my house for the pistol. I keep it there in a gun safe. I'll meet them there."

"So, have you gotten any guilty clients acquitted lately?" asked White.

"Every day is a new opportunity," he retorted.

"To *catch* bad guys, at least for us," said White. "Just wondering if we're sitting in the presence of one."

"You can waste time digging into me if you want. I can't stop you."

"Squeaky clean, are you?" she said.

"Who really is?"

"So, we'll find stuff?"

"Anything's possible. I bet I could find stuff on each of you. So what?"

"Is that a threat?" interjected Andrews.

Langley glanced at him, his expression one of indifference. "It's a hypothetical, at best." He looked at Decker. "I understand someone else was killed along with Julia."

"Where did you hear that?"

"Literally everywhere."

"A man who was employed by Gamma Protection. You know them?"

"Kasimira Roe's company."

"You know her?"

"I've met her. At some conferences and stuff. Super smart and focused."

"Did you know her father?"

"No. So, Julia needed protection? What from?"

"She was a judge. They're targets," Decker said. "Just like defense attorneys."

Langley smiled at this remark. "I can take care of myself."

"Did she mention to you about needing security?" added White.

"No, but we've been broken up for a while. Who was the guard that was killed?"

"You didn't hear that 'literally everywhere'?" said Decker.

"Guess not."

"Alan Draymont."

Langley shook his head. "Don't know the man."

"You said the breakup was mutual," said White. "You sure about that?"

"Julia was a beautiful woman with money. But I didn't get the idea that she ever intended to settle down again. Maybe that was part of it."

"Did you propose and she rejected you?" said White.

"To tell the truth, I *could* have seen myself proposing to her."

"But?" said Decker.

"But the answer would've been no."

"Maybe you weren't her type," said White.

Langley looked over at her. "I don't think it was that. I think she was afraid."

"Of what?" asked Decker. "Getting into another bad marriage?"

"No. I think she was just afraid...of something. Or someone."

CHAPTER

41

LATER THAT DAY DECKER WAS sitting in his hotel room reading over the latest report from the medical examiner. It *was* Alan Draymont's DNA on the sheets, towels, and washcloths. That meant he and the judge were having a sexual relationship. And they both died after a night of sex.

Andrews had confirmed Barry Davidson was on the Zoom calls when he said he was. And if Tyler was telling the truth, his alibi for his father made it clear that Davidson could not have killed his ex-wife. There just wasn't enough time in the firm window they had to work with. And even if you added some time on either end of the TOD, it would have been too tight to get to Cummins's place and back. And Decker didn't see Barry Davidson as capable of murdering his wife and then calmly getting on a Zoom call with clients. But even with the unusual frenzied killing, the hit man angle was still a possibility. Andrews had said he would have information on Davidson's financial records soon.

He glanced at his phone. Maya Perlman had sent him the emails detailing the messages from Gamma. Alan Draymont *had* been one of the security personnel assigned to them, among others. Alice Lancer was not on the list, however.

And then, as confirmation of his theory, Roe emailed that Julia Cummins had *not* contracted with Gamma for protection or even made an inquiry about such services. And yet Draymont's name had been given to the security people by Judge Cummins as an authorized person, so he could come and go at any time. That made sense if they were seeing each other.

He texted Andrews and told him about Roe's email.

Andrews texted back that neither Davidson's Mercedes nor Tyler's BMW had accessed the gate on the night of the murders.

Well, that made sense if Barry had hired someone to do the deed.

He called White in her room and filled her in.

"She never hired Gamma? So how did she and Draymont hook up?" she asked.

"Let's head back over to Cummins's house. Got some things to check."

* * *

They cleared security and drove to the judge's house.

Decker had a key for the police lock that had been

placed on the front door. They entered and White said, "What do you want to look at again?"

"Everything." He leaned against the wall of the foyer. "Now we know Draymont wasn't officially guarding the judge. He was here on his own dime."

"Then why did they stonewall us at that meeting then? They could have just told us that in the first place."

"Roe might not have known that Cummins hadn't hired them. And if she *did* know she was probably wondering what the hell Draymont was doing at Cummins's home. She probably didn't want to commit one way or another until she saw how things played out because it could adversely affect her company."

"Okay, I guess that makes sense. She's a sharp lady."

"In Roe's email, she said his work records showed that Draymont had been taking some time off, but he'd also been doing some daytime assignments in Fort Myers."

"So presumably he might stay overnight with Cummins when they were together? He was there late that night."

"Possibly. Roe didn't mention Draymont requesting a hotel room or anything like that as a business expense. There are probably official channels at Gamma you have to go through for that. And if he had required housing they would have just used someone from the Naples office to cover the assignment in Fort Myers."

"But Trevor Perlman said the judge asked him about Gamma. He took that to mean she was looking for security."

"That's right. And at their lunch she told Tyler that she *was* having security protection. He told his dad about it. Barry texted the judge to ask her about it but she never got back to him."

"So, she lied to everybody?"

"Maybe she didn't want Barry to know she had a new boyfriend, so she made up the story about needing protection and told Tyler, knowing that he would tell his dad."

"Well, apparently everyone knew she was dating Dennis Langley."

"We don't know that for sure. Maya Perlman just knew there was someone but didn't have a name. Doris Kline, maybe her closest friend, knew his name, but Julia swore her to secrecy. And he never came to her house, at least by his own admission. And if he's to be believed, they only had sex at Langley's house, and once went all the way to Miami to do it."

"But who would care about her having sex with either Draymont or Langley?"

"Her ex-husband, for one. And, despite what he said, Langley might have a problem with getting dumped and then replaced by Draymont. And we have to check his alibi with his new girlfriend, though she might have a motive to lie for him."

"They picked up his gun and did the ballistics. It wasn't a match for the weapon that killed Draymont."

"I know. Andrews texted me. But Langley might have more than one gun. And if he did kill Draymont, no way he gives us *that* gun. The murder weapon might be in the ocean."

"Langley said he thought she was afraid of something or someone, Decker."

"That's if Langley was telling the truth. If she *was* really afraid, why *not* hire protection? Which she didn't. But, as I said before, I think she *was* afraid of someone, too."

"But you think whoever killed Draymont didn't kill the judge. So, at least with your theory, those crimes *aren't* connected."

"Not connected at one level, but maybe at another."

"Damn, Decker, you're making this really complicated."

"If it *is* complicated, then I'm just laying it out accurately. Let's go to the bedroom first."

They headed up the stairs and looked around.

Decker leaned against the wall and closed his eyes. Something was bugging the crap out of him. And then, as he draped, one over another, the layers of conversations they'd had with third parties, along

with facts uncovered, a startling inconsistency occurred to him.

Thank you, superpower.

He opened his eyes. "We went to Gamma after
Draymont was killed. We wanted to know why
Draymont was here. We assumed he was guarding
the judge, right?"

"Right," replied White.

"They told us they couldn't reveal anything pend-
ing a review by their counsel. But we pushed it."

"Yeah, so?"

"So they brought in Alice Lancer to talk to us
about the matter."

"But she fainted dead away and then got taken
from the hospital by two fake cops."

Decker nodded. "But now we know that the judge
never contracted with Gamma or even made an
inquiry about hiring them. So why did they bring
Lancer in to talk to us about something that never
happened? What could Lancer possibly tell us?"

White looked confused. "I...she...Damn, that
doesn't make sense."

"The woman who brought her in said that Lancer
would be able to provide us information about Draymont. She didn't specify anything about Draymont
being assigned to guard the judge."

"I don't remember the exchange exactly," said
White.

"But *I* do. So we need to check with Gamma and find out why Lancer, out of all the people there, was picked to talk to us." He pulled out his phone and punched in a number.

"Who are you calling?"

"Kasimira Roe," replied Decker.

"She won't tell you anything. That lady hides behind the lawyers."

"I think she might talk to me this time...Kasimira? Yeah, it's Decker. Look, I went over your father's file, talked to Danny Garcia, and I have some thoughts and leads I'm going to run down. But on my case, I need an answer to a question."

He asked about Lancer.

"Right, yeah. Okay...Is that right? She did? All right, yeah, thanks. I'll be in touch about your father. Thanks again."

He clicked off and looked at the floor.

"Well!" snapped White. "What did she say?"

Decker glanced up at her. "Gamma didn't pick Lancer to talk to us. Kasimira said that *Lancer* approached the associate Kasimira sent out of the meeting and told *her* that she could help with the inquiry."

"You mean she basically volunteered to come and meet us?"

"Yeah, but she didn't meet with us, did she? She pulled her fainting act before she said a word, and now she's disappeared."

White looked thoughtful. "So she might have seen us come in, anticipated what we would ask about, and then seized the opportunity?"

"But why come forward and then disappear? Why not just slink off into the shadows and we'd never know of her involvement, since Gamma wasn't protecting the judge?"

"Did Roe say why Lancer came forward?" asked White.

"She didn't know for sure, but she said that Lancer and Draymont worked closely together at Gamma. He was the field guy and she was a supervisor. But still, Lancer could have just kept silent. There would be no reason for us to question her."

"But if she wanted to get away she might pull a stunt like that."

Decker said, "But why not wait a bit and then just announce you're moving or taking a new job or retiring to go paint landscapes in Tuscany? Why do it that fast?"

White replied, "Because after what happened to Draymont, she was afraid the same thing would happen to her. She had to act fast and seized on the opportunity of our being there."

Decker looked at her with respect. "Freddie, I think you might be right about that. Nice work."

She smiled at him.

"What?"

"First time you called me Freddie. I like how you say it."

Decker looked around the bedroom. "I'm thinking Draymont bought it in the study, then his killer left right away. Then the second person comes in, sees Cummins kneeling next to the dead Draymont, chases her upstairs, and kills her."

"So the second killer was there and *also* seized an opportunity?" said White.

"He might have seen Draymont go down and then he goes after his real target, the judge."

"Or *she*. Could Alice Lancer have killed Draymont? Maybe there was something between them we don't know about. They might have been more than coworkers. Remember that Lancer's neighbor recognized Draymont as being at her house a lot. She thought they were dating."

"And then Lancer left Cummins alive to tell on her?"

"Your theory of two killers is not as plausible as Lancer having killed *both* of them," noted White. "She uses a gun with Draymont because he was a big, strong guy and she didn't want to take a chance of him overpowering her. Then she waits for Cummins to come downstairs, maybe to check on the noise the shots might have made. When she does, Lancer attacks Cummins with a knife, chases her all the way upstairs, and kills her right here. If Lancer and Draymont were lovers, maybe they had a falling-out and

Lancer went all jealous when she found out about Cummins. It could happen. That would explain the frenzy of the attack on Cummins."

"And Lancer stuffs old Slovakian money down Draymont's throat?" said Decker.

"She worked at Gamma, she would know of the connection. It's a distraction only. Same with the cut-up blindfold and the 'res ipsa' bullshit."

"Well, if we can find Lancer, it might clear a lot of things up."

"Let's hope we do."

He said, "Now, let's just check the study."

They trooped downstairs, and into the room where Draymont's body had been discovered.

They both stopped so abruptly, they bumped into each other.

The electric blue light was slamming Decker from all corners.

They had just found Alice Lancer. However, she would not be telling them a damn thing.

CHAPTER

42

DECKER AND WHITE WATCHED AS Alice Lancer's covered remains were wheeled out of Cummins's house on a gurney.

Andrews spoke with Helen Jacobs, the ME, and then came over to them.

"She was shot," said Andrews. "Two to the chest. Just like Draymont."

"How long's she been dead?" asked Decker. "Seemed to me that rigor had clearly passed."

"Jacobs figures not too long after she got plucked from the hospital."

Decker looked off into the distance, obviously processing this.

"But how did they get her body inside the house?" said Andrews. "And why take that chance?"

"Symbolic," said Decker, glancing at him. "Draymont and Lancer, two peas in a pod. So the next question is obvious."

Andrews nodded in understanding. "I asked Jacobs.

She already checked. There's rolled-up money in Lancer's throat."

"Shit," exclaimed White. She looked at Decker. "Well, obviously Lancer didn't kill Draymont and Judge Cummins, like I thought. This ties into your theory of there being two separate killers."

"But other than the gun versus knife and professional hit versus frenzied attack, do you have anything else to base that on, Decker?" asked Andrews.

"Yeah, nobody stuffed Slovakian money into the judge's throat," noted Decker. "And if the killers were different, the person who stabbed Cummins would have no way of knowing about the money in the throat. It's not like it was visible on the corpse."

Andrews nodded in agreement. "Right. So we have three stiffs and no suspects. But what connection did Draymont and Lancer have, other than working together at Gamma, and Draymont being seen at her house?"

"There's at least one thing," noted Decker. "We just have to find it. And there was bruising on her face."

"Yeah, I noticed that, too."

White said, "Which means they beat her up before killing her."

Decker added, "They needed information. I wonder if they got it."

Andrews said, "What would Lancer know that they

needed? Something about Gamma? Hey, I know I thought it was a stretch, but do you think this really *does* tie into Kanak Roe's disappearance?"

"Possibly," said Decker. "But why let three years pass?"

"Maybe something just came to light," said White. "And they had to act on it."

Decker glanced at her sharply, a light sparking behind his eyes, but he remained silent.

Doris Kline and the Perlmans were in Kline's yard and watching all the police activity.

Trevor Perlman walked over to them. The man was pale and disheveled, very unlike the man they had met the first time. He said, "I know you can't tell us much, but the dead person isn't Barry or Tyler, is it?"

"No," said Andrews. "But any reason why you think it might have been?"

"With Julia dead, I just thought they would be the most likely ones to be in there."

Decker said, "Did you see anything suspicious today or last night?"

"No. I went to bed early and I've been out most of the day. I just got back in time to see all this. Should we be, I mean, do you think we could be in danger? My wife is beyond scared out of her wits. And so is Doris."

Andrews said, "I'll have the local cops make rounds until we solve this thing."

"Thank you." Perlman walked back to his wife and they went inside their home.

Decker motioned to Kline, who joined them.

"My God," she said. "Another body. What the hell is going on?"

"Did you see anything?" asked Andrews.

"When?"

"Last night, anytime today."

"Who was killed?"

"A woman, not from the neighborhood. She was killed elsewhere and placed in the judge's house," said White.

"Well, I didn't see anyone carrying a body in, if that's what you want to know. I did see you and Decker go in the front door earlier. But that was it."

"No cars in the driveway, no strangers walking by?" asked Decker.

"No, nothing like that. It's actually been pretty quiet."

"Well, keep your eyes and ears open."

"Trevor mentioned you're going to have some cops around?"

"Yes," said Andrews.

"Well, thank God. My life is passing by fast enough as it is. I don't need anyone else to hurry it along."

She walked briskly to her home and closed the door.

Andrews shook his head. "Can't blame them for being scared."

"No, you can't," said White while Decker just stared at a spot in the sky.

"What are you thinking, Decker?" said Andrews, who noticed this.

"I'm thinking how long before we find Patty Kelly, or her body."

He started to walk off.

"Where are you going?" asked Andrews.

He called back over his shoulder. "Back to the hotel. But tomorrow morning I'm going back to Gamma. Feel free to come."

"Why Gamma?" said White.

Decker stopped and turned. "Lancer and Draymont were both killed in the exact same way and placed in the exact same spot. So, in life, they must have had a direct connection. And we need to find out exactly what that connection is. Now, we know that Draymont had been to Lancer's house. They might have had a relationship of some kind. But they *worked* together, that's the low-hanging fruit."

"But Gamma didn't tell us anything before," argued Andrews.

"That's *not* an option the second time around," replied Decker.

CHAPTER

43

IT WAS THE SAME CONFERENCE room, but the only Gamma person in it this time was Kasimira Roe. She was again dressed all in black, as though in mourning. And she had a tissue in one hand.

"Alice was moving up rapidly. She reminded me of myself in some ways."

Decker, White, and Andrews were seated on the opposite side of the table.

"I can't believe she was killed. And then put where Alan Draymont was." She looked at Decker. "Did she, was the money...?"

He said nothing but his look was probably enough.

"How can I help you?" said Roe.

"You can start with telling us about the working relationship Draymont and Lancer had. We already know that Draymont would stay over at her place sometimes."

"I...I didn't know about that."

"Do you have a no-fraternization policy at Gamma?" asked White.

"We do, as a matter of fact."

"Then they probably kept their relationship secret."

"I wonder what else they kept secret?" said Decker.

"What do you mean?" asked Roe.

"Judge Cummins didn't hire your firm. Yet Lancer volunteered to come in here and tell us about . . . what, exactly?"

"Oh, I see what you mean. If Draymont wasn't over there guarding the judge, then what could Alice know about it?"

"Unless they were taking jobs on the side, but I would imagine they're prohibited from doing that," observed White.

"Yes, they are. Our agents are full-time employees. No freelancing is allowed. It would be a liability nightmare."

"I would think so," said Decker. "But before she could tell us anything she faints, gets taken to the hospital, and two fake plainclothes show up and whisk her away. At first I thought it was planned out by her. But now I'm thinking maybe those fake cops weren't her friends."

"You . . . you think they killed her?"

"If they did, they did it in a way that brought it right back to your doorstep."

"What was Draymont doing there unless he was guarding the judge?" asked Roe.

Decker said, "What he was doing there was personal, about as personal as it gets."

Roe looked confused for a moment, but then her eyes widened. "You mean...?"

"Yes, I do."

"But then why kill the judge? Because she was a witness?"

"Let's keep the focus on Draymont and Lancer. I take it they worked together here?"

"Yes, Alice was Draymont's immediate superior. She oversaw his work, was sort of his handler. He wasn't the only one. She probably had two dozen field agents she was overseeing."

"But he was the only one who ended up dead."

"Yes."

"We need to see his work schedule for the last couple of months or so. And any communications between him and Lancer."

She began to speak, but then hesitated, looking down. "I'm afraid that won't be—"

Decker interrupted her. "Okay, then we have to go to the media with this, you know, get the word out that Gamma people are dying left and right, and present and future clients might want to give the firm a wide berth for now. That way we might be able to get some help from the public to answer questions you refuse to."

Roe scowled. "Is that a threat?"

"No, it's an option."

"A nuclear option?"

"More like an assault weapon. When I go nuclear it will be unmistakable."

"And here I thought we had a meaningful working relationship."

"It's only a relationship when it goes both ways. So what's it going to be? You pull your records and help us find out who's killing your people, or we release details to the media that will probably sink your business?"

Roe looked at Andrews. "Doug, is what he's doing even legal or FBI approved?"

Andrews didn't take his eyes off Roe. "I really don't know, but I fully support it."

Decker leaned toward her. "There's one more woman out there who's disappeared. I expect her to end up dead anytime now. Maybe you're okay with slow-walking all this, but I'm not. And I don't think your dad would be, either."

Roe's face flushed. "Don't throw my father into this. You didn't even know him."

"I know all I need to know about him. He was Secret Service. He took an oath to take a bullet to keep the president alive. You think he'd let a bunch of red tape stand in the way of saving someone?"

Roe balled up her tissue and put it in her pocket. She stood. "I'll get the records for you."

"Thank you," said Decker.

"You must be a very good chess player," she said.

"Maybe, if I ever took up the game. I just can't seem to find the time."

She stalked out.

Andrews sat back and let out a long breath. "Jesus, I can't believe I just said what I did. But damn, it felt good."

"You should transfer up to DC, Doug," said White. "From what I've heard, this stuff is a daily occurrence with Decker."

"How do you not get your ass fired, Decker?" Andrews asked.

Decker said, "They know I don't give a shit. It's like body armor."

Andrews looked stunned. "Why the hell didn't I ever think of that?"

CHAPTER

44

OKAY," SAID DECKER AS HE finished both his beer and the last document he was looking at.

They were ensconced in a small conference room at Andrews's office. Spread out over the table were the records Roe had provided. White munched on the last piece of cold pizza and looked out the window, where the sun had gone down hours ago.

"Not much here," noted Andrews. "They worked cases together. Lots of them. They did the Perlman protection detail and two others in the same neighborhood. Didn't know that many people needed security in that community."

"Those people, or at least most of them, have money," noted Decker. "And other people will always try to take that money away." He sat back and rubbed his eyes. "We need to know more about Draymont and Lancer *before* they came to Gamma."

Andrews said, "You think they might have known each other before Gamma? They were both in the DC area at the same time."

"If they did, we need to find out."

The door opened and a young woman poked her head in. "Doug, we finally got the CCTV footage from the hospital you requested."

"I'd forgotten about that. What took so long?"

"It's a hospital. They have other priorities, I guess."

She brought in a laptop and set it down in front of them. "Just hit play."

Decker said, "Is this just from inside the hospital? Or did they have footage from the parking lot, too?"

"Unfortunately, with the camera angles, there weren't any clear images of them exiting the facility. And there was no footage of them getting into a car."

She left and closed the door behind her.

They crowded around the laptop and Andrews hit the play button. It took a few minutes, but then they saw two men enter the admissions area from the entrance used by the ambulance crews. They flashed badges and approached Lancer on the gurney. One of the men spoke to her. Looking stricken, she slowly rose, climbed off the gurney, and was led out by the men.

"It looks like they were arresting her," said White.

"Maybe she actually *did* faint," noted Decker.

"We can put this out to the public and other police forces and agencies to be on the lookout," said

Andrews. He looked down at his phone, which had dinged. "Damn."

"What is it?" asked White.

"We just got back some info on Kelly's cell phone before it was turned off. She got a text from an unidentified phone, probably a burner, maybe shortly before she supposedly left for the store."

"What did it say?" asked White.

In answer Andrews held up his phone. On the screen was a one-word message.

Decker looked at the time stamp. "So, minutes before Lancer walked into the conference room Kelly got a text telling her to *run?*"

"Yep," said Andrews.

"And did that text come from Lancer?" asked White.

Decker rose.

"Where are you going?" said White.

"*We're* going to see Patty Kelly's husband."

CHAPTER

45

THE LIGHTS IN THE HOUSE were all on and Steve Kelly answered on the first knock. He looked beleaguered and unfocused.

"I ... I thought you might be the police with word on Patty."

"Can we come in?" asked Decker.

He stepped aside and they moved into the house.

"Y-you're not here to tell me that she's—"

"No, we're not," said Decker. "We're doing our best to find her. Alive."

After they all sat down Decker said, "Your wife got a warning from someone shortly before she fled."

"I don't understand," said Kelly. "A warning about what? And from who?"

"We don't know, for sure. It came close to the disappearance of another person named Alice Lancer. Do you know her?"

"No, I don't. Never heard of her."

"And your wife?"

"She never mentioned that name to me. Who is she?"

"Someone of interest" was all Decker would say. "How about a man named Alan Draymont?"

Kelly shook his head.

Decker turned to Andrews. "Show him pictures of both."

Andrews did so, and Kelly pointed at Draymont. "Now, I did see that young man once."

"Where?" asked White.

"He was walking down the street and stopped to talk to Patty. I was inside reading the newspaper and saw them. When I asked her who it was, she said he was just asking for directions."

"Did you believe that?" asked Decker.

Kelly looked offended. "Of course I did."

Decker glanced around and saw some pictures on a shelf. He walked over to look at them. "Is this your wife, from some years back?"

"Yes. She was thirty-eight. I know because those are from our honeymoon in Mexico. It was my second marriage and Patty's first."

"No kids?" said Decker.

"I had two from my first marriage. Patty didn't want children and I was fine with that."

"Do you know anything of her earlier life?" asked White.

"She was from the West Coast originally. She moved to Florida at some point. She was a paralegal for a while and then got the job at the courthouse.

She had no family to speak of. Or she never mentioned any."

Decker picked up one of these photos and brought it over to show White and Andrews.

They both gaped, while Kelly looked confused. He said, "Is her picture important somehow?"

Andrews held the photo of Alice Lancer on his phone next to Kelly's picture. Now Kelly gaped.

In the photos, the two women looked like nearly identical sisters.

"My God, what the hell does that mean?"

Decker said, "We ran a check on Lancer. We know that she was adopted and her adopted parents were killed in a plane crash. But I think we may know who her biological mother was. Your wife. We'll have to confirm it with DNA."

This was the memory that had come back to Decker earlier. It was the reason why Patty Kelly had looked familiar to him when he'd first seen the woman's picture. It was because she so closely resembled her daughter, Alice, even as an older woman. Now comparing the women's images at around the same age, it was clear they were probably related.

"What in the hell is going on?" exclaimed Kelly.

"Your wife and Alice Lancer and Alan Draymont, the man she said was asking about directions, were apparently involved in something together," said Decker. "Lancer and Draymont are dead. They were killed at different times but in the exact same way and left in the exact same spot. But before all that happened Lancer, or someone acting for her, sent your wife a text message telling her to run. And she did."

The entire time Decker was talking Kelly seemed to be growing smaller and smaller until the couch threatened to swallow him.

"D-dead?"

"If your wife wanted to hide out somewhere, where would she go?" asked White.

Kelly gummed his lips and looked hopelessly confused. "I...I don't know. I mean, I never thought she would have to hide from anything."

"Okay, let me recalibrate the question," said White. "Where would she go to get away from things? Meditate? Chill?"

"We have a little beach cottage in Key Largo. I inherited it from my parents. I call it a cottage but it's really just a fishing shack. If I fixed it up I could probably get some good money for it, but I never got around to doing that. I haven't been there in a couple years, but Patty loved it. She could really get away from it all there, she said. And she loved the movie. You know, the one with Bogart and Bacall?"

"Yeah, and the murderous gangster played by Edward G. Robinson," Decker amended. "We'll need the address, right now."

CHAPTER

46

THOUGH IT WAS AFTER ELEVEN, they got on the road right away.

"Should we alert the local cops about this?" Andrews asked as they drove off.

Decker shook his head. "No. I don't want them to spook Kelly into doing something stupid or going even deeper into hiding. Let's just get there as fast as we can."

Andrews steered them to I-75 and took it across Florida west to east. Then they turned south on the Florida Turnpike and took it to Route 1.

"Okay, we're five minutes out," said Andrews.

Decker looked at his watch. The trip had taken a little over three hours.

"Stop just short of the place," he said a few minutes later.

They pulled down a narrow lane that paralleled the beach. It was quiet and still, and clouds covered the moon, throwing everything into a grim darkness.

Andrews stopped the car. He said quietly, "It must be that one down there at the end."

Steve Kelly hadn't been exaggerating. The homes here really were little more than fishing shacks, some near to falling down, others in little better shape. The tide was coming in and the breakers were noisy.

They got out and started to walk quietly toward the house, keeping off the street.

"There's her car out front," said White softly.

It was indeed the SUNNY license plate on the white Camry.

Decker took the front, and White and Andrews went around back. The yard was littered with palm leaves and trash and rotting fish heads. The shacks on either side were dark, and there were no cars in front of them. It seemed the only shack occupied was the Kellys'.

Or was it?

Decker edged up to the front door and peered into the small window to the left of the door. He slipped his gun from its holster and placed his finger near the trigger.

He stepped to the side of the door and knocked.

"FBI, Mrs. Kelly, open the door."

He could hear movement inside.

"I've... I've got a gun," said a woman's tremulous voice.

"So do we," said Decker. "I'll slide my credentials

under the door. Take a look at them. We need to talk."

He did so and a few moments later the door opened, revealing a woman who looked like a decades-older version of Alice Lancer. She had on jeans and a light blue sweater. Her feet were bare. She had a gun in her right hand and Decker's credentials in her left.

She handed them back to him and he asked her to put the gun down, which she did, laying it on a side table.

She turned around as White and Andrews came in the rear door.

"Mrs. Kelly, we need to ask you a lot of questions," said Andrews.

She pursed her lips and nodded. "I suppose so. Let's sit down."

She led them over to a couch with worn upholstery and two rickety chairs set around a small, scarred coffee table. The interior held the musty odor of having been closed up for a while.

They sat, and Kelly clutched her knees with her long, bony fingers.

Decker studied her and said, "First off, are you Alice Lancer's biological mother?"

"Yes. I gave her up for adoption right after she was born. I had no job, no way to support a baby. But it was still the hardest thing I've ever had to do."

"But you two reconciled at some point," said White.

"We did. I don't know how Alice did it, but she found me."

"Was that why she moved here, to be nearer to you?" asked Andrews.

"That's what she said. She had lived and worked in the DC area before that. Now she was only a couple hours' drive away."

"You must have been surprised when she showed up," said Decker.

"Stunned, more like it. But as soon as I opened the door and saw her, I knew she was my daughter."

"Yes, I noticed the resemblance, too."

"Have they found Alice? Is she all right?"

Andrews and White looked uneasily at one another, but Decker kept his gaze squarely on Kelly.

"She sent you a message, telling you to run?"

Kelly looked down at her lap. "Yes, yes, she did."

"We need to know all about that."

"I'm not sure I know all that much."

"Then tell us what you do know."

"Alice works at Gamma Protection Services."

"We know. She supervised Alan Draymont, who was killed at Judge Cummins's house."

Kelly's eyes filled with tears. "I can't believe Judge Cummins is dead. I really can't. She was the nicest person."

"Do you know why she wanted protection?"

"No, I don't."

"Did she receive any threats?"

"Not that I knew of." She was turning red in the face and her words were growing softer.

Decker said, "But she didn't need protection, did she?"

Kelly looked up at him. "Then why have Gamma at her house?"

Decker didn't say anything; he just stared at her. He finally said, "If you want to avoid trouble, the truth is your best path forward. If you decide to go a different route, things will get dicey. And keep in mind that Draymont *was* murdered."

"But I thought he was killed guarding Judge Cummins?"

Decker decided to bring the conversation full circle to where they started. "Then why would your daughter tell you to run? Run from what? And why?"

The woman closed her eyes, and tears seeped from under her lids. "Alice and Alan...found out something."

"What?" asked Decker.

"I don't know, she wouldn't tell me. But it was something important. And...and they were going to use it to..."

"To what? Make some money?"

Kelly opened her eyes and looked up at him. "I told her not to do it. But she wouldn't listen. I...I hope she's okay. I never liked Alan. He was too...slick."

"So why tell you to run if you knew nothing?" asked Andrews.

"The people involved in this might think she had told me something. They might learn of the connection between us. That's why Alice warned me."

"You left your husband behind," noted Decker. "They might have assumed that he knew something, too. They might have killed him."

She looked up at him in fear. "I wasn't thinking. I was so scared. They...they haven't hurt him, have they?"

"Not yet, but he's very worried about you. You left without saying anything to him. Haven't answered his calls or texts."

She let out a gush of air. "I didn't know what to do. When that text came in...I tried to call Alice, but she didn't answer. I tried so many times to call her before I turned off my phone." She looked up at Decker again. "Is she...is she...?"

"You'll need to come with us, Mrs. Kelly," said Decker. "We can protect you. But we'll need your full cooperation."

"I've told you all I know."

"I don't think so. And at the very least, there are probably things you can remember better." He put a hand under her elbow. "Let's go. We'll drive you back."

"My car!"

"Will be taken care of. Do you have a bag?"

"Just over there." She pointed to a small duffel in the corner.

White snagged it, checked her watch, and said, "Let's go. Long drive. We should be back in time for breakfast."

They stepped outside, Andrews in front and Decker next to Kelly. White closed the door behind them and they stepped off into the sandy front yard.

The first shot dropped Andrews. The second round drilled a hole right through Patty Kelly's forehead.

Decker and White flattened themselves to the sand, guns out and searching for something to shoot. When the car started up, they rose and ran forward. They both fired at the taillights of the car but missed.

They ran back to the fallen people.

Andrews was breathing, but Kelly had reached the end of her life.

White called for help, while Decker staunched the blood coming from the unconscious Andrews's shoulder.

When the ambulance showed up along with the police, Decker helped them load Andrews onto a gurney, and it sped off with the man to the closest hospital. White rode in back with the wounded agent.

Decker turned to look at Kelly, lying there dead

in the sand in front of her now-widowed husband's fishing shack. She looked at peace when her life had ended in any way but peacefully.

The electric light blue was engulfing him, like a big wave on the beach. He was surprised that he wasn't used to it by now. But it still took his breath away, still made him feel sick and lightheaded. But perhaps death deserved to have that effect, particularly the deaths Decker typically encountered.

He glanced away from the body and closed his eyes. Kelly dead and Andrews wounded, none of that was fair. Not one single bit.

Decker opened his eyes, let the electric blue dissipate, along with the nausea, and then he went back to work.

CHAPTER

47

ANDREWS WAS GOING TO RECOVER, but it would take time. He had undergone surgery and was being transported back to a hospital in Ocean View. It was now just Decker and White as the visiting team taking over for the locals.

Patty Kelly's body had been transported to Fort Myers and was currently undergoing an autopsy by Helen Jacobs. Steve Kelly had been informed of his wife's murder. They had no leads on who had done the deed. Neither Decker nor White had gotten a good look at the car. There had been no license plate on the rear.

As Decker sat in his hotel room having a late breakfast after dealing with the Key Largo cops and driving back with White, he thought about Patty Kelly's not even knowing her daughter had been murdered.

What does it matter now?

As he was having his final cup of coffee, White knocked on his door and he let her in. Her hair was still damp from her shower, and she had on a fresh set of clothes and looked ready for anything. She sat down and eyed him.

"Somebody followed us last night," she said. "Or maybe they discovered where Kelly was."

"No, if they had they would have beaten us to it. They definitely followed us from Steve Kelly's place."

"I never saw anyone back there."

"Because they knew what they were doing." He had a sudden thought. "Have our rental checked for a bug."

"You think?"

"It would explain a lot."

White made a call and then put her phone down. "Kelly managed to tell us some things before she died."

"Discovered info, probably of a sensitive type. Draymont and Lancer were using it as blackmail to make some money."

"Only what happened?" said White.

"They got their hands slammed in the cookie jar."

"Whoever they were trying to blackmail are some serious people."

"You don't blackmail the penniless and powerless."

White nodded. "I suppose. Do you really think Kelly didn't know the who and the what?"

"We'll never know now, will we?"

"So we're back at square one then. And down an agent. You want me to see if they can dial somebody else up? Either from Fort Myers or maybe Miami or Tampa?"

"No," said Decker emphatically. "Just you and me."

"Is that a vote of confidence?"

"And it's a vote of I don't want to involve another person if I don't have to. It would take too long to bring them up to speed and we don't have the time."

"FBI agent got shot. They take that seriously. I'm surprised they don't have an army of agents down here beating the bushes regardless of what we think."

"An army tends to muddy the ground. And it's not the number of agents, it's what the agents you have on the ground actually do."

"You really don't like working with people, do you?"

Decker rose. "You ready?"

"For what?"

"Another go at Gamma."

"You really think they're hiding something?"

"I do. And they may not even know they are."

* * *

"Ms. Roe is not in today," said the receptionist at Gamma's front desk.

"Where is she?" asked Decker.

"I'm not authorized to give that information out."

"Well, I can call Kasimira and ask her to tell you to give it out."

"You know Ms. Roe?"

"She's like a sister," said Decker.

The woman looked at him doubtfully. "Then you better call your *sister*."

Decker moved to the corner and made the call. It went right to voice mail. He left a message and walked back over to the receptionist. "Okay, we need to talk to anyone here who dealt with Alice Lancer and/or Alan Draymont."

"I'll have to check on that."

"Great. We'll stay right here while you do."

With an annoyed look, the woman picked up the phone and made a series of calls. She finally put down the receiver. "They all appear to be out at the moment."

"Did *you* know either of them?" asked White.

"Just to say hello."

"And now they're both dead. Mouths stuffed with money that came from the country where your founder, Kanak Roe, emigrated from," said Decker. "What a hell of a coincidence."

"I don't know anything about that, but it doesn't sound coincidental."

"No, it doesn't, does it?" said Decker. "Which explains why we're here."

"I don't know what to tell you."

"Another woman died last night. It was connected to this case. And an FBI agent was shot."

"I'm very sorry about that, but there is no one here to help you."

White glanced at Decker and clearly saw the frustration building in the man.

"Well, thank you for being so unhelpful," said White. She pulled on Decker's sleeve and dragged him from the room.

Outside she said, "Okay, I know you want to blow a gasket, same with me. But we can't. They'll have their lawyers all over our asses, and then the call will go to DC and we might get pulled right off this sucker, which I know will piss you off even more."

Decker looked sullen and uninterested in her words until he let out a deep breath and said, "You're right. That was the stupid way to go. Now we need to do the smart."

"Which is?"

"The real way to win a football game comes before you step on the field. You look at film, game plans, you study your opponent and his tendencies. You come to know him maybe better than he knows himself. It gives you a split-second advantage, but that's really all you need."

"So we're going to...?"

"Learn exactly who and what Alice Lancer and Alan Draymont were. Because I don't think this was their first rodeo when it comes to blackmail."

CHAPTER

48

THE KINGSTON GROUP," SAID WHITE as they sat in Andrews's small office at his RA in Fort Myers. "That's where Lancer was the communications director and later a lobbyist. They're a respected K Street outfit, been in business for a long time. She was there for five years. Good record, no complaints. Before that she was a corporate lawyer for a white-shoe firm in DC. I spoke to someone at the firm. They reported that nothing unusual happened while she was there."

Decker was looking over some pages on a laptop. "Connection to Draymont?"

"The people I spoke to didn't know of one. But they might have dated, hung out as friends; it didn't have to be a professional connection. She was a number of years older than he was, but so what?"

"Did they live near each other?"

"Relatively speaking, but not in the same community."

"No overlap in their jobs?" asked Decker.

"Well, the lobbying firm did a lot of work on Capitol Hill. And Draymont worked security at the Capitol complex. It was entirely possible that their paths would have crossed professionally. You know, she's up there lobbying someone while Draymont is on duty. He caught her eye. They might have dated. Those things happen every day."

Decker thought about her words. *He caught her eye.*

"But nothing firm on any nexus between them?"

"No. But they could have kept it on the Q.T."

"Were either of them married?" he asked.

"No record of that. You were thinking if one was, that would be a reason to keep their relationship secret?"

"Yes. Okay, let's just take this logically, step-by-step. You don't kill someone without a reason, particularly in this situation. Now, with Cummins we have a number of motivations, separate and apart from Draymont and Lancer. But for the latter two, you kill them if they did the killer wrong, or had information that was dangerous to the killer or whoever might have hired them." He looked up at her inquiringly.

"Okay, I agree with that. But could their killings be a symbolic act against Kanak Roe and Gamma? Remember the money in the mouths."

Decker shook his head. "I would maybe think that, if Draymont and Lancer had no connection to one another. But they did. It's beyond probability that they would both be targeted simply as symbolic stand-ins for Kanak Roe or Gamma Protection Services. And Patty Kelly intimated that they were doing something to make money."

"You thought that involved blackmail, and that they got their hands slammed in the cookie jar. So that was probably why they were killed."

"But that was somehow *also* connected to Kanak Roe and his home country. Hence the Slovakian money in their mouths."

"But, Decker, Roe came to this country many decades ago—before Draymont or Lancer were even born, in fact."

"Doesn't matter. If the connection is there, it will explain all facets of the case."

She shook her head. "Well, right now, I just don't see it. And I like to keep an open mind on cases. Going down only one alley can waste a lot of time if it turns out to be the *wrong* alley."

"And it can *save* time if it turns out to be the right one," countered Decker. "What's the latest on Andrews?"

"He's awake and in a lot of pain. But he's lucky. If the bullet had hit a few inches or so to the right, he's not waking up ever."

"And ballistics on the slug in him and the one that killed Kelly?"

"Did *not* match the rounds taken from Draymont and Lancer. They were probably from a rifle, because the shots definitely came from a distance."

"Like I said before, we need to know more about Draymont and Lancer from their time back in DC."

"Do we fly there and check it out? I'm not sure how much we would find out that's relevant besides what I learned on my phone calls."

"*You* can fly there and check it out. I'll stay here and run down some leads."

Her look turned sour. "Trying to get rid of me again? I thought we had covered that."

"We can divide and conquer." He paused, looking uncomfortable. "And..."

"And what?" she said, evidently looking for a fight.

"And I thought you might want to see your kids."

All the venom seeped from White's features as she scrutinized him. "Okay, that is the *only* response that would have saved your butt with me right this second. So, what do you want me to try to find out?"

"I said before I didn't think this was Draymont's and Lancer's first attempt at blackmail. And maybe they picked up down here where they left off in DC."

"Pretty bad blackmailers then, because Draymont drove an old car and lived in a crummy apartment. Lancer's house was pretty modest."

"Draymont also had on a Cartier watch and his

suit was an Armani. Both were the real deal. And he had a personal platinum Amex card."

"Shit," said White. "Now that I think about it, the clothes in Lancer's apartment were all designer and so were her handbags. I thought they were knock-offs. And the motivation for the people who killed them?"

"It's about something more important than money."

"Which is?"

"What we have to find out."

CHAPTER

49

DECKER DROPPED WHITE OFF AT the airport the following morning.

"Say hello to your family. Maybe I'll meet them one day."

She stabbed him with a look. "Maybe you will. If you hold up your end of our partnership."

Next, Decker drove to the hospital where they had transferred Agent Andrews. The man was sitting up in his bed appearing forlorn and defeated.

Decker sat down next to him and looked the agent over. "You feel like talking or you need to rest?"

"I'm on a ton of painkillers, but I'm still lucid *and* bored. So, your visit is welcome."

"Okay."

"Kelly's dead?" Andrews said.

Decker nodded.

"I guess I'm lucky to be alive," said Andrews.

"We all are."

"Where's your sidekick?"

"She's not my sidekick. She's my partner. She went back to DC."

Andrews looked shocked. "You're not giving up the case?"

"No, we're expanding it. Did you know Kanak Roe?"

"I told you I did."

"Tell me more," said Decker.

"What do you want to know?"

"Anything, considering I really know nothing about him."

"He was an impressive man. Everyone respected him. More than they do his daughter," he added, a bit petulantly, thought Decker.

"You seem to have an issue with her," said Decker.

Andrews rubbed at his injured shoulder and said, "Maybe I do."

"Why?"

"No particular reason," said Andrews, not meeting his eye.

"Well, let me give you one. You tried to get a position with Gamma but were rejected. Too inflexible, maybe?"

Andrews gasped, "How in the hell did you know that?"

"I didn't, not for sure, until right now. But there was something just off about you and Gamma *and* Kasimira Roe. You were a little too effusive about the firm, and you knew a lot about it. And you seem to like the finer things in life, not that there's anything wrong with that."

Andrews lay back and closed his eyes. "I guess I should have recused myself from the investigation, like you suggested."

"We're all human."

"What else do you want to know about Kanak Roe?"

"Successful, respected. Anything more?"

"You really want the observations of an *inflexible* agent who can't make the grade in the private sector?"

"I want the observations of a veteran FBI agent who was nearly killed performing his duty."

Andrews opened his eyes. "I appreciate your saying that."

"It's the truth. Subtlety is not my thing."

Andrews let out a sigh. "I'll tell you something about Kanak Roe that I don't think I've told anyone else."

"What's that?"

"I went deep-sea fishing with him once, oh, this was a little over four years ago."

"Didn't know you were into fishing."

"I was thinking about jumping to the private sector back then. I was coming up on my full twenty-five-year pension at the Bureau, and the bucks even the young punks made at Gamma were twice what the

Bureau paid. I was hoping that if I got to know Roe better it might help my chances. Unfortunately, he died before I was ready to apply. And under Kasimira's regime I didn't make the cut." He glanced sideways at Decker. "You were right, they considered me 'an inside-the-box thinker and too bureaucratic.' She'd hire you in a heartbeat."

"Go on."

"We had a good day out on the boat. His buddy, Danny Garcia, came along with us. We had our beers and caught a couple of marlins and nearly landed a big-ass tuna. We were heading back and I was feeling good about things when he told me."

"Told you what?"

"That he'd just been diagnosed with late-stage pancreatic cancer." He looked at Decker probingly. "You don't seem surprised."

"Garcia told me about it."

"Right. Anyway, he seemed to be in a contemplative mood. I guess anyone would be with death staring them in the face. He said he had about a year, eighteen months if he was lucky."

"And what else did he say?"

"Just so you know, he never really came out and said anything definitive." He stared at Decker. "But I think he wanted to make amends for something, Decker. Something he'd done in the past. End-of-life kind of remorse and penance, I guess. It happens."

"Yes, it does. Anything specific?"

"No. If there had been I would have told you before now. And frankly I didn't see how anything having to do with Kanak would be relevant to this case."

"Remorse. Recent or far in the past?"

"I don't know. He did mention his daughter. How proud he was of her. But there was something there, something else. I just couldn't put my finger on it."

"Try. Best guess."

Andrews's face screwed up in pain for a moment. His hand went to a control on one of the lines going into him and he hit a button. "Thank God for morphine."

"Yeah."

"My guess was he didn't really know if his daughter was the right person to carry the firm into the future."

"Why not? She seems very competent. Highly professional and intelligent. And driven."

"Maybe *too* driven," said Andrews.

"Meaning?"

"Meaning she might push the envelope too far. Way too far. Right over the cliff, in fact."

"Are you saying what I think you're saying?"

"If you're thinking that I'm suggesting she might have had something to do with her father's disappearance, then yeah, maybe that's what I'm saying."

CHAPTER

50

WHITE LANDED IN DC AND immediately took a cab to the Washington Field Office, or WFO as it was referred to at the Bureau. There she met with John Talbott and brought him up to speed on the case and also what she was doing back in DC.

"You okay working this with just Decker?" he said.

"Yes sir. I'm fine with that."

She didn't like the way he looked at her at all.

"He's a good agent," said White unprompted.

"If a little unorthodox."

"I think Decker and I have it under control. And the local police are involved as well. Sometimes too many cooks in the kitchen, you know."

"*Your* call, Agent White."

For some reason she couldn't explain, Talbott seemed pleased by all this.

After arranging for a series of appointments with people she needed to speak to, White called her mother on her way to the first meeting.

"How are the kids?" she asked.

"Missing Momma, of course, but all right. In school and hopefully working hard. How are things with you?"

"I'm actually in DC. I'll be up tonight to see you and the kids."

"That's wonderful. And how are you and your new partner doing?" her mother asked.

"We had a come-to-Jesus meeting and things seem to have smoothed out."

"And the case?"

"It's coming. Slowly."

"Well, I'll let you get back to it then, honey."

* * *

White's first interview was with Felicia Campbell, who had taken Alice Lancer's position as communications director at the Kingston Group, the lobbying firm headquartered on K Street. The place looked busy and prosperous. Campbell was in her thirties and full of energy.

"It was awful news about Alice," she said as they sat in her spacious office, which held the usual business trophies and pictures of her with what were probably politicians and other clients.

"And how did you learn about her death?" asked White.

"I saw it on the news. And someone posted it on the firm's social media accounts."

"What can you tell me about her?"

"We only overlapped for about a year. Even though she was a full-fledged lobbyist by then, she helped me learn the ropes. I've recently been promoted from communications director to a lobbyist here, and on a fast track to partnership."

"Congratulations. Lancer?"

"She was great at her job. Everyone liked Alice. She was really moving up."

"So why did she leave?"

"You know, I asked myself that more than once. Never found a good answer."

"Did you ever ask her?"

"She left somewhat abruptly." She paused. "I...I thought..." She looked warily at White.

"You thought there might have been some problem?"

"Not really, I mean, I never heard of anything."

"Is there anyone here that might have heard of... *anything*?"

"Mr. Drake might be able to help you."

"And who is Mr. Drake?"

"Jerome Drake is one of the founding partners. He and Alice worked closely together."

"Look forward to talking to him."

* * *

Jerome Drake was a soft-spoken, morose-looking fellow who let his gaze glide over White for a few moments before looking out the window of his corner office. The contrast between him and the energetic Campbell was startling.

"So, whatever you can tell me about Alice Lancer," began White.

"I'm not sure I can tell you anything."

"Sounds like there's a choice in there somewhere."

"Look, tell me what you want to know and then I can make that choice."

"Why did Alice Lancer leave here? She seemed to be doing so well."

"In some ways Alice was complicated, in other ways quite simple."

"You're going to have to elaborate on that."

"Alice liked success. She liked the best things in life."

"Was that the simple or the complicated?" asked White.

"As you might imagine, that was the simple part."

"And the complicated?"

"*How* she got the best things in life."

"I assume she made a good living with your firm. Then she left and joined a private security outfit in Miami. I imagine she took a pay cut with the career switch."

"She wasn't poorly compensated, I can tell you

that. Even as our communications director she made six figures. She made a lot more as a lobbyist."

"But it wasn't enough?"

"Apparently not."

"So where did it get complicated?"

He fidgeted and wouldn't meet her eye.

"She's dead, Mr. Drake. She can't sue you. I just need the truth."

He sat up straighter and said, "There is a lot of confidential information that comes through a firm like this. Part of what we do is oppo research. We perform it on opponents, but we also do it on our own clients. The theory being if we know what the dirt is, we can control and spin it. Some of it may later be leaked intentionally and strategically and with the client's permission. Some is given straight out to make a point."

"And some?" said White.

"Should never see the light of day."

"And Lancer used this to her advantage?"

"I speculate that she did. On at least two occasions."

"Can you tell me more about these instances?"

"Only that the two clients in question dropped this firm like a hot potato and would never say a word about it afterward."

"And you suspect...what?"

"I suspect that Alice Lancer used confidential

information to blackmail these clients. They paid her off but then they, understandably, cut all ties with this firm."

"Why wouldn't they have gone to the police instead?"

"Politics is a nasty business, Agent White. Dirt and mud are thrown all the time. Sometimes it sticks, sometimes it doesn't."

"But there are limits?"

"Yes, there are. And I think what Lancer had found breached those limits. The clients wouldn't go to the authorities with something that might land *them* in jail or destroy their careers."

"But why would clients ever give you, a priest, or even an attorney or anyone else confidential information of such a nature?"

"Who says they *gave* it to Alice?"

Now White sat up straighter. "She went out and found it, you mean?"

"She and whoever else she was working with."

"You have any names on that score?"

He shook his head.

"Knowing what you knew, why wasn't she fired from this place?"

"We came to a mutually advantageous separation."

"And you obviously didn't warn her new firm about her transgressions."

"As I said, we came to an agreement."

White stared at him as he looked down at his hands.

"Whatever she had on *you*, was it *that* bad?" she asked.

"I'm afraid I have to end this meeting, Agent White."

CHAPTER

51

WHITE'S NEXT TRIP TOOK HER to Capitol Hill, where she met with a rep from the police force.

Ed Nash was bald, trim, and straight backed. He looked no-nonsense and turned out to be just that.

"I remember Alan Draymont," he said. "You said he got killed?"

"At the house of a federal judge."

"Why was he guarding a judge? I thought that was what the U.S. Marshals did."

"It's complicated." White chose her words carefully. "What if I told you—hypothetically, of course—that Draymont was there for another reason unrelated to protecting the judge?"

A disgusted look swept over Nash's face. "Let me guess. Draymont was screwing her?"

"Why did that occur to you?"

He leaned forward. "I'm not into breaking confidences, but let me throw *you* a hypothetical. What would you say if I told you that while he was here some of the congresswomen and their female staffers in this building had Draymont *guard* them, too?"

"How exactly would that work?"

"DC is expensive. Quite a few lawmakers choose to essentially live in their offices, though they tried to ban that, but when do politicians listen to rules? So, they can have cozy and private meeting places after hours. And a lot of them share apartments and town houses nearby. But they're almost always out of town, so those places can be empty, too, a lot."

"What did Draymont get out of it?"

"Besides the obvious, you mean?"

"Yeah, besides that."

"Draymont kept his ear to the ground. Stuff he heard, maybe he used to his advantage."

"Like having affairs with married lawmakers?"

"I know he dressed nice and always seemed to have a lot of cash. Look, we had no proof of that or the hammer would have come down, I promise," he hastily added. "But you can't get rid of somebody here based on speculation. He covered his tracks well."

"You would think the ladies would have wised up or warned others off."

"I think that's exactly what happened. Because when we finally had enough complaints and asked Draymont to voluntarily resign, he put up no fight."

"But you didn't ding his record?"

"No, we didn't," admitted Nash. "It wasn't worth

the trouble. Besides, police forces are so hard up for cops he would have had no trouble getting another job even if we had trashed him."

"He didn't go back to being a cop. He went down to Florida and was hired by Gamma Protection Services."

Nash looked intrigued. "Kanak Roe's shop?"

"Yeah, that's right. You knew him?"

"I was just a twenty-year-old rookie cop in the Uniformed Division of the Secret Service when he was an agent there. That's before I came over here. Of course I know the success he had in the private sector. Heard him speak at some conferences, and he'd come back for Secret Service reunions every now and then. Didn't he die or something?"

"Or something. You know a lady named Alice Lancer?"

He thought for a few moments. "No, doesn't ring a bell. Who is she?"

"Worked at Gamma with Draymont."

"Was he bedding her, too?"

"Not sure. But she worked on Capitol Hill as a lobbyist for a while, and had the rep for keeping her ear to the ground and maybe profiting off it, just like Draymont." White pulled out her phone, found the photo, and held it up. "This is Lancer. She would have been younger, of course, when you might have seen her."

Nash said, "Yeah, I recognize her. I never knew her name, but I would see her at the Capitol from time to time. Good-looking woman."

Not anymore, thought White. "She worked for a lobbying firm, the Kingston Group, on K Street."

"Bloodsuckers. So, she and Draymont were a couple, huh?"

"And maybe a lot more. Did you ever see her and Draymont together?"

"No, but I probably wouldn't have. For years I've been mostly behind a desk."

"Did Draymont have any buddies on the force that he might have hung out with? They might know."

Nash picked up his phone. "I think I know just the guy."

White smiled. "You seem very eager to help me. I'm not complaining. But it is unusual."

Nash punched in the number. "I didn't like Alan Draymont. Now, don't get me wrong, I'm not happy he's dead, but if I can help you clear this matter up, I will."

* * *

Five minutes later a man in his early thirties entered the office. He wore the uniform of a Capitol Hill police officer.

"Agent White, this is Officer Stan Daniels."

They shook hands, and White showed him the picture of Lancer and asked about her and Draymont.

"Oh sure, Alice. Yeah, she and Alan were a thing. I mean, I think they were."

"Why the ambivalence?" asked White.

"He told me they were sleeping together, but Alan was sleeping with every skirt that came by. So I hesitate to call them a couple. She'd sometimes be there when I'd go by Alan's place."

"How did they meet?" asked White.

"I'm not really sure. I know she was on the Hill a lot, and of course so was Alan. She was really pretty and dressed kind of sexy, and Alan, well, like I said."

"Yeah, anything in a skirt. You ever hear them talking about stuff that seemed weird?"

Daniels looked confused. "How do you mean?"

"Stuff that sounded more like a business rather than only a sexual relationship?"

"Funny you should say that. They certainly were into gossip. They knew everything that was happening in DC, I can tell you that. I mean, folks in politics and so on."

"Anything else?"

"I went over to his place one time. The door was open so I just let myself in. Nobody was around. Alan's laptop was open on the table. I just took a peek. It was like a spreadsheet with names and, I don't know, information on each of them."

"What kind of information?"

"I couldn't really say. It was about that time I heard someone coming. I went back over to the door and pretended to open it as though I were just coming in. It was Alice walking in from the other room. She saw me and then went over and closed the laptop."

"What did you take all that to mean?"

"That they were up to something, I just didn't know what."

Nash looked at White. "I guess that's your job to find out. And I don't envy you one bit."

CHAPTER

52

GLORIA CHASE LIVED IN AN upscale part of Ocean View and only a short drive from her boyfriend, Dennis Langley. It was also about a twenty-minute drive to Cummins's house. She was a knockout in her midthirties, with long blond hair and perceptive blue eyes. She had on a short white skirt that, by contrast, emphasized her long, tanned legs. Her home was expensive and the woman seemed the same to Decker.

His creds got him in the front door, and they sat across from each other in a small, light-filled space off the kitchen.

"Are you a lawyer as well?" he asked.

"No, I have my own business. An internet services platform to help startups in Florida. Business is booming. I'm printing money."

"Congrats! The Aston Martin outside looks new."

"It is. I understand you want to talk about Dennis."

"That's right."

"I'm sure he told you that he spent the night with me when Julia Cummins was killed."

"He did."

"Dennis wouldn't hurt a fly," she said.

"No flies *were* hurt. It was his ex-girlfriend who was murdered."

She shifted, crossed her legs, and did the same with her arms. A classic defensive posture during questioning. Decker had expected to see it at some point, just not this soon.

"When did he get to your house that night?"

"Oh, around eight."

"And when did he leave?"

"The next morning. He was due in court."

"He never left you that night?" asked Decker.

"To use the bathroom."

"But he never left the house?"

She looked a little less certain and a little more defiant. "He ran to the liquor store to get some more gin."

"How long was he gone?"

"Fifteen-twenty minutes, tops."

"What time was this?"

"Around midnight."

"Twenty minutes, you're sure?" he asked.

"Yes! It's the all-night place down on the right before you turn into my neighborhood. Ricardos."

"He ever get physical with you? Abusive?"

"Never. If he did, it would be over in two seconds. I don't tolerate that."

"Some men don't care if women don't like it."

"Dennis is not that kind of guy. He's very nice and gentle."

"A gentle man with a gun."

"He has every right to protect himself."

"Did he ever mention Julia Cummins to you?" he asked.

"A few times. And I met her once."

Decker stiffened. "Really, when was that?"

"Dennis and I had been dating for maybe a month. We were at a restaurant, a little French bistro in Naples called Café Midi. She was there."

"Alone?" said Decker.

"No, she had some kid with her."

"Kid?"

"I call him a kid, but he was huge. Looked like an athlete."

"Her son, Tyler." Decker showed her a photo on his phone.

"Yeah, that's him."

"Was there anyone else with her?"

"Yes, an older woman. Rail thin with badly permed hair, and she reeked of alcohol."

"Doris Kline?"

"I don't know. She never said her name. But she looked three sheets to the wind."

"So, what happened?"

"Dennis took me over to their table and we said

hello. Frankly, I think Dennis did it to sort of show me off to Cummins."

"How did she react?"

"She was pleasant. We spoke for a bit and that was it. We left."

"What was your impression of the judge?" asked Decker.

"She seemed very put together. I could see why Dennis would be attracted to her. Her friend was a very different sort. I wouldn't have necessarily put them together."

"They're neighbors. Did you speak to Tyler?"

"No, but he did give me the eye." She smiled demurely. "He's clearly a red-blooded American male."

"Anything else you can tell me?"

"Just that I'm certain Dennis had nothing to do with what happened. I've dated guys who could be violent, creepy, and controlling, Agent Decker. They try to hide it but they give off a definite vibe after a while. Dennis has none of that."

"Some hide it better than others."

"I think you're barking up the wrong tree."

"I bark up lots of trees. Till I find the right one."

"I understand that a man was also found dead at her house," she said.

"That's right."

"Were they dating?" Chase asked.

"I'm not sure."

"How can you not be sure? Didn't anyone know?"

"It's complicated," replied Decker.

"I guess murder is often complicated."

"Actually, the act of murder is usually pretty simple. It's everything else that's complicated."

CHAPTER

———

53

HEY, TYLER, IS YOUR DAD home?" asked Decker.

Tyler had just answered his knock on the condo door. He had on khaki shorts and an untucked short-sleeved shirt.

"He's getting ready. We're going out to dinner."

"Mind if I come in and wait?"

"I guess not."

He led Decker into an adjoining room and they sat down. A storm was forming out over the Gulf. Its framing in the broad windows served as a capable analogy to what was going on in Decker's head.

"How's the investigation going?" mumbled Tyler. "Have you found out stuff?"

"We're getting there. Do you remember a guy and a woman coming up to you at a restaurant in Naples called Café Midi?" When Tyler looked uncertain, he added, "I think Doris Kline was with you, and the woman was tall, blond, and beautiful. You sort of ran your gaze over her." He kept his tone diplomatic.

Tyler grinned. "Oh, yeah. Her. Damn, I mean,

wow. She was, like, wow. And she was falling out of that dress. I wish I'd gotten a picture of her."

"Yeah. Did you know the guy?"

"No. But from how he and my mom were talking, I supposed he was a lawyer. They were talking like that anyway."

"Actually, he and your mom had dated."

Tyler looked surprised. "Really? Then it was a good thing Dad hadn't joined us yet."

"Wait a minute, your father was there?"

"He was just coming in, I think, when the guy and the lady were getting ready to leave."

"Why was your father having dinner with you and your mother?"

"It was my birthday."

"Did your father overhear anything from the man?"

"I don't know. Hell, all my attention was on the woman, if you want to know the truth. But he came up to the table right after they walked off. So Dad had to be close by. Why? What does that matter?"

"It might not."

"Tyler?" a voice called out.

"In here, Dad."

A few moments later Barry Davidson walked into the room, adjusting the cuffs of his white dress shirt. He had on dark gray slacks and brown tasseled loafers.

"What are you doing here?" he asked when he spied Decker.

"Just a few more questions, Mr. Davidson."

"Tyler and I are going out to dinner. And when the hell are you going to release Julia's remains? We have to...we have to do the service." He glanced anxiously at his son. "She...she wanted to be cremated."

"It won't be long," replied Decker.

Davidson slumped down in a chair after mixing himself a drink from the bar against the wall. Tyler silently watched him do this, his features full of disgust.

"What questions?" asked Davidson.

"I'm going to tell you some things in return for information."

"What things?"

"The man who was killed at your ex-wife's home was not protecting her. He was sleeping with her."

Tyler blurted out, "What? Sleeping with Mom?"

Decker kept his gaze on Davidson. "You don't look surprised, Mr. Davidson."

"Julia could do what she wanted. It's none of my business."

"Did you know about their...relationship?"

"No, but like I said, she could do what she wanted."

"But she obviously wanted to keep it on the Q.T."

"What do you mean, specifically?"

"She used this subterfuge that she had been receiving threats to explain his being there."

"But she *had* been getting threats," interjected Tyler. "She told me so. Right, Dad?"

"Is that what she told you, Mr. Davidson?"

"I already answered that question. She never got back to me when I texted her about it."

"I just wanted to give you the opportunity to amend your answer, if need be."

"I have no reason to change what I already told you," he said icily. "Check my phone records. I sent the one text. I haven't called her in weeks."

"I also have heard that you still loved your ex. And you told me that you hoped to reconcile with her."

"Dad?" said Tyler. "Is that true?"

Davidson wouldn't look at his son. "Okay, I told you that, but in my heart of hearts I knew it was over. I've moved on with my life. The divorce was years ago." He rose. "Now, if there's nothing else, Tyler and I need to head out or we'll be late for our reservation."

"You drive a Mercedes S600?"

"Yes."

"There are cameras in the garage here?"

"Yes, and if you check the film you'll see that my Mercedes never left the garage. And I didn't take Tyler's car, either. And there is no record of me going through Julia's gate."

Decker gave him a piercing look. "You checked?"

"I should have said I *know* there is no record of me

going through the gate, since I never left the condo, as I told you before."

"I told you all that, Agent Decker," chimed in Tyler. "My dad *was* here. I heard him. I would've known if he had left."

Davidson said heatedly, "And do you really think I could have butchered my wife and then gotten back here and then calmly held a meeting? You could check with my business clients. I wasn't covered in fucking blood when I did the Zoom call!"

"Dad!" exclaimed Tyler. "Calm down. You didn't kill her, okay?"

Decker took all this in and then said, "Who said she was *butchered*?"

Davidson glanced anxiously at his son. "You…you said she'd been stabbed. You told me that," he added.

"Oh, I *remember* exactly what I said. But I didn't say 'butchered.' In fact, I didn't say how many times she had been stabbed. It could have been only once."

Davidson nervously licked his lips. "And what about the man? Was he stabbed, too?"

Decker rose. "I guess you two had better get on to your dinner."

CHAPTER

54

As Decker was driving back to the hotel his phone buzzed.

When he answered White said, "Good, you're still alive. I didn't want to have to break in a new partner so soon."

"Find anything useful?" asked Decker.

She took a few minutes to fill him on what she had learned about Draymont and Lancer.

"So partners in blackmail from way back?"

"And both forced to pull their tent and go play in another sandbox," she said.

"Florida made sense for Lancer, since her mother was here. I wonder why Gamma?"

"They just need dirty little secrets, and they're off and running."

"And being part of an investigation firm would be a great platform to get those secrets," agreed Decker. "So, they met on Capitol Hill but we don't know exactly how?"

"She was lobbying and he was protecting."

"And they were both doing a side business."

"Maybe they were initially doing it separately and then that's what drew them together."

"Maybe," said Decker.

"So what did *you* find out?"

Decker told her about his meetings with Gloria Chase and Barry and Tyler Davidson.

"So Langley and Gloria Chase actually ran into Judge Cummins at this restaurant?"

"Yeah. And Barry Davidson might have seen and overheard it, too."

"You think he knew about them dating?"

"It's kind of a small town. Tyler was surprised by it, but his dad didn't seem to be. And despite what he told us about wanting to reconcile with Cummins, he said he'd gotten on with his life, but he was obviously lying. And another thing." He told her about Davidson's use of the word *butchered*.

"No way he could have known that," said White. "We held that detail back."

"He claims he just assumed that from my telling him that she had been stabbed."

"Do you buy that?"

"No more than I did his moving on with his life."

"So you think he had her killed somehow?"

"I don't know. Could he have made it over there in time to kill her and then get back for his next Zoom?

I guess it's possible. But Tyler was adamant that his father never left the condo that night."

"The ME was really certain on the timing of the deaths. Even without Tyler's alibi it would have been really tight for Barry to commit the murders. And then to just do a Zoom meeting right after?"

"Yeah, he actually made that point." He paused. "How are your kids?"

"I'm driving up to Baltimore to see them now. I plan to fly back down in the morning, unless there's anything else you want me to check up here."

"I guess not. You've done good work. We now know they were running a blackmail scheme up there and they were probably running one down here."

"Any word on Kelly's killer?"

"None. They found a car abandoned about five miles away. No plates and wiped clean, not a print on the damn thing. Whoever it was is long gone by now."

"Unless they're hanging around to take shots at us."

"That could be," agreed Decker.

"So watch yourself. Alex also told me you don't really care about your own safety when you're on a case."

"Yeah, I've been trying to work on that."

"How's Andrews?"

"I went by to see him. He told me that he tried to get a job with Gamma but was rejected."

"Shit, are you kidding me? And he still worked the case?"

"I think he's feeling some guilt for that one. But he's on the bench anyway with his wound. He said that he went fishing with Kanak Roe four years ago and the man told him about his terminal illness. He told me that Roe seemed to want to make amends for some things he'd done in his life, only he didn't tell Andrews what they were. He also thinks Roe wasn't sure his daughter was the one to lead Gamma into the future. She might cut corners too much. And he intimated something else."

"What?"

"That the daughter might have had something to do with her father's disappearance."

"What! Do you believe that?"

"No, but I don't disbelieve it, either. Say hello to your family. And then get back down here. I need you."

White clicked off.

And smiled broadly at his last remark.

CHAPTER

55

AN HOUR-AND-A-HALF ride later in heavy traffic White arrived in Baltimore. It was after ten and she was tired but also excited. She drove to her row house and parked out front. She had phoned ahead, and Calvin and Jacky were waiting at the front door for her.

After hugs and kisses and more hugs she took them upstairs.

Her son Calvin was growing fast. He took after his father in height and build, she noted grudgingly.

"Wait till you see this, Mom," he said.

He ran to his room and came out a few moments later holding up a martial arts belt.

"I got my green belt in Tae Kwon Do. And the teacher said I'll be ready for my purple pretty soon."

"That is so great, Cal," said White.

"I'll have my black belt in a few years and then I'll go for my double like you have in karate."

He assumed a defensive stance and smiled at her.

She grinned back and matched his posturing while Jacky watched and clapped.

"Okay, show me what you got," said White.

He did some kicks and punches and she backed up, pretending that she couldn't block them, but smiling at how accurate and smooth his technique was.

"You might be getting that black belt sooner than you think," she said, although her voice had gotten huskier and her eyes started to water.

He got his green belt when I was out of town. My mother had to take him. Because I wasn't there.

She got them into bed, and the kids told her about their days since she had been gone. They went over school and friends and special projects and sports and maybe getting a cat because Jacky really wanted one, but Calvin wasn't sure about that because he might have allergies.

She talked about the family possibly moving to DC. The kids were alarmed by this, because they didn't want to leave their friends. But she told them it wouldn't happen any time soon. She would just make the commute with some other FBI personnel she knew who were in similar situations.

After that she told them a couple of funny stories and then turned off the light. She sat with them until they fell asleep, then kissed them and left. But she stopped at the doorway, turned, and stared at her two greatest creations.

It should be three, actually.

She felt the catch in her throat, and the wobble in her chest. She could feel her heart rate speed up.

Shit!

She put a hand against the doorjamb to steady herself as she felt the anxiety build. Another panic attack was coming on, but she fought against it, taking deep breaths, thinking about good things, willing her racing heart to slow the hell down. She felt shame, she felt weak. It made her angry, which didn't help matters at all.

She walked quickly to the bathroom and washed her face and let her belly settle along with her nerves. Like some working mothers, she worried she was doing them irreparable harm by being away so much. She was missing important moments in their lives. She wasn't thinking about big things; she was thinking about being around in the morning to make them breakfast, which she planned to do before she left for the airport. But how many other such times had she missed?

Too many.

And hurried late-night catchups were just not going to cut it. But what was she supposed to do? Quit her job? Ask for a nine-to-five desk assignment that would require no travel? That was not how the Bureau worked. Not if she wanted to keep moving up. And she did. Otherwise, what was the point?

She felt an attack coming on again, and she sat on the toilet lid doing meditative breathing and thinking of spending time with her kids, until she got herself back together.

Downstairs her mother was waiting with a pot of tea and a plate of graham crackers. They had been her favorites since White was a kid.

Serena Washington was taller than her daughter and fuller figured, but their features were similar; her mother's eyes were quick and took everything in, just like White's.

"Are you coming down with something, Frederica? You look a little out of it."

"I'm okay, just a little tired." She turned so her mother couldn't see her eyes. Her reddened eyes, her unnerved look.

"And did you accomplish what you came back up here for?" asked Washington.

"I accomplished enough. I head back to Florida tomorrow." She looked around. "I wish I had something stronger than tea."

"Then I got your back on that."

Her mother rose and came back with a bottle of scotch and two tumblers. She poured out the drinks and set one in front of her daughter. "My grandbabies are doing fine. But they miss you."

"I know they do. If I didn't have bills to pay I'd spend all my time with them."

"They would hate that. Buffers make the hearts grow fonder. Closeness is a buzzkill."

"Is that how you and Daddy worked it?"

"Yes, only I had to keep reminding him. Your father didn't like buffers between him and his kids."

"You worked, too."

"But at your school. It was different. I saw quite a lot of you all." She added with a mischievous smile, "For better or worse."

"I just want my children to grow up to be good people who will take care of their momma in her old age. Or at least come by and visit me at the nursing home."

Washington glanced away at this light-hearted remark, and White bit her lip.

"I'm sorry, Momma, that came out way wrong."

"In baseball, hitting three hundred in your career might get you into the Hall of Fame. As a parent, hitting four hundred just means you failed at everything."

"Daddy getting killed like that, it messed with Randall and Frank," White said. "They were younger and went through hell. Half the town hated us and thought the racist asshole that killed Daddy got cheated somehow. And Randall and Frank got the brunt of it. I was nearly out of high school when it happened. Denise and Teddy were already in college. You were suddenly a single parent with five kids.

And two of them were getting torn up every day by something they and you had no control over. What could you do about that?"

"I don't make excuses for myself, Frederica, and you shouldn't make excuses for me."

They took sips of their scotch and let it go down slow and smooth.

White felt her anxiety rising again and took another sip.

Smooth and slow, girl. You got this. You have to have this.

Her mother reached over and gripped her hand. The two women's gazes met, and in that look White knew her mother understood exactly what was going on with her daughter.

"I'm terrified I'm going to mess up with them, you know," said White breathlessly.

"The babies will be fine."

"They're not babies, Momma. They're over halfway to adulthood. Lots of things can go wrong. And I can't expect you to always be there for me or them."

"Calvin and Jacky are my flesh and blood. You think there's anything I won't do for them?"

White looked away and shut her eyes. *If I screw up with my kids? If they turn out to go down the path that my younger brothers did? If one of them does, I'm batting five hundred and I'll be a failure at the most important job I'll ever have.*

"You will not mess up with them, Frederica. You won't allow yourself to, and I sure as hell won't let you."

White opened her eyes to see her mother staring at her with the assured look of the assistant principal she used to be.

"You promise?"

"Honey, I don't have to promise, do I? I'm here. Walk the walk, bullshit is just talk."

White nodded and squeezed her mother's hand before letting it go.

Her mother said, "So, how are things with this Decker fellow?"

"Better, actually. He told me to tell all of you hello."

"So, you said he lost his child too?"

White's gaze drifted from the half finger of scotch she had left, to her mother's large, watchful eyes. "Yes, he did."

"Then you two can understand each other."

White's brow furrowed at the statement. "What do you mean?"

"Understanding from a loss like that, Frederica. You don't get the real person from good times. You get them from the bad times, the awful ones. You both got your hearts broken and in some ways they can never be repaired. I know. I had mine broken. But that's also a bond between two people; you have something powerful in common. You can use that to turn a horrible event into maybe something positive. For both of you."

White looked incredulously at her mother. "We're just professional colleagues, Momma. We do a *job* together. No more and no less. We're not going to be besties. We're way different people even if we had similar losses. And I don't even know if I really like the man. So don't make it into something it's not. And don't tell me to go and *pray* on it. I don't have the time or the inclination. In case you didn't know, I have a lot on my plate."

"Well, if that's all you want to see in it," her mother said in a disappointed tone.

"I think that's all I *can* see in it. You don't know him like I do. And I don't really know Decker at all."

"I think you know him better than you think. At least in the most important ways."

"Why do you care about that?"

"I care about that, because I care about *you*."

CHAPTER

56

DECKER WAS JUST ABOUT TO go to sleep when his phone rang.

He didn't answer it right away because it seemed every time he did, something bad happened.

"Hello?"

Kasimira Roe said, "I need to see you."

"When?"

"Now."

"Why?" asked Decker.

"It's important."

"I'm not driving to Miami tonight."

"You don't have to. I'm in your hotel lobby."

Decker rose, dressed, and was downstairs in the span of a few minutes.

Roe was nervously pacing by the receptionist's desk. She wore jeans, low-heeled boots, and a white blouse. Her long dark hair was pinned up into a bun.

"What's so important? And how did you know where I was staying?"

"I run an investigation firm. Can we sit in my car?"

She led him outside and over to a black Porsche SUV. She climbed in and Decker wedged himself into the passenger seat.

He looked over at her. "Okay? What's up?"

"I heard what happened to Doug Andrews."

"He'll be okay. So you also heard what happened to Patty Kelly, the judge's secretary?"

"Yes."

He didn't tell her that Kelly was Lancer's biological mother. He suspected she might already know.

"Look, I haven't been entirely forthcoming with you," she conceded.

"Hell, don't tell me that. I might have a heart attack from the shock."

"I guess I deserved that."

"Yes, you did."

She glanced apprehensively at him. "Despite the positive things I said about Alice Lancer, I had some *misgivings* about her."

"Such as?"

"Her honesty, for one."

"Well, that's a big one. Talk to me about your misgivings."

"We had a client who complained. This was a few months ago."

"And the nature of the complaint?"

"That an item had gone missing during the course of Gamma protecting her."

"Lancer doesn't work in the field."

"It wasn't Alice. It was Draymont, but with Alice directly supervising."

"What item?"

"A necklace. A valuable one."

"Why did the client suspect Draymont?"

"She claimed he was the only one other than herself in the house when the jewelry went missing."

"What did you do?"

"I confronted Alice about it. She vouched for Draymont, said the allegations were untrue. That the woman was unreliable and was perhaps looking for a way to not pay us."

"Why was she getting protection?"

"Her husband was working overseas and had been threatened. He was the CEO of a subsidiary of a major U.S. company. The threats extended to his family. The company hired us."

"So the couple wasn't even paying the bill?"

"No, but Alice wouldn't necessarily know the financial arrangements."

"Which made you suspect she was lying?"

"Yes. And the necklace later turned up in a raid on a fencing operation."

"So maybe Draymont was innocent."

"No, I don't believe so. The fencing operation wasn't even in Florida. The necklace was sold to them. They are known to be a central clearing house for stolen property."

"Any firm evidence connecting either Lancer or Draymont with the stolen jewelry?"

"No."

"I don't know what you want me to do."

"I'm not sure, either." She glanced at him. "Have you found out anything that leads you to believe they were dishonest?"

"Why do I sense another fishing expedition by you? If so, I'm going back to bed."

"It's not that. I swear. This could be very serious for my business. If our reputation is no good...?"

"So your business is the most important thing in your life?"

"It was my father's business. And *he* was the most important thing in my life."

"What I can say is that from what we've uncovered, honesty did not seem to be a priority for either Lancer or Draymont." He looked at her. "Does that make you feel better or worse? I mean, they worked for you, after all."

"It doesn't make me feel great." She paused. "Have you found out anything about what happened to my father?"

"I made inquiries, like I told you. But I do have another case to work."

"I understand. I was just hoping that—"

"Why do I think there's something else hanging over your head?"

"Why do you say that?"

"Because you didn't have to drive all the way here at night to tell me what you just did. It all could have been said over the phone or via email. So *is* there something else? Because you look like you're going to throw up."

Her fingers anxiously played over the steering wheel. Then she started the engine and put on her seat belt. "Buckle up, we're going somewhere."

"Where?"

"To *show* you the answer to your question."

CHAPTER

57

IT WAS MIDNIGHT WHEN THEY pulled to a stop in the parking lot of a bargain-rate motel outside of Naples.

He looked at her, but Roe stared straight ahead.

"Okay," he said.

She turned to look at him. "I know that Alan Draymont was not a good person."

"You know personally?"

She nodded.

"Because he was blackmailing you?"

She nodded again.

"How?" he asked.

"You're with the FBI."

"So it's something illegal on your part?"

She remained rigid. "No, but it's not... something I'm proud of, either."

"Was Lancer involved as well?"

"What do you think?"

"They seemed to be quite the team, so my bet is yes. Two nasty peas in a pod." He looked at the motel. "What was the price you paid for them to keep your secret?"

"Payment was made in . . . several ways."

"One of them being here, with you doing something with Draymont you didn't want to do? In bed?"

She swallowed, perhaps choking back a sob. If he hadn't been watching her closely, Decker would have missed the barely perceptible nod of her head.

"How did Draymont find out?"

"I don't know for certain. He might have followed me."

"Followed you to where you did what you're not proud of?"

She let out a long breath and turned to him. "I went to the home of a wealthy, politically powerful, and *married* person in Miami. Later, Draymont showed me pictures, and recordings of . . . me and the person engaged in . . . certain acts. I have no idea how he managed that. I was quite shocked when he showed me."

"And did you know that Draymont *and* Lancer had a blackmail business going, in addition to what they had on you? And you looked the other way because they had you nailed to the wall, too?"

Tears seeped out from under her closed eyelids.

"I'll take that as a yes," said Decker. "And that was the other form of payment? You not exposing them?"

"Yes."

"And you didn't really push all that hard when the necklace went missing, did you? You said you confronted Lancer but you really didn't, did you?"

"No, I didn't. But I was upset. It was my business. At least with the blackmail they could keep their identities secret from their victims."

"But they didn't keep it secret from you. Draymont wanted you in his bed and they needed you to cover for their blackmail scheme."

"When you say it like that my culpability seems staggering."

"You realize that with blackmail it's a crime that keeps on giving, right?"

"I have handled blackmail cases on behalf of clients, so, yes, I am aware of that." She paused to wipe her eyes. "I just never imagined it would happen to me."

He sat back in his seat and let out a long sigh.

"Well?" she said, looking over at him. "Do you have anything to say?"

"Yeah. Now the payments *have* stopped. And you clearly had a motive to kill both Draymont and Lancer."

She leaned her head against the window. "I guess you're right about that."

"But if you did kill them, why come here and confess all this to me? If you had kept quiet no one ever would have known. You would have been free and clear."

"But not up here," said Roe, touching her temple.

"So why *did* you tell me?"

"I guess because if I want you to help me, I can't withhold the truth from you."

"You mean, not anymore, since you've been doing a real good job of it up till now."

"What are you going to do with what I've told you?"

"If you're worried about me exposing your secret, stop. I won't unless I have to in order to solve my case. I don't get kicks out of embarrassing people just for the hell of it. Now, on the blackmail piece I guess I could nail you as an accessory, but I'm down here to solve a series of murders, not get bogged down in that shit."

"I guess that's the best I could have hoped for."

"Do you love this married person?"

"I thought I did. But then I found out I was just a brief diversion from a troubled marriage."

"I'm sorry."

"If my father had ever known...it would have killed him. He was a very religious man. Adultery is a mortal sin."

"I'm not saying what you did was right. But you have to lead your own life, not the one your father may have wanted for you."

"It's...difficult to meet men when you're..."

"…a highly successful woman? Yeah, I've seen that. Not your problem, though. The fault lies with the guys. But we're not all like that, just so you know."

"But the results of their shortcomings impact squarely on women like *me*."

"I guess so. But the world of dating is not exactly my field of expertise."

"But catching killers is. And since Draymont and Lancer were blackmailing people, their targets would have motivation to kill them."

"Yes, they would. Do you have information to share on that score?"

"I might. Under certain conditions."

"Such as?"

"Such as you doing more to find out what happened to my father."

"Okay. Deal."

She looked surprised. "I didn't think you would give up that easily."

"I didn't give up squat."

"I don't understand," she said, clearly confused.

"I think whatever happened to your father *is* connected to my case. So if I solve one, I'll solve the other."

"How can you be so sure about that?"

"The currency of blackmail is money. Lancer and Draymont were in that business. The problem is they ran into a mark that bit back, hard. And stuffed that currency right down their throats. But not any old money; they used the currency of your father's homeland. So I'm thinking whatever Lancer and Draymont had on whoever killed them ties right back to Kanak Roe."

CHAPTER

58

LATE THE NEXT MORNING DECKER was waiting for White at the airport with a cup of coffee for her.

"Now *that's* service," said White, accepting the drink.

"Things to fill you in on," he said as they walked out of the terminal and got into the car.

He told White about his conversation with Kasimira Roe and the blackmailing done to her by Lancer and Draymont.

"Damn," she exclaimed. "That lady really held a lot back."

"She probably thought she was caught between a rock and a hard place. And she still has her father's disappearance to contend with."

"So we know what Draymont and Lancer were involved in. People would have motivation to kill them both."

"What about Judge Cummins?" asked Decker.

"I know you think it was two different killers, but I've never fully agreed with that. It makes a lot more sense if it were just the one."

"A lot more sense does not always equate to the truth."

"So, are we back at square one again?" she said.

"Do you think cases have this fine linear quality to them?"

"No, but it would be nice to be making *some* progress. Whoever killed them might have been blackmailed. That's a prime motivation. We just have to find out who that was and we have our murderer."

Decker didn't appear to be listening.

"I said—"

"I heard what you said. I agree that blackmail is the motivation. For at least the murders of Lancer and Draymont."

"But not Cummins?"

"Maybe a stronger motivation than blackmail."

"Which is?"

"I'll let you know when I think of it. And to my mind Langley's alibi is a little shaky."

"How so? Would he have had time to do the murders and get back to her house?"

"No, *if* Gloria Chase is telling the truth."

"And you have reason to think she's not?"

"We might find one," said Decker.

"Where are we going now?" she asked.

"To check on some money."

* * *

The internationally renowned investment house was large and distinguished and above reproach, or at least its marketing materials said so. Its Ocean View branch was housed in a granite building with marble floors and solid wooden walls and elaborate furnishings and other decorations. Oil paintings looked down upon Decker and White as they walked to their destination.

"Client commissions on the wall. Always does my heart good to see that," said Decker.

"Capitalism at its finest."

Julia Cummins's personal financial manager was Stuart Jones. He ushered them into his large corner office and offered them tea, coffee, and water, all of which they declined.

Jones was a man of fifty with hair so carefully styled, Decker thought he could see the gel still gleaming among the whitening strands. The man's suit was custom. His shoes looked expensive and no doubt were. His tie was a work of art. His teeth were too perfect to be real.

"It was awful what happened to Julia," he said as he plopped into his leather chair. "Just terrible."

"Yes it was. And we're trying to find those responsible for it," said Decker.

"And I wish you good luck and Godspeed on that," said Jones heartily.

"I alerted you in my phone call as to what we needed," said Decker.

"Yes, yes." Jones sat forward and coughed into his hand. "I hope you can understand that client confidentiality is our utmost priority."

"And I hope you can understand that finding who killed your client is our utmost priority," replied Decker. "So I think my ace beats your king."

Jones noticeably winced and looked down at his leather-topped desk. There wasn't a scrap of paper on it. Decker strongly suspected that it, like the office, was mainly for show. He had the impression of a bank of computers with proprietary algorithms loaded in doing the work that people like Jones would later take credit for.

But honestly what do I know? I don't have any money to invest.

"I understood from your phone call that you were thinking Julia was the target of some blackmail scheme?"

"She was wealthy. People are unscrupulous. That makes her a target."

"So you need to know if she made any large or irregular withdrawals or payments?"

"Yes."

Jones turned to a computer on his desk and started typing. "I would meet with her every quarter to go over her accounts. She was a very excellent investor and client. Her net worth was growing by leaps and bounds. It was so exciting."

"Yeah, I'm getting all tingly just hearing you talk about it," said White, the comment drawing a rare smile from Decker.

Jones continued, "For any truly large transfers she would have had to get on the recorded line and authorize it. That ensures there are no mistakes and the client intends for the transfer to happen."

"And that covers your end, too," said Decker. "No liability."

"Yes, that's right."

"So you would know if she made any large transfers," said Decker.

"Yes, but she could have done it through her checking account. I don't monitor that as regularly. And after all, it is her money."

He scrolled through some screens and shook his head. "I see nothing out of the ordinary. And I've gone back six months."

"All right," said Decker. "Are there any transfers of monies or checks written to Alice Lancer, Alan Draymont, or Gamma Protection Services?"

Jones typed a search request in and waited a few moments. "No, nothing under those names."

"And no large cash withdrawals?"

"No. Those would have been flagged. So, it doesn't look like she was being blackmailed," said Jones.

"Well, blackmail doesn't always involve payments of money," noted White.

"Right, yes." Jones suddenly looked alarmed. "Oh my God, right. Oh, I hope that Julia...I mean..."

"Thank you for your help," said Decker.

Outside, White said, "Well, that was a dead end."

"No, it checked a box."

"So if they weren't blackmailing her, how did Cummins and Draymont hook up?"

"I think *you* already gave the answer to that. We just came here to rule out the blackmail piece."

White looked surprised. "*I* already gave the answer?"

"I think Draymont *caught* Cummins's eye. You used the phrase to explain how Lancer and Draymont hooked up on Capitol Hill."

"Yeah, that's right. Young and handsome. It happens. But with Cummins?"

"Gamma worked protection in her neighborhood for other clients, including the Perlmans right next door. They recommended Gamma to Cummins when she asked about getting security protection. And we've confirmed that Draymont was part of her security rotation. Maybe Cummins simply saw him and became infatuated. And from what I've heard of Draymont, he could be very charismatic, and the man would not hesitate to jump into bed with a rich, lovely woman like Cummins."

"Okay, but then why the whole rigmarole about her needing protection because of threats? I know we went over this before, but it still seems a muddle."

"She really didn't want someone to know she was dating or sleeping with other men. Look at the precautions she took with Dennis Langley. They drove all the way to Miami to have sex in a hotel. He was never invited over to her house. But the only way she could get Draymont into *her* house was by pretending he was protecting her. That was probably another appeal for her to latch on to Draymont. He had that cover built right into his job."

"Decker, she must have really been afraid of someone to go to all those lengths."

"Well, as it turned out, she was *right* to be afraid, wasn't she?"

"You still think it was her husband, don't you?"

"He's the most obvious choice. But he couldn't have done it personally. With the Zoom calls and Tyler's alibi for him. But he could have hired someone. Only we had his financial records pulled and they don't show any weird payments at all. I was thinking maybe crypto, but I have no idea how that even works. But he did use the term 'butchered.'"

"Maybe he had a friend kill his wife for free. That would explain the absence of payment."

"I don't think anybody has friends that good," observed Decker.

DECKER DROVE THEM BACK TO Cummins's neighborhood. They passed through the security gate and he stopped in front of Cummins's house.

"We going over the crime scene again?" asked White. "Because I do not want to find another body."

"No, this trip is a recon of the neighbors."

He led her up to the Perlmans' door and knocked. Trevor Perlman answered the door dressed in beige golf shorts and a white polo shirt.

"Any news on what happened with Julia?" he said.

"Still working on it."

"Where is the other agent?"

"In the hospital."

"Did he have an accident?"

"There was nothing accidental about it. Do you have some time for a few questions?"

"Actually, I don't. I'm about to join a golf foursome."

"Is your wife here?"

"Yes, but is this really necessary? We've told you all we know."

"Funny how people recall new things if you keep asking," said Decker.

Perlman turned and called out, "Maya, the FBI are here. I have to leave."

He said brusquely to Decker, "Please don't upset her."

They stepped into the house as Maya Perlman came into the foyer. She had on white slacks and a polka-dotted blouse with a matching bandanna around her hair. She did not seem happy to see them.

Trevor Perlman said, "I have to go, honey, I'm already late to tee off."

She nodded dumbly and he skittered off toward the garage. A few moments later Decker saw him fly out of the driveway on his spiffy burgundy golf cart.

Maya said, "This way."

She led them out onto the lanai, and they sat down around the pool. It was already eighty degrees and sunny.

"Weather like this all the time?" asked Decker.

"Mostly. It can get pretty unbearable in South Florida in July and August but that's what you have air-conditioning for. Now, what can I do for you?"

"Alan Draymont was having a sexual relationship with Julia Cummins."

She gaped. "You *must* be joking."

"We have conclusive proof of that. And your neighbor, Doris Kline, had already suspected that was the case."

"Doris never mentioned that to me."

"Probably just being discreet," interjected White.

"So we were wondering if while Draymont was guarding you, did Cummins ever come over or have any contact with him?" asked Decker.

Perlman sat back and pondered this. "Julia did come over for drinks and dinner several times while we had protection. We talked about the reasons they were there. She was very supportive and lamented that I was having to go through this. Draymont might have been on duty then. If so, she could have seen him or even spoken with him. He would walk a perimeter, check doors and windows, or sit out in his car for a bit. He would occasionally come into the house to check around and use the bathroom."

"And then she asked you about protection for herself at some point. When was that?"

"Oh, I'm not sure I remember exactly. It might have been over drinks."

"Was your husband with you?"

"I don't believe so. No, that's right, it was just Julia and me. We'd gone out for a drink."

"And she said she had gotten threats?" asked White.

"I'm not sure it was anything that direct."

"Or did she just want to know about the company providing the service?"

"She did ask for the name. And I gave it to her. Okay, now I remember. After we got back from drinks she and Trevor and I sat down and talked about it in more detail."

"Did she specifically ask about Draymont or any other particular person?"

"I don't think so. But Trevor did show her photos of the personnel who had guarded us."

"And was Draymont one of them?" He pulled his phone and showed her the photo of Draymont.

"Yes, I believe he was one of the ones we showed Julia."

"Did Cummins zero in on the guy?"

Perlman looked a little embarrassed. "Okay, yes, now I remember. She said…that he…looked like a hottie."

White and Decker exchanged glances. Decker said, "It would have been nice to know this when we spoke with you previously."

"I just remembered it. Besides, I had no idea they were sleeping together, so I attached no importance to the man. Are you really sure they were having sex?"

"Yes," said White. "Why do you find that so unlikely? He was young and handsome. And then there are the judge's own words about him being a hottie."

"I just thought Julia was a cut above that. I mean, sleeping with any man who walks into your house? I don't care how handsome he is. Plus, he was guarding her. That was totally unprofessional, and Julia was thoroughly professional."

"But he wasn't guarding her," Decker said. "She never hired Gamma. She only wanted Draymont's name because she was attracted to him."

"Good God," exclaimed Perlman. "Julia could have had any man she wanted and she went after a *security guard?*"

White gave the woman a withering glare but remained silent.

Decker said, "Dennis Langley is the man Cummins was dating until about six months ago. You knew she was seeing someone but didn't know his name. Is *he* up to snuff for you?"

She sat back, looking stunned. "Really? Dennis? I never saw him at her place. And Julia never said anything to me."

"You know him?"

"Of course. He's very well-known in the criminal defense bar, of which I used to be an active member. It's a small legal community, everyone knows everybody." She looked pensive. "I sometimes wondered why he never appeared before her."

"What can you tell us about him?"

"He's a good lawyer."

"And?"

"And he's been known to have an eye for the ladies, and he's had a string of them."

"We met one recently. Gloria Chase?"

"Don't know her. But I assume she's gorgeous with money."

"She is," said Decker. "But why do you say that?"

"Because that's Dennis's MO. Looks and wealth are his bellwethers. I'm sure that's why he latched on to Julia."

"He's been described as controlling," said Decker.

"I imagine he is. I've seen him in court. He's good, but underneath the smooth façade is something that I don't care for. And there was that one incident."

"What incident?" said Decker sharply.

"I don't want to tell tales out of school."

"And we want to solve a series of murders, Mrs. Perlman," said White.

She placed her hands in her lap and assumed a placid manner. "It was about a year ago. It involved a prostitute. Charges were never filed and the matter got hushed up. I think she got paid off."

"Can you be more specific?" asked White.

"She was beaten."

"By Langley?"

"He denied it, of course, but he was seen with the woman around the time of the incident. And she initially named him as her attacker."

"But then...recanted?" said White.

"Yes. I'm thinking that money changed hands. But no one could ever really prove anything. And the woman left town."

White looked at Decker. "Okay, why would Cummins date a guy with that sort of rep? She must have known."

"Maybe she liked the danger aspect."

"Langley and Cummins also went to law school together at NYU. He told us that the judge was very different from the woman he'd known back then. He said she had gotten a lot wilder. Does that sound like your friend to you?"

"Well, I didn't think she'd sleep with someone who was her bodyguard, so maybe I didn't know her as well as I thought. But...she seemed to be, to use an antiquated expression, sowing some wild oats after her divorce."

"Well, apparently, someone didn't like that," noted White.

CHAPTER

60

THEY NEXT TRIED DORIS KLINE'S house, but she didn't answer their knocks.

"Car's in the garage," said Decker as he peered in the window. "But there's another space where a golf cart might be parked."

"Maybe she's teeing off at the golf course, too," said White.

"Seems to be a strong trend in this state."

They got back into the car, but Decker didn't put it in gear. He looked at White. "So, what would you do next?"

"I'd head back to the courthouse and talk to the judge's clerks, especially Sara Angstrom."

"The judge might have confided in her, you mean?"

"Women do, Decker, a lot more than men. Guys just like to keep it bottled in. Until they blow. By the way, my mother said to tell you hello. I think she likes you."

"But she hasn't even met me."

"That might be the reason," said White with a smile.

As Decker pulled off, he grinned, too.

* * *

Sara Angstrom met with them in her office. She was dressed somberly, and her mood matched her dress.

"I'm not sure what I can tell you that would be helpful."

White said, "Anything that the judge might have told you about her personal life. Even if it seemed trivial. It might be important."

"I really don't feel comfortable divulging information like that."

"Sara," said White. "Someone murdered your boss, brutally. Nothing you tell us will go any further, and it's not like the judge would mind. All we want is to find whoever took her life. I'm sure you want that, too."

Angstrom looked anxiously between them for a moment before nodding and leaning back in her chair. "I knew about Dennis Langley. Judge Cummins told me *and* Dan Sykes, I suppose so we would be aware of any potential conflict. I didn't really like him. I've seen him a lot in the courthouse. He just always seemed so full of himself. He practically struts through the place."

"Then were you surprised the judge was seeing him?" asked Decker.

Angstrom seemed to withdraw into herself at this query.

"Please, Sara, whatever you can tell us," implored White.

"When I came here the judge had been divorced for a couple of years. She was beautiful, smart, and very well off. I knew about her family money. And then I went to her house and saw how lovely that was, and her clothes were all designer stuff. And she vacationed in the South of France and Italy, and she'd even been to Japan and Australia. Pretty amazing life."

"Tell us about her life lately," said Decker.

"When I first got here she wasn't really dating anyone, I mean, not seriously. But then, all of a sudden, she started seeing a string of guys, including Langley. It was like a switch was turned on for her."

"She was nearing fifty. Maybe she just wanted to cut loose and have some fun," said Decker. "Midlife crises aren't limited to guys."

"Maybe that *was* it. She seemed so straitlaced before. But then she started dressing, well, younger, I guess. New, cool hairstyle, blond highlights. She dieted and lost weight, not that she really needed to. I think she might have had some work done on her face. Her clothes were really costly, I could tell. But..."

"Maybe not exactly age appropriate?" suggested White.

"It's no business of mine," said Angstrom firmly. "She could dress however she wanted. But it was just a change in her, I guess. That's what stood out to me."

"Any other guys that 'stood out'?" asked Decker.

"Not really. I was surprised that she was seeing Langley, though."

"Did she ever talk to you about him?"

"Only once, really, after he came to visit her in chambers and I saw them exchange a kiss. She must have noticed the look on my face. After he left she laughed and said for me not to worry. She knew what she was doing. And that it was just fun for her. She wasn't going to marry him, even if that's what he wanted."

"She said that?" asked Decker. "That he wanted to marry her?"

"Yes. I was relieved. I mean, I think the guy's a creep. There was some story about him and a prostitute around the time I first got here."

"Yeah, we heard about that. Did the judge ever mention that to you?"

"No."

Decker said, "Langley told us that the judge never asked him to her house. Whenever they were…intimate, they were at his house, and they once went to a hotel in Miami."

Angstrom blanched. "That's weird. Why would she do that? It's not like she was married or anything. She could do what she wanted, where she wanted."

"He explained it away as her perhaps being afraid of something."

"Are you sure it wasn't *him* she was afraid of?" asked Angstrom.

"Did she ever confide in you that she was scared of Langley?"

"No. But when she broke it off she told me that it was time, that he was getting too needy, too, I don't know, *obsessed*. And she had to 'cut the cord'—those were her words."

White glanced at Decker. She said to Angstrom, "Langley's girlfriend gave him an alibi for the judge's murder."

"You mean Gloria Chase?"

"How do you know her name?"

"Because Langley loves to tell everyone that he's dating her. She's apparently some amazing businesswoman. She's also gorgeous. So he treats her as some big prize." She paused. "That's funny."

"What is?" asked White.

"A friend of mine works at the county clerk's office. She told me she saw Langley and Chase there."

"When?" asked Decker.

"Yesterday."

"What were they doing at the clerk's office?" asked White.

"My friend said they were getting a marriage license."

CHAPTER

61

You DRIVE, I NEED TO Google something," said Decker after they left the courthouse.

As they got into the car, White said, "Let me guess—Florida law on spousal testimony?"

Decker nodded curtly. As they drove off he scrolled through some screens and said, "Okay, Florida has no testimonial privilege, but it does have a spousal communication privilege. So if they get married Langley could stop his wife from revealing confidential communications they had unless a couple of exceptions exist, which I'm sure the smart criminal lawyer will make sure never do."

"But she already alibied him, Decker."

"And if she was lying? If he told her to say that and then that communication is privileged and she can't be asked about whether he told her to lie?"

"But how do we even charge the guy if the lady says he was with her that night?"

"We need to talk to her before she ties the knot."

"You really think he might be our killer?"

"He sounds like an overbearing, slick creep to me, but I've met lots of them and most turn out to be scared of their own shadow. But it only takes one exception to that rule for a murder to happen. And keep in mind that if I'm right and there are two killers involved, nailing Langley only solves half the equation."

"Again, the two-killers theory is not something I'm convinced of. Although I don't see a guy like Langley stuffing foreign money down people's throats and following us to Key Largo and taking out Kelly and shooting an FBI agent. But maybe he's a sociopath."

"Let's also talk to Gloria Chase's neighbors. And Langley's. They might have seen him that night."

"The murder took place in the middle of the night. They might not have seen anything because they were in bed."

"We'll never know if we don't ask."

* * *

They struck out in Langley's upscale neighborhood. The people on either side of him had been out of town since before the murders. The neighbor across the street had seen nothing and couldn't even tell them if Langley's car was there that night, since he had a two-car garage.

"We can do traffic camera searches," suggested

White. "He wouldn't have been going through any tolls, so we can't capture anything there. We can follow the route from his house to Chase's and see if anyone might have been around that night who might have seen something."

"He drives a dark blue Bentley, so at least it's a memorable vehicle."

"How do you know that?"

"It was parked outside his office when we went to talk to him there," said Decker.

"But how do you know it was his ride?"

"The vanity plate read LAW1. Doesn't take a genius. And if his assistant or one of his associates is driving a Bentley, maybe we should apply to work for *him*."

White looked chagrined.

"What?" he asked, noting this.

"I should have seen the Bentley and the plate."

"I've got the advantage. Everything I see and hear, I remember, or pretty much everything."

"Nice tool to have."

"Yeah, but acquiring it was a real bitch."

On the way to Chase's neighborhood they stopped in at Ricardos. It was the place where Chase had told Decker that Langley had gone to get some gin the night of the murders, Decker told White.

A check of the receipts showed that Langley's credit card had been used at five minutes past midnight to buy a bottle of gin. The man on duty had not been working during that time, so he couldn't identify the picture of Langley that Decker showed him. Decker texted the picture to the clerk who had been on duty along with a message for the man to provide an answer on the ID.

They next spoke with three of Chase's neighbors. One of them remembered the Bentley being there, but she couldn't swear it was that night. The other two had not seen Chase or Langley that night, at least they didn't think so. No one saw the Aston Martin, but Chase also had a garage where it could have been parked.

"Dead end," said White as they walked back to their car.

"But at least it doesn't conclusively rule out Langley as being the killer."

"Well, if we can't shake Chase's story it sort of does."

"We can pull the traffic camera records like you suggested."

"*If* he used the Bentley. He might have another vehicle or he could have cabbed it or done a rideshare."

"Or taken Chase's car. We'll have to check all angles."

"You're starting to think this guy is good for Cummins's murder, aren't you?"

He glanced at her. "I don't know, Freddie. That's why we do the dance."

"But if so, Chase must be in on it."

"You'd think, wouldn't you?"

"But you don't?"

"I'm not sure that lady would take that kind of risk for anyone. She strikes me as being very much into self-preservation."

"But if she loves the guy? Love can mess you up. Makes you do stuff you wouldn't have ever contemplated."

Decker thought of Mary Lancaster taking her own life, because she had briefly forgotten her beloved daughter. "Yes, it can."

62

THEY LATER HAD SOME DINNER at the hotel and it was well past dark when Decker steered the car back to Cummins's house. They parked in front and got out. Doris Kline's house was still dark and there was no sign of her car.

White said, "You want to talk to Trevor Perlman?"

"I'm not sure what else he could tell us that his wife couldn't. Let's go through Cummins's house again. Something might pop."

He unlocked the police lock on the front door and they went inside.

Decker immediately held up his hand and looked around.

White had heard it, too. Someone was inside the house.

They both pulled their weapons. Decker pointed up the stairs, where the noise seemed to be coming from.

They slowly made their way up, stopping at each riser to listen. When they reached the second-floor landing, Decker eased his head around the wall.

He whispered to White, "There's a light on in Cummins's bedroom."

She nodded.

As they edged down the hall the noises became clearer.

Decker glanced in confusion at White.

It sounded like someone sobbing.

They reached the doorway leading into the bedroom, Decker on the right, White on the left. The door was partially closed.

Decker held up three fingers, then lowered them one by one. With the drop of the final finger, he kicked open the door and they surged inside, their guns arcing in front of them.

And then coming to hold on the man sitting on the bed.

Barry Davidson was the source of the sobs.

They did not lower their pistols, because Davidson also had a gun in one hand and a bottle of scotch in the other.

He looked up at them in bewilderment.

"What th-the f-fuck are you doing h-here?"

"Mr. Davidson," said Decker, "we need you to put that gun down, right now."

Davidson glanced at the gun, his expression one as though he were seeing the weapon for the first time and wondering how it had gotten in his hand.

"I-it's m-my gun. B-bought and p-paid for."

"I'm sure, but guns and liquor don't really mix," said White.

"It's my g-gun."

"Put it down," said Decker.

"O-only had one l-little d-drink."

"I think it was more than one. But let's talk about it. *After* you put the gun down."

"This is m-my h-house. Can b-be here if...if I want t-to."

"Let's talk about it, downstairs. After you put the gun down."

Instead Davidson lifted the gun and placed the muzzle next to his cheek.

"You don't want to do that, Barry," warned Decker, the imagined images of Mary Lancaster in her final moments lurching back into his head.

"J-Julia's gone. G-gone. G-got nothing l-left. Wh-what's it m-matter? You tell me."

His finger edged closer to the trigger.

Decker said, "You have Tyler, you have your son left. You going to leave him all alone? Is that what a father does? Leave his teenager to pick up the pieces?"

Davidson looked up at Decker, maybe seeing him for the first time.

"T-Tyler deserves b-better than me."

"But you're all he has left. So give me the gun and we can talk about it."

Davidson didn't move the gun, but his finger did slip away from the trigger. He shook his head stubbornly. "Y-you think I k-killed her."

"We never said that."

"I know you do!" shouted Davidson. "D-don't lie to me."

"We're just doing our job, investigating lots of things and people."

"Wh-who else then? Huh? You're lying. Nobody else. Nobody else." He dipped his head.

"There's Dennis Langley. You know about him, right?"

Davidson looked up once more. "L-Langley?"

"You met him, right? At the French bistro. You were there for Tyler's birthday."

Davidson slowly nodded. "Why him?"

"He was dating Julia."

Davidson smiled. "H-he's a shitty golfer. S-seen him play. Swings his club l-like a f-fucking a-axe."

"I bet. Let's go downstairs now and we can fill you in on our investigation."

"Dad!"

They turned to see Tyler standing there drenched in sweat.

"T-Tyler?"

"Dad, what are you doing with that gun?"

"M-my gun."

Tyler stepped forward. "Come on, Dad. Let's go

home. Where are your keys? I'll drive you back. Come on. It's late."

He took the gun from him, and helped his father off the bed.

"Let's go."

White scooted forward and secured the gun.

As they half-carried Davidson down the stairs, Decker said, "How did you know he was here, Tyler?"

"I was riding my bike and saw his car parked on the side of the road about five hundred feet from the entrance. I figured he was here. He'd just walked around through the golf course side to avoid the gate."

"Why wouldn't he just drive through the gate?"

"I think his electronic pass was expired, or something," Tyler replied, not looking at Decker.

"Expired?"

"Or something, look, I'm not really sure."

The two of them got Davidson out to the rental car and loaded him in, as White got into the driver's seat.

"We'll drive you to his car and you can take him from there," said Decker. "Where's your bike?"

"It's foldable, so I put it in the back of my dad's car. He left it unlocked."

"We can follow along if you need help getting him into the condo building."

"I'm fine. Won't be the first time I've carried my dad inside," said Tyler, looking embarrassed.

After Tyler drove off in the Mercedes with his father lying down in the back seat, Decker turned to White. "We need to run ballistics on the gun."

"You don't think…?"

"I'm not sure. That's why I want to run the test. And there's something else."

"What?"

"Tyler said his father parked his car off the road and slipped into the neighborhood through the golf course side to avoid the gate."

"Meaning he could have done the same the night of the murder. But his car didn't leave the garage that night, *and* he has an alibi."

"He could have borrowed or rented a car. And maybe Tyler isn't as sure of the times that night as he said he was."

"You think he's covering for his dad?"

"His dad is the only thing he has left."

"But at least we know one thing for certain."

"What's that?" said Decker.

"The man was clearly lying when he said he was over his ex-wife."

CHAPTER

63

WHITE COULDN'T SLEEP, SO SHE left her room, trudged down to the hotel lobby, and went out the rear entrance. She sat by the pool and slipped out a single cigarette from her jacket pocket. She had smoked some in high school, and college, but then swore off the habit when she became pregnant the first time. But when her panic attacks had begun, she had allowed herself an occasional flutter. It was no coincidence, she knew, that her panic attacks had commenced right after Donte's death.

When it had happened she had caught the first flight back and driven straight to the morgue to see her baby lying lifeless on a slab. They had not conducted the autopsy yet. They had held off so White could see her child before the required procedure took place. For that she was grateful. That had been the only thing she had been grateful about.

It had taken her seemingly an eternity to open her eyes and look down at his small body with the sheet pulled up to his chest. A part of her was thinking that if she didn't open her eyes and see him, he couldn't possibly be dead.

Yet she had to accept the reality of her son being gone. And when she had looked down at him...?

She suddenly felt panicked as her heart commenced to beat rapidly. The dread ate into her belly and her lungs heaved, making her breaths erratic.

With a shaky hand she used a Zippo to light her cigarette. In the momentary flicker of flame she saw Donte—not the boy on the slab, but the child she had birthed and raised until senseless violence had taken him away from his mother.

She controlled and slowed her breathing, letting the cigarette smoke drift from her. It lazily moved over the pool and then disappeared into the night.

Like Donte had.

"Didn't figure you for a closet smoker."

She whirled to see Decker standing off to the right, in the fringe of flickering shadows.

White said, "I allow myself one every once in a while."

Decker nodded and drew closer. He stared at the still waters of the pool. "Couldn't sleep?"

"Apparently just like you couldn't."

"I never sleep well. *Apparently*, it's just not my thing," he added.

"I sent you a file on the incident with Langley and the prostitute."

"I read it and saw the pictures. She's lucky to be alive. And then she dropped her complaint and left town. Leaving Langley free and clear."

"For guys like him, there's never any accountability." White took another puff. "And Barry Davidson's weapon is a Sig nine-mill. Same caliber round found in Draymont and Lancer. If ballistics confirms that it was the gun used to kill them, that blows your theory of two killers."

"Maybe," said Decker.

"I don't see any way around it."

"We also need to see Gloria Chase and Dennis Langley, *separately*."

"You think you can get her to flip on him?"

Decker shrugged. "Who knows? And we won't be able to do it if Langley *didn't* kill Cummins."

"The way I see it, we have two primary suspects for Cummins's murder: Barry Davidson and Dennis Langley. But if the gun matches, Davidson did all three and Langley is innocent. Do you agree with that?"

"There are problems with that theory," said Decker. "One big one is that Cummins was stabbed and not shot."

"I know that. But if Davidson was there shooting Draymont, odds are he knifed his ex-wife."

"And the Slovakian money in the mouth?" asked Decker.

White finished her smoke, tapped it out, and threw the butt away in a trash can. "Could just be an intentional distraction."

"And the two men who took Lancer from the hospital? Are they Davidson's or Langley's associates? And where did they keep Lancer all that time? And why beat her? What did she know that could hurt them? And if Draymont was only killed because he was there when either Davidson or Langley showed up to murder Cummins, why kill Lancer at all?"

"Decker, I thought you believed it was one of these two guys," said a frustrated White.

"I never said that. They're suspects, sure. And they could have killed Cummins, but not Draymont and Lancer. And not Kelly. They would have had no reason to."

"But you think Davidson or Langley might have killed Cummins?" asked White.

"It's certainly possible. They had motive and means and maybe opportunity if their alibis don't hold up. So we have to follow that through. Especially since we now know Davidson knew how to avoid the security gate."

"Okay but if Davidson's gun comes back as the murder weapon on Draymont *and* Lancer? What then?"

"Then maybe I've been looking at this case completely wrong," conceded Decker.

CHAPTER

64

THE CALL CAME IN AS Decker and White were having breakfast at the hotel the following morning. Decker listened and then put his phone down.

"Well?" asked White.

"That was the U.S. attorney's office. Based on the ballistics test, they went before a federal magistrate and had an arrest warrant issued for Barry Davidson for murder. The Feds are leading the prosecution because of Cummins's connection. Their theory is Davidson killed all three."

"So the ballistics matched on Draymont and Lancer. Which means you *were* looking at this case all wrong."

Decker finished his coffee. "The U.S. marshals are making the pickup on Davidson. I do want to talk to him. Hopefully he'll be sober."

"What about Tyler?"

"Shitty all around. If his father gets convicted he'll go off to college with an albatross wrapped around his neck."

"If he even goes after all this."

"Maybe the best thing for him to do is to get away from this place."

* * *

Later that day, Decker and White arranged to interview Davidson at the federal lockup in Fort Myers, where he had been processed and jailed. They met him in a small, windowless room. He was in his prison-issued one-piece, his wrists and ankles shackled.

The man was stone-cold sober and also looked utterly bewildered. And he had, surprisingly, not requested a lawyer, at least not yet.

Decker had confirmed this with the marshals, and then with Davidson himself.

As he settled in across from Davidson, Decker couldn't help feeling sorry for the man. He was either innocent or the most hapless murderer Decker had come across. And he had confronted some real doozies.

"They...they tell me my gun killed two people," he began.

"Ballistics matched, yeah," said Decker. "It's why you were arrested."

"I didn't kill them. I didn't even know them."

"Well, one of them was in your ex's house. He

was killed at the same time she was," pointed out White.

"And I *didn't* kill Julia," Davidson snapped.

Decker said, "How did you end up in her house last night?"

"We have a key in case Tyler needed to get in. I went in the rear door because there was a funny lock on the front door."

"A police lock," said White. "So same door that was left open by the killer."

"I didn't kill anyone!"

"Okay, but why were *you* there?" asked Decker.

"With a gun," added White.

Davidson sunk his face into his hands. "I was drunk. I was...out of my head. I guess I just...missed her."

"Why'd you take the gun?" asked Decker. "Why would you need it?"

Davidson shrugged and didn't answer.

"You put the muzzle against your cheek. I was afraid you were going to pull the trigger and that would've been the end of you."

Davidson again didn't reply. He rubbed at his shackled wrists.

White said, "Some might see your wanting to kill yourself as a guilty conscience."

Davidson shook his head but remained silent.

Decker said, "Tyler mentioned that your car's security pass had expired?"

Davidson glanced up. "What? No, it hadn't. It's on auto renewal."

"Then why not just come in through the gate?"

Davidson looked confused and troubled by the question. "I...I don't remember."

"Tyler intimated that you had previously cut through the golf course parking lot on foot to avoid the gate. Why do that, Barry? You must have had a reason to go to all that trouble."

Davidson's features were now guarded. "I *don't* remember."

"Did you make a habit of going over to her house, to *check* on things?" asked Decker.

Davidson glared at him. "You mean *spy*, don't you? You think I was stalking her?"

"I think you hadn't gotten over the divorce. My partner here feels the same."

Davidson shot White a questioning glance but said nothing.

"Before last night, when was the last time you had seen or used your gun?" asked White.

"I don't really remember. It's been a long time."

"Where do you keep it?" asked White.

"When Tyler was younger, I had a gun box. But lately, it's been in my desk drawer."

"So last time you saw it, just ballpark. Weeks, months, years?" said White.

"Maybe six months. I bought it after Julia and I

were married and were living in another house. We were robbed there."

"Anybody been to your home recently who could have taken it and then returned it?" asked Decker.

"No, it's just been me and Tyler."

"Anyone have a key to your place?" asked White.

"Tyler does, of course. And Julia had one. In case of emergency."

Decker glanced at White. "Nothing like that was found at Cummins's house, was it?"

"Not that I know of, but they probably weren't looking for a key."

"I didn't shoot those people," barked Davidson. "I'll take one of those polygraphs if you want me to."

Decker said, "But you can see why you were arrested, can't you?"

He looked at them in desperation. "I have a damn alibi."

"But some alibis are better than others. And maybe Tyler has a reason to give you one," noted Decker.

"He wouldn't lie. He said I was there because I *was* there!"

"Okay," said Decker. "Just keep calm."

"How the hell am I supposed to keep calm! And Tyler was at school when they arrested me. I don't think he even knows where I am."

"We'll fill him in," said Decker.

"I guess I need a lawyer."

"Yes, you do. Have you given an official statement yet?"

"No."

Decker said, "Don't without talking to an attorney, and he'll probably recommend against it. Your arraignment is tomorrow. You'll make your plea, and bail will be set."

"I'm pleading not guilty."

"Okay," said Decker.

"Will I need to stay in jail?"

"Depends on what the prosecution asks for and what the judge decides," answered White. "But given that we're talking about multiple homicides, don't be surprised if you're remanded into custody until your trial date."

"But Tyler!"

"Can take care of himself," pointed out Decker. "But get a lawyer, okay? A good one."

Davidson laughed, a bitter expression on his features.

"What's so funny?" asked White.

"I wonder if Dennis Langley is available? I hear he's really good."

"But he also might have a conflict," said Decker.

"Why? Because he and Julia dated?"

Decker didn't answer. But he thought, *No, because he might be a suspect, too.*

CHAPTER

65

AROUND FOUR THIRTY THAT DAY Decker and White stood near the football field and watched Tyler run his routes and catch balls thrown to him by what looked to be a coach.

"Funny time to be doing that," opined White.

"Actually, it makes perfect sense. This is his comfort zone."

"You think he knows about his dad?" she asked.

"Oh yeah. That's why he's here."

As they stood there another young man walked over to them. He was about six-two and weighed around two thirty, beefy in the legs, core, and shoulders. He was wearing Under Armour gear and was sweating profusely.

"You guys waiting to talk to Tyler?" he said.

"Yeah," replied Decker. "We're with the FBI. Who are you?"

"Drew James. I'm on the team with Tyler. Left tackle."

"You got the blindside then, unless your QB's left-handed."

"He's not. I *am* the blindside tackle. Just finished up in the weight room."

"Never stops, does it?" said Decker.

"Not if you want to play in college." He stared out at the field where Tyler was running hard. "Tyler's got a chance at the big time, D1 Top Ten. I'm not nearly big enough for the O-line at a D1 college, and I can't play another position. And I don't have the frame to grow much more. I'm shooting for a decent D2 scholarship."

"You make it sound like a business," noted White.

"I just want my *business* degree," said James. "No way I can go pro. I'd have to grow three more inches and put on a hundred pounds and be a lot more athletic than I am."

"Tyler doesn't think he can make the jump to the NFL, either," said Decker.

James leaned on the fence and watched Tyler run routes. "I think he has a shot. Or did."

"What do you mean by that?" asked Decker.

"Tyler is super focused with discipline like nothing I've seen. His mom was a big part of that. She really believed in him. Now? He's out here, but I think he's just burning off some shit in his head. He usually does two hours in the weight room five days a week. He hasn't been in at all lately. And he didn't run with us the morning she died and hasn't since. And we used to all go surfing a couple times a week. But he hasn't done that in more than a month."

"Why do you think that was?" asked White.

"I think he's worried about his dad."

"Why?"

James looked at them. "Look, I don't want to get anybody in trouble."

"Just tell us what you know," prompted White. "It goes no further."

James looked back out at the field, his elbows resting on the fence top. "His dad never got over his mom. Tyler said his dad would sneak over there just to watch her."

"Is that right?" said White, shooting a glance at Decker.

"And he was seeing all these young girls, but Tyler said his dad really had no interest in them. Tyler thinks he was just trying to make his mom jealous. He'd get drunk at night and cry about the divorce. I think it took a lot out of Tyler. I mean, a lot. He'd have to sit with his dad and listen to that. He's only seventeen; he's not going to know how to handle stuff like that."

Decker studied him. "It's rough what he's going through, for sure."

"Kid shouldn't have to be a parent, too," chimed in White.

"You ever been over to Tyler's condo?" Decker asked him.

"Sure, lots of times." He grinned. "The girls his dad dates? I don't mind hanging out with them."

"His dad conducts his business from there."

"Yeah, even before COVID, he did that. He has clients all over the place, and he can't travel to see them all so he does it online. I listened to him practice what he would say to clients sometimes. Tyler said his dad would record it, play it back, and then, you know, improve on it. Get it just right before he did it for real. He told me that's what separates the winners from the losers." He looked out at the field. "Sort of what Tyler is doing right now. So maybe his dad was teaching him some good stuff, too. Practice makes perfect."

"Right," said Decker.

"Yeah. Well, see ya. I gotta go do my protein shakes." James walked off.

Tyler glanced over and saw them watching, White impatiently and Decker with interest. But he kept running his routes for another half hour.

He finished up and jogged over to them, toweled off, and guzzled down a bottle of water.

Decker said, "You've already made improvements on the dominant leg issue. Your cuts are more balanced, sharper, and cleaner."

Breathing hard, Tyler stared at them in anger. "You arrested my dad. That's bullshit."

"Evidence says otherwise."

"Fuck evidence. My dad never left the condo."

"It looks like at least his gun did," observed White.

"I'm telling you, I heard him there pretty much all night."

"Talk to me about the gun," said Decker.

"He's had it forever. I doubt he's ever even fired it."

"When was the last time you saw it?"

"It's probably been years. He used to keep it locked in a box when I was a kid."

"Your dad said no one had been over to the condo for a while."

"Why does that matter?"

"It matters because if your dad didn't use that gun to kill two people, then someone took it, used it, and then returned it. There were four rounds fired from it, Tyler. Those four bullets killed two people."

"Do you think that's what happened? Someone's trying to frame him?"

"It's possible. In fact, the way I see it, it's the only way your dad gets out of this."

Tyler looked down at the grass. "I can't lose him."

"I understand that," said Decker.

"Can I see him?"

"That can be arranged."

"What do I tell him?"

"That you love him. That you'll always be there to support him."

Tyler nodded, wiped his face off with the towel, and trudged from the field.

"That kid is right on the edge," noted White.

"Hopefully we can bring him back."

"Is that our job, Decker?"

He looked at her. "Maybe it should be."

"You earlier gave Barry Davidson some good legal advice. I didn't think that was our job, either. So why was that?"

"Everyone deserves a fair shake. And something about this whole thing is off. I mean, someone who kills someone else with a gun rarely offers up the murder weapon so freely to the cops. If he did kill with it, there's a big body of water right around here he could have dumped it in."

"So someone really might be framing him? Who?" asked White.

"Who stands to benefit if he goes down for this?"

"Tyler already gets his mother's money, so he's out. Maybe Langley framed Davidson."

"Motive?" said Decker.

"Just to screw over Davidson. I think both men were still in love with Cummins."

"If so, he would have had to kill Cummins, too."

"Lots of men kill the women they supposedly love," noted White.

"Let's talk to Gloria Chase then, and see how much she loves Langley."

"Apparently enough to marry him," said White.

CHAPTER

66

Chase was at her office located in the downtown area. The space was done in a minimalist but costly manner. There was an energetic flow of young, enthusiastic people and large computer screens with fascinating images and reams of data pouring over them. Decker felt like he was on some hip film set where they drank flavored sparkling water, wore chic clothes, and drove exotic cars, which meant he was as far out of his element as it was possible to be.

She met them in her spacious, light-filled office that was full of high-end build-outs and expensive furnishings. She looked equal parts indifferent and bored.

"I hear the ex-husband has been arrested," she said.

"News travels fast," said White.

"Like a *bullet.*"

The emphasis on the word showed them its use was intentional.

"So if he killed his wife and her guard, why are you here?" she asked.

"That 'presumed innocent' thing," said Decker. "But first, I understand congratulations are in order."

Chase smiled and held up her hand. A four-carat diamond rose from her finger like a miniature crystal mountain.

"Nice," said White. "Even if it doesn't work out, be sure to keep the rock."

"Oh, it *will* work out. We love each other very much." She glanced at White. "He did the knee and everything. Very romantic."

"He's close to fifty, right? Big age gap," White noted.

She frowned for a moment, but then smiled. "But he looks far closer to forty. And wants kids, same as me."

"Big wedding planned?" asked White.

Chase looked a bit crestfallen by the query. "No. Um, we're getting married next week in a very low-key affair, just the two of us. And then flying to Vegas for our honeymoon."

"Vegas, interesting choice. Do you like to gamble?"

"No, but they have great restaurants and shows."

"And as soon as you say your vows, everything he might have told you about Julia Cummins or anything related to her death will be confidential," pointed out Decker.

Chase glanced sharply at him. "What are you talking about?"

"Florida has a spousal communication privilege.

So Langley can invoke it to prevent you from talking to the police or anyone else about any communications he might have made to you about Julia Cummins or anything else that might be incriminating. He could have told you that he killed her, but once you're married, your lips are legally sealed."

"He didn't kill her. He was with me!"

"So no worries there. I'm just wondering if that law was the impetus for a quickie marriage as opposed to some societal extravaganza. But maybe you didn't want that." He looked around the posh space. "I mean, you don't strike me as someone who likes to make a big splash."

"Look, I won't deny that I had plans for something here that was going to be pretty fabulous, but Dennis explained things to me. I mean, why pay all that money for what's basically a big party for everybody else? Instead it'll just be us and we'll pamper ourselves, not three hundred guests."

"Makes perfect sense," said White. "What every woman wants, right?"

Chase scowled at her and finally said, "Well, *this* woman does." She turned to Decker. "And besides, didn't Barry Davidson kill his ex-wife?"

"He's been charged with murder, but not *that* murder," pointed out White.

"What?" said a confused Chase.

"Did you know that your fiancé wanted to marry Julia Cummins?" said Decker.

"That's crazy. Who told you that?"

"Someone close to her said the judge broke it off because Langley wanted to tie the knot but she didn't."

"I don't believe it."

"And you know about the prostitute?" said White.

"The what?"

"Your fiancé was charged with assaulting a prostitute and nearly beating her to death. But the charges were dropped."

"Because they were untrue! The woman was trying to blackmail Dennis. I remember now, he told me all about it."

"So he admits being with a prostitute?" asked Decker.

"No...he...he...it was a stupid thing to do. He was drunk."

"Then did he beat her up in a drunken stupor? Because I've seen the photos of her from that night. She was in the hospital for several days." He took out his phone. "I have the pictures of her if you want to look at them."

"I don't!"

"Twenty minutes, liquor store and back, you're sure?"

"Yes! Now if there's nothing else, I have a meeting."

Decker stood. "I wish you a happy marriage."

"Yeah, sure you do," she said with a sour expression.

As they walked out White said, "So, what do you think?"

"She's either telling the truth, or, more likely, the truth she desperately wants to believe, because she's invested a lot in this guy and doesn't want the deal to go south."

"And the quickie marriage?"

"Maybe Langley is cheap when it comes to stuff like that. And I wouldn't put it past the prick to be marrying her for another reason. But we need to refocus and grab a new angle, or Barry Davidson is going down for this."

"But what would be Davidson's motive to kill Draymont and Lancer?"

"Draymont obviously because he was there when Cummins died."

"And Lancer?" asked White.

"What if she and Draymont were blackmailing Davidson somehow?"

"How?"

Decker said, "Maybe they found out he was spying on Cummins. They were going to expose him if he didn't pay up. So we need to check his finances again to see if payments went out to any unusual parties that might be connected to Draymont or Lancer."

"That could be."

"Yeah, it could. But I don't think that's it. I still think there were two unrelated killers."

With hiked eyebrows she said, "You do have unusual ways of working a case."

"Oh, you've just barely skimmed the surface so far."

CHAPTER

67

YOU LOOK TIRED," DECKER SAID to White as they later sat down to dinner at a restaurant near the hotel.

"I was just on a Zoom call helping Calvin with math. I hate math, I'm no good at it. And it wears me out."

"Is he good at it?"

"Better than me. And I don't remember doing the kind of math he is when I was that age."

"And your daughter?"

"Jacky's still easy. I've got a couple more years before I *can't* help with her homework."

Decker idly stacked his fork on top of his spoon. "My daughter was good with numbers. She could see them line up in her head. Made it easy to do the math problems."

"That's cool," White said quietly, watching him closely.

"She got that from her mom, not me. Cassie was a nurse. She was good at figures and stuff, too."

"What were you good at?"

"Before I became what I am, you mean?"

"Yeah."

"I don't remember, really. Maybe just football."

"I thought your memory was infallible."

"Yeah, well, what's really infallible? Clearly not people."

They ate their meals and discussed the case.

"It seems to me that we're no further along than when we got here," said White in a frustrated tone. "We've got a hodgepodge of clues, all pointing in different directions, one guy under arrest, another guy who might have done it. But with both of them the clues add up one way, but not all the way."

"Maybe we're looking at the wrong suspects then," said Decker, plunking a fry in his mouth and chewing it. He hefted his beer and took a drink.

"Which means we have to find new suspects. And if you think those people dying are also tied to Kanak Roe's disappearance, we need a whole new set of facts. And maybe a parallel universe to reside in."

He put his beer down. "You know what I wonder?"

"No, Decker, but I'm sitting here with bated breath just waiting to hear."

"How did Kanak Roe, after leaving the Secret Service without his federal pension, manage to start a security business in Miami and grow it into Gamma?"

"Hard work, perseverance, some luck?" she suggested. "Isn't that the American Dream?"

"Lots of people try to do that, and yet most of them don't build their dream into a billion-dollar enterprise."

"So, what are you saying?"

"I'm just wondering if he had help," said Decker.

"Help? What kind of help?"

"Any kind of help."

"You mean from his Secret Service days?" asked White.

"Yeah."

"Well, he guarded presidents, met a lot of wheeler-dealers, no doubt. They might have supported him in the private sector."

"I'm thinking about something other than legal means," said Decker.

"Why are you thinking along this line all of a sudden?"

"I've been thinking about it ever since I learned the man was terminal and headed out on his boat never to be seen again."

"What's the connection with his illness and a boat ride?" asked White.

"I just think researching his past might not be a bad thing. Like we did with Draymont and Lancer. That definitely panned out for us because we found out they knew each other in DC and were running a blackmail business."

"How do you propose to do that?"

"We can start by talking to his daughter," noted Decker.

"You want to call her or go see her tomorrow?"

"The night's still young. Why don't we drive there? I'll call her first."

"That's not a quick trip," White pointed out.

"Pack a bag. We can stay over in Miami."

"Okay, but she might not know much."

"She strikes me as a daughter who knows pretty much everything about her old man. Maybe more than he wanted her to," added Decker.

"If you're wrong, then we are wasting time on something totally unrelated to four homicides. John Talbott back in DC will not be happy."

Decker gazed at her. "Is that how you judge your work performance? By how happy your boss is?"

"Not necessarily. But it is how I keep score on my career trajectory. And, unlike you, apparently, I need my job and my path to keep moving upward."

"I'll make a deal with you, Freddie. We go to Miami and talk to Roe. Nothing pops from that, we come back here, stay in our lanes, and make Talbott a proud poppa."

"I don't need you to patronize me, either."

"You want to hear something?"

"I don't know—do I?" said White.

"You got great instincts. You read people well. You know what to look for. You know when to hold a suspect's hand and when to bring the hammer down."

"But?"

"Who says there's a but?"

"Just tell me, Decker."

"I got this shit going on in my head that gives me insights sometimes, but also makes me a pain to work with. I've got no family to support, and if the FBI wants to can me, so be it. Fuck them and I'm on my way somewhere else."

"So where does that leave me?"

"I don't know. But it leaves *me* in no position to second-guess you and your career choices. I haven't walked in your shoes. In fact, I don't own any heels in your particular color."

"Why do I think, in a really screwy roundabout Amos Decker sort of way, you're trying to pay me a compliment?"

He rose. "I'll call Roe. When will you be ready?"

"Just as soon as you are. And in every way you can think of."

CHAPTER

68

"OKAY, WOW, THIS MIGHT MAKE me think of jumping to the private sector one day," said White as she looked around the wraparound deck of Roe's palatial high-rise Miami Beach home. Roe had gone to get them some coffee. The woman had not been put off by their late visit.

"It's a little over the top for me," noted Decker.

"Well, I'd like the opportunity to try, at least once in my life."

Decker looked out to the Atlantic Ocean, where Kanak Roe had disappeared from the face of the earth. Since people and large boats didn't just vanish, something had caused them to do so.

Kasimira Roe came out onto the deck carrying a tray of full coffee mugs and a pot with cream and some sweeteners and spoons. The women doctored their coffees while Decker drank his black. The air was refreshingly chilly and the breeze invigorating as they sat around the flaming outdoor gas firepit.

Roe was casually dressed in jeans and a sweater, and boat shoes without socks. Her hair was pinned up and she wore rimless glasses.

"Thanks for agreeing to meet us on such short notice and this late," said Decker.

"No problem. I haven't been sleeping much. I heard about the arrest. The judge's ex. Think it will stick?"

"His gun was the murder weapon for Lancer and Draymont," said White.

Roe looked at Decker. "What do you think?"

"He had motive, means, and maybe opportunity."

"But?"

Decker glanced at White. "There's not always a *but* in my remarks."

"I'm sure. But why would you be here if you thought you already had your killer?"

"Maybe to discuss your *father's* case?"

"But you said you would only do that if you thought it was connected to these killings."

"Maybe I do."

"So there *is* a but," noted White.

Decker leaned forward. "What can you tell us about your dad founding his firm?"

"What do you want to know?"

"Pretty much everything. He joined the Service right out of college. He put in sixteen years. If he put in twenty-five he could have retired with a full ride.

That's a big sacrifice to go off and start your own firm. He could have finished his tour of duty with the Service, banked his pension, and then started his company. That's what lots of people do."

"But *not* my father."

"Did he ever talk to you about why he left the Service?"

"Not really. But *I* left after only five years."

"There's a big difference between five and sixteen years invested," noted Decker.

"And Gamma was already established and successful," added White. She looked around the luxurious space. "You had some place to go. Groomed to take over an empire."

"I don't think it's suspicious that my father was naturally an entrepreneur. Lots of immigrants build businesses."

"Yes, they do. But a lot of them do it right away. So I'm not sure how *natural* an entrepreneur he was."

"What exactly are you suggesting?" said Roe in a bristling tone.

"I'm not suggesting anything," said Decker. "I'm just trying to fully understand your father's motivations."

"Then I don't know what to tell you."

"Did he keep in touch with anyone he worked with in the Service?"

She sat back and mulled over this. "There was one

agent that he was good friends with. I don't remember the name offhand, but I can look it up."

"Can you do it now?" asked Decker.

She glared at him. "You're very impatient."

"I like to think of it as very motivated to do my job."

"Let me get my phone, it might be on there."

She rose and left them.

White turned to Decker. "Okay, where are you going with all this?"

"We have one definite lead, Freddie," Decker said in a low voice. "Slovakian money in the mouths of two dead people. That does *not* tie into either Barry Davidson or Dennis Langley. But it might be connected to Kanak Roe and Gamma Protection Services. And the two dead people worked for Roe. So unless leaving that money behind was some giant coincidence—which stretches plausibility beyond belief—it's symbolic, and all symbols have meaning."

"So Lancer and Draymont, and, I suppose, Patty Kelly, are dead because of Kanak Roe and something he did, what, while he was still in the Secret Service all those years ago? For me, *that* stretches plausibility to the breaking point. Why wait so long to take action?"

"That's what we have to find out. And maybe they already took action, three years ago."

"You mean, when Kanak disappeared?"

Roe came back out at that moment looking at her phone.

"Okay, his name is Arthur Dykes. He and my dad were close friends for a long time. Came up through the Secret Service ranks and worked side by side for quite a few years. He should be able to tell you some things I might not know."

"Can you give him a heads-up that we'll be in contact?"

"Yes. But I can't believe this has anything to do with my father's past."

"That's why we're checking. To either rule it out or not."

"Did your father have any enemies?" asked White.

Roe stared directly at her. "In this life, we *all* have enemies."

CHAPTER

69

THEY STAYED OVER IN MIAMI, and the next morning Decker called Arthur Dykes, who had long since retired and was living in Punta Gorda, north of Fort Myers. They made arrangements to meet with him, then left Miami and drove straight to see the retired agent.

Dykes lived in—*What else?* Decker thought—a golf community. They took the elevator up to his condo and were invited in.

Dykes was medium height and had kept a trim, active figure, though he was now around eighty. He also had a full head of silvery hair. His home was free of knickknacks and the clutter one sometimes saw in the homes of the elderly. He was a widower, he told them, as he invited them in. His four kids were spread out over the country.

Over iced teas as they sat at an outdoor deck, Dykes told them about his time with Kanak Roe and the Secret Service.

"Kanak was driven, focused, wanted to make a career out of it," he said.

"But he didn't," pointed out Decker. "He left nine years short of his full pension. Do you know what changed his mind?"

Dykes looked uncomfortable. "You could retire with twenty years' service at age fifty, but Kanak wasn't close to being that old. He wasn't even forty when he left the Service. He was hard to read. I mean, he was a really good friend for many years, but we came from really different backgrounds. He left his home country when he was a kid, but he saw some crazy shit, let me tell you. And I know it affected him. As good friends as we were, there was a side of Kanak that no one else ever saw, including me."

"Anything unusual with his Secret Service career?" asked Decker.

"We joined up at the same time. Went through training together. We did normal rotations, worked on protection details for several presidents, including Reagan. Everything was going smoothly. Then, bam, he checked out."

"So he never talked to you about his abrupt career change?" asked White.

"Not in so many words, but Kanak became...different."

"When and how?" asked a suddenly tense Decker. "Be as precise as possible."

"I've given it a lot of thought, particularly after I found out you wanted to meet. And I can actually pinpoint it to one specific time."

"Let's hear it," said Decker.

"We were protecting Reagan at the time. This was about eight months after Hinckley shot him. The Service, of course, had changed its protocols to make sure that wouldn't happen again. Anyway, we'd been on that particular protection detail for about three months. And don't believe what you see on movies or TV, there's nothing glamorous about it. It's just a grind. Tedious as hell ninety-nine percent of the time. The other one percent? You're screwed if you mess up one little bit."

"I'm sure," said White.

"We were in Miami for a speech Reagan was giving. Nothing special, just another fund-raiser. When it was over, we rotated off duty after the president got back to his hotel suite and went to bed. Some of us guys went out for a late dinner and drinks. But Kanak didn't. He stayed at the hotel. The next morning he...he was different."

"How?" asked Decker.

"He was normally the first down for the briefing, but I had to go up and get him. He was still dressed in his clothes from the previous night. Looked like he hadn't slept. At first, I thought he was hungover because he just seemed out of it, but he assured me he hadn't had a drop. There were no bottles that I could see, and no smell of liquor on his breath or clothes. And he was pretty much a teetotaler, so I believed him. I asked him what was wrong, but he wouldn't say anything. He...he just looked stunned, I guess."

"Keep going," prompted White.

"He pulled himself together and did his job that day. But after that things got weird."

"How so?" asked Decker.

"He'd get phone calls in the office but would never say a word about them. Who was calling or why. He'd leave early to go meet someone, but he never said who. His work suffered, and he got written up a couple of times. I would have thought he was having an affair, but he wasn't married back then."

"Maybe he was seeing someone who *was* married," suggested White.

"Maybe, but Kanak was such a straight arrow, I just couldn't see that. I had him over a few times for dinner with me and my wife, you know, trying to get him to open up. But he never really did."

"Did he say anything at all that might explain what had happened?" asked Decker.

Dykes mulled over this. "He and I were sitting in my apartment just shooting the breeze one day. Suddenly, he looked over at me and said, 'Artie, I wish one thing.' He said, 'I wish to hell I had gone out with you guys that night in Miami.'"

Decker and White glanced at each other. He said, "Did you ask him why?"

"Of course I did, but he clammed up like nobody's business. Couldn't get another word out of him on the subject. And believe me, I tried. I talked to some other agents who had stayed at the hotel that night, but they couldn't tell me anything useful. They just hit the sack and woke up the next morning. Seems like whatever happened, only happened to Kanak."

"You ever tell anybody about this?" asked White.

"Just my wife."

"I'd keep it that way, for now," said White. "Until we figure this out."

Dykes glanced at her with an anxious expression. "Yeah, okay."

"Anything else you can tell us?"

"Just that it was about six months later when he resigned from the Secret Service and moved to Florida to start his business. Then he got married and, later, his daughter was born. He sent me an announcement."

"Career change, marriage, baby. That's a lot in a very short period of time," noted Decker.

"Yeah, it was."

"Were you surprised?" asked White.

"Flabbergasted was more like it. Me and every-body else. I mean, he was walking away from a great pension, health care, everything. But, as it turned out, he made the right decision. I mean, the guy became rich."

"Did you see him after he left the Service?"

"Yeah, he came to some reunions, birthdays, retirement parties. He was a big shot by then. Drove up in a Rolls-Royce one time, with a driver and everything. I could only shake my head." Dykes chuckled. "He brought his daughter to one event. Hell, she was probably only ten or twelve, but you could tell he was already grooming her to be his heir apparent. She was clearly in awe of him. Heard she went the Secret Service route, too. That was long after I retired. Now she's running the show at Gamma."

"You heard what happened to Kanak?" said Decker.

"Yeah, I did. Crazy. I mean, we'd lost touch by then. Last time I saw him was maybe ten years ago. Ann, my wife, was still alive. He looked good, happy, content."

"Did he mention anything when you saw him last?"

"No, it was all superficial 'how ya doing' bullshit. He was just a totally different guy by then. We just had our years at the Service in common by then, and it had been a long time. When I heard he went missing on his boat, I thought, what the hell was that about? It was like he just wanted to disappear. I mean, they never found any wreckage or anything. And you'd think they would have found something if the boat went down."

"You'd think," said Decker. "You ever see Kasimira again?"

Dykes nodded. "I went to his memorial service. They couldn't really have a funeral, of course. She spoke at it. Very moving stuff. I was crying like a baby. She loved her father, that was for sure."

"You have any inkling what could have happened back in Miami that night?" asked Decker.

Dykes eyed him. "All I can say is, whatever did happen, must've been goddamn life changing. Because it *did* change Kanak Roe's life."

Decker glanced at White before asking, "What hotel in Miami?"

Dykes took on a wistful look. "The Fontainebleau. Reagan liked it because the hotel had been used for a bunch of movies and TV. Jerry Lewis and Sinatra did stuff there. Lucille Ball, Bob Hope, and Judy Garland all stayed there. They filmed some of that Bond movie *Goldfinger* there. Reagan just ate it up. You know he was an actor before he was president."

"Yeah, I heard. Was anyone else of note staying at the hotel at the time?" asked Decker.

Dykes shook his head. "I mean, after POTUS, everyone else is way down the pecking order."

"Was his wife with him on the trip?" asked White.

"No, Mrs. Reagan was back in DC. It was only the one night. We flew back home the next morning. All routine stuff."

Decker handed him a card. "If you can think of anything, give us a call."

Dykes took the card and looked up at him. "What is going on here, Agent Decker?"

"I wish I knew. But we're going to find out."

As they walked to their car, White said, "Let me guess. Back to Miami and the Fontainebleau?"

"Where else?"

CHAPTER

70

IT WAS NOW KNOWN AS the Fontainebleau Miami Beach. It had undergone a two-year, billion-dollar renovation and reopened in 2008. There was a Michael Mina steak restaurant, a slew of bars, and also Italian and Cantonese cuisine. The lobby was vast and expensive looking.

"Surprised the Service could afford the rates here on their per diem," said White as they walked toward the concierge desk.

"It was cheaper back then, no doubt. And what the president wants the president gets."

"Yeah, you'll catch me at the local Marriott, thank you very much. A meal here probably equals one of my paychecks."

"You know what they say, if you have to ask the price..."

They flashed their creds at the concierge, who, after they had told him what they needed, made a phone call and then directed the pair to a small office off the lobby. There a young woman rose to greet them.

Pamela Lawrence was in her twenties with an energetic manner and dancing blue eyes. "FBI, huh? That's not something we see every day."

"I hope not," said White.

They sat down across from her. Decker said, "We're interested in the hotel's history."

Lawrence said enthusiastically, "It *is* very historic. It's on the National Register. And in 2012 the Florida chapter of the American Institute of Architects ranked the hotel number one on its list of Florida architecture."

"Congratulations," said Decker. "We were interested in another part of its history."

"Okay, what?"

"In 1981 President Reagan gave a speech here."

She looked at him blankly. "Reagan? I wasn't aware of that. But that was almost twenty years before I was even born."

"Do you have records that might address that event? I mean, it's a pretty big deal when the president comes to your place."

"We've had lots of big names here. When the hotel reopened in 2008, Usher and Mariah Carey performed."

"Wow," said White. "That's some firepower."

"Right?" said Lawrence, smiling. "I mean, I was only eight back then, and I don't really follow their music, but I'm sure it was pretty cool."

"Now you're really making me feel geriatric," quipped White.

"But a president, now that's *really* cool," said Decker in a prompting manner. "So, do you have an archive or something we could look at?"

"We do actually, but I helped put it together, so I know it doesn't include this speech by President Reagan. I'm sorry. Maybe I should go and research that."

"I suppose there's no one working now that was here at that time?"

Lawrence went on her computer and checked. "Our longest-serving employee started in 2010." She glanced up. "Hospitality has a high turnover rate, even in a place like this."

"I'm sure it has nothing to do with the attitude and behavior of the guests," said Decker.

"Isn't the customer always right?" said Lawrence brightly.

"Ask yourself that in two years."

They left. White drove while Decker checked his phone.

"Okay, Google was no help, maybe we need to do it the old-fashioned way."

"Meaning?"

"The local newspaper. Reagan's in town to give a speech? It might be in their news morgue."

"Now *you're* really showing your age."

"And there's something else."

"What?"

"Arthur Dykes said that Reagan was there to give a fund-raising speech."

"Right, so what? Politicians do those all the time."

"Dykes also said it was eight months after John Hinckley shot Reagan. Well, Reagan was shot in March, so eight months later was November of 1981."

"Which was before *I* was born!"

"The point is, why would Reagan be doing a fund-raiser not even a year into his term? I know how politics has gotten nowadays, but back then you didn't need a billion bucks to run for president."

"I guess that *is* odd."

"But he might have been doing a fund-raiser for someone *else*."

CHAPTER

71

THEY SAT IN THE PARKING lot while Decker accessed the digital archives of the *Miami Herald*. To do the searches necessary Decker had to activate a free membership. He plugged in Reagan's name and the year and hit the search key.

A story came up about Reagan's speech. Decker read that it was well received, but he didn't really care about that. What he did care about was the fact that the fund-raiser was being held for the benefit of Mason Tanner, who was seeking the seat of a retiring U.S. senator in Florida.

Decker looked at a picture of Reagan and Tanner shaking hands. Tanner was tall, in his midforties, with thick dark hair and an easy smile. However, Decker didn't like the look of the man. He seemed fake and smarmy. Then again he didn't care for most politicians, so that might just have been his own bias.

He held up his phone so White could see the image. "Mason Tanner. Candidate for the U.S. Senate."

"The fund-raiser was for him?"

"Yeah. Although according to this, he didn't really need the money. The story says his grandfather was a bigwig in Standard Oil and he inherited a ton. And his wife was one of the heiresses to the E. F. Hutton fortune."

"Nice birth luck, if you can get it."

Decker Googled something on his phone. "Says here he won the following year, by quite a large margin." He looked at another article. "He served three terms and is now retired and living in New York."

"Whatever happened to Kanak Roe back in 1981 may have nothing to do with the speech or Tanner."

"We won't know for sure until we rule it out."

"So do we go to see Tanner and try to get some answers from him?"

"I don't think it would be much help."

"Why?"

"According to this article he's now in his late eighties, lives in New York City, and has late-stage Alzheimer's."

White let out a long sigh. "Great. Nothing like running into a brick wall around every corner." She glanced at him. "I thought you solved your cases fast?"

Decker shot her a look. "We've only been on this sucker a few days."

"Says Superman."

"You called me shrimpy before."

"I didn't know you then," she shot back.

He wrote out a long email and sent it off.

"Who did that go to?" she asked.

"Alex."

"Trying to replace me already?"

"She's in New York. I asked her to check and see if Tanner maintained an office there, or had relatives who we could talk to."

"Good idea."

"For a guy to change his whole life over something that happened one night, it must've been something really terrible. I mean, Kanak was a seasoned agent by then. And whatever happened rocked him to his core."

"If that's what happened, yeah."

"Yeah," said Decker thoughtfully.

"But?"

Decker didn't answer. He had nothing to say.

CHAPTER

72

As she sat in her car, Alex Jamison glanced up at the four-story brownstone located on New York's Upper East Side. This was the home of the extremely wealthy octogenarian Mason Tanner.

In his email, Decker had given her a rundown on where his investigation stood, and Jamison knew she was taking a risk coming here. She was not assigned to this case, and Tanner, a former U.S. senator, was a very prominent citizen. Still, when Decker asked, her instinct was to deliver as much as she could. And she thought, as he did, that whatever had happened in Miami that night might have something to do with Tanner, or someone connected to him. At the very least, if she could help rule it out, that would assist Decker.

The problem was she couldn't just knock on the door and ask to speak to Tanner, who she had found out had round-the-clock care. And she had no idea if there was anyone around now who was with him back during his time as a senator.

Then she had an idea and called the man she was dating. She was thinking of breaking it off with him because their priorities were very different. She had struggled to rationalize why she had begun dating him in the first place and decided she had allowed herself to be swept off her feet by his family wealth, and the prestige of his position in the financial world. But he was part of the same world that people like the Tanners inhabited, so it was worth a shot.

"Hey, Kevin."

"Alex, great to hear from you finally. You've been avoiding my calls."

"It's just work, Kevin. Being an FBI agent means I don't control my days."

"Well, like I've told you, you could just chuck it. I'll take care of you."

"Not really what I want. I worked hard to get where I am."

"I know it's not PC for me to take care of you. But the reality is, I can. And want to."

She decided to cut through his me-me ramblings. "I was actually calling for a favor."

"Name it."

"Do you know Mason Tanner?"

"The former U.S. senator? My grandparents did when they were alive, and my parents do. I hear he has dementia or something."

"I was wondering if you know anyone who might still be with him from the early 1980s."

"Why the interest? You're not investigating him, are you?"

"I just need to talk to someone who might have known him back then. Nothing is going to happen to Mr. Tanner."

"I'll have to ask my parents."

"Could you check with them as soon as possible? "

"And you swear this will not reflect badly on Tanner?"

"I'm sure he's done nothing that would get him in trouble, right?" she replied, neatly turning the tables on him.

"Well, my parents always spoke very highly of him."

"I'll wait to hear from you. But as quickly as you can."

"I'll call them now. When can we get together again? I was thinking of taking the family jet down to St. Barts. We have a compound there. It would be fun."

"I don't have any time off now, Kevin, I'm sorry."

"See, another reason to let me take care of you," he said.

He clicked off, and she slowly put her phone away.

A kept woman? Yeah, really my life's ambition.

She couldn't deny that it had been fun flying around on private wings, going to great restaurants, and being driven from one fabulous family estate to another. But she could not see herself doing that for the rest of her life. It would seem a cop-out after all she had worked for. And she could only imagine how much Decker would hate it.

She settled back in her seat as a light rain began to fall. She thought about Decker down in Florida doing what Decker did better than anyone she had ever met.

And while I love the guy, and admire all that he can do, I can't see myself working with him for the next twenty years, either. It's just too exhausting. And while I like unpredictability to a certain extent, I can't take it every single moment of every single day.

That was one reason she had sought the transfer to New York in the first place. Not to exactly get away from Decker, but just to have a reprieve, for a bit.

An hour later her phone rang.

Kevin said, "Okay, I spoke with my mother. Mrs. Tanner died three years ago, but there's a daughter, Deidre. She's in her fifties. She might be able to help you. I have her contact information. I'll text it to you."

"Thank you, Kevin. I owe you."

"I'll hold you to that," he said. In a more earnest tone he added, "I really do love spending time with you, Alex. And I'm sorry for what I said before about chucking your job. That was stupid. And you don't need anyone to take care of you. You do fine all by yourself."

"Why this sudden change of heart?" she asked, her tone suspicious.

"Talking to my mother. Listening to her made me think how narrow-minded and shallow my family is."

"Your family gives a lot to charity."

"We only give enough to keep up with our ilk and put our name on buildings."

"But you still do it, when you don't really have to."

"I suppose."

This sort of talk was unusual for him, Alex noted, and she wondered where it was leading.

"I spend all my time making money because that was what I was taught that you did with your life. The fact is, my family has enough money. You've showed me another slice of life, Alex. One I needed to see. But for you, I'm just another guy born with a silver spoon in his mouth who thinks he made it all on his own. I had no clue about the reality of most peoples' lives. Not that I couldn't have discovered that on my own, and I should have. But I can thank you for showing me that side of life. It's ... it's made me think. It's made me think about what's important. And what's important is ... I love being around you. Because ... you're just a terrific person. And you make me want to be a better person."

This caught her by surprise. "That's ... that's really nice to hear you say, Kevin."

"Do you think we can get together at some point?"

She hesitated. "Yes. I'll give you a call. And thanks for doing me this favor."

"Okay, Alex, I hope it will help."

"Me too."

He clicked off and Jamison sat there, once more full of doubts.

CHAPTER

73

THANKS FOR THE INFO, ALEX," Decker said. "I really appreciate it."

She said, "No problem. I hope it helps."

"So, this guy you're seeing? You don't think it's going to work out? Does that mean you'll be heading back to DC at some point?"

"Um, I'm not sure, Amos. I'll have to let you know. But keep me in the loop on your case."

"Sure, okay."

He clicked off and stared down at his phone.

It's her life, Decker, not yours.

He looked at the contact information she had forwarded him. Deidre Fellows. Divorced and in her midfifties. That meant she would have been a teenager back in 1981. He wondered if she had been in Miami that night. Fortunately for him, Fellows now lived in Florida. On Sanibel Island, not that far from Fort Myers.

He called White and filled her in.

"Sanibel tomorrow morning then?" she said.

"Yeah. I'll call the woman ahead of time. Hopefully, she'll agree to meet with us."

"And if she won't?"

"A bridge to cross *if* we get to it."

*   *   *

The next morning they set off.

"So she said she'd talk to us?" asked White as she guided the rental out of the hotel parking lot.

"I left a message. She didn't call back."

"Okay, so why are we going there?"

"To cross that bridge."

There were actually *three* separate bridges to cross to get to Sanibel from the mainland, although all three were referred to collectively as the Sanibel Causeway.

When they arrived at the house, there was a large gate blocking access. Between Fellows's house and the property next door, they could see the water. A call box was set up next to the gate. White rolled down her window and pushed the button.

"Yes?" a voice said.

"It's the FBI. Agents White and Decker to see Ms. Fellows." She glanced at Decker before turning back to the call box. "We left her a message last night."

"Ms. Fellows is not available."

"When will she be available?"

"You'll have to call and make an appointment."

"We did. But no one called back."

"Thank you."

"Hello? Hello?" White looked over at Decker.

"Roll your window back up," he said.

She did.

Decker said, "Okay, I'm sure someone is watching us. Let's drive away. Off this street we turn right, go halfway down, and wait in the parking lot of the dry cleaners we passed. That's the only way in or out."

"Okay, but wait for what?"

"A black Mercedes convertible was pulling out of the garage up there. But then it stopped and reversed out of sight. You didn't notice because you were talking to the person on the box. I think that was Ms. Fellows. If we leave, she might just go on her way. And we can follow."

"And if it's not her?"

"Then it's someone who knows her and we can talk to that person as a way to convince Fellows to see us. Short of that we'll need a warrant or a subpoena, and we don't have nearly enough evidence to get either one."

White did as Decker asked, and they parked in the lot with the dry cleaners.

A half hour later, a black Mercedes convertible drove past. Its top was down, and driving it was a stylishly dressed woman in her fifties.

"I looked her up online last night," said Decker. "That's her. Hit it."

White pulled out into traffic and kept three cars behind the Benz. They followed for about ten minutes until Fellows pulled into the parking lot of a spa. She got out and headed toward the door.

"You want to snag her now?" asked White.

"No, let the lady have a nice spa treatment. She might be in a better mood to answer our questions."

White looked at him in surprise. "Decker, I didn't expect that nuance from you."

"Yeah, I actually shocked myself with that one."

White parked the car and they settled down to wait.

"How is Alex doing?" asked White.

"Seems to be doing fine," he replied. *If conflicted.*

"Nice of her to score this lead for us."

"Yes, it was."

"Guess she'd do anything for you, huh?"

He glanced over at her. "And where exactly is this going?"

"Just making an observation."

"Uh-huh."

"What do you expect Fellows to tell us?"

"Everything."

"Seriously?"

"Why not shoot for the stars?"

"And end up always being disappointed?"

"There are far worse things in life than that."

White was about to launch a retort but said, "I guess you're right about that."

An hour and a half later, Fellows walked out of the spa, her skin glowing, her fingernails and toenails painted aquamarine, and her hair shiny.

"I wonder how much all of *that* cost," said White.

Decker opened his car door. "Who cares? Let's go swing for the fences."

CHAPTER

74

THE FLASH OF THEIR CREDS made Fellows's large eyes widen even more.

"You were the one who left a message last night. Look, why are you harassing me? Talk to my accountants. They're handling everything. I just spend the money, I have no idea where it comes from. And I know nothing about taxes!"

"I don't know what you're talking about," said White. "We're investigating a series of murders."

Fellows almost fell against her car. "Murders? Why the hell do you want to talk to me about *murders*?"

"Maybe we can go someplace *very* private and talk it through?" suggested Decker. "Like your home?"

They followed her back to her house, driving through the open gate after her.

"Wow," said White as they pulled up in front of the three-story mansion set right on the water. "So *this* is how the other half lives."

"It's not half," replied Decker. "It's more like a handful."

They were led inside by Fellows and passed a woman in a maid's uniform. "Coffee, Jane, by the pool," Fellows said to her.

"Yes ma'am."

Decker looked around and noted a large shelf full of photos. He walked over and ran his gaze along them. "Your father?" he said, indicating one large photo of a group of people.

She crossed the room and joined him. "Yes. This actually is his home and all of his things are still out." She gazed at her father's picture. "He *looked* every bit the politician, didn't he?"

"Were looks deceiving?" asked Decker.

"Did you ever watch the film *The Candidate*, with Robert Redford?"

"Yes."

"Well, God bless him, that was my father. He was a delightful man. Loved to campaign, loved glad-handing people, loved the limelight, but was clueless about what the job entailed and didn't want to put in the work. He never managed to write and pass a single piece of legislation in all his years on Capitol Hill. I'm not telling tales out of school, it was common knowledge."

"And yet they reelected him over and over," said Decker.

"Seems to be the norm now, doesn't it? Okay, let's get to it, shall we?"

They followed Fellows out to the rear lanai, where an infinity pool was situated along with luxurious plantings, furnishings, and sculptures. Just beyond was an enormous dock, where a boat large enough to qualify as a yacht was tethered.

"So, you have *tax* problems?" said White, looking around as they sat down at a table.

"Everyone in my income bracket has tax problems. As I said, my accountants are handling that."

"And your husband?"

"Divorced. That's *why* I have tax problems. My father inherited a lot of money. He had great financial advisors who turned that inheritance into a lot more money. He set up trust funds for me starting when I was a little girl. I was a millionaire many times over by the time I was a toddler. My ex-husband did his best to make me poor. But because of my prenup *he's* poor, and I'm just working through some issues. I'll still be rich when I die. Now, why are you here?"

Decker gave a brief description of the case before getting to the night in Miami in 1981. He did not mention Kanak Roe.

"Were you there with your father?" asked Decker.

She said sharply, "Where are you trying to go with all this? My father has Alzheimer's."

"We know. And where we're going with this is, if you were there with your father, do you have any recollection of anything unusual that happened the night of the speech?"

"Okay, yes, I *was* there. My father was originally from New York, but we moved to Florida when I was little. My parents liked the weather, and the taxes were a lot lower than New York's. We lived in West Palm at the time. I traveled with my father to Miami. I wanted to meet the president. I was only fifteen."

"So, anything unusual?"

"Unusual how?"

"Anything out of the ordinary."

"Not that I can think of. The president gave his speech, then my father followed him with his remarks. There was the photo op and shaking the hands of all the big donors. I got to meet Reagan. He was quite charming. And looked quite robust, considering he'd almost been killed not that long before. Then the president left. No one could leave before him—that's standard procedure, you know."

"And then what?"

"And then I went back to the hotel with one of my father's aides. Then I went to sleep."

"And your father?"

"I'm sure he came along later. He had some more people to glad-hand."

"But you didn't see him that night?"

The maid brought the coffees out and then departed.

Fellows took a sip of hers. "I don't think I saw him after I got back to the hotel. I mean, I wasn't a little child he needed to tuck in." She paused and added, "Why do you think anything unusual happened that night?"

When she said this last part her gaze dipped, and her hand shook a bit, Decker noted.

White said, "That night a Secret Service agent saw something that, let's just say, changed his life completely. He was never the same since."

Fellows looked startled. "A Secret Service agent? You mean from Reagan's detail?"

"Yes."

"You're not suggesting that the president—"

"No, of course not," said Decker. "Reagan was in bed long before then, surrounded by his protection detail. And the agent in question was off duty. Some of his fellow agents went out for dinner and drinks, but he didn't. He stayed at the hotel."

Fellows looked thoughtful. "And that's when you think he saw something *unusual*?"

"Yes."

Decker watched her closely. "But since you never left your room and saw nothing, I guess you can't help us...?"

White added, "And that means the recent murders we're investigating, I guess the guilty people go free."

Fellows shot her a stern look. "So now you're trying to guilt me into talking, I guess?"

"We're just trying to get to the truth," replied Decker.

She took another sip of coffee and then looked down at her freshly done nails. "I was very excited that night. After meeting the president and all." She glanced up, seemingly trying to read their reaction to this. "It made it difficult to sleep."

Decker shifted his large bulk in his small seat as he perceived what she was trying to do. "And when you couldn't sleep, what did you do?"

"I might have gone out into the hall and...walked around, gotten some fresh air."

"And saw...something, perhaps?" interjected White.

"What did this Secret Service agent look like?" Fellows asked abruptly.

Decker took his phone from his pocket, pulled up a file, and showed her a photo of a far younger Kanak Roe from his company's website.

She looked at it and nodded. "Yes, that looks like the man I saw that night. At least I think so. It was a long time ago, after all," she added with a touch of defiance. "Memories are not infallible, you know."

"Yeah, I know," said Decker, drawing a surprised glance from White. "What was he doing?"

Fellows suddenly became rigid, closed her eyes, and shook her head. "I really don't want to revisit this. There's no point in dredging up the past. No good can come of it."

White leaned forward. "I know this is hard, Ms. Fellows. I really do. But there are some people who could unfairly be found guilty of murder and go to prison, or worse, if we don't get to the bottom of this. And what you tell us will go no further. We just need some information, that's all."

Fellows pulled a tissue from her pocket and dabbed at her eyes. After a few moments she said, "I...I heard raised voices from a room."

"Could you hear what was being said?" asked Decker.

She shook her head. "But the door *was* open a crack. I...I took a peek."

"What did you see in the room?"

"This agent, and another man...and a woman. A young woman."

"What were they doing?"

"The..." She looked away and rubbed at her eyes with the tissue. "I really had forgotten all this. And now you come here and stir everything back up again. It can't possibly matter one bit now."

"It *does* matter," said Decker. "A great deal to some people. Enough to kill over, in fact. And I don't think you ever forgot it. You just didn't want to ever think about it again. Because the possibilities were too frightening."

She shuddered. "Are there really innocent people who might go to prison, after all this time?"

"There is no statute of limitations on murder," White pointed out.

"Oh my God. I can't believe this has come back to bite me in the ass." She looked out toward the Gulf for a few moments before turning back to them and saying in a low voice, "They were...wrapping her in...sheets."

"Was she dead?" asked White.

"I...I don't know, but I think so. She wasn't moving. She looked...limp."

"Who was the other man?"

"I...I think he might have worked on my..."

"On your father's campaign?" prompted White.

"Yes, but I never knew his name. Hell, I'm not even sure he did work for my father. He just looked the type."

"Didn't they see you?" asked White.

"No. I was very quiet and just peering through the slight gap."

"So they were wrapping up the *body*?" said Decker in a prompting manner.

She closed her eyes and dipped her head. "They...they put her in a suitcase. I...I ran away before...they could see me."

"So you don't know what they did with it?"

"No."

"Did you recognize the woman?"

Fellows shook her head.

"Can you describe her?" asked White, taking out a notebook and jotting some things down. "I know it was a long time ago."

Fellows said quietly, her gaze downcast, "She was Black, in her twenties, long dark hair, slender, quite beautiful, even in...death. And she...was naked."

"You saw all that peeking through a crack in the door?" said White skeptically.

"Well, maybe it was open more than a crack."

"Why would they have left the door open at all if they were putting a dead, naked woman in a suitcase?" asked White.

"It wasn't the door going into the hotel room. It was a two-room suite. It...it was the door going into the bedroom."

"But then how did you get into the room?" asked White.

Decker held up a hand. "Just continue with your story," he told Fellows. "Did you see any wounds? Any signs of trauma, or blood?"

"No, nothing like that. And I think I would have on the white sheets. She was just...not breathing, or moving."

Decker leaned in. "Why didn't you alert someone in the hotel? Or call the police?"

"I...I don't know. I was just a kid, really. I was

scared. Confused. I...I just wanted to run away and forget what I saw. And I have, all these years." She snapped, "Until you showed up."

Decker said, "I think there was more to it than that. Far more."

"What the hell do you mean?" she exclaimed, looking fearful.

"It was your *father's* room, wasn't it? That's how you got in, right? You had a key to his room."

Fellows broke down and started to sob.

CHAPTER

75

So, WE HAVE TO FIND a missing and maybe murdered person from over four decades ago, no problem," said White as they drove back to Ocean View.

"We have some things to go by," noted Decker.

"Fellows also said her father wasn't in the room and had nothing to do with the dead woman."

"What else did you expect her to say? And he might have left by then so Roe and the other guy could clean things up."

"What do *you* think happened that night?"

Decker shrugged. "Young Black woman dead in the bed of an older, powerful, rich, and married white guy running for the Senate? That's a career-ender. Either things went sideways and he killed her, or she had some sort of medical emergency and died in his bed. He called a trusted aide to deal with it, and Kanak Roe stumbled on it somehow. I think the fact that Roe didn't raise the alarm leads me to believe the woman wasn't murdered but died of natural causes. Otherwise, I think Roe would have blown the whistle."

"But still, even if it wasn't murder, why cover it up? Why would Roe take that risk?"

"The guy in question had just done an event with the president that Roe was guarding. If the truth came out, it would not have been good for anybody. And Roe probably didn't want to drag his boss into something that he had nothing to do with and knew nothing about. With news like that everybody tends to jump to conclusions."

"So he helped with the coverup in return for what?"

"Maybe enough money to start his company."

"So Kanak wasn't so much of a straight arrow then. He saw an opportunity and took it."

"A lot of people do," replied Decker.

"Okay, how do we locate the dead woman?"

"More to the point, how do we locate the other guy in the room?" said Decker.

"Fellows thought he worked on her father's campaign, but wasn't sure about that."

"He might be easier to track down than the dead woman."

"How?"

"We can check on Tanner's campaign staff. He was a senator for nearly twenty years. The Bureau should be able to get some names for us."

"Okay, I'll get on that. And the woman? I'm sure her friends and family would like some closure."

"I'm sure they would, too," Decker said quietly. "I know I would."

White glanced at him, but didn't comment on this. "Then we need to start digging. Missing persons reports in November of 1981. We have her description. Cold case file may be in some police storage facility."

"If anyone filed one."

"Shit, who would have thought this case would end up dragging us into the past like this? And someone might be killing people in the present over it all."

"And maybe in the not-too-distant *past*," noted Decker.

"What are you talking about?"

"Kanak Roe."

"Roe. He kept silent all this time. Why would they worry—" She broke off as the possibility occurred to her.

"Right," said Decker, looking at her. "Kasimira said her father was very religious. He was dying with a guilty conscience and wanted to clear that conscience."

"And he let it slip to someone who didn't want him to do that."

"And he and his boat disappear as a result."

"You going to share that theory with Kasimira?" asked White. "She might be a suspect. Andrews clearly doesn't trust her."

"Andrews's view is 'clearly' biased, since Gamma wouldn't hire him."

"Children sometimes murder their parents, if those parents are a threat to them. And if Kanak was going to tell the world that his and now *her* empire was built on murder and blackmail?"

"If she did kill him, why ask me to find out what happened to him? That makes no sense."

"That's true. So, what do we do?"

"We keep digging. That's all we can do."

"On this case we might hit China before all is said and done."

"And if my initial theory is right, this piece is only half the equation. So while you start making inquiries about Tanner's aides and the missing woman, I'm going to follow up on who killed Julia Cummins."

"How are you going to do that?"

"By talking to Barry Davidson again."

"But you don't think he did it."

"But he might have some idea who did. And then I'm going to interview Dennis Langley again."

"That asshole won't say anything."

"But by now his fiancée will have spoken to him. And maybe shared our suspicions about the timing of his marriage proposal. He might be rattled enough to let something slip."

"Why does it feel like we're back at square one on the game board?"

"Maybe because we are. Only now it might be a different game we're in the middle of."

CHAPTER

76

BARRY DAVIDSON HAD BEEN REMANDED into custody after his bail hearing. He had pleaded not guilty, he told Decker as the two men sat across from each other at the jail. Davidson had hired a lawyer but had agreed to speak with Decker without his attorney being present.

"My lawyer has a stellar reputation as an obnoxious son of a bitch," said Davidson.

"I'm sure you had your pick, since there are a lot of those around. And we spoke to Tyler."

"He came by to visit. He's pissed I'm in here. He keeps bringing up the alibi. The judge didn't seem to give a crap."

"Alibis are for trials, not bail hearings."

"And the judge said I had to stay in here until my trial. I got a business to run."

"Piece of advice, Barry. You need to focus on this right here. Not your business. Not even Tyler right now. Because if this goes sideways, you lose both, for the rest of your life."

"Shit, you think I don't know that?"

"Not from your attitude, no."

"Why are you here other than to bust my chops, Decker?"

"I was the one who told you to get a lawyer and not make a statement."

"I told my guy that and he was surprised. He tried to turn it into you trying to trick me, but he couldn't figure out how."

"I'll lay my cards on the table. I'm not convinced you killed your wife, but a lot of the evidence says otherwise. And juries and prosecutors could give a crap what I think. They just care about what the evidence says, okay?"

Davidson sat up straighter, his expression focused. "Yeah, okay, I get that. Sure."

"Now, your alibi is not foolproof, because your son is supplying some of it. Your gun killed two people. You have a motive. You had means, and the prosecution will argue you also had opportunity. They'll grill Tyler on every second of the alibi and he might not make it out the other end in one piece."

"Does he really have to go through that?"

"Yes, unless you plan on changing your plea to guilty."

"I told you I hadn't held that gun in years."

"But you were holding it in your ex-wife's bedroom, so your prints are all over it. You also told me no one went into your condo who could have taken it. But you said Julia had a key to your condo."

"Right, she did."

"So anyone who had access to *her* house could have gotten that key, gone to your place, taken the gun, used it to kill two people, and then returned it. Are there cameras in the condo building or in the elevators? Do you have cameras in your condo?"

"No, they've got them in the garage, but that's it. I don't think people want to feel like they're being watched all the time. I know I don't."

"I noted you don't have a security system."

"The building is very secure and it's part of a gated community. Guests have to check in with the guard, and residents have an electronic tag on their car that activates the gate. And after hours you need a key card to get into the building."

"And Julia had one of those, too?"

"Of course. But who could have taken the key and security card and gotten into my place and stolen the gun?"

"Anyone who was at your ex-wife's house."

"Julia was very outgoing. And when we were married, we had a great many people over for dinner and social events."

"In fact, they could have made a copy of the key and taken or cloned the security card at any time," mused Decker.

"Who would hate me that much?" asked Davidson.

"I'm not sure it's a question of hate, but of *convenience*," said Decker. "You make a very appealing patsy. You obviously were still in love with her. That's motive enough. She lied about the reason Alan Draymont was at her home. She wouldn't even let Dennis Langley come to her house. Why was that, Barry? The truth!"

"I've told you all I know."

"No, you haven't. I think you don't want to say because it will be embarrassing for you. So you have to ask yourself: Do you want to be embarrassed, or do you want to spend the rest of your life in prison? It will probably come out at your trial, so you might as well get it out now."

Davidson looked shaken by this blunt talk. He let out a breath and said, "She...she caught me watching her house."

"So she knew you were stalking her? Did she feel threatened?"

"I would never have hurt her, Decker. I swear."

"But that was probably why she did what she did. And she was having sex with Draymont, but it had the added benefit of him being an experienced security person. She might have felt protected."

"Didn't turn out too well for him, though, did it?" retorted Davidson.

"Keep talking like that, Barry, and they'll convict your ass for sure."

Davidson changed color and looked down. "I didn't mean it like that."

"When she saw you that time, did you say anything that might have led her to fear for her safety?"

"I...I might have been a little drunk. And I might have said...some things."

"So the answer to my question is yes. You know, the longer I sit here, the more I think you might have actually killed her."

Davidson looked up, scowling. "Then get the hell out of here, Decker. I shouldn't be talking to you anyway without my lawyer present."

"You're still the executor and trustee of your ex's estate?"

"Yes," he replied in a calmer tone. "But in light of everything, I've talked to Duncan Trotter about assigning those duties to someone else, maybe a bank."

"Why?"

"It's actually what Julia would have wanted. And if I get convicted, I can't perform those duties for the estate. And it's a large one. It needs professional management."

"So you knew how rich your wife was?"

"She made no secret of it."

Decker nodded and rose. "Okay."

"What are you going to do now?"

"Go talk to Dennis Langley."

"You really think he might have killed Julia?"

"What do you think?"

"I don't think the guy cares enough about anyone else to commit murder. From what I've heard, he's too self-absorbed."

"You might be right about that. He's getting married, by the way."

"Really, to whom?"

"Gloria Chase."

"Oh right, I heard they were an item."

"What do you know about her?"

"Blew into the area about five years ago and took it by storm. She reminded me a little of a younger Julia, actually. Strong, independent, take-no-prisoners sort of mentality. And beautiful and brainy on top of it. Langley is a lucky guy."

"Maybe luckier than she is."

"How do you mean?"

"Only time will tell," said Decker.

77

"WHY ARE YOU BACK?" ASKED Dennis Langley after his assistant, Rose, had escorted Decker in and left his office. She didn't look like the same woman as before, Decker thought. Her shoulders were slumped, and the sunny smile he had seen during his first visit here was gone. And she hadn't sashayed out the door with twitching hips like before. And the reason for all that was clear.

Langley had told her about the marriage.

"Like a bad penny, I guess," said Decker as he sat down across from the man.

"Make it snappy. I'm a busy man."

"If you're cooperative, I'm sure we can knock this out pretty quickly."

"Knock out *what* pretty quickly? My alibi is solidly established, so there's really nothing more to discuss."

"You say you never went to the judge's house?"

"That's right."

"So you wouldn't have had access to the key she had to her ex's place?"

"Of course not. I didn't even know she had one."

"She never mentioned it?"

"No. And how would I even know what it looked like, or where it was?" He cocked his head. "Why is that important?"

"I understand you're getting married next week, and then flying to Nevada right after. Why the rush?" ·

"I don't see how that is possibly any of your business."

"Why don't you just imagine it is and answer the question?"

"Why don't you just *imagine* we're done and get out of here? You know, Decker, you have no cards in your hand, not a one. So don't try to pretend to play any. You keep this up, coming to see me and my fiancée, I'll file harassment charges against you, and I'll make them stick. And then where will you be?"

Decker said impassively, "I don't know. Where?"

"Okay, we're done. You obviously have nothing better to do with your time. But I do."

"Why did you move down here?"

"Again, none of your concern."

Decker glanced at the man's collar. "You going to see Gloria later?"

"Yes, why?"

"Piece of advice. Change your shirt."

"Why?"

"You have lipstick on your collar. Interestingly, it's the same shade of red that your assistant, Rose, is wearing."

Langley pulled a hand mirror out of his desk drawer, checked his collar, and used a tissue to rub off the lipstick. "She was congratulating me on my upcoming marriage and got a little carried away."

"Really? I assume she kissed you *before* you told her that you were betrothed."

"Think whatever you want."

"How exactly did you get the prostitute to drop the charges against you?"

Langley rose. "You are very, very close to a defamation suit."

"Don't think so."

"Oh, so now you're a lawyer?"

"No, everything I said was true. She was a prostitute, you were charged with assaulting her, and she then dropped the charges and left town. I hope she's still alive."

"Goodbye, Decker."

Decker walked out of his office and closed the door.

He stopped in front of Rose's desk. She was crumpling up a tissue and wouldn't look at him.

He sat down across from her. "I take it you heard about the wedding plans?"

She nodded and blew her nose.

"And you two were...?"

"At least I hoped so. I mean, I know he was seeing her, but I never thought..." She glanced up at him, her eyes brimming with tears. "He told me he loved me."

"I'm really sorry," Decker said as she blew her nose again. "That was not a nice thing for him to do." He looked around. "This is pretty expensive office space, and it's built out top dollar. And the guy drives a Bentley. I mean, I know lawyers do well, but is there something else going on here?"

She looked at him guardedly. "I don't think I can talk to you about anything having to do with this firm."

"That's fine. I don't want you to do anything you're uncomfortable with. Seeing as how he's been so loyal to you."

He heard her say something under her breath that sounded basically like, *Fuck it*.

She glanced at her computer and a few seconds later tapped some keys. "In addition to being Mr. Langley's assistant and paralegal, I also handle the firm's accounts. Now, I have to go and see someone about something. I'll be back. You can just *hang around* here if you want."

She walked off and Decker immediately sat down behind her desk.

The pages he was scrolling through were financial

in nature. He took screenshots of all of them and then studied the pages as he walked out.

The embittered Rose had just given him a piece of low-hanging fruit. Langley should treat his employees better.

When he passed by the Bentley, he smiled and patted its hood.

Now he understood Dennis Langley quite clearly, not that it was so very difficult.

But was he also the murderer of Julia Cummins?

CHAPTER

78

WHITE HAD MADE A DOZEN calls and come up essentially empty.

The senior members of Tanner's former Senate staff were almost all either deceased or long retired. She had gotten some names and a few pictures online of these people from their younger days. She supposed they could show them to Deidre Fellows to see if she recognized the man in the bedroom helping Kanak Roe to wrap up a dead woman and stuff her into a suitcase.

But if the person had been a young aide, a secretary, or some very junior member of the staff, it was going to be really difficult to track that person down now. It wasn't like they kept exhaustive lists of such personnel in some neat and tidy archive. A lot of the staff had probably gone on to work with other members of Congress after Tanner retired, or left the political arena entirely. If the man was a personal aide of Tanner's and not part of his political operation, they still might be able to identify him, but she wasn't sure how. Mrs. Tanner was dead. Mr. Tanner would be of no help. Deidre was an only child, and she hadn't recognized the person that night. Kanak Roe would know, but he was probably dead, too. And all of this had happened before Kasimira Roe was even born.

She had contacted the Miami–Dade Police Department and spoken with someone from their Cold Case Squad. Without revealing specifically what her case was about, she gave the woman's description and the date and location in question. The officer said he would get back to her—but she was in a long queue, he had warned, and without a name it was not going to be quick or easy. In fact, he said, it was going to be pretty much impossible.

There was a Cold Case database run by an independent organization that covered forty-six states and fifty Florida counties, but, again, without a name White's search turned up no hits when she put in the information she had.

Shit. She rubbed her eyes and wondered how Decker was getting on.

She got some email responses on other lines of inquiry they had started. The traffic cameras had turned up nothing on Langley's Bentley or Chase's Aston Martin at the time in question. Barry Davidson had made no suspicious payments. They hadn't heard back from the liquor store, so she had called and was told the night clerk had remembered seeing Langley come in that night at the time he said he had.

Three strikes and we're out.

She forwarded all of this to Decker, and then called her mother to check on the kids. She had refrained from getting her children phones yet, but she knew that would change soon, especially for her oldest.

And in no time they'll be in college and then married and off living their lives far, far away from their mother.

And you are wallowing in self-pity, Freddie, and it is definitely not a good look.

"Hi, honey," said her mother. "How's it going in sunny Florida? Sunny Baltimore is currently in the forties."

"It's going slowly. I'm not sure when I'll be back again."

"I meant to ask you, don't they have FBI down there? Why did you and Decker get called in for this?"

"I've been asking myself that from day one. And the agent we've been working with down here was not particularly happy about it."

She had not told her mother that Agent Andrews had been shot, and that she had been shot at, too. And she prayed her mother did not see it in the news somewhere.

"Well, it could be that the Bureau considers you and Decker crackerjack agents and you get sent out only on the tough ones."

"Yeah," said White sarcastically. "I'm so crackerjack I'm two promotions behind. But that might just be due to my winning disposition."

"And the fact that you don't take crap from anybody, particularly from male agents who try to put you in a place they want you to be. But you keep fighting the good fight, honey."

They spent some time going over how the kids were doing, and White told her mother she would get up to see them as soon as possible.

She clicked off, sat back, and wondered again why they had been sent down here when there were FBI agents all over South Florida, and the Bureau also had large field offices in both Tampa and Miami.

It's not me, that's for sure. So, is it Decker? I mean, I know the guy is good, but is that it?

She couldn't very well ask her superior about it.

Hey, sir, why did you send our sorry asses down here when you already got all that manpower in the Sunshine State?

On a whim she decided to call Jim Pollard, a friend of hers at the Hoover Building who kept his ear to the ground and knew all the Bureau gossip.

"Hey, Freddie, how goes it?" said Pollard in a booming voice.

His voice matched his stature, she knew. He was a big, gregarious guy with the rep of a good agent, but he had a secret desire to act—and did so in local productions. Everything about the man was larger than life. He also loved the inner drama of the Bureau, of which there was an endless supply.

"I'm down in Florida on a case."

"I know you are, Freddie. With the one-of-a-kind Amos Decker, no less."

"So you knew that?"

"Hell, everybody knows that. Sorry you got stuck with him as his new partner. I heard his old one ran away to New York."

"Actually, Alex Jamison thinks the world of him," retorted White, who was surprised at how angry his comment had made her.

"Not what I heard."

"What did you mean everyone knows about us being down here?"

"You mean you haven't heard?"

"Heard what?"

"Ross Bogart was Decker's protector. Now that he's retired the Bureau is getting tired of the man. Granted he's had some success, but word is Decker is an absolute dick to work with."

"He's a little out of the mainstream, but he's got a brilliant mind and a softer touch with people than I would have imagined."

"Wow, I didn't expect to hear that from you."

"I just call them like I see them," she replied

coldly. "And what do you mean they're getting tired of him?"

"They want to get rid of him, that's what. I've heard scuttlebutt from the executive suites that they just want to cut bait on him. He's rude, won't follow orders, won't toe the Bureau line, and is never going to fit in."

"He gets results, Jim. I looked at his record. He has a *one hundred percent* solve rate. Name me another agent who has that. He got an innocent guy off death row. And he saved a U.S. president's life once, and got a medal for it."

"The execs don't care about that. They want people who will walk the walk and talk the talk on the *Bureau's* terms. And he never even wears a suit. I've seen him a few times at the WFO when I was over there. He looks like he's homeless."

"He's not an official FBI agent. He's a consultant."

"Which makes it easier to cut him loose. I'm stunned he's lasted this long."

White had to bite back the comment she was about to make and calm her rising anger. "But that doesn't explain why we got assigned to this case. Last time I looked Florida had lots of agents."

"Federal judge and a private security guard, right?"

"Right. How did you know those details?"

"Grapevine. It looked to be a really complicated case where nuance was required."

White did not like his gleeful tone. "Where exactly is this going, Jim?"

"I think the powers that be sent Decker down there to fall flat on his face. With his termination to come right after."

"Why run the guy around by the nose like that? Why not just fire him?"

"He's made some enemies here, Freddie. It's payback time. They want to rub his face in it."

"And I'm down here with him, so what happens to me if we don't solve this sucker?"

"I don't know."

"I've made enemies, too, but it's mostly because some male agents don't want me around."

"Look, Freddie, what you need to do is make sure you stay far enough away from the fallout so that *you* survive this intact."

"What the hell are you talking about, 'stay far away'? Not do my job? Sabotage the investigation?"

"Of course not. I'm just saying don't go down with the ship."

"But what about Decker?"

"What about him? Don't tell me you *like* the guy?"

"I haven't known him that long, but—"

He interrupted, "Well, hopefully, you won't have to *know* him much longer. Hang in there. Gotta go, hear the boss coming. Bye."

White slowly put her phone down.

CHAPTER

79

SOMETHING ON YOUR MIND?" ASKED Decker as he stared across the width of the table at White in the hotel restaurant.

"Why do you ask?"

"You seem off."

White shrugged and drank from her glass of water. "It's the case. It's frustrating."

Decker kept his gaze on her for a moment longer and then looked away. "Yeah."

"So, you found out Dennis Langley is broke?"

"He should have cut off his assistant's access to the financial files *before* he told her he was marrying Chase."

"What are you going to do with the info?"

"Info I'm not supposed to have."

"Look, it's not like I have any love for the woman, but I have even less for Langley. And he *did* attack that prostitute and got away with it. And I don't want any woman or any person to suffer the same at his hands."

"Then you'll be happy to know that I printed out what I took pictures of, put it in an envelope, and dropped it through the slot at her office. I also added an unsigned note telling Chase to make sure to do a prenup if she decides to go through with the quickie wedding. And I highlighted the fact that the bill for her engagement ring already went to collection. Apparently, Langley bought it a month ago and then stiffed the dealer. And the Bentley's not far behind."

"Wow, I wish I had a ringside seat for that."

"Who knows, we might."

"At least you had something positive happen. I struck out on Tanner's aide and the dead woman. And I sent you the results of the other inquiries. A bunch of nothing."

"The Tanner piece is not surprising, since it was over forty years ago. It might take a miracle."

She eyed him nervously. Decker was quick to pick up on it.

"If you don't tell me what you want to tell me, I think you might actually explode with the built-up pressure," he said.

She sighed and sat back. "I might need a cigarette before I do."

"Or you could just tell me and save your lungs."

"Decker, have you made enemies at the Bureau?"

He shrugged. "I don't dress the part. And I'm a little annoying to work with. You might have noticed."

White smiled weakly. "I did, but just a bit."

"Why do you ask?"

"They have a lot of agents down here. They didn't need us to come down and investigate this. And they didn't even let Andrews know we were coming. That way he had no path to object."

He eyed her shrewdly. "Any idea why we *are* here?"

"You're really good, Decker. I mean, really good, if unorthodox. And that might be your undoing."

"Meaning?"

"Meaning maybe this case is a way for the Bureau to pull out a thorn in its side."

He drank his beer down and set the glass on the table. "So I blow this, I'm history?"

"I'm not saying it's fair or right."

"How did you score this information?"

"A gossipy friend at the Bureau. I began to think about Andrews being blindsided by our assignment to this case. Bureau doesn't usually do things that way. So I called the gossipy friend. He filled me in. They want to jettison you and decided this would be a good way to do it. And that also explains the strange way Talbott was acting when I reported in with him. It was like he was glad Andrews was out of the way, and that we didn't want any reinforcements."

"So the blame would fall on us and no one else?"

"You should be pissed. I would be," said White.

"Being pissed doesn't change anything."

"What does?"

"I imagine if you and I manage to solve this sucker, they won't be able to kick me to the curb."

"I wouldn't think so, no."

"But if we don't, you shouldn't be collateral damage, Freddie. So you can jump ship and go do something else."

"I was assigned to this, Decker. I can't just leave."

"Blame it on me. Impossible to work with. Goes against everything the Bureau stands for, at least that part will be true. That way you don't go down with me."

"My gossipy friend suggested something similar. But, see, you're not the only one the Bureau doesn't like, Decker. Why do you think my ass got dragged from Baltimore on a moment's notice to come down here with you?"

Decker cocked his head. "So is the Bureau planning to clean house with me *and* you?"

"My gossipy friend either didn't know or wouldn't reveal it to me for obvious reasons. If the latter, I need to make new friends. And in any case, he was really gleeful over the prospects of your getting cut down to size. And he probably won't shed any tears if I get canned."

"You don't deserve this crap. You're a good agent, Freddie."

"And that apparently is not enough. I'm a woman

and I'm Black on top of it. And while everyone who doesn't know shit about how the world really works seems to think that's like the golden apple combo package, those of us in the trenches know different. You get smiles and applause and the media sucks it all up, but then when the applause dies down and the public attention gets turned away, everyone misses the knife that stabs you in the back minute by minute, day by day. Which is exactly what is going on right now."

"So why have you stuck around this long?"

"Because I've put a lot of time and effort into building a career, and I'll be damned if I'm going to let a pack of assholes take all that away from me just because they think they can. I hope you feel the same way."

"I do." Decker leaned back in the booth. "So where does that leave us?"

"I figure our only way out is solving this case. Together."

"Hell, I intended to do that for free. Sticking it to the suits is just an added bonus."

White laughed. "You are really starting to grow on me, Decker."

"Look out then, Freddie, because there's a lot of me to grow on."

CHAPTER

80

DECKER HAD TAKEN OFF HIS shoes and socks and was walking on the beach after dinner.

I might get used to this sand thing, and how ironic would that be?

There were a lot of moving pieces with this case, and even his superior memory was having a difficult time keeping track and syncing things up properly. He decided to take them in different silos.

Julia Cummins's murder. If his theory was right, whoever had killed Cummins had not killed Draymont, or Lancer, or Lancer's biological mother, Patty Kelly.

Ten stab wounds, the justice-is-not-blind symbol left behind, the legal phrase, all smacked of a highly personal killing. She'd had a sexual relationship with Alan Draymont, which she'd tried to hide under the subterfuge of her needing protection. But there had been no actual threats, at least that they knew of, and she hadn't hired Gamma to protect her.

At first, it would have seemed logical that there was only one killer. Whoever had stabbed Cummins would have also murdered Draymont. The motive would have been jealousy perhaps, because the two had had sex that night.

But the two crimes were as different as possible. Knife versus gun. Frenzied and personal versus methodical and perhaps transactional. And then there was the money stuffed down first Draymont's throat, and then Lancer's. No money had been forced into the judge's mouth, which bolstered the theory that Draymont had died first, then the judge had heard the shots and come down to check. She had found Draymont's body, but his killer had already fled. However, the person who would end up murdering the judge was just arriving on the scene. That person had chased the judge back upstairs to her bedroom, where the slaughter had taken place, with the blindfold and note left behind.

Decker stopped and looked out to the water. The winks of ship lights far out in the Gulf were the only interruption to the darkness.

That's what this case feels like. Almost total darkness with a few feeble points of light. But will that be enough?

It didn't surprise him that the Bureau was trying to get rid of him. After Ross Bogart had retired, Decker had sensed a subtle shift of opinion about him, and not in his favor. When Jamison had departed to New York, he had no one really in his corner, and he had no interest in fighting office political battles.

I can be annoying. I don't like playing by other people's rules. Solving cases should be the only goal, and the bullshit part of the job doesn't interest me at all.

He imagined that he and Frederica White were in complete agreement on all that. But the last thing he wanted was to see the woman go down with him.

She has a family. The Bureau is her career, and she's worked her butt off for it.

So absorbed was Decker in these thoughts that he did not notice the two men emerge out of the darkness until they were right upon him.

They were both dressed in jogging outfits and tennis shoes.

They stared at Decker and he stared back at them.

"Can I help you guys?" he said.

One man drew a knife; the other pulled a pistol.

Decker had left his weapon back in his room.

Well, this sucks.

He was about to try to tackle the guy with the gun when he saw a blur of movement to his right. A foot struck the gun and it went spiraling off into the water. Another foot hit the man in the gut, and he went down to his knees with a grunt of pain.

Another side-winding kick to his jaw and he went down to the sand.

The knife guy slashed at their attacker, which gave Decker time to clamp down on his arm and twist it until the man cried out in pain and dropped the knife. Decker drew his fist back to land a haymaker on the man when a foot whipsawed against knife guy's chin. There was a dull thud, his head shifted violently to one side, and he fell to the sand yelling in pain and holding his face.

Then a hand grabbed Decker's.

"Come on!" yelled White. "Run."

They hustled back up the beach and through the gate into the pool area of the hotel.

White pulled her phone, called 911, and relayed what had just happened. She clicked off and looked up at Decker.

"You weren't kidding about that double black belt," he said breathlessly. "That was pretty amazing."

"I don't kid, in general," she replied just as breathlessly. "And you were lucky I was out there getting some fresh air and spotted the two guys coming up on you."

"I was very lucky."

"Okay, first thing, you need to be more careful."

"Yeah, I can see that."

"Second thing, I'm going to be beyond pissed if you get your ass killed."

"Duly noted. But this happening is a positive sign, too."

"How so?"

"We're making certain people nervous, which means we're getting closer to the truth."

CHAPTER

81

DECKER CAME DOWN THE FOLLOWING morning to the hotel lobby to meet White. As he crossed the lobby to go into the restaurant, someone approached him.

Gloria Chase was dressed, at least for her, in a subdued fashion. The dress was just above the knee, not all that tight, and the heels were barely two inches tall.

She held up an envelope. "Was this from you?" she asked.

"Have no idea what you're talking about."

"I'll take that as a yes. Got a minute to chat?"

She led him over to a seating area where they wouldn't be overheard.

They sat, and she crossed one long leg over the other, her expression dejected.

"Just when you think you know someone well enough to walk down the aisle with them."

"Trouble in paradise?"

"Do we have to play this game?" she snapped.

"Have you spoken to him?"

"More than that. I told him I would not be marrying him, ever. I also gave him back his crummy ring before the collection people came after *me* for it."

"Was he living beyond his means?"

"My people did a quick check on him, which I should have done when I first met him. He owes everybody. It's not that he's a bad lawyer. He makes good money. It's that he has a gambling problem, which is why he really wanted to go to Vegas for the honeymoon. To gamble away *my* money."

"I'm sorry."

"Are you really?"

He glanced at the envelope. "Proof's in the pudding, as they say."

"Right. You could have let me marry him and there would go all my money."

"I wasn't so much worried about your money as I was about your safety."

"You really think he's dangerous?"

"That prostitute didn't assault herself."

She pursed her lips. "Have I been a complete fool?"

"The hardest thing for someone to do is admit they've been suckered. It's easier to say the emperor is wearing his new clothes when he's really stark naked, right up until the moment everything goes to shit and you have to pay the price for your bad judgment." He leaned forward. "But moving on—do you stand by your alibi for him?"

She played with the latch on her purse. "Let's just say that I was not counting the minutes when he was gone. I was actually in the shower and getting...spruced up."

"So, longer than twenty minutes?"

"I think he found out when he needed an alibi for and then 'reminded' me how long he was gone. I can't say for sure how long he was out, actually."

"An hour or more?"

"I take a while to spruce up. So, yes, clearly an hour or more."

"And you'll stick to that if it comes to legal proceedings?"

"Count on it."

She rose and so did Decker. She put out her hand, which he shook.

"Thank you, Agent Decker."

"Thank you for being candid."

"It's not my usual forte, but an old dog can learn new tricks, I guess."

"I guess so," said Decker, thinking about himself.

* * *

As Chase was leaving, White walked over to Decker. "The cops turned up nothing on the two guys from last night. They were long gone and left behind no clues."

"Not surprising."

White looked in the direction of Chase. "What did she want?"

"To tell me she's not marrying Langley, and she has no idea how long he was gone the night Cummins was killed. But it was at least an hour. So that puts Langley right back onto the suspect list for Cummins's murder."

"The motive? I mean, he was seeing Chase. They were planning to get married. She was loaded. She was his ticket out. So why would he kill the judge?"

"It doesn't have to be about money. Cummins rejected him. With a guy like Langley, I doubt he took it well. So with what he thought was an ironclad alibi, he probably figured he could kill Cummins and he'd just argue he couldn't be in two places at the same time and Chase would back him up. And even if she didn't, once they were married, her lips would be legally sealed."

"So now you think *he's* good for the murder?"

Decker said, "Well, we know he is capable of violence."

"Yeah, and he's also a jerk."

CHAPTER

82

As they were heading out White got a call. It was the officer from Miami's Cold Case Squad.

"Didn't expect to ever hear back from you in my lifetime," said White.

"Yeah, I surprised myself. But even though you didn't have a name, you had a specific date. I ran it through our missing persons database for the day after, and got one hit that matched your physical description. Her name is Wanda Monroe, African American, age twenty-three. She was reported missing by her roommate. According to her rap sheet, Monroe was a known prostitute who worked the strip back then, including the Fontainebleau."

"Can you send me a photo?"

"Soon as I hang up."

"I assume she was never found?"

"Nope."

"Okay, thanks a lot."

A minute later the photo dropped into her inbox.

They looked at the young woman with long dark hair, a fetching smile, and lovely features.

"What a damn waste," said White.

"Yeah, it is. Send that photo to Deidre Fellows and see if she recognizes it as the woman in her father's hotel room."

"It was over forty years ago, Decker."

"Sometimes a memory like that gets seared into your head."

"Is that how all your memories are?" she said curiously.

"For better or worse, yeah."

She sent the email off. "Now what?"

"I was thinking there was one thing we didn't check."

"What's that?"

"Where did the killers get all that old Slovakian money to stuff down Draymont's and Lancer's throats?"

White shot him a glance. "I just assumed—"

"Yeah, so did I, and that was a mistake. I looked online, and it's sold on Etsy and eBay for the most part."

"I can run a check on recent purchases of the currency. I can't imagine there's a big market for it."

White made a call and got this in motion. "I told them to make it a priority. Hopefully, they won't need a warrant or anything."

"Yeah."

"Now where?"

"Let's talk to Doris Kline again."

"Why?"

"She lived next door to Julia Cummins and knew her maybe better than anyone else. And she held back before. Maybe she's still holding back something."

* * *

Kline was out on her lanai reading a book and having orange juice, though knowing the woman now, Decker doubted it was solely juice in there.

She was dressed in a salmon-and-white-striped shirt and white capri pants. A pack of cigarettes sat next to the juice. An ashtray with a few butts in it sat next to that.

"Long time, no see," said Kline, laying her book aside. "Have you solved the case yet?"

"Not quite."

"Where's the other FBI guy?"

"In the hospital."

"What? Is he sick?"

"No, he was shot."

Kline had picked up her glass and nearly spilled it.

"My God, was it connected to—"

"Maybe," interrupted Decker.

"Okay." She gingerly set the glass down. "I understand Barry has been arrested."

"That's right. And charged with the murders of Alan Draymont and Alice Lancer," said White. "But not Julia Cummins. At least not yet. What do you think about that?"

"If you want the truth, I don't think Barry has the guts to kill anyone."

"We understand that he sometimes watched Cummins's house?" said Decker.

Kline nodded. "And Julia caught him at it. They had words. And he ran off with his tail tucked between his legs."

"And you didn't think to mention this before?" asked White.

"Like I said, I don't believe Barry did it."

"His gun *was* used to kill Alan Draymont and Alice Lancer," noted Decker.

"I didn't even know he had a gun."

"He had it at Cummins's house the night before he was arrested. Looked like he was going to kill himself with it. Fortunately we were there in time to stop him."

"Jesus, Barry?" She reached for her Zippo and slid a cigarette out and lit it, blowing smoke off to the side.

"That surprises you?" asked Decker.

"I always thought Barry was having too much fun

in life to want to end it. But then you think you know people and it turns out you know squat."

"He was clearly not over the divorce," observed White.

"I just hoped he would eventually move on. Do you really think he killed those people?"

"Doesn't really matter what I think if all the evidence points to him."

"Okay, Julia and the guy she was sleeping with, I get. But what about this other gal, you said her name was Alice?"

"Alice Lancer. She worked with Draymont. She was killed separately, but with Barry's gun."

"Why would Barry kill her? Did he know her?"

"We've turned up nothing to show that. But she might have seen him next door that night. Maybe she was blackmailing him."

Kline shook her head and puffed on her cigarette. "And here I thought I had nice friends."

"It's not been conclusively proved that Barry did it," pointed out Decker. "His son will testify that he was at the condo when his mom was killed. But since he's Barry's son, a jury may not believe him."

"Okay, but from all you just said, who else could it have been other than Barry?"

"Cummins was a judge. Judges *do* make enemies."

"That's true."

"But she wasn't receiving threats. She just used that

to disguise the real reason Draymont was over there. Why would she feel the need to do that?"

"Maybe she was afraid of someone's finding out," said Kline.

"Other things being equal, that might also point to the stalker ex-husband," interjected White.

Kline eyed White, blew out a final mouthful of smoke, and stabbed out her cigarette.

"I guess that makes sense, but, again, I never would have figured Barry as the violent type."

"Did they ever have fights?" asked Decker.

"What couple doesn't? But nothing bad. Hell, my ex and me? We'd light up the neighborhood. I could never hear Barry and Julia going at it. Julia would always talk to me later about it, though. And Barry always backed down, usually because Julia was right and had the facts to back her up. At least that's what she told me."

"How about the Perlmans? They seem pretty compatible."

"Yeah, they get along fine. Most second marriages do. You figure it out by then, and even if you haven't you don't have the energy or lungs to scream like you used to."

"Maybe I should think about getting married again, then," quipped White.

Kline eyed her. "Honey, I would advise against it unless you're damn sure, and what woman really is?"

"True, we met one recently who thought she had Prince Charming in a bottle, only to find out it was Pandora's Box."

"Did she manage not to open the box?" asked Kline.

White eyed Decker and smiled. "Yes, with a little help from a good Samaritan."

"So is Barry going to prison over this?"

"He could," said Decker. "Unless we find another plausible theory."

Kline shook her head. "That means Tyler will have lost both parents. Poor kid."

"He believes in his father's innocence, although he's clearly not happy with Barry's drinking and lifestyle."

"Barry's all he has left. That's pretty scary for a kid."

"Yes, it is," said Decker, rising to leave.

* * *

Later, back at the hotel, White rapped on Decker's door. When he opened it she looked triumphant.

"We got a hit on the Slovakian currency purchase," she told him.

"That was fast."

"Sometimes the good guys get lucky. And the Bureau has a team devoted to online purchases that might later figure in prosecutions. Apparently criminals really like to get their felonious shit on platforms like that. And as you said, not much trafficking in the currency. It was purchased on eBay. Happened three weeks ago."

"They have a name?"

"Yep."

"Who?"

"Kasimira Roe."

CHAPTER

83

DECKER IMMEDIATELY CONTACTED ROE AND asked for a meeting without mentioning what they had just uncovered.

White showed Decker the documentation on the currency purchase. "I don't remember the bills that came out of Draymont's and Lancer's throats. But we can get them from the evidence locker."

"No need. I remember them."

"Seriously, I mean, to that level of detail?"

"I can see them in my head, Freddie, including serial numbers."

"Well, look at you, Rain Man. Maybe *we* should go to Vegas."

They left their hotel and got into the rental. As she drove them to Miami, he went over the pictures of the money in the email.

"Well?"

"It's the same money."

"Shit, I did not see that coming."

"It doesn't necessarily mean what you think it might."

"How could it not?"

"That's why we're heading to Miami. To ask her."

"And you think she'll really answer truthfully?"

"We'll see, won't we?"

He had been told to go to Roe's home instead of the office. They took the elevator up, and the woman herself answered their knock.

"Not working today?" said Decker.

"I've decided to take some time off."

She was not her usual put-together self, Decker noted. She was dressed in faded jeans and a T-shirt, and was barefoot. Her hair was unbrushed, and her face, normally made up to an exacting degree, was apparently free of anything other than the woman's actual skin.

She led them into a room set up as a small study. Decker looked around, his gaze first fixing on the object over the door, and then moving to two items resting on a small table. He glanced at White but said nothing.

They all sat and Roe looked across at them.

"How can I help you?"

"Are you a fan of eBay?" asked White.

"Excuse me?"

"It's an online market—"

"I *know* what eBay is. Why do you want to know if I'm a fan?"

"Have you ever used it?"

She sat back. "Well, I guess I have purchased a few things from them over the years."

"What sort of things?" asked Decker.

"Look, where is this going?"

"Did you buy something around three weeks ago?"

"What exactly are we talking about?"

Decker said, "You should be able to remember if you bought something on eBay three weeks ago."

She looked put off. "Why won't you tell me what this is about?"

"We'd prefer to hear an answer from you first," said Decker.

"Okay, I don't specifically remember buying anything on eBay three weeks ago. In fact, I don't think I've bought anything from there since I was in college."

"Okay." Decker looked over at White.

She held up her phone. "We got confirmation from eBay that you purchased Slovakian money from one of their vendors three weeks ago. And Decker has confirmed that the bills purchased are the same ones found in the throats of Draymont and Lancer."

Roe stared at White like she couldn't really understand what she was saying. "Why would I buy old Slovakian currency?"

"It was your father's homeland," replied Decker.

"But my father has been gone for three years. Where did you get this information?"

"From eBay." White showed her the screen. "It shows the credit card account you have on file to make the purchase and a PO box delivery address."

"I don't have a PO box. And since I haven't bought anything on eBay since college, any credit card would have long since expired."

"Okay, then somebody could have hacked into your current credit card account and linked it to a bogus account set up on eBay. Can you check your statements to see if that charge appeared on it?" asked Decker.

Roe rose and got her laptop. After a few minutes on it she glanced up. "Okay, there is a charge here from eBay that matches the amount paid for the money. But I did not purchase it."

"So why didn't you challenge the amount?"

"I don't go over all my charges line by line. If it's over a certain amount the bank contacts me. This purchase wasn't even close to that. Less than fifty dollars."

"The PO box is in Naples."

"Like I said, I have no PO box. And even if I did, why would I have it in Naples?"

"Then somebody stole your credit card information, bought the currency, and had it shipped in your name to the PO box. Why go to all that trouble?" White wanted to know.

"To frame me for two murders, apparently," said Roe.

"Interesting, since we've already made an arrest and the gun used for the killings has been tied to that person."

"I don't profess to understand it."

"If you're telling the truth, it seems like someone is trying to punish you, Kasimira," noted Decker.

She shook her head. "I can't imagine what I've done to elicit that sort of hatred."

"I don't think it's connected to you. I think it's connected to your father. And something he might have done."

"What are you talking about?"

Decker took a few minutes to tell her about what had happened in Miami back in 1981.

As he finished, Roe looked devastated by these revelations. "And...and you think my father—"

"I don't know how he saw what he did, but he was in that room, helping to put a dead prostitute in a suitcase. The body has never been recovered."

"And Senator Tanner?"

"Was probably very grateful. Which might explain how your father was able to quit the Secret Service and start his security firm. It might also be that as a senator and wealthy, well-connected businessman, Tanner managed to throw a bunch of business your father's way."

"In return for keeping his mouth shut?"

"I'm not sure I see another reason, unless you

do?" said Decker, who was watching the woman closely.

Roe seemed to hover between screaming or crying, and he was unsure, ultimately, which way it would fall.

She surprised him by doing neither. She sat up straight and said, "Then why, after all these years, did this happen now? My father presumably kept the confidence."

"You told me your father was religious. He obviously raised you the same."

"What?"

Decker pointed to the crucifix over the doorway into the room, and a set of rosaries lying on a credenza next to a bible.

"Yes. He was a devout Catholic. That's how I was raised."

"And when people are dying, someone like a devout Catholic harboring a guilty secret, what might they do?"

Roe walked over to the credenza, picked up the rosaries, and began fingering them. "They would confess their sins for absolution of their soul in the eyes of God, so they could be forgiven and go to Heaven."

"And if your father went further, and told others who were also involved in that secret that that was his intent? To make his secret public, and not just confess it to a priest in private?"

Roe walked over and sat back down.

"So you think those people killed him to prevent him from confessing his guilt, and theirs?"

"It's certainly one plausible theory."

Finally breaking down, Kasimira Roe put her face in her hands and started to weep.

84

AFTER THEY LEFT ROE'S CONDO, White received another email.

"It's from Deidre Fellows." She read over it. "She said she believes that the photo I sent of Wanda Monroe is the woman she saw back in 1981."

"Okay, so she was a prostitute and she was in Mason Tanner's hotel suite when she died. We just don't know *how* she died."

"Fellows didn't see any blood. But Monroe could have been strangled."

They got into the car and drove away.

"And what about Roe?" asked White.

"She seemed stunned by her father's secret."

"Nice call on the Catholic piece."

"End-of-life guilt can be immense," noted Decker.

"You really think Kanak Roe was killed by the people he worked with all those years ago to cover up Tanner's having a dead prostitute in his bed?"

"It certainly fits the facts as we know them."

"What about Tanner? I know he has Alzheimer's now, but what about three years ago?"

"No, he's been incapacitated for at least the last five years."

"So we have to find the guy in the room with Kanak. If he's still alive. We should get a description from Fellows."

"The other thing is, whoever killed Draymont and Lancer might have tried to implicate other people. Barry Davidson, by using his gun, and Kasimira Roe, by buying the Slovakian currency with her credit card."

"Well, if they really wanted to implicate someone successfully they should have picked one and stuck with it."

"I think I might know one reason why they didn't."

"What?" asked White.

"Let me think about it some more. But let's see if we can find that man."

* * *

"You son of a bitch!"

Decker and White had just walked into the lobby of their hotel when Dennis Langley jumped up from a chair and confronted them.

"Excuse me?" said Decker.

"Don't play bullshit games with me," said Langley.

"I'm going to sue you for theft and defamation and anything else I can think of. Your fat ass is going to jail."

"Well, maybe we'll be cellmates then."

Langley looked taken aback by this. "What do you mean? I've broken no laws."

"Really? So you won't have a problem with the authorities checking into your business and financial dealings? And I would imagine a full accounting of any funds you hold for clients would probably be a good thing, because a man with a gambling problem doesn't tend to care where he gets his money from to pay off who he owes. And you have to pay them off, because Vegas casinos can get really nasty if you don't. I'll contact the necessary organizations and get that inquiry into your finances rolling."

Langley's hand balled to a fist.

White stepped between the two men. "Don't even think about it. Assaulting a Fed gets you a minimum of five years in the pen."

"You think you've really got me, don't you?" barked Langley as he looked over White at Decker.

"I *think* you really don't have Gloria Chase and her money anymore and you needed to take it out on somebody and I'm it. But your being here saved me a trip to see you. When your marriage play with Judge Cummins didn't pan out because she saw right through you, was that motive enough to kill her?"

"I have an alibi."

"Not anymore you don't. Chase recanted."

Langley glanced nervously at White. "I didn't kill Julia."

"I've yet to meet a murderer who openly confessed to killing anyone," replied Decker.

"Why would I kill her? I had Gloria."

"With some people it's not about money. It's about ego. How is your ego? Strong enough to handle rejection like that? Or should Chase hire security to protect her now? From you?"

Langley took a step back. "You're an asshole."

"Well, it usually takes one to know one. And I definitely *know* you. And if you didn't kill her, why did you work so hard to have Gloria as an alibi that night? You went to the liquor store, sure, we confirmed that. But where else did you go?"

Langley turned and stalked out.

White let out a breath and said, "Okay, I thought I was going to have to pull out my karate again. Though it would have given me great pleasure to put my foot right against that jerk's square jaw."

"He's a bully. You pop him in the nose, he runs away crying. That's not really important. What is important is does he have it in him to stab a woman ten times?"

"And remember the card left behind with that legal phrase. He's a lawyer. That fits."

"But the blindfold with holes? How does that tie into Langley?"

"I don't know," confessed White.

"Neither do I. But that may be because he didn't do it."

"Then there must be someone else out there that we're not aware of yet, Decker."

"Maybe we *are* aware of them."

CHAPTER

85

LATER THAT NIGHT WHITE KNOCKED on Decker's door. He let her in and they sat across from each other.

"Andrews left the hospital today. He's starting rehab."

"Good. Hope it goes well."

"And I got a call back from DC. No one matching the description that I got from Deidre Fellows worked at Senator Tanner's office or on his campaign."

"At least that anyone can remember."

"Right. But we end up in the same place—nowhere," said White.

"If he wasn't working on the campaign, what was he doing in Tanner's room cleaning up that mess?"

"A good Samaritan passing by would not have stuffed a woman into a suitcase. They would have called the police. Same for someone working at the hotel."

Decker said, "There's something we haven't thought about yet. Why would Tanner, on the very night of his big fund-raiser with the president, and all those Secret Service agents around the hotel, have invited a prostitute up to his room? Why take that chance? He could have done it another night, or at some hideaway of his. The guy was rich."

"You're right—it doesn't make sense."

Decker pulled out his phone and made a call. "Ms. Fellows, Amos Decker. Thanks for getting back to us on that photo, but I have another question to ask you, and some new information to share. Please don't take it the wrong way, because it might be shocking to you...Okay, all right...Thanks. We found out that the woman you saw in your father's hotel room that night might well have been a prostitute. Her body was never found. Now, I know you were just a teenager back then, but was that something you could see your father doing? Hiring a prostitute?"

Decker listened for quite a while before saying, "Well, thank you for being so candid. We'll let you know what we find." He clicked off and looked at White.

"Well?" she said.

"She said she wasn't aware at the time of her father's sexual *endeavors*. But she said as she got older she discovered that her father had a wandering eye as a younger man, though he and his wife apparently worked through those issues, at least according to Deidre. And they did stay married all these years."

"So that was why Wanda Monroe was in his bed?"

"Not necessarily. She still might have been placed there."

"But you just said the man had a wandering eye?" she pointed out.

"Even if he did, like we just discussed, would he risk having a prostitute in his bed on the night of his big event with Reagan, and while Secret Service agents and media people are swarming all over the place? That's just too risky."

"So they *knew* he was promiscuous and they set him up."

"Tanner was running to be a U.S. senator. That's a useful position if you want to blackmail someone." He took out his phone and performed a search. "Mason Tanner was a member of the Senate Intelligence Committee and ended up chairing it for four years."

"Meaning he would be privy to national security intelligence," said White.

"Right. And back in Miami he ends up with a dead woman, possibly a prostitute, in bed. Then this man shows up to take care of things. And then Kanak Roe appears and together they get rid of the body."

"So they were setting up Tanner for blackmail, and Roe shows up by chance and they enlist him to help? Why not just kill Roe? How could they be sure he wouldn't pull his gun and arrest them all? I mean,

I know we went over this before, but that's what I would have done. It's what *you* would have done."

"The Secret Service is a little different. Reagan was Kanak Roe's boss, the most powerful man in the world. The repercussions if the truth came out might have been really bad. Better to bury it than have it become a national scandal. And Roe probably only had seconds to make a decision. And keep in mind that he might not have known that anyone had set up Tanner or was planning to blackmail him over this. He might have only been told that the woman had died by natural causes and they just needed to get her out of there to save Tanner's reputation and chance at winning his election. She had no obvious wounds, so he might have believed that she had a heart attack or maybe overdosed. And they might have made him an offer of payment, or he might have come back later with that sort of demand. Since he might have wanted to confess decades later, my thinking is he decided to demand payment for his silence. Tanner had enough money to pay him off. And that's also why they didn't just kill Roe. Maybe you could make a prostitute disappear without consequences, but you can't do the same with a Secret Service agent. There would have been a scorched-earth investigation and they couldn't chance that. So they paid him off."

White shook her head. "God, dirty all around. And Lancer and Draymont?"

"They were already in the blackmail business. I think they stumbled onto all this, or maybe something else just as incriminating, and believed it could be a big payoff for them."

"So you think the fix-it guy in Tanner's hotel room is down here now?" asked White. "And they tried to blackmail him?"

"I do. Only this guy decides to bite back. Hard. He kills Draymont. And then snatches Lancer from the hospital, and kills her after getting whatever information they could out of her."

"But why the Slovakian money?"

"Whoever is behind this might have seen it as Kanak Roe's having taken the money years ago to build his empire, then deciding to rat them out. They would not have been happy about that. And that's why they killed him."

"Okay. But trying to implicate Kasimira?"

Decker said, "If she goes down for murder, what happens to Gamma Protection Services?"

"It would probably go down the tubes. And you still think the murder of Julia Cummins is unconnected to all this?" she asked.

"I do."

"Damn, Decker, this is getting to be the messiest case I've ever been involved in."

Decker didn't respond to this. He was thinking something else entirely.

Maybe in some ways, it's finally beginning to clear.

His phone buzzed. Decker listened, mumbled a few words in response, and then clicked off.

"That was the U.S. attorney. They let Barry Davidson go."

"What? Why?"

"A neighbor on the floor just below him was out on his balcony that night. He came forward to make a sworn statement that he heard Barry in his office—I guess the doors were open—from around eleven thirty until around three."

"Why was the guy up that late and why didn't he come forward before?"

"He went out of the country the morning the bodies were discovered and just got back and found out about the murders and Davidson's arrest. And he was up late because he'd been in Asia for a month and was still on that time zone. But he swears that Barry was in his office that whole time."

"So Tyler and Barry were telling the truth."

"Yeah. They still have his gun as evidence, but he could not have pulled the trigger. And the U.S. attorney is of the same mind I am. If Barry knew that his gun was the murder weapon he would have gotten rid of it."

"So now the pendulum swings back to Langley?"

"Yes, it does."

CHAPTER

86

DECKER TOOK OUT THE PHOTO of his wife and daughter as he lay in bed in his room.

Recently, he had felt compelled to take it from his wallet each night before turning in. He looked at the twin faces, studied the eyes, the mouths, the slopes of their necks. He, of course, remembered exactly when it had been taken. He had actually been the photographer. It was just a picnic at a local park. A rare day off for Decker that had coincided with Cassie's scheduled time away from the hospital where she worked as a nurse. Molly had been home because it was a teacher workday, and she was the one who suggested the picnic. At first, Decker had not been too thrilled with the idea. There were some chores for him to do around the house, and social outings, even just with his family, were awkward for him. But Molly had persisted, and they had all joined in to make the food for the picnic. And it had been a truly glorious day. The sun bright and warming, the flowers in bloom, the breeze invigorating, the company the best in the world. Every bite of the simple luncheon the most wonderful food that Decker had ever had.

Because it was the last time.

A week later he had no family left.

He slowly put the picture away in his wallet and closed his eyes.

I would much prefer to be at that park with them, instead of being here trying to solve another crime.

White had turned out to be fine as a partner, but even with that...Change, way too much damn change.

And then there was the letter from the Cognitive Institute. Things happening. Things changing.

Me changing. Irreversibly so.

Alone.

He slept and then awoke when the night was about its darkest.

He rose and went to the window and looked out at the paradise of Ocean View, Florida.

Some paradise. Stacked with bodies and blackmailers.

He went back to sleep and woke at nearly eight o'clock.

As he showered, he thought about the case, not at a broad, macro level, but at the building-block stage because that, he had come to believe, was where the real answers were to be found. That and the little inconsistencies that later turned out to be important.

First up was the revelation about Barry Davidson. Tyler had said his father had not left the premises. And now this neighbor had come forward to corroborate that. The result: Davidson was a free man. Then who had killed Cummins?

The key to the murders of Draymont and Lancer was finding out who they had been blackmailing. And to blackmail someone, you had to find out a dark secret. On Capitol Hill they had done that by, presumably, listening at keyholes, shadowing people, taking photos or recordings of indiscretions.

He thought back to something that Kasimira Roe had said. She had been blackmailed by Draymont and Lancer after they had discovered that she was seeing a married person. But she had also said that the pair had blackmailed other clients, and, in one case, Draymont had stolen some jewelry.

He sent Roe an email and got a reply back a few minutes later.

Judith Kilroy, with an address in West Palm.

* * *

After traversing the state of Florida once more, Decker and White arrived at Judith Kilroy's home, a large, oceanfront stucco house with wavy palm trees out front. Decker knew he could have simply called the woman, but he liked to see the people he was talking to. And doing that on a computer was just not the same thing, at least to him.

Kilroy was in her early sixties and dressed casually, although the jewelry she had on was anything but casual. She led Decker and White into a room with a lovely view of the Atlantic, which, for some reason, Decker found slightly nauseating.

"I'm as certain that that man robbed me as I am of my own name. How dare they claim I was trying to get out of paying the bill? My husband's firm was footing that. And besides that, we're rich, for God's sake."

"And who made that claim?" asked White.

"Some woman. I forget her name. She called and made up a pack of lies. I was never that insulted in my life. When it first happened my husband was considering legal action, but then we decided it would be too much of a hassle, and the necklace *was* insured."

"I understand. But why were you so sure he stole it?"

"I caught him in my bedroom. That's where I kept my jewelry. That necklace was there before he went in there, and then it was gone right after he left. No one else was in the house during that whole time. Oh, he did it all right." She took a deep breath and composed herself.

Decker looked around the grand space. On one wall were photos of Kilroy and presumably her husband and their children over a series of years.

"The passage-of-time wall, I call it," said Kilroy as she noted what Decker was looking at. "It goes by so fast. But when your kids are little and the days seem like they're forty-eight hours long, you just can't see that. And everyone with grown kids tells you that they grow up in the blink of an eye and will be out of college and on with their lives before you know it. And young parents listen but never really believe it." She paused. "Until it happens to them. I was fortunate to be able to stay home with my kids while my husband worked his way up the corporate ladder. I will never exchange that experience for anything. I understand a lot of people don't have that opportunity. Still, I miss the days when my kids were all at home."

Decker glanced at a stricken White, who looked like she might be sick to her stomach.

He said quickly, "Anything else you can tell us about Alan Draymont?"

"When I found the necklace missing I confronted him, but he denied having taken it. He was so smug and condescending. Said I was mistaken, but he could understand my being upset at having misplaced something so valuable. Can you believe that? The arrogance."

"That must have been traumatizing," said Decker.

"Yes, indeed it was."

"Did anyone contact you later?"

"Contact me? What do you mean?"

"We think that the man and the woman you spoke with were involved in a blackmail ring. So I was wondering if they tried to do something like that with you. Perhaps to get you to drop your claims about the necklace being stolen."

Kilroy set her lips firmly. "In order to blackmail someone, they have to find something to blackmail with. And my husband and I have led an exemplary life. A scandal for my husband was wearing a brown belt and black shoes."

"I'm sure."

"Is there anything else?" she asked.

"I guess not," said Decker, rising and pulling up a still-distracted White with him.

"Sorry about that," said White as she drove them back to Ocean View.

"Sorry about what?"

She glanced at him and let out a curt laugh. "Thanks."

"My wife, Cassie, worked long hours. She was a nurse. She hated being away from Molly, but we couldn't make it on just my paycheck. And my schedule was beyond ridiculous, so she worked full time *and* carried the laboring oar at home, too."

"I think you've just described a lot of marriages, Decker."

"Yeah, I suppose so."

"Did she regret it? Your wife?"

Decker glanced over at her. "Some days she'd come to bed crying."

"What'd you tell her?"

"If you want the truth, I never really knew what to tell her. I just held her until she stopped crying."

"Maybe that was exactly what she needed," said White in a wistful tone.

"I hope so," replied Decker.

87

LATER THAT AFTERNOON, AFTER GETTING back from West Palm, Decker and White sat out in their rental in front of Cummins's house.

"In some ways it seems like we've been investigating this thing a lot longer than we have," observed White.

Decker wasn't listening. He looked at Doris Kline's house and then at the Perlmans'.

"Not easy transporting Lancer's body into a house unseen."

"They could have just brought it in the trunk of a car," noted White.

"And then what? Pulled into the driveway and hauled the corpse out?"

"Well, they obviously did it late at night when no one was around."

"The security here makes regular rounds. And how does a car with no special tag get in the gate after hours?"

"Well, that's true. But I don't see Kline carrying a

body around. And the Perlmans were in New York when Cummins was killed. We confirmed that."

"Remember the guys on the beach? The person behind the killings didn't have to be here that night if *they* were."

"By that logic, they could be working for Davidson or Langley."

"True."

"Do you think they're the same guys who pulled Lancer from the hospital?" she asked.

"It was dark on the beach, and the video at the hospital wasn't great, so we can't be sure. But it certainly could be the case. They were the same sizes as the guys on the CCTV footage."

Decker rubbed his eyes and shook his head.

"What is it?"

"My perfect memory isn't so perfect right now."

"What do you mean?"

"There's something in there but it won't connect."

"How do you mean it won't connect?"

"Two images I have that should be connected, but I can't remember what they are."

"You'll think of it, just give it time."

"How much time do we have?"

"What do you mean?"

"Before the Bureau declares the investigation a clusterfuck and yanks us both back to DC for our professional execution?"

White sank back against her seat. She said, "Well, I won't go quietly."

"I wouldn't expect you to."

"How about you?"

"I don't know."

"You don't want to do this anymore?"

"Not necessarily. I just don't know if the Bureau is the right place for me to be doing it." He opened the car door. "Let's go talk to the Perlmans. Maybe something will pop."

She killed the engine and opened her door. "And why the Perlmans over Doris Kline?"

"The Perlmans recommended Gamma to Cummins. And Draymont was in their house."

"Wait a minute—you think he might have been blackmailing them? But if so, why recommend Gamma to the judge?"

"Maybe they did that *before* they got blackmailed."

CHAPTER

88

Maya Perlman greeted them at the door. She was dressed in a light blue skirt and white blouse with sandals.

"I'm afraid my husband isn't here right now."

"More golf?" said Decker.

She smiled. "Something like that. He enjoys his retirement."

They sat in the living room. She offered them coffee or tea but they declined.

"I know that Barry has been arrested. But I just can't believe he would have done that. I knew the man well. He wasn't the type to stab anyone, much less his wife."

"His *ex*-wife. And did you know he was watching her house?" asked Decker.

Perlman looked uncomfortable with the question. "Where did you hear that?"

"From someone who would know."

"Doris?"

"Neither confirm nor deny. But Barry also admitted it."

"I see. But that doesn't make him a killer."

"You like him, I take it?" said White.

"He had his faults just like all of us. But he was always wonderful with Julia. Very kind to her, and he's been a good father to Tyler. And we had so much fun together."

"There was that tax issue."

"I don't know anything about that," she said quickly—maybe a little too quickly, thought Decker.

"Well, you'll be happy to know that he's been released from custody."

Her face brightened. "He has? That's wonderful. What caused that?"

"Another alibi came in for him. Couldn't be in two places at the same time."

"I'm sure Tyler is thrilled."

"We've learned some more about the man who was found dead at Cummins's house," said Decker.

"Oh, yes, what?"

"He had been involved in some blackmail schemes. And he had been accused of stealing jewelry from a woman he was guarding."

"Oh my God, really?"

"Yes. Just to be clear, did you find anything missing?"

"What? No. I mean, I haven't inventoried my

jewelry lately. We keep it in a large safe. He couldn't have gotten in there."

"And no blackmail demands?"

She sat back, looking offended. "He would have nothing to blackmail us about, Agent Decker."

"I'm not suggesting otherwise. But it doesn't have to be anything illegal. Just, well, something you wouldn't want anyone to know about. Hell, I wouldn't want anyone to be able to see my online search history."

She now looked uncertain. "Yes, I see what you mean. Well, we certainly didn't get any blackmail demands from this person. If we had, we *never* would have recommended the firm to Julia."

"Of course." Decker looked over her shoulder at the wall of photos he had seen on his first visit to their home. "I take it you like to sail?"

Perlman glanced at the picture of herself and her husband on the sailboat. "We used to, quite regularly. Trevor kept a sailboat and cabin cruiser, but it got to be so much upkeep we ended up selling them. Now if want to go out we just charter something."

"Did you keep it here?"

"No, in Key West. We used to take it over to Cuba."

"I thought there were restrictions," said White.

"This was when relations had thawed. It's harder now, and you need a permit once you're past the twelve-mile limit. It's a beautiful country. Have you ever been?"

White shook her head.

While Perlman had been talking Decker ran his gaze over the other photos on the wall, until he came to the very end. He glanced at Perlman, who was looking at him curiously.

"We know you were a lawyer, but what did your husband do for a living?" he asked.

"He was already retired when I married him. He was a consultant. His work took him all over the world. He speaks several languages."

"A consultant in what?"

"Raising capital for companies engaged in emerging markets. He was very successful."

"Was he married before?"

She smiled. "No, he said he was waiting for the right woman to come along. I had already made my mistake with my first marriage. Trevor was a godsend."

"He's a good-looking guy," said Decker, pointing to one of the photos on the wall. White turned to look at the image of a young Perlman in a suit and tie. Decker had actually seen it earlier, but back then it meant nothing to him. Now it meant pretty much everything.

Perlman said, "He was barely thirty then. It's the only picture I have of him from that time. He doesn't like to look back, only forward."

"I don't blame him. When do you expect him back?"

"Sometime this evening. Do you need to speak with him?"

"Probably. If you could let him know, I'd appreciate it. Just routine stuff. Well, thanks for your time."

They walked out the door and got into the car.

"Okay, what was all that about?" asked White.

"That connection I was talking about? It just came together."

"You mean that picture of a younger Trevor Perlman?"

"Yeah. I'd seen it when I was over here before, but I had nothing to compare it to then."

"What do you mean? Compare it to what?"

"The picture of Trevor Perlman with Senator Tanner at Deidre Fellows's house."

89

I NEED EVERYTHING YOU HAVE on Trevor Perlman ASAP," White said into the phone as they sat outside of the Perlmans' home. She gave the person the Perlmans' address in Florida and also informed the person of his connection to Mason Tanner.

White clicked off and turned to Decker. "Okay, what now?"

"I emailed Deidre Fellows. She's agreed to see us again."

They drove to Sanibel Island and passed through the gates to Fellows's oceanfront mansion.

She was waiting for them by the infinity pool when the maid escorted them through. Fellows had on a colorful muumuu and a sun hat.

On the way, Decker had taken a picture off the shelf in the other room.

They sat down, and Fellows eyed the photo frame. The picture was turned away from her. "Did you bring something for me to look at?"

"No, this is one of your photos from the other room."

"Then it's my *father's* photos. As I said, this was his house. I've only lived here for about six months. It was fully furnished. The house I shared with my ex is on the market."

Decker turned the picture around so she could see it.

She glanced at the group of men and women in the photo. "That's my father, and the woman is my mother, and the man next to her was my father's chief of staff at the time. He's dead now."

"And the young man on the very end?"

Fellows's gaze traveled down there and then she gaped.

"Miami, 1981?" said Decker. "The man packing the woman into the suitcase?"

She nodded dumbly.

"I thought so."

She looked astonished. "My God. It was here all that time. But I never looked at those photos. I'm not in any of them, you see. What's his name?"

"Trevor Perlman. Ring any bells?"

"No, none."

"I doubt he was part of your father's staff. And that may not have been the name he was using back then."

"Then why is he in the picture?"

"Politicians take lots of pictures."

"Yes, but why would my father keep that one in particular? There are lots of others with my mother and his staff."

"I don't know. But I'm very glad he kept this one."

"What does this all mean, Agent Decker?"

"Hopefully, it means a killer is about to get caught."

* * *

After a long discussion with Fellows, and White making some phone calls, they drove back to Ocean View and to their hotel.

In White's room they held a quick conference.

"Okay, let me try to get this straight," began White. "Trevor Perlman helped clean up the mess in Miami back in 1981."

"As we talked about before, he also may have *created* the mess."

"You mean a setup?"

"A consultant? Traveled the world and speaks several languages? Goes to Cuba by private boat?"

"What exactly are you saying?"

"I'm saying that I would bet more money than I have that Kanak Roe's boat is in Cuba, where Perlman took it after killing him and dumping his body in the ocean."

White stammered, "Are you...was Perlman working for—"

"—enemies of this country, yeah. He sets up Tanner, who was a shoo-in for election. The guy owes his political life to Perlman and his handlers. In return for their taking care of the dead woman in his bed and never revealing the truth, he would do anything they asked. You heard Deidre describe her father. He had no stomach for actual legislating. He just liked the glitz and glamour of it. He'd do anything not to be exposed."

"Like leaking information to our enemies?"

"Yes. And voting in certain ways to help whoever Perlman was working for."

"But if the guy was blackmailing him, why would Tanner keep a photo of the man in his house?" White asked.

"Tanner might have had no reason to believe that Perlman was involved in the blackmail scheme. He might have just thought Perlman tried to help him, but then someone else found out about it. And that way Perlman could blackmail other politicians. Getting compromising dirt on politicians and using it to further an agenda isn't exactly a new concept.

"And Roe somehow sees what's going on and Perlman has to co-opt him into helping, probably using the story that he was just trying to prevent a scandal and maybe the girl had overdosed or something. I'm sure he poured it on thick that the truth coming out would not be good for POTUS. That probably cinched the deal for Roe. But then decades later Roe finds out he's terminal and maybe stupidly tells Perlman he needs to spill his guts, which Perlman can't allow to happen."

"And Draymont and Lancer?" asked White.

"Draymont was in their house. I bet he was snooping around and found something incriminating, because I don't think Perlman is really retired. I bet Perlman knew Cummins's interest in Draymont was solely sexual and he would have an opportunity to get to Draymont at the house. So with that scene set, he nicks Cummins's condo key and security card to Barry's place in order to get Barry's gun. They were longtime friends, and Perlman probably would have known of its existence."

"Okay, that makes sense."

"Then Perlman's people hacked Kasimira's credit card and ordered the Slovakian currency. Later, they kill Draymont while the Perlmans are out of town. They probably followed Draymont and learned about his ties to Lancer, and through her to Patty Kelly. They kidnap Lancer and store her somewhere, and make her talk. She had warned Kelly, who ran for it. They kill Lancer and stuff her mouth with the money. They could have transported the body in Perlman's car easily, and then transferred it to Cummins's house when the coast was clear. Then they put a trace on our car, followed us to Kelly's getaway place in Key

Largo, and took her out just in case Lancer had told her anything. After Lancer's murder they put the gun back in the drawer at Barry's condo, and Barry helps them out immeasurably by pulling it out and taking it to his ex's house. We get the gun and it turns out to be the murder weapon. So down goes Barry."

"Damn, Decker, it all adds up. But why not kill Cummins at the same time?"

"They had no beef with her. And they were friends. Barry was still the perfect patsy because he had every reason to kill Draymont. Perlman just thought the judge would find the body, call the police, and they would investigate, and poor Barry would be left holding the bag. And then the cops would track down the source of the Slovakian money, think it was Kasimira Roe also involved somehow, and Gamma goes down in scandal."

"But can we prove it?"

"We have the ID of Perlman by Fellows and what she saw that night in Miami. That should be enough to take him down."

"Let's hope so, before he takes *us* down."

CHAPTER

90

At nine o'clock that night Decker knocked on the door of the Perlmans' home. A lot had happened between their leaving Deirdre Fellows's estate and now. And the next few minutes could go any number of ways.

Trevor Perlman, dressed in beige slacks and a collared white shirt, answered the door. "Agent Decker. My wife said you had come by earlier. Please come in. Where is your partner?"

"Working on something else."

"I see."

Perlman closed the door and escorted Decker into a small furnished room off the main living area.

"Now, let's fill out the rest of the group," said Perlman.

Another door opened and a man came in. He was one of the same men from the beach. He had a pistol pointed at Decker. They searched Decker. Perlman took Decker's gun and laid it on a table behind him.

"And now this," said Perlman.

He took out a wand and ran it all over Decker. When it didn't beep he said, "I'm surprised. I thought for sure you would be wired. Please sit."

Decker sat. "Where's your wife?"

"Off doing some things, like your partner."

Decker looked up at the other man, whose face still showed the effects of White's karate skills. "I bet you didn't think a person so small could inflict that much pain."

"We plan on taking care of her later," he said.

"We have a witness to what happened in Miami," Decker said to Perlman.

"Oh, you must not have checked your news feed. There was a terrible accident in Sanibel Island. A woman died. The daughter of a very prominent former senator. She apparently fell off her balcony. It was so sad. My other colleague just happened to be in the area when it happened and texted me the sad news. A Deidre Fellows—you may have heard of her. She might have seen something long ago and told you about it? I'm just speculating here."

Decker took a moment to absorb all this. "How did you arrange for the dead woman in Tanner's bed?"

"We hired her to be there. As a gift to the soon-to-be senator. He was giddy about the fund-raiser and was appreciative, without ever thinking it through. We knew this would be the case. We had a thick dossier on the man. His brain was in his pants. But, unknown to him, she had been given a drug that would soon kill her. And it did, right in his bed. Tanner freaked out, as we knew he would. I was there right on cue and took care of everything. I told him I was with the president's team."

"And then Kanak Roe showed up."

"That was a complication. He must have heard something. But I'm used to complications. It worked out all right. And Deidre Fellows's death leaves you with no evidence at all."

"How did you blackmail Tanner?"

"He never knew it was me, of course. But the room had been wired for picture and sound. After he won the election, he was given a sample of the evidence and he had a choice to make. He chose wisely."

"I'm not sure this country would think so. And your guy here? My partner and I can identify him as one of the men on the beach that night who attacked me."

"I received a text informing me that my man who was near Fellows's home when she died has already left the country. And this gentleman will be on the other side of the world by this time tomorrow."

"I suppose Draymont and Lancer had no idea who they had run into when they tried to black-mail you."

"I ate amateurs like them for lunch. I almost

laughed when Draymont tried to use something he overheard, and a piece of paper he found, against me. I pretended to be a cowering, helpless target just waiting to pay him money. But what I was doing was collecting intelligence on him and his associates. And when the time was right I returned the favor. I recommended Gamma to Julia. Even if my wife was clueless, I could easily tell what Julia wanted from Mr. Draymont. She even confirmed it when I asked her." He smiled. "It was our little secret."

"So you stole the key and security card from Cummins's house to get the gun from Barry. And you ordered the Slovakian money in Kasimira's name. Then you had Draymont killed while you were out of town."

"He was about to leave the house after his little sexual encounter with Julia when my men arrived. They were under strict instructions not to harm her no matter what. We later searched his apartment and took his electronic devices and the information he had on me. We did the same at Lancer's place. I had learned they were working together when I did my research on Draymont."

"And Patty Kelly?"

"We saw the text that Lancer sent her. We beat the information out of Lancer and it became apparent that Kelly was a loose end that needed cutting. Her husband, we determined, knew nothing. The fact that she left him behind confirmed that."

Decker looked at the other man before glancing back at Perlman. "When we told you the judge had also been killed, your wife was stunned, but you were merely confused. Because you knew it was only Draymont who had been killed by *your* people."

"Yes, that was puzzling. My men reported that they never saw her. They killed Draymont downstairs, stuffed the money in his throat, and left."

"*You* killed a lot of people, Perlman, or whatever your real name is."

Perlman sat down across from Decker. "What you don't understand is that the number of people dead is of no significance. This is a war, Mr. Decker. And in any war there *are* casualties. The key is to have more on the other side than on your own."

"How many people died from the secrets you blackmailed Tanner into leaking to you?"

"Apparently not enough, since the Soviet Union fell anyway."

"We did a search on you. Everything was perfect, all the way back to childhood. Too perfect. So perfect it had to be made up."

"Good, thank you for that. Though technically retired, I will have our people inject such flaws in future background profiles."

"How did you kill Kanak out in the Atlantic? Were

you hidden on the boat, or did you overtake him in yours?"

Perlman shook his head, a weary expression on his features. "What does it matter? After all we did for him. Stumbled onto an incredible opportunity in Miami that ended up making him rich. And he wanted to betray all that simply because he was dying and felt the need to publicly confess. Well, people die every day. As did he."

"He wanted to save his soul in the eyes of God."

Perlman pointed a finger at Decker. "That is why religion is so dangerous. It makes you do stupid things. That is why I am an atheist. As Marx said, religion is the opium of the masses."

"And what happens with me? My partner knows I came here and why. If I don't show back up, things will get really bad for you, really fast."

"You have no proof of anything. I could let you go right now and you can go and spew all the theories you want, claim that we all confessed, and what will it amount to?"

"Not much."

"But I am a man who does not care for loose ends. And you like to go for walks on the beach at night. There is a beach here. You will walk on the sand." He pulled out a syringe from a drawer of a credenza. "And then your heart will feel funny, like it is racing. You will not be able to breathe. You will stumble and fall and that will be that. And you are a large man and not a young one, so nothing unusual about such a man having a heart attack. And by the time the postmortem is done, what is in this syringe will no longer be detectable in your body." He uncapped the needle. "So, shall we begin your last walk, Mr. Decker?"

Decker looked at each of the men. "I suppose I can't convince you to turn yourselves in?"

Perlman shook his head and smiled. "I don't believe there is a phrase for that in Russian."

"Yeah, I didn't think so." He rose. "Well, okay, I'm sick of this case. Let's do it."

The door was kicked in and a team of armored personnel poured into the room pointing automatic weapons. Perlman's accomplice quickly dropped his gun, and Perlman the syringe, as they backed up against the wall.

Perlman snapped, "What is going on? You have no right to be here. This is a private house. This man broke in and we were simply defending ourselves."

One of the armored people took off their helmet. White brushed hair out of her eyes. "You good, Decker?"

"Much better than I was a minute ago."

Perlman shouted, "You will leave my house now. You have no proof of anything."

Decker walked over to the table and picked up his

gun. He turned, pointed the gun right at Perlman, and pulled the trigger.

Perlman screamed and fell to the floor, his hands over his face.

Instead of a bullet coming out of the gun, though, they all listened to the conversation that had gone on in the room before White and the others had shown up.

"A recording device disguised as a gun?" said Perlman in disbelief.

"It smacks of the old Cold War days, doesn't it?" said Decker. He lowered the gun and turned off the recorder by pulling the trigger again. "And just so you know, Deidre Fellows is alive and well. As soon as she became a key witness, we put her under protection."

"But my man, the news feed," snapped Perlman.

"Yeah, your guy is in custody. We caught him sneaking into the grounds, made him talk, and then we used his phone to text you that the mission was complete and he was leaving the country as planned. And the news feed was set up by the Bureau to make you think what we wanted you to think."

He looked down at Perlman. "And you walked right into it, *amateur*."

CHAPTER

91

He keeps asking to call his damn embassy," reported White to Decker after Perlman and his men had been arrested and charged.

"He can call Vladimir Putin for all the good it will do him."

They were at the police facility where the men had been brought to be booked for the murders.

White had contacted Agent Andrews and filled him in. As they were standing there, Maya Perlman rushed in, looking alarmed.

"There was a police officer at my house when I got back. He drove me here. Can someone please tell me what the hell is going on?"

"Your husband and two of his associates have been charged with murder and attempted murders," said Decker.

"Murder? That's ridiculous. Who is Trevor supposed to have murdered?"

"Alan Draymont, Alice Lancer, Patty Kelly, and Kanak Roe. And the attempted murders were a woman named Deidre Fellows and *me*."

She gaped. "You?"

"We have it all on audio," said White. "Your husband is some kind of Soviet spy from way back."

She looked at White. "A Soviet spy? You must be delusional."

White squared off with the woman. "Are you saying you knew nothing about any of it?"

"Of course I didn't. Because none of it is true."

Decker said, "Well, then you might want to ask your hubby why he keeps demanding to speak with someone at the *Russian* embassy."

Perlman shot him a terrified look. "The *Russian* embassy?"

"Yeah. If you listen closely you can hear him."

She looked down at the floor. "Oh my God, what is happening?"

White said, "A lot is happening, Mrs. Perlman, and none of it good. Your husband is a bad guy, a real bad guy who blackmailed Americans into turning against their country."

She put a hand to her mouth and sobbed. "This isn't happening. It can't be."

White's look softened. "Okay, I know this is a lot to process. Let me get you some water before you pass out. Then I'll find you a room where you can have some privacy. I recall you have kids from your first marriage, right?"

Perlman dumbly nodded.

"You can call them. They can come and be with you. Okay? Help you get through this?"

Perlman shot her a grateful look and nodded. "Y-yes, thank you."

White led her away and then returned to Decker.

"She's either a Viola Davis–level actress or the woman was clueless about old Trevor."

"He probably didn't tell her. No reason to. Need-to-know spy bullshit."

She sat down next to him. "You solved this sucker and brought the bad guys down."

"*We* did, Freddie. I wasn't solving anything without you."

"Thank you for saying that," she said warmly. "But it seems like Perlman didn't have the judge killed. And Barry couldn't have done it. So are we back to Dennis Langley?"

"I don't know."

"Who else is out there? Langley has no alibi, really. And Barry now has two alibis, Tyler, and the neighbor."

Decker looked at her funny. *Barry has two alibis. Tyler and . . . But the neighbor's alibi was enough. Tyler's wasn't needed.*

"Decker, I know that look. You thought of something, didn't you?"

He didn't answer her. He was suddenly feeling sick to his stomach. *What if Tyler wasn't Barry's alibi? What if Barry was Tyler's alibi?*

CHAPTER

92

DECKER FINALLY PUT HIS HEAD on his pillow at two in the morning, and yet his mind would not shut off. It was racing like it had never done before; images flashed across the spectrum of his brain at a frightening pace. Yet he could see every single image with great clarity, though what was being presented held little rhyme or reason. But still, it was unnerving.

New lesions, new anomalies. Maybe this is what my future looks like.

But I'm not going to let it control me.

He focused, pushing the stream of consciousness away, and willed himself to concentrate on the case. Four murders had been solved, but there was one outstanding.

Julia Cummins's killer was still out there. And he couldn't leave here with that unresolved. *And why did I never consider the possibility that it might be Tyler? Because he was a football player working his ass off? Because he...reminded me...of me?*

They would have to follow up on Langley, but

Decker's gut was telling him the man was not Cummins's murderer. Langley believed he had a new sugar momma in hand. Why risk that? But had Perlman's men killed the woman and lied about it to Perlman? If so, they might never reveal the truth.

But things about Tyler's potential complicity were now clicking into place and taking Decker to conclusions that he didn't want to draw. The mother always demanding perfection. The mother with all the rules. The mother always hovering over her only child. Then throwing out Tyler's father, and maybe Tyler as well, and going off on her own midlife crisis, while complaining about her husband doing the very same thing. What might that have done to her son?

Decker knew that Tyler could have slipped out of the condo while Davidson was on his Zooms. He could have run to his mother's home; he had done it the night they'd found Davidson there. If he had found his mother there with a dead man? Dressed as she was? What would have happened? A kitchen knife snatched, a chase ensuing, a slaughter to follow? Then he could have run back, gotten back into bed, and no one the wiser.

Shit.

He turned over on his side and stared at the wall. His old bedroom had been painted a similar gray color. It was soothing and Cassie had liked soothing things, particularly after stressful days at the hospital.

He recalled the time when Molly, unnerved by the night terrors she sometimes suffered with, would climb into bed with them. Decker could never really understand what was troubling his daughter, but Cassie would hold her, and speak soothing words into her little girl's ear. Eventually, Molly would calm and fall asleep between them, her fingers usually curled around her father's huge hand.

What I would give to have that right now. To feel those fingers around mine?

He had wanted to help Tyler through this, to get him closure on his mother's death. It was evident now, to Decker, that Tyler was a younger him, maybe the son he never had, basking in the glory of his youthful football prowess. But Tyler was also mired in the expectations and uncertainties that came with constantly being thrown against greater and greater competition until the day came when he would realize he was no longer the fastest or strongest, or most athletic. That, in the spectrum of elites, he was mediocre at best. Decker had first tasted that bitter rinse at Ohio State. And then he had been completely humbled when entering the NFL. Those expectations had come close to breaking Decker. The question was: Had they broken Tyler?

Guys like Drew James, Tyler's teammate, would never experience that dilemma. They would be stopped well short of that lofty—

Decker sat up in bed as the memory plates re-ordered themselves and fell into place so perfectly that it seemed he had nothing to do with the process. It was like his mind was on autopilot.

James had said that Tyler hadn't run with them since the morning his mother died. But Cummins didn't die in the morning, she died at night. So if James really meant that Tyler had not run with them beginning with the morning his mother's body was found...several hours after Tyler would normally run with the other players? But James had also said something else that was far more critical.

And suddenly Decker knew two things: His super-power had not failed him, regardless of what the Cognitive Institute had said.

And he had just solved Julia Cummins's murder.

And it wasn't as simple as *one* killer for the dead woman.

CHAPTER

93

IN THE MORNING DECKER AND White drove out to the Davidsons' condo. They took the elevator up, but to the floor right below the Davidsons'. They spent time inside with the owner, and Decker and White learned what they needed to know.

As they headed back up the elevator to the fourth floor, White looked at Decker.

"So, this occurred to you last night?"

He nodded, looking somber.

"I just don't get you, Decker. You snatched victory right out of the jaws of defeat, and you act like the criminal got away with it."

"It all depends on how you define victory and defeat, I guess."

* * *

Barry Davidson met them at the door with a frown.

"I'm not sure I should even let you in."

"*We* didn't arrest you," White pointed out. "And

now you're free and clear, so I would hope that smiles and good cheer are in order."

He stepped aside to let them pass and then escorted them into the living room.

"It does feel good to be home," he said. "I made some coffee if you want some."

"Sure," said White. They headed into the kitchen, where Davidson poured them all cups.

"Where's Tyler?" asked Decker.

"He left for school already," Davidson said. "But we're going out tonight to celebrate. Did my heart good to see him so happy. I sort of feel things are turning around for us both."

"You mind if I have a look at Tyler's room?" asked Decker.

"Why?"

"I saw his place at his mom's house. I wondered if it was the same here."

Davidson grinned. "Help yourself. You'll find that here, Tyler is allowed to be a teenager. At his mom's, not so much. Down the hall, third door on the right."

"Next to your office, got it."

Decker left them and went to Tyler's room, glancing in the open doorway of Davidson's office as he went by.

As Davidson had intimated, Tyler's room looked like a typical teenage boy's space. Movie, music, and sports posters were on the walls. The place was sloppy and cluttered with piles of dirty clothes, athletic equipment, dumbbells, a football helmet and shoulder pads, books, and an iPad lying on the floor. There was an Xbox and a set of VR goggles. There was also a poster of someone named Kaia Gerber in a bikini. And another poster was of a woman called Olivia Rodrigo. Decker didn't know who either of these beautiful young women were, but he was pretty sure most seventeen-year-old males would recognize them.

And his father was right—this place couldn't be more different from his room at his mom's.

He picked up a *Black's Law Dictionary* from the desk, flicked through the pages, and found what he thought he might. Then he picked up a book on psychological disorders that had been checked out of the local library. Some pages were marked with Post-it notes. He read through them. He dropped the book and gazed out the window at the Gulf.

Normally, solving a case brought a rush of euphoria. *Not this time.*

He left the bedroom and poked his head into the laundry room, where'd he spoken with Tyler previously and the young man had broken down in tears over the loss of his mother. He opened the washing machine and looked inside.

Last night his memory superpower had come back

just in the nick of time. Decker had taken everything that he had seen and heard during the course
of this investigation and laid it next to everything
else. Layer after layer of conversations, seemingly
innocent remarks, certain observations, and assorted
other evidence had been plucked from his personal
cloud and analyzed with one another. And the truth
had come out of all that with startling clarity.

It really all was in the smallest details. The ones
that seemingly had no importance, right up until the
moment they became the only things of importance.
People lie really well on the big stuff. But no one can lie
well enough to take care of the small inconsistencies.

He rejoined White and Davidson in the kitchen,
where she was pouring out more coffee and Davidson was making some eggs and toast. "Don't know
about you, but I'm hungry."

"Knock yourself out," said Decker.

They sat down and White watched Davidson eat
while Decker stared down at his coffee cup.

Davidson said, "So, I heard something about
Trevor Perlman being behind all this? What the hell
is that all about? He was a good friend and he
adored Julia."

"He had some people killed, including the man
and woman found at your ex-wife's home, but he
didn't have Julia killed," said Decker.

Davidson slowly put down his fork. "Wait a

minute, how is that possible? Whoever killed them also killed Julia."

"Decker has a theory that there were two different killers," said White.

Davidson gazed at Decker in disbelief. "Two killers who killed two different people in the same place at the same time? What, are you on drugs?"

"It's what happened," said Decker.

"Was it Dennis Langley then? Did that son of a bitch do it?"

"Finish your meal and then we'll talk."

Shooting them curious glances, Davidson continued eating.

When he was done, Decker said, "Follow me."

CHAPTER

94

DECKER LED THEM NOT TO Tyler's room but to Davidson's office.

Decker closed the door behind them, then reached into his pocket and pulled out a phone.

"The cops forgot to give you this. Remember they took your phone and computer when they arrested you."

"Yeah, I remember," groused Davidson. "And I need it all back. I conduct my business on that computer." He reached out for his phone but Decker didn't hand it over.

"What gives?" said Davidson. He glanced at White. "What games are you two playing?"

She said, "We talked to your neighbor downstairs, the one who gave you the alibi when he got back into town."

"Right. Lou Perry. I wish he hadn't gone out of the country. I never would have been arrested."

Decker pointed to the set of French doors leading

outside. "He was out on his balcony watching some news from overseas on his iPad."

"So I understand."

"He said he told you earlier in the day he was going to be out there smoking a cigar, having some scotch. He invited you to join him and maybe play some cards. He'd been in Asia recently and his body clock was still in that time zone. And he knew you were usually up late. But you had meetings."

"Right again. So?"

"So you knew he'd be out there that night."

"Okay. So what?"

"He said he called up to you around ten thirty. Heard you outside."

"I was out on my balcony getting ready for my first Zoom at midnight. I called back to him."

"Perry also said he heard you off and on from around eleven thirty until he went inside and went to bed close to three. He remembered seeing the times on his iPad."

"Which is why he knew I couldn't have been at Julia's during the time she was killed. Nobody can be in two places at the same time."

"Yeah, they sort of can."

"What?"

"A friend of Tyler's said you record your practice sessions."

"That's right."

Decker held up the phone. "You recorded your 'Hong Kong practice session' from that night on a voice memo on your phone."

"So? I do that a lot."

"We never had much reason to look at the memo until Lou Perry's alibi came up, and a few possibilities occurred to me. We played the recording for Perry. He said it was pretty much verbatim what he heard from you that night between one and nearly two."

"Of course it was. I was getting ready for my second Zoom with the client in Hong Kong then."

"Not between one and two o'clock you weren't." Decker held up the phone again. "Voice memos are time stamped. You recorded your Hong Kong practice session starting at ten fifty, which is shortly after Tyler went to bed, and you finished it at five minutes before midnight."

"Then how the hell did Perry hear it at one o'clock?"

In answer Decker opened the French doors, went out on the balcony, and set the phone on the top of the waist-high wall that encircled the balcony. "You put it here, turned the volume all the way up, hit play, and left. That made Perry think you were up here the whole time. You used Tyler's electric bike parked in the foyer. You took it down the back stairs, most likely. On the bike using the motor you could cover the two miles in a few minutes. You went to Julia's house. You killed her. And then you came back here in plenty of time to clean up and do your next meeting at two."

"That is crazy."

"You recorded the Zoom videos, Barry. We watched them. You had on a different shirt between the first and second ones. Why was that?"

"I...I spilled something on my shirt."

"The geolocator on your phone shows it never left here that night."

"Because *I* never left here that night. Look, this is all bullshit. A good lawyer would make mincemeat out of it. You think I murdered my wife and came back here and did a Zoom!"

"You used the word 'butchered' before. How did you know that? Because you were the one who did it."

"You're nuts!"

"Perry told us he also called up to you around one twenty. But you didn't answer him."

"I didn't hear him, obviously. I was focused on practicing for my next Zoom."

"No you weren't. You were probably still at Julia's. You finished with her, planted your evidence, and rode back here. At that time of night no one would be in the elevator or stairwell to see you coming back in with the bike and the bloody clothes. You cleaned up, changed your clothes, threw the bloody ones in the washing machine, and got ready for your next

Zoom. Later, you showered to get the rest of the crap off you."

"That is all a fantasy, nothing more."

" 'Res ipsa loquitor'?"

Davidson just stared at him.

"Tyler highlighted the legal phrase in the law dictionary in his bedroom. That phrase was on the card left with Julia's body. I talked to the medical examiner this morning. She said when Tyler came to ID the body—because you were too upset to do it—the card in the evidence bag was out and clearly visible. I think Tyler saw it. And I think he had heard his mother use that phrase before. With *you*. And he wanted to know what it meant."

"You leave my son out of this!" Davidson said warningly.

"I'm not sure that's possible, Barry. The way I see it, either you killed your wife—or Tyler did. Or you did and he covered up for you. That's accessory after the fact. That means prison time for him. And he can kiss his college dreams goodbye."

"Bullshit!" Davidson lunged at Decker, but Decker easily pushed him away. Davidson fell back against his desk.

"I'll sue your ass off!" bellowed Davidson.

"He was also looking up information on bipolarism. Is that what he thinks you have?"

"My son loves me."

"Yes, he absolutely does. So are you going to tell us the truth and save him? Or are you going to take your son down with you?"

"What did you mean he was covering up for me?" Davidson said darkly as he slowly got to his feet.

"He washed your clothes that night. They must have still had stains on them even after you laundered them. Then he spilled your drink on purpose, the first time we met you and him. He did that so he could run another load. Probably to get the blood out of the machine and the drains, and all that. Even though you never really can. We'll be checking that next. Julia Cummins's blood shows up in one of your drains, Barry, it's over, for both of you. So what's it going to be? You, or *both* of you?"

Davidson snarled, "You son of a bitch. You asshole!"

White put a hand on the butt of her gun and stepped forward. "That is not a solution, Barry. That does not make the problem go away."

"What do you want from me!" screamed Davidson.

Decker said, "It's real simple. The truth."

Davidson slowly sank to the floor, his head in his hands.

Decker sat in a chair and looked down at the man. "You must have been stunned when you walked into Julia's house and saw the dead guy. And her maybe kneeling next to him. She made up the bullshit about needing a security guard, and then not letting her other gentlemen friends come over to the house. She was afraid of how *you* might react, wasn't she? What did you do to make her afraid, Barry? Was it just the stalking, or something else?"

He sat up straighter, leaned back against a desk leg, and wiped at his eyes. "I said some shit. And did some stuff. But she deserved it. She walked out on me when I needed her. Tyler was devastated by the divorce and she didn't give a shit. She was always on my ass because I just loved life. I wanted to go out and party and feel young. But, no, she was having no part of that. And then what happens? She dumps me and she's out partying and dressing younger and having the time of her life. All the stuff she said she hated in *me*! She was a liar. Just a fucking liar."

"Or maybe she was a single woman approaching middle age who just wanted to have some fun," said White. "Without *you,* because she was tired of cleaning up your messes."

"Go to hell," barked Davidson.

"Did you go there that night planning to kill her?" asked Decker.

Davidson shook his head. "I didn't tell you, but I called her that day, from *Tyler's* phone. She wouldn't answer my number. When Tyler told me about his mom needing security I really was concerned. That's when she told me it was all bullshit. That she was actually screwing the guy. That's what she said, 'screwing the guy.' She basically told me to eat shit and die and then hung up. So I decided to go over that night and find out what was really going on."

"Did you see the men who killed Draymont?" asked Decker.

Davidson shook his head. "No. When I got there, there was a strange car in the driveway. The rear door was open. I went in, and there they were. At first I thought they were doing it right there on the floor. She barely had any clothes on. Then when I saw the blood I knew something bad had happened. I was going to try and help her. Call the cops. But she saw me, and screamed at me, accused *me* of killing the guy. Then she said all these horrible things about me, and then it hit me that she had never really loved me at all. Then I just snapped. I grabbed a knife from the kitchen drawer and...chased her upstairs. And I...did what I did. Then I put the blindfold on her and I wrote out the words on a piece of paper and left it on her chest."

" 'The thing speaks for itself'?"

"She used to use that term with me. Every time something got messed up, she blamed me. That tax thing? It was just a misunderstanding. But no, she could never see it that way. Res ipsa fucking loquitor. She always threw that in my face. Oh, something got screwed up? It must be Barry. It fucking speaks for itself."

"You used the ruse with the voice memo to establish an alibi. You sure you didn't go there to kill her?" asked White.

"I swear I didn't. Part of me...a little part of me thought we might, I don't know, hit it off that night. Maybe get back together."

Decker and White exchanged glances at the utter absurdity of this comment.

Decker said, "No fingerprints of yours showed up at the house, Barry. No footprints either. There were no prints on the card you left with the legal phrase. No prints on the handkerchief you used to blindfold her. You took the knife you used to kill her, and presumably the pen you used to write the note. For someone in a daze you were pretty damn careful."

"I...I watch cop shows. I used another of her handkerchiefs so my prints wouldn't show up. I took that and the knife and pen with me. Later, I threw them all in the ocean."

"And your footprints?" asked White.

"I smoothed out the carpet on my way out and used the handkerchief to wipe out any marks on the hardwood floor."

"I think you *did* go over there to kill her, Barry," said Decker.

Davidson glanced at him. "She pleaded with me, you know. The woman who was always in control, always was right about every little thing, was on her hands and knees begging me not to do it, not to hurt her. But it was too late. And once I started...I couldn't stop. Then I just looked down at her lying there." He stopped and choked back a sob. "And...and maybe I did go over there to hurt her. But...now that it was over, I couldn't believe what I'd just done. It was like somebody else had done it."

"Why did you put the mask on her?" asked White.

"So...I thought the cops would think whoever killed her did it because she was a judge. You know...justice is supposed to be blind, but not really. I thought that would confuse everybody, especially since she had been telling people she needed protection."

"So, again, you were thinking that clearly at that moment in time?" said Decker as he stared impassively at the man. "To try to throw suspicion off you?"

"I...I don't know what I was thinking. I was scared. I'd just killed Julia, for God's sake!"

"You might have been scared, *after* the fact, because of what *you'd* done. But Julia must have been terrified. You stabbed her ten times, Barry. You took your son's mother away, in the most brutal way possible."

Davidson composed himself and said, "But Tyler had nothing to do with this. I'll say anything, sign anything, but only if nothing happens to my son.

I've ruined pretty much everything, but he still has a life to live, and he's going to get a chance to live it. If you can't promise me that, then I'll deny everything and fight you like hell in court."

White looked at Decker, who kept his gaze on Davidson.

"I think we can promise you that," said Decker quietly. "You must have been shocked when you found out your gun had been used to kill Lancer and Draymont."

"'Shocked' is too mild a word," he said dully.

"Did you go over there to kill yourself that night with the gun?" asked Decker.

"I thought if I did it where I killed her, it might, I don't know, equalize things."

"It doesn't work that way," interjected White.

"Do you have to tell Tyler what I just told you? I...I don't think I can live with that."

Decker said, "I'm not sure he can either, Barry. But I think I might know how to do it best. For him, *not* you."

SHOULDN'T YOU BE IN CLASS?" Decker called out to Tyler.

Decker was leaning on the fence that surrounded the football field, and was watching Tyler run pass routes all alone.

"Teacher workday—thought I'd get in some reps."

Tyler glided over to Decker and wiped down with a towel he pulled from his duffel. "You know they let my dad go, right?"

"Yeah, I heard."

"I told you. You just wouldn't listen. And now our neighbor said the same thing."

"Right. Can I ask you something?"

"Sure, what?"

"Did you really want your dad to get away with it?"

Tyler slowly let the towel fall to the ground. "Wh-what?"

"Could you really live with the knowledge that your father murdered your mother?"

Tyler's lips started trembling and he looked away. "What are you talking about?"

"He confessed, Tyler. He...he couldn't live with the guilt anymore. So he did the right thing. He came in and confessed. He asked me to come here and tell you that. And that he was sorry for everything. He didn't mean to do it. He just snapped."

"He...my dad confessed?"

"Yeah. He's in custody now."

Tears slid down Tyler's cheeks as he cried out, "Why couldn't you just let it alone?"

"It's not my job to let things like that alone. It's my job to catch people who commit crimes. He used your electric bike, did you know that?"

Tyler slowly nodded. "I keep a really accurate record of mileage because it's part of my training. It had four extra miles on it that morning."

"Right, over and back from your mom's. And 'res ipsa loquitor'?"

"She was always saying that to him. I never really knew what it meant. When I found out it was on a note left beside her body..."

"But you knew what he'd done before that, right? The laundry? You spilled your dad's drink on purpose so you'd have an excuse to run another load of clothes while we were there. The clothes he wore from that night were in the machine when you tossed in the clothes you spilled the drink on, weren't they?"

Tyler shook his head, his eyes clenched tight. "He washed his clothes that night, which he never did. I heard the machine going from my room. But there were still some stains on them when I checked them early that morning. I...I didn't know what they were."

"I think you did know what they were, Tyler. I think you saw the mileage on the bike and the bloodstains on the clothes. And then your dad showering at three in the morning? You said that was normal, but I don't think it was. And, I spoke with Drew James earlier. He confirmed that you didn't run with them that morning. *Before* you supposedly even knew your mother was dead."

Tyler's eyes glistened with tears. "I'd seen a *CSI* episode where they check the drains for blood. I thought if I ran it multiple times and used bleach..."

"It's harder than you think to get rid of that evidence."

He finally looked up at Decker. "Look, I didn't want to think that my dad..."

Decker's tone softened. "I know."

"I...I was hoping it was all in my head. That I was just thinking crazy stuff. I made myself believe that my mom was fine. That I'd see her soon. Right until the police showed up to tell us she was dead."

"I understand, Tyler."

"No, you don't fucking *understand* anything. Now,

thanks to you, I've lost my mom *and* my dad. I've got nobody. I've got nothing. I'm all alone," he screamed.

Tyler threw his duffel at Decker and sprinted flat out to his car. He slid into his BMW, fired it up, and roared off.

Decker just stood there and watched him go before slowly walking back to his car.

96

THEY HAD CHECKED OUT OF the hotel and were heading to the airport after saying their goodbyes the night before to Agent Andrews, who was doing well in rehab. He offered free golf lessons to Decker and White should they ever be back in his neck of the woods again.

"Is it relaxing?" White had asked.

Andrews had grinned. "Only if you play well. So, not really."

On the drive to the airport White asked, "So, why was Langley trying so hard to work up an alibi for that night if he didn't kill Cummins?" asked White.

Decker said, "Gloria Chase called me. She hired a detective to do some more digging because she was puzzled about that, too."

"And?"

"And turns out Langley had another relationship going. He left from the liquor store to have a quickie with a married client while her husband was out of town."

"What a scumbag."

"I don't think that term actually goes far enough."

They dropped off the car and walked into the terminal.

And found Tyler Davidson inside waiting for them.

He looked like a pale shadow of his former self, but he walked resolutely up to them and said, "I found out you were leaving from Agent Andrews. I...I just thought I'd come out to see you."

Decker said, "Okay, Tyler. How are you holding up?"

He shrugged. "My dad has a good lawyer. They might plead insanity or something like that. I don't know what that will do. He's going to go to prison, I know that."

"I'm sorry," said White. "I can't imagine how hard this is for you."

Tyler looked up at Decker. "I just wanted you to know that my dad isn't really a bad person. When I was a kid my parents really got along. We had so much fun. We were a great family, we really were."

"I'm sure, Tyler. But sometimes life is good and sometimes it's bad, and sometimes it's good and bad at the same time. Otherwise, it wouldn't be real. And you can't assume either one will last forever. So while things look really bad now, that won't last, Tyler. I promise you."

"I don't know if I can believe that."

Decker took this in and said, "I played ball against a guy in college. Best pure football player I've ever gone up against. He was a running back at the University of Texas, and every time we played them the guy killed us. He was a finalist for the Heisman his junior year, and he would have easily won it his senior year."

"What happened? Did he go pro early? What's his name? If he was that good, I probably heard of him. I follow stuff like that."

"He never played a down of pro football."

"Why? If he was that good."

"He got framed for murder and spent twenty years in prison. Over half of that time was on death row."

Tyler gaped. "Holy shit!"

"His innocence was finally established and he was released. He got a big payment from the government for what they did to him, and he's now married and living a wonderful life in California."

"He deserved it."

"He never got to realize his dream of going pro, of being maybe one of the best of all time. But my point is, Tyler, no matter how bad it ever gets, it can also get better."

"I...I guess if things turned out okay for him, they could turn out okay for me."

"And, remember, you have a lot of money coming your way," pointed out White.

"I don't care about that. I don't even want it."

White said, "But your mother wanted you to have it. And it won't be coming for quite a few years, so make no decisions until then. You can start that business that Decker told me you talked about. Or you can give it away to worthy causes. The choice will be *yours*."

Decker gave Tyler one of his cards. "And let me know where you land for college. I know more about football than most people. I'd be happy to help you any way I can. And not just with football, but anything, or you just want to shoot the shit. Call me, anytime, anywhere."

"Really?"

"We husky football guys have to stick together."

Tyler slipped the card into his pocket. "My dad told me what you did for him. How you managed things for...me. So nobody would...the police...would leave me alone."

"You didn't ask for any of this. And what you did, or didn't do, under those circumstances? Well, I don't know that I would've handled it any differently, particularly at your age. So what right do I have to judge you?"

"Thanks for that, Mr. Decker."

"Call me Amos. All my friends do."

This drew a surprised look from White.

Decker put out his hand, but Tyler bypassed that

and hugged him. Decker could feel the young man squeezing him with all his strength, even as he trembled like a frightened child. Like Decker was the only thing keeping him tethered to reality.

Decker closed his eyes, and in his mind he was holding his daughter after a bout of night terrors. Holding her tight, saying soothing things into her ear. Making her feel safe. And Decker felt himself starting to tremble, and then his eyes filled with tears as he hugged the young, frightened teenager as tightly as he could.

After Tyler left, Decker just stood there, while White, her gaze averted, waited with him.

Finally, Decker picked up his bag and lumbered off to the security gate, wiping at his face.

White followed silently.

CHAPTER

97

THEY BOARDED THE PLANE AND flew back to DC. Right before they landed White got an email.

"Uh-oh."

"What?"

"SAC Talbott wants to see us as soon as we get in."

"Okay, this is not looking good."

"But we solved the case, Decker. What can he do?"

"He can do anything he wants."

They landed and took a cab to the WFO.

Talbott was waiting in his office. He rose with a smile on his face and his hand held out. "Just wanted to congratulate you on a job well done."

He shook Decker's hand but did not acknowledge White. She managed a smile while Decker just stood there like a stone wall. He said, "You might have missed my partner standing right there. But for her, I'm lying on a morgue slab in Florida."

Talbott changed color and glanced at White. "Yes, thank you too, Agent, um, White."

He turned back to Decker. "Our sister intelligence

agencies are very pleased with us. They had their suspicions of Senator Tanner for a long time, but could never prove anything. You solved that problem for them."

"Yes, we did," said White, but Talbott kept his gaze on Decker.

"We were thinking that a promotion was in order for you, Decker. Since you're not an actual special agent, our options are somewhat limited. But you are a valuable asset to the Bureau and we will find a spot for you. You have my word on that. It won't be in the DC area, but I know that you're from the Midwest, so maybe Kansas or Nebraska?"

"Agent White has young kids in school on the East Coast. She can't make that transfer."

Talbott glanced at White and then back at Decker. "I was just speaking of *you*."

"But you just made us partners. You pulled her down from Baltimore."

"We're actually promoting Agent White as well, for the exemplary work she did."

White looked surprised but pleased. "Promoting?"

"Absolutely, and it's well deserved. You will be the head agent overseeing a dozen other FBI special agents. It's quite a career move up for you."

"My God, sir, thank you. And where is it?"

Talbott smiled. "In Boise, Idaho. I'm sure you'll fit right in."

"Idaho!" barked White, looking stunned.

"There *is* crime in Idaho," said Talbott.

"My kids. I can't—"

Talbott's look turned stern. "Well...that's *your* choice. But the Bureau is cutting back on field agents. Budget concerns and all. Everyone has to tighten their belts. So it's either Idaho or..."

"She's not going to Idaho," said Decker.

"That really isn't your concern," said Talbott sharply.

"Well, considering that we're partners, it's very much my concern."

"Decker," interjected White. "It's okay. I can work this—"

"No, it's really not okay. So we'll just stay here and remain partners and do our job."

"That is not your call," Talbott barked, the kid gloves now off. "You'll do what you are ordered to do, or—"

"Or you'll can my ass, which is what this whole bullshit thing is about. Fine. Do it. Like you said, I'm not a real agent or anything, which means I'm not bound by the same crap as real agents are."

"What exactly do you mean by that?" exclaimed Talbott.

"What I mean by that is the media would love to hear our story."

"What story?"

"Two heroic FBI agents who solved a major crime and a decades-old spy case get kicked to the curb because they won't play the stupid reindeer games to suit the fucking stuffed shirts that run this place."

White stepped back, closed her eyes, and said a silent prayer.

"*What* did you just say to me?" barked Talbott.

"Maybe your *sister* intelligence agencies, who are so grateful for what Agent White and I did, would like to take us on. I mean, don't they love it when they can kick the Bureau in the nuts? And they have media people there who I'm sure could get the word out about what the FBI does to people who just do their job and keep the country safe. But maybe, since you're just biding your time until you retire so you can go and sit on your ass somewhere, or play fucking *golf*, you don't want to deal with all that shit, because it might end up getting your pension screwed. You know, budget cuts and all, so be prepared to tighten *your* belt if you go that route. But there's a way for you to avoid all of that, and you know exactly what it is. Your call."

The two men stared at each other for what seemed an eternity.

Finally, in a muted voice, his gaze averted, Talbott said, "You will carry on your normal duties until further notice."

"Yes sir," said White immediately. She pulled on Decker's arm and forcibly dragged him out of the room.

As they walked down the hall she said, "Do you realize you pretty much just *blackmailed* the man?"

"Must be all that crap in Florida rubbing off on me."

As they got outside, White said, "Look, we have a ton of stuff to talk about, but I really need to head home and see my kids."

"Absolutely."

"I do have to say one thing."

"What?" said Decker warily.

"After hearing what you said to Sandy Lancaster, and then seeing you with Tyler...you must have really been a wonderful father, Decker."

Decker appeared stunned, and White had the look of a person who suddenly realized she had just gotten way out over her skis.

"My friends call me Amos," said Decker finally.

White smiled. "Well, would you like to come up to Baltimore to meet my kids, *Amos*? And my mom is a great cook, and I've been known to open a decent bottle of red for the right guest, although I have plenty of beer, too. And Calvin's been talking about wanting to play football. You could teach him some stuff, maybe."

"Yes, I would like that. But not today. You need some time with them alone."

White's expression turned somber. "Thanks for standing up for me back there."

"If there's one thing I've learned about you,

Frederica White, you don't need anybody to fight your battles. You do that just fine all by yourself."

She reached up on tiptoes and gave him a hug, surprising Decker. He surprised himself again when he squeezed her back.

"I'll see you at the office, *partner*," she said.

"Yep."

He watched her walk off and then he trudged the other way.

CHAPTER

98

DECKER HAD ONLY BEEN IN his apartment for about an hour, and he'd had only two beers with more to come, when the knock came.

He opened the door to find Kasimira Roe standing there.

"I missed you by a few minutes in Florida and jumped on the corporate jet."

"Why?"

"Can I come in?"

He stepped back and let her pass. She had on jeans and a dark green sweater and low-heeled leather boots. Her hair was down around her shoulders, making her look younger, but she appeared anxious, at least to Decker.

"How did you know where I lived?"

"I called in a favor at the Bureau, I hope you don't mind."

"No. You want a beer?"

She hesitated and then said, "Sure."

They sat in the small living room. As she looked

around at the modest space he said, "Not exactly what you're used to, I know, but if you stand at the corner of that window and lean to the left you get a pretty good view of the Anacostia River."

She sipped her beer. "This is fine. I didn't always live where I do now."

"So, what can I do for you?"

"First, I wanted to thank you personally for finding out what happened to my father."

"I'm sorry it couldn't have been better news."

"It's closure. That's far more than what I had."

"You could have just called or emailed, you know. You're a busy CEO."

"In many ways my father was the most important person in my life. So I wanted to do this face-to-face."

"I can understand that."

"I also realized that the man I had placed on a very high pedestal all my life was a human being, with the flaws and faults we all have."

"Some more than others."

"And in addition to finding out what happened to my father, you taught me a lot about him, far more than I knew before."

Decker glanced over at the trash can, which held the torn-up letter from the Cognitive Institute. "We all keep things hidden, Kasimira, all of us."

"That certainly applies to me," she said, her gaze downcast. "As you know."

"That doesn't make you any less of a person, it just makes you more of a human being. I've never met a perfect person in my life, nor would I ever want to."

"I know that. Now. Also thanks to you."

"I think you would have figured it out, with or without me."

"And then there's the other reason I flew up here."

"Oh yeah, what was that?"

She glanced up and smiled. "Would you like a job with Gamma? I know you are not an office person, but how about running our field investigation division? I think you would be a wonderful addition to the Gamma family, and I would consider it an honor to work alongside you."

"That's a great offer and I really appreciate it."

Her smile weakened a bit. "But?"

"But I've got a brand-new partner who's probably going to be moving down here from Baltimore, and she's got little kids, and I can't leave her high and dry."

"That's very good of you, Agent Decker. Very loyal."

"I'm not a real agent, Kasimira, and I sure as hell don't play one on TV. Just make it Decker."

"Okay, *Decker*. I think Agent White is lucky to have you as a partner."

"Funny, I was feeling pretty lucky to have her."

She took out a card and slid it across. "If you ever

change your mind, or just want to talk. And if you're ever back down in Florida, please look me up."

"I have to admit, I was almost getting used to that sand thing."

They shook hands and he saw her out. He went back to the table and finished his beer while he looked down at her card. He glanced over at the trash can, rose, and lifted out the torn-up letter from the Cognitive Institute.

He slowly and methodically pieced it back together, just like he would any case he was working on. He still remembered what it said, and yet he reread every word twice over.

He popped another beer, placed it in a paper bag, put on his jacket, and walked out of the apartment. There was a bench down by the river where he liked to sit and just watch the water flow and the occasional boat pass by.

The letter from the Institute had predicted a great deal of change coming his way, at least in the way his brain functioned. That might be good, or that might be bad, he had no way of knowing. And neither, really, did they.

My superpower served me well on this case, even if it all dropped into place near the end. Better late than never.

And then his thoughts turned to his old partner.

Mary Lancaster didn't have the best memory, but she had all the other attributes of a good detective.

She actually read people better than Decker ever could. And her instincts had become so refined over time that her deductions sometimes had been truly eye-popping. A great many people thought she was just the tugboat sidekick to Decker's ocean liner. But the fact was, Mary Lancaster had more than held her own with him and everyone else. And she had taught Decker a lot.

And I will miss the woman every minute of every day. Because she understood me better than anyone other than my wife. And she was my friend.

As Decker stared out at the water, he began to wonder what his new partner's kids looked like. Whether they took after their mom. And he thought of Donte, the child she had lost. And whether White's mother would actually like him when they met. And whether she really was a good cook. And what the next case they would work on might be about. And about how Freddie White might become just as good a friend to him as Mary Lancaster had been.

And me to her.

Just regular stuff that people thought about every day.

That was the thing about life. You actually had to spend time living it.

Or else what the hell did any of it really matter?

So he sat there with his beer and his thoughts and watched the river cruise on by.

ACKNOWLEDGMENTS

To Michelle, the ride continues and I'm so happy you allowed me to come along for it!

To Michael Pietsch, Ben Sevier, Elizabeth Kulhanek, Jonathan Valuckas, Matthew Ballast, Beth de Guzman, Ana Maria Allessi, Rena Kornbluh, Karen Kosztolnyik, Brian McLendon, Albert Tang, Andy Dodds, Ivy Cheng, Joseph Benincase, Alexis Gilbert, Andrew Duncan, Janine Perez, Lauren Sum, Morgan Martinez, Bob Castillo, Kristen Lemire, Briana Kuchta, Mark Steven Long, Marie Mundaca, Rachael Kelly, Kirsiah McNamara, Lisa Cahn, John Colucci, Megan Fitzpatrick, Nita Basu, Alison Lazarus, Barry Broadhead, Martha Bucci, Ali Cutrone, Raylan Davis, Tracy Dowd, Melanie Freedman, Elizabeth Blue Guess, Linda Jamison, John Leary, John Lefler, Rachel Hairston, Tishana Knight, Jennifer Kosek, Suzanne Marx, Derek Meehan, Christopher Murphy, Donna Nopper, Rob Philpott, Barbara Slavin, Karen Torres, Rich Tullis, Mary Urban, Tracy Williams, Julie Hernandez, Laura Shepherd, Maritza

Lumpris, Jeff Shay, Carla Stockalper, Ky'ron Fitzgerald, and everyone at Grand Central Publishing. Every day you toil away not just to publish and promote my books, but those of so many others. You make the world a better place, because books make people more informed and engaged.

To Aaron and Arleen Priest, Lucy Childs, Lisa Erbach Vance, Frances Jalet-Miller, and Kristen Pini, for always going the extra mile for me.

To Mitch Hoffman, for understanding Amos Decker almost as well as I do.

To Jeremy Trevathan, Lucy Hale, Trisha Jackson, Stuart Dwyer, Leanne Williams, Alex Saunders, Sara Lloyd, Claire Evans, Eleanor Bailey, Laura Sherlock, Jonathan Atkins, Christine Jones, Andy Joannou, Charlotte Williams, Rebecca Kellaway, Charlotte Cross, Lucy Grainger, Lucy Jones, and Neil Lang at Pan Macmillan, for continuing to push the boundaries on how books are published and promoted.

To Praveen Naidoo and the wonderful team at Pan Macmillan in Australia, who have made me a number one bestseller.

To Caspian Dennis and Sandy Violette, can't wait to see you in person again. It's been too long.

To the charity auction winners, Julia Cummins (National Multiple Sclerosis Society) and Kasimira Roe (The Mark Twain House & Museum), I hope you enjoyed your characters.

To Arthur Dykes, I hope you enjoyed your character—and his full head of hair. Thanks for all your great work over the years.

And to Kristen White and Michelle Butler, who keep me sane!

ABOUT THE AUTHOR

David Baldacci is a global #1 bestselling author, and one of the world's favorite storytellers. His books are published in over forty-five languages and in more than eighty countries, with 150 million copies sold worldwide. His works have been adapted for both feature film and television. David Baldacci is also the cofounder, along with his wife, of the Wish You Well Foundation, a nonprofit organization dedicated to supporting literacy efforts across America. Still a resident of his native Virginia, he invites you to visit him at DavidBaldacci.com and his foundation at WishYouWellFoundation.org.

Facebook.com/writer.david.baldacci
Twitter @davidbaldacci
Instagram @davidbaldacciauthor